Sterlen
And a Mosaic of Mountain Women

The third book in the trilogy of the saga of the
Tom Ammons and Wiley Owen Families

By Amy Ammons Garza

Edited by
David Franklin Ammons
Sherilyn Ammons

Cover Illustration by
Doreyl Ammons Cain

PUBLISHED BY
Catch the Spirit of Appalachia, Inc.
WESTERN NORTH CAROLINA

FIRST PRINTING

The stories told in this novel are based on actual family
incidents. Some may have been rearranged or expounded
upon for effective storytelling. This is the third book
of a trilogy about the Tom Ammons and Wiley I. Owen
families of Jackson County, NC.

Other books & CDs by Amy Ammons Garza:
    Retter, *a novel of the mountains*   (1st in the trilogy)
    Cannie, the hi*lls of home*   (2nd in the trilogy)
    Matchbox Mountain, *a storytelling book*
    Catch the Spirit of Creativity, *a writing & art workbook*
    I Am Somebody, *the story of Tony Queen*
    Blue Ridge Mountain Stories, *a storytelling CD*

Some of the original photos published in this book were given to
the author by family members Lillie Ammons Owen
and Linda Owen Vinson. Illustrations within the book
by Doreyl Ammons Cain and David Franklin Ammons.
Song *"Lord Are you Listening?"* — Score written by
Phillip A. Scopelite, words by Amy Ammons Garza ©
Song *"Blue Ridge Mountains Call For Me"* — Score & words
by Phillip A. Scopelite ©

PUBLISHED BY
Catch the Spirit of Appalachia, Inc.
29 REGAL AVENUE, SYLVA, NC 28779 — PHONE: 828-631-4587

LIBRARY OF CONGRESS CONTROL NUMBER: 2005900287
ISBN: 0-9753023-2-9

DEDICATED TO THE ORIGINAL AMMONS SISTERS
LILLIE AND CORA AMMONS

AND TO THE GENERATIONS TO COME

WITH A SPECIAL DEDICATION TO THE DESCENDANTS
OF STERLEN AND MARTHA GALLOWAY

Families intertwined within the following pages:

Tom and Retter (Bryson) Coggins Ammons
Wiley and Ellen Canzadie Galloway Owen

and their children:
Jim and Libby Owen Ammons
Frank and Cannie Owen Ammons
Sterlen and Martha Ammons Galloway
Ray and Lillie Ammons Owen

i

The Recording of the Saga

of the Tom Ammons and Wiley Owen families all began with "Retter," my grandmother on Daddy's side.

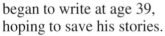

I remembered and loved the way they talked, the way they said their words, so I wanted to save their style of Old English.

Grandpa Ammons loved to tell stories about Grandma. She had given him nine children and when he was knocked off of a railroad trestle at age 39, she had saved his life. It seemed natural that I began to write at age 39, hoping to save his stories.

The Ammons Place, as the 3-room cabin on Cullowhee Mountain was called, sheltered those nine children and two adults, providing the setting of what was to become the drama of three novels about my family in Jackson County, NC.

The second book, "Cannie," once again brought my loved ones alive. It told the story of how my mother Cannie Owen met and married Frank Ammons, the 5th son of Tom and Retter Ammons *(photo to the right)*. It told of the hardships, the isolation, just as it told of the joys of family, of neighbors, of the creativity it took to live in the back woods. Most importantly, it told of the love of the land itself.

Wiley I. and Ellen with Cecil & Dohonov.

Ellen Canzadie Galloway Owen

Wolf Mountain in "Little Canada" was the setting for this second book, the home of Wiley I. and Ellen Canzadie Galloway Owen. Wiley and Ellen had also birthed nine children, three of whom wound up marrying into the Ammons family.

The integration of the Ammons and Owen families had it's start when Jim Ammons met and married Libby Owen *(photo on top left next page)*. Their union brought about the marriage of Frank Ammons and Cannie Owen.

The third marriage between the

families came about when Martha Ammons married the mountain man Sterlen Galloway, Grandma Ellen's brother. (Sterlen was 25 years older than Marthie.)

And finally, the fourth marriage was that of Ray Owen and Lillie Ammons *(photo below).*

Sterlen, the man whom my third novel in the trilogy is centered around, was a musically gifted mountain man. His marriage to Martha Ammons, Tom and Retter's eldest daughter, thrust this

man of music and song into the darkness of an abused woman's emotional pain.

It has taken nine years to tell the stories of Sterlen and Martha, of Jim and Libby, of Frank and Cannie, and of Ray and Lillie. What fun it was to talk with them and others who shared with me their most interesting and compelling life experiences. Seven of the eight passed

away before and while I've been writing this book. The only one still living today is Lillie Ammons Owen, my aunt who has helped me tremendously with her memories and photos.

There are no pictures to be found of Sterlen in the family, and the only picture of Martha is taken much later in life, after she had lost her husband and her grown children had left home.

Cousins Michael Owen of SC and Denton Higdon of NC have been a blessing with their help in compiling the lineage of our large family. Five of the major families are listed at the end of the novel—Ammons, Owen, Bryson, Coggins, and Galloway.

All five families crossed the mountains into Western North Carolina along with many others in the 1700's to pioneer what is now Jackson County.

Doreyl Ammons Cain, my sister, has given Sterlen a presence with her illustration on the cover. David, my brother and his wife Sherilyn (retired teachers) spend days and hours with the editing of the novel. Another teacher, my sister-in-law Candy Scopelite, also gave time proof reading.

Once I decided to include the full family lineage, I began calling my cousins... men and women whom I remembered to be children. (It had been years since I had spoken with some of them.) What a bless-

Martha Ammons Galloway

ing! They openly and honestly gave freely the information I needed to complete the lineage--all of it, down to babies!

How warm my heart grows as I know that once again, this novel is a "family affair!"

—Amy Ammons Garza

Amy, Doreyl, and David

v

Sterlen

And a Mosaic of Mountain Women

Sterlen
And a Mosaic of Mountain Women

Icicles on Wolf Creek Road

Sterlen

and a Mosaic of Mountain Women

By Amy Ammons Garza

CHAPTER 1

The 1960 Blizzard
Wolf Creek Lake, North Carolina

Marthie crouched on the floor in the corner of the room, her glassy gaze darting from the closed bedroom door to the young people sleeping on pallets of quilts nearby.

If I listen carefully, he'll come...I know he will. I won't move.

A child stirred, moaning in her sleep. Marthie squeezed her breast with crossed arms, pushing her neck down into a nest of shoulder blades, cradling her head. Her eyes, scratchy red from lack of sleep, glowed wild out of the paleness of a mad face.

Ellavee, stay still...ye havta stay still. Listen fer yer daddy.

From the fireplace came a sucking sound. Marthie's darting glance flew to the sight of smoldering ashes. Even in her madness she knew the last chair was gone. There would be no more to burn. Her gaze flashed again to the children. With a twisted face, her attention once again turned to the closed door.

Sterlen...the young'uns...they're gonna...die...if'n ye don't fetch some wood. The snow's done fell s'deep it's...God! Oh, God! it's covered the winders.

She waited for the door to open, one hand unconsciously pulling at the heaviness of her hair. The walls creaked as the howling wind outside pushed against the drifted snow closeting the cabin.

"STERLEN!" she suddenly cried aloud. "Sterlen! Ain't ye carin' 'bout yer young'uns! Sterlen! We're all set to die!"

The bundles on the floor moved, then one young teen-ager sat up, staring at the crouching woman. "Momma!" he whispered loudly.

"Jay, yer pa won't answer me...'n the fire's done gone out." She tightened her grip on her arms as she began to silently rock back and forth.

"Momma! Don't! I'll find something to burn." He struggled to his knees.

"STERLEN!" The cry seemed to come from the depths of Marthie's soul. She had no control of it; it had a will of its own. "STERLEN! I NEED ye!"

"Momma, please...please don't cry out. ye'll wake the others." The young boy crawled across the floor to his mother and tried to put his arms around her. "Momma, I'll fix the fire. Momma...please!"

Marthie pushed him away, looking desperately around his working face to the front door.

"Where er ye, STERLEN! Yer family's in a bad way!"

Her body rocked with heavy motion, her hair whipping across straining eyes. A deep rasping sound crawled up out of her stomach, pushing against the back of her tongue. The horror it carried could not get past the tongue. It lodged.

He ain't comin'! He ain't comin'!

Truth struggled to win in her grieving mind with such force her body ceased it's rocking. She flung her gaze to the face of her wide-eyed, terrified son.

"Mom-ma...," the boy's voice cracked, hardly more than a whisper, "Pa's...."

"NO! NO!" Marthie grabbed her head with both hands, staring at her oldest son, her mind now passionately refusing to listen. She swayed, falling back against the roughness of the cabin walls, once again wrapping herself with her arms, holding on to what had been...crouching, holding on...slowly slipping from reality.

Sterlen will come. He always has, ever since that first time I seen him. He wuz so beautiful--him with his white hair there at the old place...on the mountain....

The boy in the corner swallowed, then rose to drag the remains of a small table to the fireplace. In seconds, he had the fire stoked and kindled. Flames, surprised and hungry, lapped at the dry wood. The boy moved back underneath his quilt, his eyes—full of reality—stone quiet in the dark clutches of double sorrow.

Smoke fingers stretched and hissed toward Marthie, but she saw only another time and place. Faint images that had hung in the chambers of her mind grew stronger, slowly materializing, swaying like whiskery moss on a dying tree. She concentrated. She could see him standing in front of another fireplace, one from long ago, in her daddy's cabin. She could see him...there...framed by the firelight.

"Sterlen," she whispered.

Red-blue flames rolled around bark and wood strips, the fire's light fanning the floor in front of Marthie, pulling her in, warming her, transporting her. Wolf Creek and her plight faded as she drifted back nineteen years in time to Cullowhee Mountain, to the Ammons Cabin, her father's homeplace.

And into the ageless shadow-light of her memory stepped Sterlen Galloway.

CHAPTER 2

Destiny on Cullowhee Mountain—1941

He gave the impression of being a big man, when actually Sterlen Galloway was of medium height and build. It was especially his wide shoulders and warm eyes that drew attention. He was not yet fifty years old, but rippling muscles, pushing at his shirt, belied his age. The sun had bleached the bearded mountain man's hair white and tanned his skin rawhide brown. And when he laughed, a deep, resounding voice filled the room.

Sterlen was a most welcome visitor in the Ammons cabin. Light from the open fireplace cast flickering shadows on the faces turned in the direction of his voice. Stories of the past, woven with nostalgia and humor, touched all hearts in the semi-circle near the rock fireplace. The mountain man's stories made his listeners forget their daily struggles in the backwoods of these western Carolina mountains and brought smiles to their faces.

On Sterlen's right sat Retter and Tom Ammons, the couple who had pioneered the mountain and raised a brood of nine children. Three of the sons, Frank, Albert and Bryson

4

Ammons, were on the other side of Sterlen, each leaning forward in his chair. On the far left, Libby, Sterlen's niece, sat next to her husband Jim Ammons. The younger children, Lillie, Corie and Nealie were all supposed to be in bed, but from where he sat, Sterlen could hear faint sounds behind him at the curtain covering the doorway to the back bedroom. He smiled.

In the shadow of the far corner of the room, sat Marthie the oldest Ammons daughter, in a rocking chair. She gave no outward sign of enjoying the company of the visitor. The sound of her chair as she rocked was her only contribution to the evening.

"Wal, now, yawl have listened to my yarns 'n' my tall tales long enough...how 'bout a little music?" said Sterlen, a smile in his eyes. And with that, he leaned toward the wall, picking up the banjo he had left near the doorway.

"Hey, Sterlen! L-l-lessus hear a fast'un!" said Frank, the grin on his face stretching even wider.

Sterlen smiled. *The young son of Tom's is tall, sorta bashful and always stalls up on his words,* he thought, *but he gits them out...all at the same time.* Then he resumed his chair, set the banjo in his lap and the small room was suddenly transported from the back woods to the deeper South as "Swanee" danced off the strings of the banjo.

In the shadows of the room, eyes sparkled as feet tapped to the tune. Each face shone with deep enjoyment and excitement. It had been a long time since they had heard music in this cabin hidden on the mountain.

The banjo slowed time for over an hour; the rhythm sometimes joined with song and laughter, and always with the tapping of feet.

Finally, Sterlen set the instrument back near the door, and shook his hand in the air. "Whew! It's been a month o' Sundays since I picked fer s'long."

"It wuz a fine bit o' pickin', Sterlen. We're all much obliged," said Retter, nodding her head at the others. They all agreed, clapping their hands.

Out of the corner of his eye, Sterlen had caught the

slightest movement, as Marthie started to applaud also, but then quickly stopped. This young woman in the back of the room had become a source of curiosity for Sterlen. Beautiful in a dark sort of way; yet the man sensed a deep sadness in her, or was it something else. She couldn't have been more than in her early twenties. Deep down, in a strange way he felt drawn to her. She didn't join the others, preferring to stay by herself. Still, there seemed to be a longing in her to be near them, but not a part of them. He decided he'd have to think about this curious girl, but at another time. He turned back to the others.

From the back of the room, Marthie looked through lowered lashes at Sterlen as he turned away. She had felt his gaze upon her, so she hadn't dared to look up. The older man fascinated her. She longed to walk close to him, to touch his white hair.

Her gaze moved across the hearth to the sparkle of Libby's chatter. How she despised her! But, for a moment, she wished she could talk as freely as her sister-in-law. Try as she might, Marthie could not join in the fun with her family and their visitor. She had no laughter in her.

Rising suddenly, Sterlen walked to the side of the room across from Marthie. He had spied a fiddle on a shelf high on the wall. He brought the fiddle down, dusted it off with his shirt sleeve, and turned to the glow of the faces in the room.

"Y'know, I try my hand once in a while at writin' words to the tunes in my head. I'd like to play one fer ye I wrote a while back."

The mountain man's presence seemed to fill the room as he now stood with his back to the fire, his white hair gleaming in the midst of the flickering light, the bow poised. The fiddle in his big hands melted into him as he played, his shadow on the wall swaying to the music. A soft, sweet tune glided through the small mountain cabin, haunting the hearts of his audience.

Softly, he began to sing....

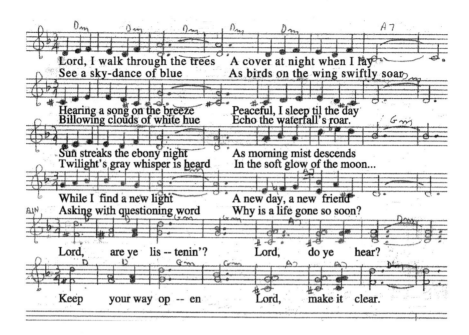

"Lord, I walk through the trees, A cover at night when I lay
Hearing a song on the breeze, Peaceful, I sleep til the day
Sun streaks the ebony night, As morning mist descends
While I find a new light, A new day, a new friend

Lord, are ye listenin'? Lord, do ye hear?
Keep your way open, Lord, make it clear.

See a sky-dance of blue, As birds on the wing swiftly soar
Billowing clouds of white hue, Echo the waterfall's roar.
Twilight's gray whisper is heard, In the soft glow of the moon...
Asking with questioning word, 'Why is a life gone so soon?

Lord, are ye listenin'? Lord, do ye hear?
Keep your way open Lord, make it clear."

The last note of the song gently died to the stillness of the room, the crackling of fire logs the only sound. Then,

without warning, Marthie stood in the dark of the corner and
ran quickly out of the room. As she passed Sterlen, he saw
the sparkle of wetness on her cheeks. The older man turned
surprised eyes toward the others as the stab in his chest
almost bent him.

"The song wuz lovely, Sterlen," Retter spoke up
quickly. "It seems to have touched us all." Her piercing eyes
met Sterlen's and then moved to the door that had closed
behind her daughter. "She's grievin' fer one who's gone from
her," she continued quietly, "Ain't nobody can help."

In the quiet that followed, all gazes rested uneasily on
the closed door.

Jim broke the silence. "Sterlen," he began, "ye ready to
light out fer the back woods tomorrow?"

With Jim's words the tension eased out of the room.

"Yep! I'm lookin' fer a new patch o' 'sang I'm hopin' to
tuck away fer this comin' September...when the diggin's
good. There's a patch over to the ravine t'other side o'
Cherry Gap they tell me. They're offerin' ten dollars a pound
fer the stuff down to Sylvie!"

"Speakin' o' Sylvie, Sterlen," spoke up Albert. "Ye
didn't brang one o' them papers they put out from there--the
'Jackson County... er...Journal?'" As he spoke, the lithesome
man rose from his seat beside his brothers and walked to the
fireplace, pulling a packet of cigarette paper leaves from his
shirt pocket. He removed a single leaf, reached for the tin of
Prince Albert on the mantle, and turned to gaze at Sterlen,
waiting for his answer.

"Naw, shore didn't...had no nickel to buy one, Albert.
Somethin' happenin' ye wanta know 'bout?" Sterlen leaned
forward, his elbows on his knees, gazing in surprise at the
quietest male member of the Ammons family.

"Jest wanted to read up on that war in them foreign
countries that started a couple o' years back." Albert deftly
held the cigarette leaf in one hand, tapped the tin of tobacco
to fill the leaf; then rolled the cigarette, licked the edge and
each tip, caught it between his lips and then spoke around it.
"Been readin' that Roosevelt asked fer a bunch o' money to
build up our fightin' forces. Yawl reckon he thanks he kin

raise that money and...take us to war?"

"I-I-I 'spect so, myself...I read where that feller Hitler thanks he'll take over the world!" said Frank from his position next to Bryson. "H-H-He better not thank o' comin' up the road yonder!"

"Jest means we need to keep Roosevelt in office all the more. 'Least he knows what he's a'doin'!" Tom Ammons stated as he lifted his crippled leg up and across the other. He pulled his knife and a plug of tobacco out of his pocket, cut off a slug, and placed it in his mouth. "Who knows what could happen! Sure hate to see my boys off 'n' gone—might come another flood like that one last year."

"Ain't it awful, Sterlen, how ye gotta dig a passel o' 'sang 'fore ye kin git one pound o' roots," spoke up Bryson, watching the workings of his mother's suddenly frightened face. "It weights nigh onto nothin'."

Sterlen obliged the shift from war talk. "Wal, Bryson...I got all the time in the world, 'n' I like the woods in the sprang. It's cold at night 'n' warm in the day; jest right fer trampin' through the brush a'checkin' on that 'sang. Should be a'sproutin' by now." Sterlen's gaze strayed to the corner of the room where the rocker sat, still and alone. "Always carry a root o' 'sang to chew on whilst I walk...stirs up my blood!"

"Come on by the Golden Place tomorrow, Sterlen, I'd like to go with ye," said Jim. "I thank I'll see if I can scout me out a groundhog or two. Got me a hankerin' fer some greasy meat...'specially after the sip I'm fixin' on takin' right 'bout now! Ye boys wanta lift a dipper er two?"

No one noticed Libby's hand slip from Jim's arm as her gaze fell to the floor. Her deep auburn hair glowed in the lamplight as she folded her hands in her lap. Chairs scraped the floor as the younger men stood; their laughter and banter following them outside.

That night Sterlen slept with the Ammons brothers in the attic of the mountain home. He shared Frank's straw-tick mattress, feeling dwarfed next to the young man.

"S-S-Sterlen, I cain't tell ye how much yer song meant

to me." Frank spoke softly, for his ear alone. "I-I-I got some decisions to make in my life that ye have...helped me with tonight...y'know, that's what songs ought to do! B-B-Be real to the listener!"

"Thank ye, son." Sterlen felt deeply drawn to this young man, and surprised at his intenseness. "That's sayin' some-thin' comin' from somebody yer age."

"Y-Y-yer a good man, Sterlen! I'm right proud to know ye. S-S-See ye in the morning." Frank turned over and went promptly to sleep.

The older man had trouble falling asleep. In his threshing about on the straw, his thoughts kept returning to that silent form in the shadows of the front room. He had felt her sadness; it had cried out to him of her loneliness and her need.

Surprised at his feelings, Sterlen finally settled himself to studying his reactions. Even though he, himself, had never found the right girl, loneliness had never bothered him much, for at the first sign of this feeling, he would grab his banjo and play to the tall blue-green spruce and shiny-leafed laurel around the small cabin he had built on Wolf Mountain. His visits to his sister Ellie, Libby's mother...and to the friends he had all over these hills had satisfied his desire for companionship and provided ears for his tall tales and singing. His life was full and he had been happy.

But now, he sensed this life was about to change. The face of Marthie had found an empty spot in his mind and had lodged there. For the first time in his life he realized a deep need to know more about a woman. Confused, but warmed by his thoughts, he finally drifted off to sleep.

CHAPTER 3

Sterlen Galloway, the Mountain Man

The next morning Sterlen found himself still deep in thought, opinions rambling around in his head as he prepared himself for his journey. He knew as well as birds fly south in fall that Jim had experienced a rough night. "Drink's a demon, 'n' Jim's got a'holt to his tail," muttered Sterlen to himself as he gathered his pack together. "Shore is a pity."

Attempting not to disturb the people of the house, Sterlen's breakfast consisted of a cold biscuit he found in the warmer of Retter's wood stove, and a quick dipper of water. Then, wiping his mouth with the back of his hand, he lifted his banjo case and quietly left the dark cabin.

A heavy dew covered the ground as Sterlen made his way up the path leading from the Ammons homeplace. At the top of the first incline, he turned and looked long at the shadowed cabin, searching in vain for a sign of the troubled girl, Marthie. Sighing, he decided he had best put her out of his mind. He had no business even considering what had entered his thoughts the night before. There was no getting around it...he was old enough to be her father.

As the trail turned to the left and gradually led upward, Sterlen's face was touched by a thin gray mist, lightly swirling, then vanishing before his eyes. Gold from the rising sun tinted the sky overhead as he breathed in the cool air, relishing the beauty that surrounded him. In the early beginnings of light, his quick eyes caught the flutter of tiny yellow wings as butterflies danced around the white of dewberry flowers. In the distance, a bobwhite added its voice to the throng of bird calls.

A sweep of wind played with his clothes, pushing the tip of his felt hat down into his eyes. Sterlen's body responded and tightened in mild excitement and he stretched his legs in energy born of long hours in the freedom of the outdoors. And as usual, all thoughts vanished for a time as the mountain man became one with the earth.

A rustling came from the undergrowth that hung above the trail. Slowly, limbs parted and softened eyes watched the back of Sterlen disappear over the rise of the mountain.

He was gone. Why did she feel as if she had lost the world? He had been to their home many times, but she, herself, had only seen him for the first time the night before. What made this man different? Whatever it was, she knew she had to find out.

The Golden Place...he's goin' to the Golden Place.

Marthie stood quickly. She whirled, and then the force of her turn billowed her hair in long strands that reached out in all directions. As quietly as she had hidden, she was suddenly gone.

Sterlen's legs stretched. He could feel the presence of the forest around him, each tree, each bush, each fern, each flower; they were now all a part of him. Born on Wolf Mountain, twenty miles from this spot as the crow flies, Sterlen had spent all his life out of doors. The freedom it gave him had shaped his body and mind.

As a child he had found his music drifting through the boughs of the swaying Balsams, the song of the whippoorwills, and in the bubbling of the many creeks he splashed through. The sounds followed him as he played alongside the terrains and cliffs of Wolf Mountain, of Horseshoe Rock, of the chestnut grove near his home; so much so, that at around age four without knowing it, he had mastered the music scales.

When he had grown in size and had the arm to reach around the arm of a banjo like he had seen others do as they played, his need to have one permeated his mind. He wanted one in the worse way. But when he asked his mother if he could have an instrument, she refused. She didn't hold with string music, and she would make no allowances for it to be played at home.

So Sterlen decided that he would make his own banjo and not let his mother know. He slipped off into the woods and cut a piece of cherry wood, then found just the place to work...high above the house on the top of Horseshoe Rock. There, alongside the summit of the rock that had horseshoe prints embedded in it, he found an old hollow log.

He sat for long hours there, backed by the draping forest, covered by the bluest of sky, and fronted by the most spectacular view in that part of the Balsam Mountain range. The boy Sterlen held the piece of wood gently, caressing it, raising it in glory to the sun as if in an offering. Then he stripped off the bark and began to whittle, to shape, to shine that piece of cherry wood. Pretty soon he had whittled himself a banjo.

What'll I use for the head? he thought. *I read where it wuz made out of cat's skin.*

But he had no cat's skin...and he wasn't about to kill one. And then, it came to him. His daddy had trapped a bobcat and had his pelt hanging on the smokehouse door. He hid his banjo inside the hollow log and ran to ask his daddy if he could use some of the pelt. But the closer he got to home, the more he doubted that his daddy would help him. *Maybe,* he thought, *I can just take part of it without anyone knowing.*

Sterlen stood looking at the pelt. There would be no way to take part of it without it showing.

Well, I best git up my nerve and ask Daddy!

And lo and behold, his daddy agreed.

In no time the boy had his banjo together. Then he began to play. He played to the sky above, to the forest at his back, to everything and everybody below and beyond where he sat on top of Horseshoe Rock.

The skin gave the banjo a gentle sound...a sound that matched the young boy's heart. Music he had never heard before moved through his body and the creation of it began to shape his entire being. The gentle mountains all around were a part of it, the hawks that soared close to his log were a part of it, the small rabbits hiding in the shadows of the rhododendron hugging the clearing were a part of it. He basked in the glory of his pure unabated God-given talent and lost time and thoughts and cares, gaining as the months passed a personality filled with only the natural love coming with creativity.

With this insight, the boy Sterlen became the man Sterlen, who made his home within the hallowed mountains in a small cabin on his sister's land and his living in the forest as an herbalist, trapping for pelts, and digging for ginseng. His entertainment followed him wherever he went, for he would visit people who lived alongside the mountain trails he walked, bringing with him the banjo and the stories that had become a part of him. Sterlen Galloway was a happy man and had been that way for all of his forty-eight years.

As he now neared his destination, Sterlen stopped deep in the coverlet of hemlock, balsam and laurel thickets. Taking a deep breath, the older mountain man rested, leaning on nothing except the quiet of his experience. His gaze swept the pathway ahead, a trail made only by the footprints of fellow inhabitants of the forest. It was a good day. Taking another deep breath, Sterlen moved forward, placing his foot into what lay ahead.

CHAPTER 4
Watching from the Chinquapin Grove

Pine needles combing her hair, Marthie sped along, her bare feet digging into the moist earth and decaying leaves. The disappearing mist, seemingly sucked up by the coming dawn, evaporated in her pathway. Strangely, everything moved aside as she passed. Limbs and branches turned back, touching her only slightly, and settled into place with hardly a movement of the leaves. A second after she passed, it was as if she had never been there. Even her footprints in the soft ground vanished under a blanket of brown pine needles.

Darkness ran beside the woman, drinking in her every glance. She knew these trails, she knew these trees, the strength within the power that held the universe together.

Her heart beat loudly in her ears, drowning out all other sounds. Why had it all been against her? Why had her elders deep within the soil, within the earth, let the devils take away her soul? She was lost...lost! And yet, she knew exactly were she was within this land of her six generations. Six genera-

tions of people who had come before her here on this very
land! Why had they not stopped her pain, her dying?

Her life as she had known it—a life of innocence, care-
free openness—had ended eight years ago when she was sixteen. It had come to an abrupt finish. But then, a year later, a
new life, a son, opened a small clearing for love...six years of
it. Six years. And then, through no fault of her own, he too,
was taken away.

For two years, she had thought that interest in life most
likely would come never again. All she had to sustain her
had been the forest...the peaceful forest; for here she could
forget for a time the hate that burned within her. She hated all
men, she hated Libby...even though she had been nowhere
around when those men had.... She couldn't even think the
words! She hated God! She hated all who stood in her way.

Suddenly, now, somewhere inside of her, a spark had
ignited. She had seen something in the eyes of this
Sterlen...something she wanted but didn't know what it could
be. Control was gone for the moment. She had to find out, to
follow, to watch at a distance until she could understand. She
would have to go over the devil's back and under his belly to
sneak past her own madness...but, maybe....

Given the name of one of it's past residents, Jim Golden,
the Golden Place was a small cabin, weathered and old, set
among an orchard of apple trees. A fence of palings ran
along one side of the house, circled a garden plot, and then
pushed away the forest along the back with its sharp points.
A spring house covered the head of the spring to the left of
the cabin, the spring bubbling up and rushing from underneath the rough logs to twist its way down the mountain. A
strong stand of chinquapin bushes had conquered the cliff
above the spring, walling the edge of the first incline to the
north and west of the Golden Place.

It was into this stand of chinquapins that Marthie ended
her run. The girl stood for a moment staring toward the
cabin, then she turned an anxious gaze back to the edge of the
woods. She dropped to the ground beside a large crumbling
rock. Not even breathing hard, she waited.

The barn was not much more than a lean-to made of split oak and pine. Poison ivy crept up one side, its roots digging into the aged wood. A path coming from the cabin had been worn down into the dull red dirt, forming an almost perfect "Y," one walkway stopping at the barn door and then running on to the forest beyond, the other going past the spring toward a cove underneath the northern end of the chinquapin stand.

Just as Sterlen came into view, a dominecker rooster jumped to the top of an old tree stump, flapped its wings and crowed a welcome.

The man stopped, set his banjo case on the ground, took off his hat, and leaned against an apple tree. Smoke rose from the chimney, testifying that someone was up and stirring. Sterlen took a deep breath, and rolled his head around on his neck once, then twice. He needed this time to adjust, to bring himself back from a world foreign to most. His body and mind consumed the lacy forests in beds of tender fern, bits and pieces of sky and mountain springs, mossy earth and foamy waterfalls. His heart still vibrated with the noiseless sounds of the unchartered trails of the lingering souls of the Cherokee, the songs forever unfolding like the petals of dogwood blossoms.

From the door of the barn, the rooster crowed again. For some reason, the slight breeze against Sterlen's brow seemed to suddenly carry the presence of an unknown quality. He narrowed his eyes, studying the scene before him. Uneasy now, the man pulled away from the tree, his gaze sweeping the edges of the clearing in the woods. Nothing moved except a hawk circling slowly above; yet Sterlen still bided his time.

Marthie's heart pounded incredulously. *He knows I'm here. He feels me!*

She sank lower, still further behind the crumbling rock, disturbing no leaf, almost melting into the earth itself. *Please, don't let him see me.*

The barn door suddenly opened, and Jim came out, his tall head ducking as he leaned heavily on Libby. From their vantage points, neither Sterlen nor Marthie could hear what they were saying to each other. Their walk to the door of the Golden Place had interrupted Sterlen's thoughts, thereby directing his attention away from the ghost of uneasiness. Shaking his head, Sterlen retrieved his banjo case and began to cover the ground between him and the yard quickly. He had wasted enough time day dreaming.

The sun's rays now beginning to warm the path into the Golden Place gave the hiding eyes full opportunity to observe the man who strode with intention. Marthie, wide-eyed, drank in the strength of the older mountain man, kindling a desire she would never lose. The walk to the cabin lasted only a few short minutes, but it left Marthie almost breathless. As he knocked at the door, then disappeared inside the cabin, she knew without a doubt that this was the man of whom she had dreamed. But that had been before....

Oh God! Oh God!

Marthie dropped her head to the soft earth, her hair spreading out into the high grass. She moaned.

I ain't fittin' fer no man like him! No man would ever want me now!

CHAPTER 5

To Kill The Pain Of It All

While Sterlen had been walking through the woods, another story had been unfolding at the Golden Place.

Jim stirred, turning his face away from the morning sunlight that streamed through a crack in the barn. The straw on which he lay rustled as he moved. Caught within the cold, he slowly realized the pain in his left leg was beginning to rival the pain in his head. He moaned aloud, his callused hand covering his face.

Lying still, he tried to think. This Sunday morning would be like all the Sunday mornings he'd had since he and Libby had married and moved into the Golden Place in October of last year. He would have to pay for the good time he'd had last night.

He grimaced. What he needed was a drink. His hand slid from his face as he realized he would have to move. Rolling his heavy tongue around in his foul-tasting mouth, he

19

tried to pull himself up. Pain ran across the top of his head from one temple to the other. Funny how he always forgot about this pain every Saturday night.

With difficulty he staggered to his feet, his hands going to his head as he tried to soothe the pain driven like a spike into his head.

A drink! he had to have a drink!

His bloodshot eyes sought and found the quart jars he had set high on a beam overhead. In his haste to reach a jar, he almost fell.

The ring lid wouldn't turn at first in his trembling hands, but strength flowed gradually into his arms as the desire for the liquor grew. Then, the long drink from the fruit jar, taken in big gulps that burned all the way down, made him feel much better. He wiped his mouth with the back of his hand, and rocked to and fro on the balls of his feet. He took another drink and screwed the lid back on the jar.

Remarkably after his second drink, Jim's countenance seemed to change; he straightened to his full height, and slowly looked around for his hat. He absently brushed at the bits and pieces of straw sticking to his clothes and hair. The pain that had filled his head had dulled, tapering off to a mild ache.

He spied his hat half hidden in the straw, and stepped forward, bending to pick it up. But then the pain in his leg hit him sharply! It hurt so badly tears sprang to his eyes. He must have gotten cold in the old wound again. Jim stumbled to the corner of the barn, and leaned against the wall, only to slide slowly downward, sitting once again in the straw on the dirt floor.

Jim gently stretched his leg out before him, eased his head back against the wall of split pine, and closed his eyes.

That's how Libby found him an hour later. She stood in the doorway, wrapped in a heavy coat, looking at her husband with mixed emotions. Anger clouded her eyes, yet she could see the pain on his face.

"Jim! 'er ye all right?" her voice so loud it startled him.

He swallowed visibly, careful not to move his head, and watched her through lowered eyes as she walked toward him.

"Jim! kin ye hear me?" she said, more anger rising.

"I'm nigh onto dead, Libby," came Jim's rough voice.

"Ye got drunk agin last night, Jim. Why do ye do it when it hurts ye so?" Libby's voice continued to rise.

"Libby, I can't argue with ye...I'm 'most dead. 'Sides, it's my leg that pains me."

"Yer leg!" she exclaimed. "Don't ye know yer drinkin' is makin' yer leg worse! Ye sleep out o' doors here in this barn in the cold, 'n' ye can't figger out why yer leg hurts? Jim Ammons...use yer head! Or does that hurt ye, too?"

"Can't git any sweetness outta ye today, kin I?" said Jim, glancing at her, his chin resting on his chest. "Kin I git ye to help me to the house?"

"No, sir! Ye want somethin' to lean on? Wal, I'll tell ye what! I'm gonna have yer daddy whittle ye out a walkin' stick like his'n. That's all the lean onto's yer gonna git!"

Jim had begun to push himself up as Libby spoke, but the pain on his face was so evident that she began feeling regret at her words. Love pushed away her anger as she walked over to help him.

"Oh, Jim...ye are in a lot o' pain, ain't ye! I'm s'sorry fer it." Libby's tone now showed deep concern. As she leaned down to him, from the open door of the barn behind her, Libby heard the old dominecker crow. *"Means we gonna git a visitor,"* she thought absently. *"Gotta git this feller o' mine into the house."*

Unaware that they were being watched, the two made their way slowly from the barn, Jim's left arm draped over her shoulder and her right arm around his waist. Libby moved her thin frame close to Jim's side, giving him the support he needed.

A pleasant smell of burning wood greeted them as they entered the small kitchen. Jim was happy to see the walls that had become his new home. He had been content here with Libby these first months of marriage.

Libby helped Jim sit down at the table and pulled up another chair for him so he could rest his leg. He loosened his coat and, trying to grin, looked up at Libby. "Yer the best walkin' stick I ever did have, honey."

"Oh, go on with ye!" grinned Libby. "Ye say that jest to git on my good side."

"All yer sides are good!" laughed Jim as the warmth of the room cradled him. Suddenly, there came a pounding at the front door.

"*Hello!* Hello the house!"

"My goodness, who on earth...oh...the old dominecker told me somebody wuz a'comin'! That rooster's always right...." Libby's voice trailed off as she went toward the door.

"Dagnab it! It's Sterlen!" called Jim behind her as he shook his head at himself. "I wuz supposed to go on out to Cherry Cap with him this mornin'... I fergot!"

"Howdy, Jim. Howdy, Libby. How yaw'll faring this mornin'?" Sterlen came stamping into the room, rubbing his hands together. "Me, I'm doin' fair ta middlin'; the walk over the mountain sure stirred up my blood this mornin'!"

"Wal, I ain't feelin' none too good, Sterlen, if ye wanta know the truth. My leg's actin' up agin."

"Sorry to hear it, Jim. How 'bout some coffee? Libby, ye got some brewin'?"

"Shore do, Uncle Sterlen. Pull up a chair 'n' sit a spell. I'll git us some cups." Libby scurried around the kitchen, and soon there were three steaming mugs on the table.

"Yer leg's been a chore fer quite a spell, huh, Jim?" said Sterlen, sitting down at the table, gazing at Jim's obviously bloodshot eyes.

"Yep, it shore has! I reckon I won't be goin' on over to Cherry Cap with ye today, Sterlen...don't reckon I'll be doin' much at all." Jim set his empty cup down on the table and wiped his mouth, shaking his head.

Libby got up to refill Jim's cup.

"Whatever happened to yer leg anyway, Jim? How'd ye git in such a bad fix?" Sterlen leaned toward Jim, taking a sip of coffee. "Heard tell ye got buckshot in it."

"Yep, shore have; it wuz an accident ...a long time ago. If ye got some time, I'll tell the story." Jim sat up, straightened himself, a far-away look coming into his eyes.

"I always got time fer a story, Jim!"

Libby refilled their cups and silently seated herself near Sterlen at the table, sipping coffee as the two of them listened to Jim.

"I wuz twelve years old...er near 'bouts, 'n' our oldest brother, Bryson, wuz 'bout fourteen. Grandmaw, Mama's mama, wuz feelin' porely, so's Momma 'n' Daddy wuz gone to see her when this thang happened. In other words, we wuz all alone." Jim paused to make sure his audience was listening, then he continued.

"Homer--ye remember our cousin, Homer Coggins, don't ye, Sterlen? Homer had come to see us boys. We wuz all in the sittin' room a'playin'. Homer wuz a mite littler'n me, 'n' him 'n' Thomas had been playin' with a blindfold. Homer suddenly sees that old shotgun o' Bryson's hangin' on the wall. Bein' he wuz such a nosy soul, he pulls down that old gun 'n' commences to look it over.

"Bryson, he comes off the bed where he'd been layin', 'n' starts to take it away from Homer.

"Whilst this wuz goin' on, I wuz puttin' on my socks Momma had made me. I had jest got one on, 'n' begun puttin' the other one on. My leg wuz up to jest 'bout here," Jim held up his leg to illustrate. "Then I retched over to git me a string to tie my sock up, when the gun went off 'n' knocked me over under the table 'side the wall. Blood wuz a'gushin' outta my leg like it wuz a sieve.

"Homer, he musta had his fanger over the barrel, cuz the shot purt near blew it off! He commenced throwin' such a fit that at first nobody even knowed I wuz hit. But Albert comes in 'n' sees me with the blood a'spurtin' out all which a'ways.

"Wal, sir, I rose up 'n' hopped over to a chair 'n' Bryson tuck off up into the attic to git some spiderwebs to stop the bleedin'. He piled 'um on thick, 'n' then him 'n' Albert finally got a sheet wrapped hard 'round my leg.

"'N' while this wuz a'goin' on, Thomas done run outta the house 'n' on over to Grandmaw's. Pretty soon they all come runnin'...bringin' old Doc Wilkes. He wuz a Army doctor in the first war, ye know. Like to cut thangs up...."

Jim paused and took a long drink of coffee, gazing at the widened eyes of his wife and the interested face of Sterlen. He smiled faintly as he continued.

"Old Doc, ye should've seen him! He'd been the doc fer ever s'long in our parts, 'n' he wuz old--real old. I kin see him as if it wuz yesterday! His hair wuz white—like yourn, Sterlen—'n' he had a white mustache stained with tabaccy juice. The black coat he wore jest seemed to hang from his bowed shoulders. He shore wuz a sight!

"But, what I remember most wuz his eyes! They wuz red 'n' shiny, 'n' seemed to glare at me from underneath them bushy white eyebrows. All I could think o' then wuz that he must be close to lookin' like the devil. Why, he jest 'bout scared me to death!

"Wal, sir, he takes his time a'gittin' his black bag open. Then he lays out onto the table some long silver-lookin' sizzers—'n' a knife. I remember his fingers wuz all crooked 'n' drawed up together.

"Then, he turns 'n' he looks at my leg, 'n' says in a real deep voice, 'Looks like I'm gonna have to cut it off, boy!'

"I jest 'bout died right there! He wanted to cut my leg off!" Jim's expression seemed to be once again one of total disbelief. "Wal, Daddy wouldn't let him, thank God! He told him to jest git the pellets out 'n' he'd trust to the Lord fer the gittin' better o' it.

"'N' then, Doc looks at Homer's fanger...'n before any-one kin blink an eye, he cut off the rest o' Homer's fanger 'n' throwed it in the fire!" The tall man paused for effect, swinging his arm toward the pot-bellied stove, and then repeated, "Jest like that, he throwed it in the fire!

"When Doc wuz wrappin' his hand up, Homer jest stood there, starin' into the fire. He had the quarest look on his face. Everbody wuz standin' there with their mouths open.

"But as we watched Homer's fanger burn up, that old

doc started in on me. He commenced jabbin' my leg with a long needle. There'd be a 'ping,' 'n' then he'd pull out the pellet...'n' then there'd be another 'ping,' 'n' he'd pull another pellet. He went on doin' that 'til he thought they wuz all gone. Then he rubbed my leg with some black salve 'n' wrapped it up. By then, the pain had hit me, 'n' I wuz yellin' somethin' fierce! I all but chewed up my piller in amongst it all.

"I wuz never s'glad to see anyone go as I wuz old Doc Wilkes. He left a'ridin' on a mule...it wuz the same mule he'd come on, I reckon."

Jim sat still for a moment, gazing out the window near the kitchen stove. After straightening out his leg, he went on.

"It dragged on fer days--the pain--the awful pain. 'N' then it got worse, till I took the wrappin' off myself. That wuz when Momma pulled the strangs outta my leg...strangs that'd come from my britches. They had gone into the holes in my leg betwixt the pellets. She pulled the strangs out, 'n' there wuz the awfulest smell...the awfulest pain!" The kitchen had gotten so quiet the listeners could almost hear the boy Jim cry out.

"At last I begun to git some better. Daddy even built me a wagon so I could roll myself around...but it took nigh onto three years 'fore I could walk good."

"That's some story, Jim! But I gotta tell ye...I've heard some o' it before! Don't rightly recollect where, though." Sterlen rubbed his chin.

"Reckon ye heard it at church." Jim laughed.

"Wal...now that ye mention it, that's so. Howsomever, it wuz a while back."

"Yep! Had to be from Homer hisself ye heard it. Fer, ye see, Homer never did forgive Bryson fer shootin' his fanger off. Since Bryson got religion, he sometimes runs into Homer at church, 'n' ever chance Homer gits, he stands right up 'n' testifies agin us mean Ammonses fer ruinin' his shootin' fanger!"

Sterlen laughed. "Reckon that would addle a feller a mite, Jim!"

Libby stood to gather the empty coffee cups, shaking her head. "All I gotta say is that ain't nothin' to testify 'bout in church! Now...a feller quitin' his unholy drinkin' would be, though!"

Jim's face lost its smile. And just as suddenly, there was the scrape of wood against wood as he rose unsteadily from his chair. Slowly he made his way over to the far wall. He reached up to a shelf above his head and brought down a half-full jar of moonshine.

As he unscrewed the lid, he turned to the two who were now watching him in somber silence. Then, with an almost sarcastic smile on his face, he saluted them with the jar. "To kill the pain o' it all!" he said, and putting the rim to his mouth, he turned the jar up.

CHAPTER 6
The Praying Cove

"Here, Jim, put this buckeye in yer pocket," said Sterlen, as the two men prepared to set off on their venture. "If ye rub it evertime yer leg acts up, it'll take away some o' the pain."

"Mebbe it'll brang me some luck, too!" Jim laughed as he put the glossy brown nut into his pocket, and then picked up his rifle.

Her apron knotted in her hands, Libby watched Jim limp away with Sterlen. She supposed she should be happy her uncle Sterlen had talked Jim into going with him, telling him that he could surely get that groundhog he wanted. After all, it was Sunday...his day off from logging, and he didn't seem to be too happy with her for complaining about his drinking in the presence of Sterlen, anyway.

Sunday! Poppy's preaching today...preachin' 'n' prayin'! I miss it. I miss Mommy 'n' Poppy...'n' the young'un's!

Libby's uplifted face wrinkled as a tear slid across her cheek, rolling into her ear. She loosened her hold on the apron and wiped at the tear with her wrist.

Now don't go feelin' sorry fer yerself! Yo're married now; ain't no call to drag out yesterd'y's fatback drippin's! I can't go to preachin'...but I surely kin pray!

Libby set off toward what she called her "prayin' cove."

Sheltered by the deep-green of laurel bushes, the hollow in the side of the mountain opened like a half-moon at the mouth of the creek that snaked it's way down the mountain beside the Golden Place. It took Libby only minutes to walk to this place that had become her refuge away from home. For a moment, she stared intently into the recessed dark rocks of the mountain, once again marveling that the spring had never ceased to run, even in the driest of seasons. At least, that's what Jim had told her when they had moved up here, an hour's walk from the Ammons homestead.

Libby relished this time in prayer. Jim had no patience with her prayers in the house, so Libby had found her own little world out here in God's cathedral. On a mossy knoll, cushioned near the sweet smell of earth and dampened vegetation, Libby knelt. She did not feel the burn of the hidden eyes above her, watching.

Taught from early childhood to pray by her daddy, Wiley Owen the circuit-riding preacher from Wolf Mountain, the preacher's daughter began her prayers for Jim...prayers that sometimes lasted all morning or all evening.

"Well Lord, here I am agin..." she raised her face and began as if she were addressing a friend, "here on bended knees in this cove! I'm a'prayin' fer my Jim -- fer my Jim to see the error of his ways. This drankin' is gonna be the death o' him...er me, one! He don't know what he's doin', Lord. If he could but see what I see.... But Lord, he does come by it rightly, I reckon. All his family dranks...them brothers all started drankin' from a water bucket...they warn't any more'n seven years old, Jim says. They been drankin' it by the dipperful fer ever s'long.

"Jim's a powerful strong man...them arms are like steel...'n' them hands are so big 'n' calloused! He sure does put his heart into what he's a'doin'. Sometimes he fergits when he's a'huggin' on me, 'n' I git a'feared he's gonna squeeze me s'tight I'm gonna wind up cross-eyed. But, Lord, he don't mean it! He's got the kindest o' hearts...but o' course he hides it. Folks 'round these parts call him the meanest of the 'mean, fightin' Ammons' boys.' He kin be mean et times...but I do know, Lord, that he works his fangers to the bone! Why...Bryson says Jim's the best of the loggers in the territory...he cuts 'um, trims 'um, rolls 'um, 'n' does it all by hand.

"Don't ye think, Lord, he'd make a mighty fine preacher? I been thinkin' on it some fer quite a spell. It's settled into my soul with a stayin' power...'course I know better'n to say anythang like that to Jim!

"The devil's got him now 'n' he's pushin' hard to keep him. I think that devil's sunk low enough to slosh 'round in that jar o' moonshine! He keeps on a'whisperin' in Jim's ear, a'hangin' onto him like a cat in heat!

        "That devil's smart...cuz he knows Jim would make a fearsome foe! Jim don't even know hisself what he could do if he takes a hankerin' to.

"Ain't there nothin' I kin do, Lord?

"Yeah, I know I kin pray...but...I been prayin' down on my knees a goodly part o' ever day since we got married...'n Jim's only got worse!

"Lord...I worry some that yer s'busy up there that ye don't have time fer jest one prayer risin' up outta this cove. Kin Ye hear me up there, Lord?"

A cool wind began slipping through the limbs above her, moaning quietly in an almost sing-song fashion. Libby ignored it, continuing in her attempt to be heard.

"If Ye kin hear me, Lord, I thank ye! I thank ye...fer givin' me this sweet man to love me. I thought I'd be an old maid, cuz I had already done aged outta my young years when ye finally sent Jim.   In all that time, I never thought I'd git the chance to find a man to love me like he does.

"'N'...I thank ye, Lord, fer testin' me now. Poppy always says we all gotta be tested some how. I jest reckon it takes a month o' Sundays to git the job done. I know ye got somethin' planned fer Jim that's a'waitin'. I begun to feel that now. I been sent to help him, ain't I..cuz there ain't nobody up here on Ammons Mountain that's gonna help him find the thing he's bound to do...nobody but me. None o' 'um kin see how special he is!"

Libby paused and swallowed, bringing her hands up to her breast.

"But, Lord, while I'm at it, I jest wanted to say that I cain't figger out why...Ye took my little'un I wuz a'carryin'...a few months back. I warn't more'n a month along, Miz Ammons says. Now, here I am agin, missin' my time two months...soes, I reckon I'm carryin' another little'un.

"I...want this baby, Lord! There ain't nobody up here on the back o' this mountain to talk to...'ceptin' Jim...'n' I don't much like to talk to Jim when he's been a'drankin'. 'Sides, I want a little'un to hold...close here in my arms.

"Please, Lord...can I have...this baby. Please, Lord...please...."

The wind ceased its prowl. Libby's chin had slowly sunk until it rested on her collar bone. The earnestness in her plea wrapped the cove in stillness. Then, as if in answer to the woman, a soft warm rain began to fall. Libby's quickly dampening head rose and a sudden small smile tugged at her lips as she turned to look back down the pathway.

"My Jim! A preacher," she said to the rain, "I kin see him now, a'comin' up the mountain yonder, a'totein' a Bible under one arm, 'n' carryin' a young'un in the other'n." She paused, and raising her face into the rain, she continued, "Are Ye up there, Lord...Kin Ye hear me.... Please give me this baby."

CHAPTER 7

Within the Smoky Mist

A baby! *Libby's gonna have a baby! Why should she? It's not fair! It's jest not fair!*

Hidden within the bushes above the cove, Marthie's now hard, cold eyes narrowed. Even the caressing rain could not dilute their intensity. All thoughts of Sterlen had vanished. Hidden above Libby's cove, she had listened to the words of this woman and had come to a conclusion. Libby had married Marthie's brother, taken the place of her beloved Bell. Why should she even like her! Libby was a stranger on this mountain. She should have stayed with her own people. Jim drank...he would always drink! Even Bell couldn't make him stop! Just who was Libby to think she could come into another family and change their lives!

And it simply was not fair for Libby to have a baby when she had lost her own. Something had to be done; this woman needed to be taught a lesson.

An image of her son's face tugged at Marthie's mind.

Jhon Fred! Oh, Jhon Fred!   Why?

Below, Libby rose from her kneeling position, and
leaned over for a time rubbing the feeling back into her
knees. Marthie pulled herself out of her memories, more
determined than ever that Libby should suffer some of her
own pain.

A breeze picked up, warmer than usual for this time of
year, bringing the rain in earnest, forcing Libby to hurry
toward the house. Marthie followed, passing the spring,
veering onto the other path, and coming to the door of the
barn. There she stepped inside, lingering by the
opening...planning as she watched Libby enter the cabin.

About midday the rain quit, yet thick heavy gray clouds
remained in the sky.

At noon, Libby stood on the back porch of the Golden
Place, gazing out at the dismal weather. The day matched her
spirits. Through the raindrops that slowly fell from the
eaves of the porch, Libby stared at the now misty mountains
in the distance.

"How-do, Libby," came a flat voice beside her.

Startled, Libby turned quickly to view Marthie. Libby's
eyes grew large and she shivered.

"Libby, I been wonderin'," Marthie's emotionless voice
continued, "would ye care to see my most favor-rite place in
the whole world?"

Libby's eyes grew even larger. These were as many
words as Marthie had ever said to her at one time.
Something seemed to be telling Libby to move away, not to
listen to this woman. But Libby shook off the feeling and
answered her.

"I ain't done nothin' this whole day. I shore would!"

"Wal, ye cover up right good; it's a'ways over that
mountain yonder." Marthie half-turned from Libby, her eyes
lowered. Then, as Libby hurried into the back room, a
curious look darkened Marthie's features as she smiled
through tight lips.

The world was wet and still dripping as the two young

women made their way up the trail. Marthie was in the lead, and with her back to Libby, there was no conversation.

Libby tried to keep her sense of direction as she followed Marthie, but before long she was totally lost. When they had left the Golden Place, they had started out toward its upper pasture, so at first Libby had not thought much about being in an area that was unknown to her. Soon, however, Marthie had turned away from the worn trail and had gone deep into the forest. Libby knew then that she had made a big mistake. She must now depend upon Marthie, a woman who truly frightened her.

The air had grown heavy and damp. All around her, Libby could hear the sound of water dripping. Drops came sliding down the pine boughs and fell onto brown oak leaves. Then they glided silently through the still air, only to reach the earth with a soft pitter-patter.

Libby began to wonder just what kind of place Marthie would think of as her favorite spot. Her own favorite places were in clearings blessed by the sun.

It was apparent that Marthie was leading Libby down the side of the mountain into a valley or hollow. Cool air began pushing aside the moist breeze that had been following the women. A light wind whispered softly in the treetops.

Suddenly, a misty fog began to rise from the cold earth, appearing as if from nowhere. Stealthily, the fog crept, clinging lovingly to the folds of Marthie's ankle-length skirt, then dancing out and slowly rising.

"Marthie! We best turn back, there's too much fog!" Libby's voice trembled. She hugged her arms closer to her body and shivered.

"Don't be a'feared, Libby, jest follow me. We're 'most there now anyways." Marthie's voice floated back to Libby. There was a calm in her attitude that soothed Libby's growing fear...almost.

Against the thickness of the close growth, shadows moved in on the two women. To Libby, the scene before her seemed unreal. Marthie's dark figure was immersed almost to the waist in the white sea of fog.

Libby's shoes began to slip on the wet leaves and pine needles, making it difficult for her to keep her balance.

"Marthie, please! Let's turn back. I can't see where to step."

This time Marthie didn't answer. She only walked faster, not even turning her head. It seemed to Libby that Marthie's feet had been over these leaves so many times that she could have been walking blindfolded.

Fear almost consumed Libby. Why hadn't she listened to her misgivings?

Where is this woman takin' me?

Her gaze darted to either side of Marthie. In the fog, she could see only dark limbs, as if somehow, mysteriously, they had no beginnings. She listened to the drip...drip...drip of the spruce's tears, to the low voices of the tree frogs, and to the padding of Marthie's footsteps on the wet ground.

Then, Marthie stopped. Slowly she turned and smiled at Libby. Even through the mist, Libby could see Marthie's eyes flash. It seemed unnatural. Libby noticed that some strands of hair clung to Marthie's face, drawing attention to the pallor of her skin.

"Wal, Libby, this here is it!"

Libby turned around, trying her best to appreciate Marthie's favorite spot. They were deep in a hollow, surrounded by undergrowth and trees. The now bare limbs of sycamore intertwined with the branches of full-chested white pine, heavy twisted vines of muscadine clutching the boughs. The fog still drifted among the trees and bushes, claiming them. The place gave Libby an eerie feeling. Her body quivered. She felt as if she were slipping down inside a tight-fitting glove. There was nowhere to turn, except back to Marthie. Libby spun around, taking a step forward. But the hollow was suddenly empty. There was no Marthie.

"MARTHIE! WHERE ARE YE? MARTHIE!" Libby's voice resounded in her own ears.

There was no answer; not even an echo. Her voice had been absorbed by the white blanket that still covered the woods.

"Marthie...?" Libby's voice, now soft, belied the fast beating of her heart. Her arms fell to her sides.

Deep in the secluded hollow, the fog closed in on the lone figure.

CHAPTER 8

Hair of Fire

L ibby couldn't speak. The words wouldn't come from
around the lump in her throat. As darkness fell and
tears slowly rolled down her cheeks, she listened
fearfully to the sounds around her. She could hear the
weeping of the forest. She stood still as the fog enfolded her.

God. . .Oh, my God!

Suddenly, her legs would no longer hold her; she sank to
the wet ground. Her arm brushed against the side of a fallen
trunk and she felt a soft cushion of moss. In the darkness,
she explored the size of the log and found that she could use
it as a bench. She pulled herself up and sat down, her move-
ments stirring the white misty thickness.

There was nothing Libby could do except wait. When
the fog lifted, she could try to find her way back. As she sat
in the grey darkness, her imagination went to work. The
sounds of the forest seemed to magnify. The drip of the rain
became approaching footsteps, and the croak of the tree frogs
became the cry of faceless creatures in the night. Libby
clenched her arms with cold hands and squeezed her eyes

shut so that she would be less conscious of her plight.

Time passed slowly. She brought her feet up onto the log, covered her legs with her skirt, and found that she could lean against the wet bark of a tree. Her head slumped to her knees and she wrapped her arms around her legs. Tears eased from the corners of her closed eyes. Her thoughts began to drift. Thoughts of Jim and Sterlen came to her. There would be no help from them. Scenes of her old home and family came to her. She could see Poppy's face, floating at first small and far away, then coming closer and closer. He smiled and his lips moved. Words crept into Libby's mind, "Weeping endureth for a night, but joy cometh in the morning." The words were calming and she slept.

Night claimed the small figure. All around her, layers of white swayed to the dark music of the pines. And then, almost without warning, the fog slowly began to dissipate, pushed gently by a strange, crying breeze. Then even it ceased and the earth became still.

Suddenly, Libby awoke. Immediately, she realized that there were no night sounds about her. The silence hurt her ears. Her eyes grew wide. Oddly, moonbeams had found their way through the now thin mist, through the boughs of pine and sycamore, to illuminate the hollow before her. Her gaze caught the flicker of a campfire. There was a pleasant smell of burning oak. And suddenly, before her, stood a Native American. His long white hair flowed over his buckskin shoulders. Wrinkles lined his face, his eyes alert. He carried a staff decorated with a knot of eagle feathers.

Libby stared. *It's an Indian! I've never met an Indian before!* She jumped to her feet, and then froze, feeling only the pain in her hands as she tightly gripped her arms.

"Woman rise from ela [earth] with hair of fire!" he said. At first the old man sounded as if he were as startled as she. Then he spoke again, a question in his voice.

"White woman lost?"

Libby's tongue was paralyzed. She couldn't answer. Working her mouth, but with no effect, she continued to stare, her eyes still wide. She thought that if she blinked, he would disappear.

The Native American dug his staff into the wet pine needles. He repeated, "White woman lost?"

Finally, Libby managed to answer. "Yes...I'm lost...I reckon."

"Be not afraid, ste Tsi [child]. Great Spirit is here...all around." The Indian moved his staff in a circle, tracing the shadows of limbs that edged the firelight. "Come, sit with me by the fire."

Libby picked her way gratefully toward the warmth. She sat, following his lead, the two of them positioned across from each other, he crossing his ankles. She could see him clearly, the early morning greyness replaced by the gold of firelight.

Then he spoke again.

"Here in the forest lives all truth. By day, the light of the Creator shows the way. In the dark of the moon the eyes and mind rest, but still the Creator sees." The old man crossed his arms, his face calm. "Wind is the breath of the Creator."

Still, she could not speak.

His face softened. "Hair of Fire is afraid? Listen...."

High above them, Libby could hear the swish of the pines. In her mind, she could almost see the wind gathering the smoky mist, sweeping it away with limbs of pine. The woman began to slip into a cocoon of warmth.

"Only the soul can see in the dark. The soul needs a path to follow, so the Creator, in His wisdom, gives eyes to the soul. Then the soul rides on the wind. It's good to listen to the wind. On the wind comes voices of all souls--all spirits. They come to help, they come to warn, they come to tell of the future.

"Retter's girl child comes here many times, not knowing why. She comes to weep—on down the trail by the waterfall. I watch, but it is not time to speak to her. She is too full of sorrow to hear the voices. Time will come when I will speak to her. Hair of Fire will tell Retter?" His piercing eyes took in Libby's quick nod, then he rose, and moving slowly, the old man covered the fire with black dirt, pushing it with the toe of his moccasin. Taking his staff, he turned to walk into the trees. Over his shoulder came the words, "Hair of Fire, come--follow."

Libby didn't question his command. She rose and followed silently. The smell of the fire lingered in the folds of her skirt as she trudged behind the imposing figure.

A pathway seemed to open before the old man as he led her up, up, and then back down again. There were no sounds made by the footsteps of the man she followed. Slowly Libby again heard the sounds of the night, a chorus chanted by unseen caretakers of the darkness.

She set aside her fear, the feeling replaced by a strange curiosity.

Who is this Indian in front of me? Where has he come from?

When he stopped, Libby halted only a few feet from him. He turned to face her. Behind him, in the moonlight, she could clearly see the trail that led down to the Ammons homestead. Relief flooded her.

"Hair of Fire see Retter's cabin?" The old man spoke softly beside her.

"Oh, yes, I can't begin to thank ye enough," said Libby. She started to move around him.

"Wait...woman with crying heart comes," spoke the old man. His arm, holding the staff, went out before him. Libby could see a dim shadow approaching from below.

Stepping closer to Libby, the old man continued quietly, "Retter's girl child is full of sorrow. Listen...." He turned his head. "hear the wind in trees cry?" He stared deep into Libby's eyes. "It's hard to hear a heart cry."

Still puzzled, Libby glanced again toward the figure that would soon be upon them. Then she looked back to the Indian. He was gone.

I don't know who he is! My spirit of the wind...didn't tell me his name.

Her mind full, Libby waited.

"Marthie!" Libby's voice caused the woman to come to a

complete stop. Her searching eyes quickly found the shadowy figure. She appeared to be only slightly surprised to find Libby waiting here for her, instead of miles away.

"Wal, here ye are. I wuz jest comin' to fetch ye," Marthie said, her voice unfeeling.

"Marthie, why did ye go off 'n' leave me?"

The woman standing before her didn't answer. Her back was to the full of the moon, so Libby couldn't see her face. She saw only the black outline of her body against the circle of yellow behind her. Libby felt surprise at her lack of fear before this woman who had deserted her only hours before. The words of the Indian had somehow strengthened the spirit of the woman with the hair of fire.

Libby spoke again. "Marthie, why don't ye like me? What have I done to ye?" She didn't look at Marthie as she spoke. "Marthie, I kin be yer friend...honest I kin."

Again Marthie held her silence.

If Libby had looked up, she would have seen Marthie's hand move toward her slightly, almost reaching out to her. But it was only the smallest gesture, quickly withdrawn.

"'Pears ye have a little gumption, after all. Ye found yer way back here." Marthie's voice rose and fell in the darkness.

"Marthie, I want to be friends with ye." Libby turned toward Marthie as she spoke.

Quickly stepping back, Marthie shied away from the offered friendship. As Libby hesitated, Marthie spoke again, in a softer tone. "'Way back, when ye wuz sick 'n' layin' in Momma's bed that first month ye wuz here, I felt kinda sorry fer ye. Once er twice, I even went fer enough to pull up yer covers. 'N' my boy did seem to like ye."

Libby quickly took advantage of her seeming change of character. "Marthie, I don't remember much those first few days—but I could see that Jhon Fred loved ye so much he wuz jealous 'bout the care o' ye. He tried to do anythin' in his power to make sure ye wanted fer nothin'! I could see how easy it wuz fer ye to love him. Why, everybody loved him! Did ye ever wonder how he could show so much love when ye seemed...to have none to give him?"

"I loved my boy!" Marthie's voice came back strong as her body began to jerk.

"Yes! Yes ye did!" Libby hurried on, moving closer to the woman she had finally moved. "Ye loved him...I loved him, too! Yer heart cries fer him! My heart cries fer him! Although we are so different, Marthie, we have our feelin's fer Jhon Fred in common. We have each loved yer boy, in different ways, but we loved him! We must learn to get along with each other, for the sake of Jhon Fred's memory!" She moved even closer to Marthie, this time touching her arm. She continued talking, "I wuz yer son's friend...I'm yer friend!"

Marthie stood still, this time not drawing away. She seemed to be studying what the red-headed woman had said. Then quietly, she spoke, "I'll think on it some. Come on down to the house. Ye might as well have breakfast with Momma." Marthie turned, and started off quickly.

Without answering, Libby first glanced around her, half expecting to see her Indian spirit, but seeing nothing but trees, she hurried to follow Marthie. Her mind churned with the sudden change in the situation. Maybe this trip into the unknown had turned into the best thing that could have happened. She felt strong. She watched the shoulders of the woman before her. Yes, there was a resemblance here. In the sway of the shoulders, Libby could once again see the swagger of a little figure--the figure of Jhon Fred. How she had loved Marthie's son...the little man of Ammons Mountain in little boys clothes. In her mind, she could still see his eyes—big, brown and shiny—peeping at her from behind the door of the Ammons cabin....

CHAPTER 9

Cowboy Boots

Libby's thoughts went way back to when she had first visited the Ammons homestead to meet Jim's family. During their walk through the area, a falling rock had struck her head. For days she had laid abed with the family caring for her. It was then that she came in contact with the angel of a boy, Jhon Fred.

From where she sat on the porch she could see the grin on his face, showing small, white, even teeth. She could tell he wanted to come to her, but he had to wait, she thought, until his mother was out of sight.

Libby watched Marthie turn the corner of the cabin on her way to the spring house. Then, again glancing at the boy, she resumed the sewing in her lap and waited. She knew he'd come to her before long.

It was but a minute or two before she saw the worn, muddy shoes inching their way closer. She kept her eyes cast down to her sewing.

Suddenly, there was a small brown hand on her knee, as the boy strained his head closer to see what lay in her lap.

"It's a new shirt fer ye, Jhon Fred," she said softly as she held it up for him to see.

"Fer me?"" came the whispery voice, his face lighting up with an even bigger grin. He turned his head to one side as he gazed at the piece of blue broadcloth. Then, wiping his nose with the back of his hand, he said, "It ain't got no buttons, Libby!"

She laughed. The expression on his face was softly questioning, but the grin obediently stayed in place.

Laying the sewing on the shelf nearest her, Libby held out her arms to the small six-year-old, and he quickly climbed into her lap. Looking up at her, his brown eyes did not leave her face. "Does Libby's haid hurt?"

"No, Jhon Fred, my head's almost well now. I think I kin go on home tomorrow. Will ye miss me, sweetheart?"

Jhon Fred's face lost the wide grin, and his eyes glistened. He struggled with his tears, then threw his arms around Libby's neck.

"Please, don't go, Libby! I don't want ye to go! I won't have nobody to play with!" And his tears overflowed onto his cheeks.

Libby put her arms around him and hugged him close. Tears came to her eyes also, and she laid her head against his dark brown hair, and rocked him to and fro.

In the week since Libby had been injured, she had found that Jhon Fred held everyone's heart in this home, for the love he gave to each member of the family was genuine. His displays of temper were frequent though and at times he was somewhat mischievous. But he always knew when someone felt sad or hurt, and was the first to try to console, to help and to show true concern. The older Ammons children, Nealie, Corie, and Lillie cared deeply for Jhon Fred. However, they left him out of their games and adventures into the surrounding woods. Because of his short legs and the trouble he had breathing, he couldn't seem to keep up with them. There had been many a time Libby had seen him come back dejected after being left at the edge of the forest. To Libby, he seemed so alone. Her heart went out to him.

It was sometimes not easy to see that Marthie loved anyone. But even though Marthie often concealed her emotions, after only observing the woman and the boy just a short time, it finally began to dawn on Libby that this woman truly adored her son. However, that was where emotion started and ended with her.

At first, Marthie had not allowed Jhon Fred anywhere near the bed where Libby lay. But he waited at a distance, grinning shyly at Libby every time he caught her eyes on him. He played on the creaky floor near the door to the front porch, waiting for his chance to get closer to the red-headed woman in his grandma's bed.

His patience had finally paid off when Marthie went to help her mother with the wash. He had come to the end of the bed, crawled up between the iron bedposts, and perched at Libby's feet, his brown eyes full of concern. Patting her feet gently, in a fatherly tone he spoke his first words to her. "It'll be all right...I'll take keer o' ye."

He had nodded his head as he spoke. A grin broke out as he saw the smile Libby gave him. Instantly, they were friends from the heart.

As each day passed, the two became even closer. To Jhon Fred, it was as if he had found the playmate he'd always wanted. Libby wasn't allowed to do too much, and Jhon Fred made her recovery a time of happiness she would never forget.

At first Marthie had tried to interfere, but when she saw how happy Libby made her son, she finally gave in and just watched with a puzzled expression.

The oldest of nine children, Libby had had plenty of experience taking care of youngsters. In other children, she had seen unexpected selfishness and lack of responsibility ...then, moments later, just the opposite—complete acceptance and love. But somehow, it was different with Jhon Fred. He seemed to know that there was no special man he could call "Dad" or to care for his mother, so he had already assumed that position.

Responsibility had become a big factor in his child life. However, there were times that this position grew to be too much for him. His temper would explode when he was told that he was too little to carry water; that he could not chop wood; and that milking the cow needed stronger, larger hands. He would take his revenge by sulking somewhere off by himself, but Libby had noticed that these times would not last long. He would soon be back into the middle of everything.

But, to Libby, the most important difference she had noticed in Jhon Fred was that he had no malice in his heart for any living thing, even to a flower. Once she had found him in Retter's flower garden, trying to put a petal back onto a daisy, talking aloud, as if to a baby. To Libby, Jhon Fred was love itself.

The boy had Marthie's dark hair and eyes, along with her dark complexion, but his facial features were unlike those of any other member of the Ammons family. His chin was sharp and his cheeks were round. He had short, chubby legs and wide shoulders...and when he walked in the wake of the Ammons brothers, he imitated their gait almost perfectly. But, of course, he could never catch up, so he just ran as fast as he could. Libby noticed early in their relationship the trouble he had getting his breath. In answer to her questions, Retter had told her that "Jhon Fred's chest seemed to fill up a right smart."

"Jhon Fred, listen to me," she said to the boy with his arms still around her neck. "I'll be comin' back to see ye, fer Jim 'n' me are gonna live jest over the mountain at the Golden Place. Ye can even come stay with me some, if your momma will let ye!"

The boy pulled away from Libby, gazing at her to make sure he had heard her right. "Ye're gonna live here on the mountain...fer ever 'n' ever?"

"Yes, sweetheart, soon as Jim 'n' me git married."

His grin was back, and he was again sniffing.

Libby pulled a handkerchief out of her pocket and wiped his nose, then kissed him on the cheek.

"We're gonna be together always! Jest ye wait 'n' see.

Jim's takin' me down to Pickens, South Carolina and then over to my momma's at Wolf Mountain. I'll brang ye back a present. What do ye want most o' all?"

Libby laughed as Jhon Fred jumped down to the wooden porch, and just kept on jumping. But suddenly, he stopped and began breathing deeply, his breath coming in loud, hacking coughs.

By the time Libby was out of her chair and on her knees beside him, he had quieted down, almost breathing normally. "Are ye all right, Jhon Fred? Where does it hurt?"

The boy looked up at Libby, his nose running freely, and said, "I want cowboy boots! Kin I have cowboy boots? Please!"

Libby burst out laughing, and then after again wiping his nose, she answered, "If ye're gittin' anythin', ye're gittin' cowboy boots!"

She and Jim were gone a week. Jim had used an old logging truck for transportation, and on the long drive back from South Carolina, Libby at times had sung to the clank and rattle of the vehicle. They had already gone by Wolf Mountain, visiting her family and catching up on all the news of home.

Jim left the truck at Grassy Creek at the bottom of Ammons mountain, and the two of them began the long climb. They went as far as they could without resting so as to reach the cabin before dark. The closer she got, the more she thought about Jhon Fred. She would see him again before long. And in the packages that Jim carried in the gunny sack over his shoulder were cowboy boots, and also a cowboy hat!

The crest of the mountain in sight, and the fatigue that Jim and Libby had begun to feel suddenly vanished. As the homestead came into view, the sun was going down behind the mountain, sending streaks of warm pinks and reds in all directions. It was a beautiful sight. Tonight they would stay with the Ammons family. Tomorrow they would walk over to the Golden Place, their home.

"Let's go in the back way 'n' surprise them, Libby," Jim whispered as they neared the cabin.

They veered around, passed between the chimney and rock wall, and came upon the back porch. They found Frank sitting with his head in his hands.

"Howdy Frank! We're back!" Jim spoke loudly.

"H-H-Howdy Jim, Libby. I'm right proud to see ye both...but I got real bad news to tell ye." Frank stood up and shook his brother's hands as he spoke.

"What bad news?" Jim asked quickly, a startled look on his face.

Frank glanced at Libby, then spoke, "I-I-It's Jhon Fred. He's got pneumonia real bad 'n'...."

Libby had started running from the two men before Frank had finished speaking. She burst into the front room and rushed to the bed she herself had occupied some weeks before.

Marthie was sitting on one side, holding a cloth on the small boy's head. With her face drained of all color, against the darkness of her hair she looked half dead. Her hazel eyes seemed glassed over. Retter and Tom sat close together near the fireplace, pain in their eyes.

Marthie looked at Libby, and spoke quietly, "There ain't nothin' ye kin do...he's gone."

Libby reached out to the boy who loved everything—his hands were cold.

Slowly she began to realize that Jhon Fred was already gone. Her hand moved slowly to touch the small feet, covered and still. She began to pat his feet as sorrow took over. Between her sobs, she spoke brokenly, "Oh, Jhon Fred...ye asked...fer so little.... Ye didn't even get to see your cowboy boots."

The black-clad figures were strung out in single file. It was a dark caravan that followed the small wooden box. Some of the sunshine had been taken from their world. None of the mourners could understand why God had taken the boy.

Just behind the small wooden box carried by the Ammons brothers, walked Marthie. The family had not yet seen her cry over the loss of her child. After their first attempts to show sympathy had been ignored, they had kept their distance, respectfully.

Double Springs Church of God sat by the edge of the road with the graveyard curving downhill. Jhon Fred would be just at the beginning of the graveyard, a little to the right of the pathway beside the church. From her position behind Jim, Libby watched the straight-back shoulders of Marthie. Libby realized that the pain in her own heart must be as nothing compared to Marthie's agony. She longed to help her sister-in-law in some way, but Marthie was keeping everyone locked out of her world.

Just yesterday, results of the testing had come back from the hospital in Sylva. Jhon Fred had not only been suffering from pneumonia, but he had contracted a form of polio. It was a disease people were just beginning to hear about.

"The pain the boy must have had!" Jim had almost sobbed when he'd heard. "We took care o' his cough fer so long...'n' now this!"

The grave site was under a young pin oak. The only tree in the graveyard that still bore its brilliant brown-red leaves in this wintery scene, it stood out in a vivid contrast against its own rough gray bark. Libby could hear Poppy giving the eulogy, but she couldn't concentrate on what he was saying. She had helped dress Jhon Fred for the small wake given him. The last time she touched him, she had slipped on his cowboy boots.

Wanting reassurance, Libby's eyes moved slowly up from the cold ground to catch a flutter of golden wings. She watched in awakened amazement as a swarm of butterflies hovered over the bowed heads. They were Monarchs, the patterns of their wings almost lost in a whir of silk. She knew it was too cold for Monarchs to swarm. It had to be a miracle.

Jhon Fred had been like the butterfly, beautiful and fragile. Pain has a way of making spirits strong, she thought. So, it must have been that he had come to value life around him because his own acute pain made him sensitive to pain in others. And because of his determination, he seemed to have wrought a change in most of the people he encountered. Just as the butterfly nurtured flowers, so Jhon Fred had inspired blossoms in the hearts he'd touched.

But after his death, Marthie had hidden him in her heart and refused to talk about him. Until tonight!

She had said that her boy seemed to like me—that she loved her boy!

As Libby followed the straight-back shoulders of Marthie—this woman who walked like her son—her own shoulders began to straighten and her head went up. A "Jhon Fred" determination began to live within her. There was indeed hope!

Oh, I so want to be her friend. Jhon Fred would like that.

CHAPTER 10

Beautiful Bell

As Marthie led Libby down the mountain toward the Ammons place, her thoughts in no way matched Libby's—they swarmed like hornets coming strong and heavy laden. Her memories swelled, buzzing, buzzing in her head.

Her life as she had known it on the mountain had not gradually changed. It had came to a full stop on that day long ago...her sixteenth birthday. The end had all started with Bell...beautiful Bell—Jim's first wife. Funny how she had not seen it in just that way...until now. She could see Bell and hear her clearly, as if she were there in front of her.

"Oh, Marthie! don't be a ninny! Yer're pretty! Well, pretty enough. I'll tell ye what I'll do...I'll take ye next time I go to town. Ye'll have FUN!"

Bell sat in front of the old cracked mirror at the dresser in the back bedroom of the Ammons Cabin. As she leaned closer to the mirror, she painted her lips a brilliant red and then straightened to gaze at her reflection. Suddenly, in the mirror, her gaze shifted to Marthie, who stood behind her, watching. Bell whirled around to lean toward the thin young girl.

"Marthie," she continued, "I'll see to it ye git a chance to live! That wuz more than I had at your age! I'll take ye with me!"

"But, Bell," said Marthie, "I ain't never been off this mountain alone before...only with Momma...'n' a few times with my brothers. I did go with Daddy once, up to the courthouse on the hill; but I fell down! I fell down a goodly portion o' them court house steps. Hurt my head bad...ain't been the same since. Sometimes...."

"Well, fergit all that! We're goin' tomorrow. It'll be yer birthday present from me. We'll go down to town, 'n' maybe go to the Lyric!"

"The Lyric Theater to see a movie!" Marthie's breath caught in her throat.

"We'll sneak out early, 'fore everbody's fully aware that I'm not sleeping late...like I sometimes do." Bell turned back to the mirror, smiling widely.

"But, Bell...what will Jim say?" Marthie came closer to the old dresser, gingerly reaching out to touch the rounded cylinder of lipstick Bell had tossed onto its top.

"Oh, heck with Jim. He has his own fun—drinkin' with his brothers! He's forgot I ever existed. He's yer brother, but I made a big mistake by marrying him!"

Bell's gaze in the mirror caught the motion of Marthie's hand and her momentary frown vanished as she rested her own hand atop Marthie's, catching her eye.

"Wanta try the lipstick?" she continued softly, squeezing the young girl's fingers.

"Momma won't like it." Marthie's voice was yearningly soft.

"We'll wash it off...come, try it!"

Marthie quickly looked over her shoulder, then smiling, she moved her hand away from Bell's touch. She opened the lid. Turning the cylinder, Marthie brought the brightness toward her face. Her hand shook so much with excitement that Bell had to help steady her as Marthie smoothed a line of red over her slightly opened lips.

Then, standing back, the excited girl gazed into the mirror. The change in her appearance pleased her. She felt the surge of a strange new feeling--a feeling that grew as she again turned toward the smiling Bell.

"Okay, I'll go! But don't tell Momma!"

That next morning, through sips of hot coffee, Marthie remembered she had noticed early morning dew covering the budding hollyhocks outside the kitchen window. Later, she had thought about the flower's paleness as she had followed Bell's striding steps down the mountain. She had felt as the hollyhocks had looked...for she, too, was at the budding of her life. The excitement of the thought had put a pink sheen on her face, and had pushed her to hurry to Bell's side.

"Ain't it a pretty day!" Her voice seemed to dance beside them.

"Goodness, Marthie, it always perks a person up when ye're doin' somethin' excitin'! I can't stand it...I mean I HATE it...up here on the top of this mountain! I feel like I'm chained here. I only start to breathe when I'm goin' away from all this quiet! I like laughter, 'n' the touch of a man on me. Your brother don't understand me, Marthie...I have to have pleasure 'n' he ain't givin' it to me!"

Bell's outburst almost frightened Marthie. "What do ye mean...a man's touch?" For some reason, Marthie didn't want to look at Bell. She struggled to keep step with her.

"I like to feel needed, to feel the...." Bell slowed her rush in the obvious delight of her own thoughts. "I like the chase...to be chased! But best of all, I like to be caught...'n'...well, ye know." The young woman's' eyes lowered, almost as if she suddenly felt embarrassed by her own words.

Marthie said nothing, but she thought to herself, *No, I didn't know.* She wanted to know, though, in the worse way. She heard herself say, "How is it, Bell...with a man?"

"Ye really don't know, Marthie?"

"No...ain't no man ever touched me, even though there's some old men who have wanted to. With my brothers all 'round me, they don't come near. Ye know, Bell--I got these four great big, older brothers....'"

"Oh, it's the best feeling! Let's stop here, Marthie. Let me tell ye! I've had it a lot of times, 'n' I never git tired o' it. Here...here's a sittin' rock. Let's sit down."

Spreading her long skirt out, Bell sat, motioning for Marthie to sit on an old log next to her. "Listen real careful now, Marthie, cuz what I'm gonna tell, your Momma will never tell ye. See, it's this way. He'll look ye up 'n' down-- this man who is interested in ye--'n' that's when it starts...this real excitin' feeling inside ye. He talks real sweet, lettin' ye git used to him, all the time he's gittin' closer. Then...," Bell paused, letting the tip of her tongue slide over her lips. "Then, he's real close 'n' his hand suddenly touches yer shoulder. It sorta burns, 'n' then his hand slides a little, until...." Bell's voice dropped as her eyes looked beyond Marthie. Unconsciously, Marthie's gaze shifted from Bell's face to her hands clutched in her lap.

"That don't sound like fun to me!" she said.

The indignant look on Marthie's face made Bell laugh and jump up.

"Well, ye'll change yer mind later on. Ye're such a little girl! Come on, let's go! The sun's movin' farther up in the sky 'n' we need to catch Doc Watson 'fore he leaves fer town."

The Lyric Theatre set right on main street. Marthie had always heard about the theater from her brothers. It was the first movie house in Sylva to have sound. Bell pushed a total of 80¢ through the glass window for the two of them.

Marthie had enjoyed the movie, but she was glad to be leaving. The dark of the theater in the middle of the day was new to her.

Bell had talked to just about everyone she had come into contact with since the two of them had left that morning. Standing beside Bell--with her newly painted lips--Marthie

had felt important...more important than she had ever felt.
She had also received more attention than she had ever
received. Even if she could never come with Bell again, she
would never forget this day.

As the fading sunlight warmed her face, Marthie stopped
to blink her eyes and to readjust her vision. Bell was just
ahead of her, talking to two men in a shiny new car pulled up
in front of the theater.

The younger of the two men was staring at Marthie. She
felt uneasy and moved to shield herself behind Bell's figure.
She waited for Bell to finish her conversation. The woman
seemed to be truly enthralled with the car.

"Marthie." Bell was looking at her. "Marthie!"

"Yes...yes, I hear ye. What is it?" Marthie turned
trusting eyes on Bell.

"Marthie, this here is Lester...'n his friend...Bill. They
want to drive us up to Doc's house in this beautiful black
car!"

Marthie's uneasiness grew as the young man got out of
the car and held the door wide.

"I...I don't thank we aught to, Bell. Doc said...."

"Doc's gone, Marthie! The movie lasted longer than I
thought." Bell smiled at Marthie, taking her hand. "Let's
go...come on. I know these men. This is Bill here. Bill,
meet Marthie Ammons."

"But, Bell...." Marthie was being pulled through the
car's door by the young man. She didn't ever hear her reply.
Pushed into the rear seat, Marthie suddenly felt Bill squeeze
in beside her. His hand already on her knee, he smiled
crookedly at her.

"Please...don't...." she began, then louder, "BELL...."

But Bell's chatter from the front seat drowned the
frightened words.

The man's smell came to her--a smell of tobacco, liquor
and perspiration. He moved even closer, his arm now going
over her shoulders, while the other hand moved up her leg.

"Don't...TOUCH...me like that!" Marthie had found her
voice. She picked up his hand and threw it from her,

struggling to move, yet being held in an iron-like grip.

But the man only laughed, and brought her even closer with the pressure of his arm around her neck. His right hand moved to her neck, his fingers searching her shoulder, then pulling at the collar of her dress. The buttons strained as the top few came out of the button holes, sliding out so easily.

"Please...," she began, still struggling. "I don't...." She couldn't finish. Emotion closed around her throat like a vise.

In the front, Bell continued to talk, not even glancing around. Marthie's eyes swam, tears washing over the brims, her breath seeming to vanish.

Bill's fingers now found what they were seeking. His breath hot against her cheek, he forced her face around and kissed her mouth. At first, the kiss was soft, then brusingly hard. His teeth pressed against her lips--she had no way even to resist as his mouth suddenly covered hers, and his tongue found its way into her mouth. And then, suddenly, he ripped her dress open.

Horrified, Marthie's body jerked, and she freed herself enough to scream.

"Marthie, what on earth!" Bell's voice grew louder. "Bill, ye're not.... Bill, what are ye doin'!"

"Let 'um alone, Bell," came Lester's voice. "Bill's only helpin' hisself to the pickin's! Soon as I kin git this car stopped, I'm gonna do the same! We're almost there! Fact is, here's the house now! Come on, I gotta have ye!"

The car came to a stop. Through the shadows of impending night, Marthie couldn't make out where they were. Lester opened his car door and pulled a strangely quiet Bell out the side.

The next thing Marthie knew she was being dragged from the back seat. Lester and Bell had already disappeared inside the dark frame of a cabin. The man Bill loomed over Marthie. He did not wait to get her inside. He pulled at the loosened front of her dress; the cotton gave way.

And then, as the child screamed inwardly to a God she felt had deserted her, a lusting man growled in a gratingly low tone as he lay across the girl. In horror, Marthie felt the man's body. Somehow, it suffocated her. She could not move, nor could she speak. His smell engulfed her senses, her eyes glazed over, and she passed out. When she came to, she could not budge the heavy man. But her actions brought his growl back, and he began all over again.

But then, just before dawn, a silent Lester came to stand over them. He rolled Bill from atop her; and then, it was he who brought the blood.

The sun, breaking the new day, rubbed the eastern edges of the mountains a blood red as Marthie, with Libby following her, descended onto the road beside the Ammons' freshly plowed fields. Ahead a pale light shown from the kitchen window of the cabin. In no time, the silent Marthie deposited Libby at the door to the kitchen, and vanished around the side of the house.

CHAPTER 11

A Whimpering At The Door

Libby brushed her feet, turned the handle of the door and entered the kitchen. Retter Ammons looked up in surprise, a hand pausing in her biscuit dough.

"Miz Ammons! I'm so glad to see ye." Relief filled Libby's voice as she sank onto the bench beside the table. "I need to talk to somebody!"

"My goodness, girl! yer a mess!" Retter exclaimed. "What'er ye doin' here this time o' the mornin'? Ain't nothin' wrong with Jim, is there?"

Shaking her head, Libby proceeded to talk fast, gesturing emphatically with her hands. Retter listened as the story unfolded, her eyes flashing as the young woman told of being left in the fog alone.

"That does it! That girl of mine has gone too far this time! But...she did go back fer ye, didn't she? How else could ye have got all the way back here!" Retter's floury hands now rested on her hips as her voice rose and fell.

"We did git here together, Miz Ammons, but I had help gittin' up outta that holler. I ain't told ye the most unheard of

thang yit! An Indian with white hair found me there...'n'....."
Libby stopped talking and stared at the amazed expression on
the older woman's face.

"Indian...with...white...hair!" Retter's words crawled
out.

"Yes, he had white hair cuz he wuz old. He wore skins
fer clothes. He carried a stick with white 'n' brown feathers
on it. 'N', oh yes, he mentioned ye a lot...come to think on
it!" Excitement grew in Libby's voice as Retter suddenly
came closer to her.

"What did he say, girl?"

"He said...that Retter's girl child wuz full o' sorrow...'n'
that it wuz hard to hear a heart cry." Libby spoke quickly,
full of curiosity about Retter's reaction. "Who is he, Miz
Ammons? Do ye know him? He wuz gone 'fore he told me
who he wuz." Then, as if in afterthought, she continued, "He
called me 'woman with hair o' fire.'"

Retter turned quickly and walked to the window. Libby
watched as the morning sunlight touched the outline of the
heavier woman. A moment later, Retter stood facing the
younger woman, softly smiling.

"Once, long ago," she said, "I had a friend, an Indian
friend named Cooweesucoowee...I called him 'Charlie.' He
taught me all 'bout herbs 'n' all 'bout healin'. I met him in
the woods when I wuz 'bout ten year old. I loved him 'n' he
loved me, I know. He promised to be with me always." The
older woman paused, then went on, "Then I found out that
he wuz really my grandpa after all—my real one. But that's
another story! What I think, girl, is that ye met him yerself
last night. Ye must be really special to have seen him, Libby."
Her warmth enveloped Libby.

"Yer grandpa! But, Miz Ammons...that would make him
powerfully old!"

"Libby...Charlie died over thirty year ago."

"But, Miz Ammons...I saw...."

Libby's voice trailed off as the older woman turned
abruptly away. Over her shoulder came the words, "Strange
things...strange things happen in these here mountains. Ain't

none of us kin explain it. Strange, wonderfully strange." In the wake of her words, Retter washed her hands and began rolling out her biscuits.

Libby sat quietly at the table watching the white-headed woman. Her hair, twisted into a soft braid on top of her head, framed a face soft with memories. Libby knew she shouldn't dare interrupt those thoughts now.

For the first time, the younger woman felt as if she had been accepted in her new family, and as if she suddenly belonged in this kitchen. Having been in the presence of "Charlie" had given her a special status. She herself, believed in "spirits" and that miracles could happen. This must be why she had been singled out.

She looked around at the kitchen's cleanliness. The younger girls, Lillie and Corie, had told her many times about how their mother had made them scrub the kitchen after every wash day; especially the heavy, long table. In their description, they had given Libby a mental picture of two girls turning the table upside down, and brushing the underside with the wash water full of soap suds. One time they had added their play to this chore and the table had slid almost through the wall on the other side of the room. The thought brought a smile to Libby's lips and she glanced at Retter, to see her now looking directly at her, the softness of her expression gone. Instead there had developed a deep sadness. "Libby, I 'spect I had better tell ye 'bout Bell," she said.

"Jim told me, Miz Ammons. He told me 'bout his divorce...'fore we left fer South Carolina to git married."

"Did he tell ye what Bell done...to Marthie?" Retter picked up her biscuit pan and walked to the woodstove.

"No...nothing more than that he wuz married before." The clank of the oven door opening and closing drowned Libby's answer.

Retter, her shoulders slumped, continued talking as if she'd heard her response. "When Jim 'n' Bell first got married 'n' they come here to live, we got to know Bell. We saw that she liked to carry on with all the men folk. She went

to town more'n she ought! 'Fore long, she started workin' on
Marthie to go with her. Marthie begun follerin' her 'round
like a sick puppy. She learned Marthie to fix her face with
make-up." Retter paused and sat down heavily at the table
across from Libby, then she sighed and continued.

"Jim worked all day fer his daddy, 'n' when he'd git
home, his wife would still be gone. Then, one day, Bell 'n'
Marthie went into town, 'n' didn't come back when they wuz
expected. At first, I thought they wuz with Bell's family. But
then three days went by 'n' I 'bout went crazy worryin'. Jim
asked 'round down to the store in town 'n' talked to the
sheriff, 'n' brought back a story that made him s'mad he had
trouble hangin' onto his all togethers. People said Bell 'n'
Marthie had got into a spankin' new car with two men; that
they didn't look like they wuz forced. Jim 'n' the sheriff
looked all over, but they wuz nowheres to be found."

Tears formed in the older woman's eyes. She dabbed at
them with her apron. In a moment she began again. "Then,
one night there wuz a...whimperin' at the door...so low I
hardly heard it. I went to open the door real slow, 'n' there
on the doorstep wuz my beautiful Marthie. She wuz dirty, 'n'
her clothes wuz torn 'n' ripped s'bad I had to throw 'em away
later. She wuz bloody 'n' had been cryin' s'much, she didn't
seem to have no tears left. She had got away from the men
who had been holdin' her."

Retter's voice now grew even softer. "Somethin' wuz
gone from her eyes. There wuz no sparkle like before...only
blank, starin' eyes looked back et me. She had
been...hurt...bad. I fixed her up, 'n' held her real close.
Sometime in there I asked her 'bout Bell. Marthie said Bell
wuz afraid to come home, afraid that Jim would kill her. She
wuz right! Jim had to git over it...took him a long time."

"Did Jim ever see Bell agin?" whispered Libby.

"Yes, it wuz sometime later, 'bout three months, when
Bell finally come home. Marthie still loved the
woman...don't ask me why...less'n it wuz cuz Bell had made
such a fuss over her 'n' showed her some attention. It's
crazy! But that's when Jim throwed Bell out 'n' divorced
her."

"But..whut 'bout the men who took 'um?"

"They...they suddenly wuz...jest gone," said Retter with eyes averted. "Musta left these parts."

"'N' Marthie. Did she git over what happened to her?" asked Libby softly.

Retter again quietly wiped at the tears in her eyes as she gazed at Libby's wet face. For a moment, she said nothing. Then slowly it came, "I don't know if ye can call it gittin' over it er not, but when her time had passed, Jhon Fred wuz born."

The room grew quiet.

Oh, Marthie! Oh, Marthie!

Libby's heart cried out for her! Marthie had endured almost unrepairable trauma. Then...had to carry a child inside of her, all the time knowing and remembering what had happened, and go through the pain of having a child of rape. She must have had to learn to love him..and then Jhon Fred had died six years later.

Oh, God, how awful!

The only way she could truly help Marthie, she knew, was to seek petition for her on her knees in the cove at home, to pray as hard as she could for her as she had been praying for Jim. She would pray for the Lord to heal the pain, the deep pain that still filled the dark-eyed woman.

CHAPTER 12

Gathering Herbs and Hearts

Sterlen left Jim at the Golden Place still grumbling because Libby wasn't there. The rain from the previous day had not helped in their trip through the mountains; both had been wet and hungry, looking forward to a fresh cup of Libby's good coffee. Jim decided to take solace in his moonshine.

Gazing at Jim, Sterlen felt he would leave Libby a poultice to help relieve the pain in her husband's leg. Some of the ingredients were not in what he called his "cure-all sack"— so he decided to write the recipe down for Libby. With pencil in hand, he laboriously wrote:

Libby
fir Jim's leg, in pot put in sage, rosemary, tyme,
lavender, camomile flowers & melilot, then stew
all in a splash or two of Jim's brew. or else make
some lye with oak leaves, just a little vingar, and
a half fist of salt. use as paste. put the poultice
on leg. rap warm cloth round. will help.

With this completed, he lay the information on the kitchen table. After saying goodby to Jim, he headed out for the other side of Cherry Gap, still looking for a new patch of the ginseng herb.

It was a tired, but happy man that left Cherry Gap that evening. Sterlen had stayed longer than he had planned, for he had found the herb patch for which he had been searching, and he knew it would be more bountiful than he had ever hoped for.

It had been a long day, and he knew he couldn't make it home that night. So he headed once again through the dense forest toward the Ammons cabin.

Shadows crept up the trunks and vines around him as he made his way through the late evening. Tree frogs and crickets began to sing; bright lavenders and pinks lingered as the sun bowed out of the western sky, bringing the curtain down on the soft spring day.

Then a new sound joined those of the tree frogs and crickets. Sterlen stopped and turned his face in the direction of the sound. He recognized the voices of two men. The calls of nature vanished as the voices grew louder.

The man moved toward the new sound, curiosity filling him. The closer he got the louder the voices became.

Sterlen topped an incline, and parting the limbs of a white pine, he gazed down into an almost hidden valley. Even though there was no smoke, he could still smell the burning. *Ivy leaves...it's ivy leaves and vines,* he thought. *Somebody's making moonshine.* And sure enough, down below he saw what was unmistakably a working still.

Loud voices rode the unseen veiling of smoke that drifted up toward the darkening sky. "What 'er we gonna do with her? She's found us! She'll fetch her daddy er them brothers up here, sure as shootin'! No tellin' what them Ammons boys will do!"

"We jest havta shut her mouth...if...ya know what I mean, Sam!"

"But, Zeb...I ain't done nothin' like that a'fore. I don't hold with it! Moonshining ain't worth that! 'N' jest look et her—she's kinda pretty."

"Yep, she's got some promise. She sure wuz a passel to catch! Say, ain't she that oldest girl...that one that's already been had? Now...that's an idee!"

Hidden from the two men below, Sterlen suddenly felt a surge of anger. He watched as one of the men grabbed the arm of a young woman. She was struggling. The bigger of the two men reached out and jerked the chin of the woman sharply, tilting her face toward his. High above, Sterlen's breath caught in his throat as he recognized Marthie, the dark one who had been in his thoughts most of the day. His heart began to pound as he felt his stomach tighten.

"LET GO, LET GO!" Marthie cried, struggling to hit the men with her fists, being held back beyond the reach of her arms. "Ye bastards ain't doin' nothin' to me agin! I'll kill ye first!"

"Ye got no right to call us names, ye bitch!" yelled the man called Zeb, batting off her attempts to hit him. "Ye? Ye—the one who had yer own bastard!"

"AGGGHHH!" Marthie's passion grew with her strength. Both men received scratches and bruises in just the seconds Sterlen watched.

Sam caught both of Marthie's arms and held her in an iron grip, letting her kick and scream at the two of them.

"Sam Mason!" she cried. "My brothers will be down on ye like a dog on a bone—ye and yer brother here!"

"What wuz ye doin' up here anyways, woman!" said Sam. "We been makin' our liquor right here in Jim's back yard fer over a year 'n' ain't nobody's ever found us...till ye had to go 'n' stumble in on us!"

"Ain't no never mind what I wuz doin'! I'm always out in these woods! LET ME GO!"

Zeb, growing angrier by the minute, realized Marthie was in the control of his brother and suddenly caught Marthie's hair and began jerking her toward him. His laugh filled the valley. "NOW, I got ye!"

Sterlen, who had waited to make sure his actions would not bring more harm to the girl, suddenly could not stand it any more. Through the undergrowth he strode, pushing the brush aside.

"WHAT'S GOIN' ON HERE!"

Below him, Marthie's heart seemed to stop. She gazed up at the form of the white-haired man as he descended. She felt Sam's and Zep's surprise as both of them eased their holds on her. She took advantage of this moment to pull away. Quickly she ran to the edge of the clearing. There she stopped. With trembling hands caught in the collar of her dress, she turned to watch.

"Who the hell are ye?" yelled Zeb, still grasping at the emptiness where Marthie had been.

"I'M ONE HELL OF AN ENEMY! JEST WHAT DO YE THINK YER DOIN'?"

As the Mason brothers watched this seeming giant of a man descend upon them, suddenly neither one wanted any part of him. They looked at each other, then turned and ran, each in a different direction.

Sterlen strode right into the now empty clearing. From her position, Marthie could see that anger filled the big man. For a moment, he gazed after the two who had run, then his gaze took in the clutter and debris that surrounded the still.

Without even looking at her, he swung his case down, and pulled a long burning limb from the fire beneath the container of sour mash. With mighty swings, he proceeded to destroy the still and all the tubs.

Marthie's eyes were fixed on the sight before her. Emotions struggled within her--so many that she felt momentarily confused. However, deep satisfaction at seeing the still destroyed slowly began to make its way up through the uncertainty. She had been right about this man; he was strong willed! She admired that. But, then heavy sadness descended upon the emotional woman once again. This man must now know about her...it seemed everybody did. Even those worthless no-good moonshiners knew of her. Her eyes grew salty...they burned with bitterness. A lump found its way into her throat.

When Sterlen finally tossed the limb aside, he also tossed away the last of his anger. Turning, he gazed at the quiet form of the woman. He walked over to her, his gaze tender on her upturned face. Big hands rested themselves on her slender shoulders.

"Are ye all right, chile?" He spoke softly.

His tenderness and concern seemed to dissolve the lump...and whatever reserve Marthie may have had. And although she hated to show her emotions, this time she could help it. She began to weep. Sterlen quickly stepped closer, and she almost collapsed into his arms. Surprisingly, she was almost as tall as he. In his warm embrace, she let go completely, laying her head on his shoulder, sobbing with abandonment.

Sterlen's arms tightened as he drew her still closer, guiding her head to lay against his chest. She cried into his heart, feeling the muscles beneath her tighten against her cheeks. The warmth of the big man filled her. She felt protected.

She allowed him to hold her, while all her pent-up feelings poured out in a rain-spout of relief. He held her until her sobs finally subsided and she became still in his arms.

"Chile, what's this powerful sadness I feel in ye?" His voice gentle, he laid his cheek against her hair.

After a moment, she whispered, "I'm so...so alone."

Sterlen cradled her chin with his hand. He instantly realized that this was no child! A heart that had been empty suddenly overflowed with love, and Sterlen knew that he'd never again be the same.

Gripping her arms, the mountain man gently held her out from him. With earnest intent he looked deep into her eyes.

She felt herself being drawn inside quiet pools of ice blue. Her heart pounded so loud that she was sure he could hear it.

"Marthie." He only mouthed the word, but she heard.

Her hands touched his face, and then, almost shyly, she leaned toward him and softly touched her lips to his cheek.

It was then that, without Marthie knowing it, a heart of love gathered in her heart of sadness and a new intent found its beginning. Sterlen folded her once more into his arms and held her.

Incredibly, there for a time in the silence of the forest, the woman felt safe and warm within the embrace of the mountain man. Never before had she experienced this particular sensation. But, a shadow began to form, pushing its way up from the depth of her most inner being. She became aware that her mouth had grown so dry that her tongue stuck to its roof. Backing away, she dropped her head, muttering, "Thank ye...I best be gittin' on home now."

The dazed Sterlen only slightly hesitated. "I'll walk with ye," he said, "and take keer o' ye."

As they set off through the woods, the broken-hearted Marthie could only think one thought.

That's what Jhon Fred used to say.

CHAPTER 13
A Hoss of a Different Color

The next morning Sterlen rose with the dawn. He determined to know the truth about this young woman he now had fastened into his heart. He wanted to speak to Marthie about how he felt about her, but not before he knew all the details, and she refused to talk about her sorrows. What he did know was that he could see the flag of "caution" in her eyes. It was the same look he had seen in a beaten dog's eyes.

I must go slow. I must know what I'm up against.

Not wanting to ask anyone here at the Ammons cabin, he had decided to go back up to the Golden Place and have a talk with his niece before heading on home. Libby had married into this family. If anyone would know, she would, he decided. In the most proper manner he could muster, Sterlen said his goodbyes to Marthie. Making sure she knew he would be back to see her soon, he took his leave in the direction of Wolf Mountain, but then doubled back to go to the Golden place.

Jim and his horses were headed for the lumber camp

when the older man came out of the woods, so Sterlen found Libby alone and happy for company. She prepared a fresh pot of coffee and served it on the porch in the crisp morning air.

Sterlen took a sip of coffee and stared out over the mountains.

"Uncle Sterlen, first I want to thank ye fer the poultice recipe ye left. I'm already gatherin' what I need to make it," Libby said, pausing to see his nod, and continued excitedly, "Then I want to tell ye that I'm the happiest I've been in months!"

"Goodness, gal, what's happened!" Sterlen smiled at the flush on her face.

"Some time back, I pushed Jim's brother Frank into writin' to Irene...he's such a good looking young man, 'n' not so much of a dranker like his brothers...anyway, he done it-- 'n' guess what happened!"

"They like each other!" Sterlen laughed, enjoying the enthusiasm Libby showed.

"Well...no. When Frank went to see Irene, he found Cannie instead!" Libby leaned back in her chair to watch Sterlen's reaction.

"Cannie. The little one...why she's 'bout thirteen, ain't she?

"Lord, no. Cannie's all o' fifteen! Just a year younger'n Irene." Libby righted the chair, calming herself. "This all happened back in the winter. Cannie's jest wrote me that she 'n' Frank er gittin' married. Daddy's gonna sign fer her 'n' all. We're gonna have another wedding 'twix the Ammons' 'n' the Owen's!"

Sterlen smiled deeper into his beard. He liked the boy. "So that's what he wuz inferrin' to the other night! He's one o' the tallest Ammons' I know, fer I've slept next to 'em...his feet goes off the edge o' that old strawtick. Ain't Cannie kinda short?"

"She's just over five feet tall; they'll make a pair!" Libby laid a hand on Sterlen's arm. "But Uncle Sterlen, that's not all the news...Cannie 'n' Frank er gonna live with us fer a while! Ain't that something! I'll have my sister here; I won't be so...alone."

Sterlen's warm hand covered Libby's. "Ain't that good! Ain't that good!"

Libby's eyes had filled with tears. She quickly wiped them away and turned back to Sterlen. "Pretty soon I'm gonna...need a little help, fer I'm with child, Uncle Sterlen."

"Good God 'A'mighty! Yer full o' good news! Everbody knows how much ye wanted a chile. I'm ever s'happy fer ye. I feel like dancin'!"

"Thank ye, Uncle Sterlen, but ye jest drink yer coffee instead, 'fore it gits cold," Libby laughed. "Tell me what's the news with ye. I see there's somethin' different in yer eyes."

Sterlen sobered and looked intently at Libby. Clearing his throat, he said, "I done what ye 'n' Cannie done...I'm a'lookin' et one o' them Ammons' myself."

"Who? It can't be...Marthie...can it?" her eyes widened in shock.

"It's Marthie all right," Sterlen smiled. "I reckon I'm right smitten; but I know I'm headin' fer trouble. Can't help it...fer the first time in my life, I feel like goin' on with it; but I've heard all kinds o' stories 'bout Marthie's past, 'n' I'd like to know what's true gospel...'n' what's hogwash."

"Oh, Uncle Sterlen, Marthie's life has been jest plum-full o' sadness. She sure could use some gladness!"

"Libby, I can't get her to talk to me 'bout what's botherin' her. Kin ye tell me anythin' that could help me?"

"Well, Miz Ammons told me 'bout some o' her troubles...ye got some time to listen?"

Sterlen nodded as his eyebrows rose in question and he leaned back in his chair. "I'm ready to listen to anythin' that's gonna help me know that woman. I can't seem to git her out o' my mind. If she needs help, I'm prepared to give it to her...if it's the right thing...'n' she'll let me."

For the better part of an hour Sterlen listened to the compounded life of the woman he loved. The expression on his face did not change; only his eyes showed feeling. One minute they were full of sadness, then anger, and finally sadness again.

With the passage of time, the morning sun climbed higher in the sky, moving its warmth to rest in Sterlen's white hair. Libby listened as he made his decision.

"Wal, Libby, gal...seems as if my Marthie jest might need a lot o' patience 'n' an out 'n' out passel o' understandin'."

"Uncle Sterlen, yer gonna need a soft hand 'n' the right words. Jest since I've been here these...er, seven months now...I know that sometimes Marthie can be worse'n a den o' rattlers!" Libby shook her head.

"Lord knows I don't know much 'bout womenfolk, Libby, but I do know all there is to know 'bout me! Even as a boy, I learned how to trust my instincts. From age five I had to handle jest 'bout anythin' ye er anyone else can name—storms, animals, people—man er woman."

Sterlen squared his shoulders, leaned forward in his chair, and turned toward the warmth of the sun. Then he continued, "In fact, jest this mornin' I wuz reminded o' somethin' that happened to me when I wuz jest 'bout ten er eleven year old."

"What happened?" asked Libby, settling more in her chair, her curiosity kindled.

"Them hosses o' yer husband's jest pulled a good one on him. They tried to run away, but Jim kept his head, 'n' held 'em. I stood 'n' watched him as I came outta the woods."

"Ye said it reminded ye o' a story...tell me." Libby turned her complete attention on the big man. Like everyone else, she loved his stories of the past.

The quiet of the early morning lingered on the rough-cut boards of the porch. For a moment, Sterlen continued to stare off into the blue haze of his memory, slowly locking his scarred hands together in a restful position.

"I wuz always a big feller, ye know, 'n' a mite strong, too—powerful big fer my age. It wuz sprang, plantin' time, 'n' Daddy had decided that he wuz gonna train a pair o' three-year-old fillies. One wuz a bay with a blazeface, 'n' the other'n wuz a sable with white stockin's. Pretty hosses! But skittish, I'm here to tell ye! Them young thangs would try to run at the drop o' a hat.

"Wal, sir, my daddy 'n' me wuz takin' turns plowin' a new piece o' ground that we'd cleared. The stumps had been pulled out o' the field, but the ground wuz still a little hard to get the plow through on the first run.

"All 'round us wuz the forest. We seemed to be cut off from the rest o' the world. It shore did give me a funny feelin'—almost like we wuz the only folk left on the face o' the earth. I'll never fergit it!

"Daddy wuz on his turn with the walkin' plow, 'n' I wuz waitin' fer him at the end o' the row, under a walnut tree. He pulled up 'n' asked fer a drank o' water from the quart jar we had hid out in the weeds by the fence row.

"Sweat wuz drippin' from Daddy. He turned 'n' propped hisself up on the middle bar o' the plow, his back to them hosses. The reins wuz draped 'round his chest, so he jest let them hang there whilst he wiped his brow. I noticed that them hosses' tails wuz jest a'flappin' when I handed the mason jar to Daddy.

"Then, all o' a sudden, them fillies took off! I jest stood there—shocked! I watched as they veered off to my right, draggin' that plow 'n' my daddy, too! The reins had slid up on his chest and were caught under both o' Daddy's arms. The dirt went a'flyin' everwhere!"

Sterlen sat back in his chair again, the memory of the plight of his father rich in his mind. The blue of his eyes flashed, and he swallowed, rubbing his bushy white beard with an anxious hand.

Libby sat on the edge of her chair, her eyes big. "Go on! What happened then?"

"Daddy hollered fer help, 'n' I reacted...doin' what I done by jest plain wits. I run, fast as I could, to git to the head o' them critters. I shore musta run hard, cuz I got right there alongside o' 'em almost et the flick o' an eye! Then, there I wuz, betwixt their heads, grabbin' their bridles, my hands touchin' their cheek pieces. Ye got to remember now, I wuz a big boy. I reckon that's the reason I could do what I done."

The older man's strong arms had risen while he was telling his story, his hands gripping the air as if he was actually living that day again.

"Wal, I pulled back on them bits, 'n' dug my heels into the ground, holdin' on fer dear life, puttin' all my strength into it. I reckon the weight o' my daddy 'n' the plow, 'n' me, is what stopped 'em, all right. I wuz s'scared, I don't remember runnin' back to my daddy, but all o' a sudden, I wuz kneelin' down beside him. He wuz only scraped, thank God, but he come up cussin' them fillies! Doggone! but them Smokies shore did turn blue that day!"

Sterlen threw back his head and burst into loud laughter. Libby joined him, as the two relished the picture of Sterlen's daddy.

"I never reckoned ye wuz s'strong as a little boy to have stopped two run-away hosses!" Libby paused, and then continued, "But are ye shore ye kin hold the bridle on Marthie?"

"Like I said, Libby, I don't know too much 'bout women, but I reckon I kin trust my wits like always! I never wanted to git married cuz I never did find one woman that I wanted to take keer of...till now. I'm gonna ask Marthie to marry me."

Libby's smile almost instantly left her face as she grew sober at his words. "If ye kin make her happy, ye'll have done a great deed, to be shore...to be shore! But I can't help but worry fer ye a little. She could hurt ye, Uncle Sterlen. Please don't let anythin' take away yer laugh 'n' yer...come-to-gethers! I couldn't stand that! Ye know, Marthie's a hoss o' a different color."

Sterlen smiled at his niece, and stood up, pushing his chair back to the wall. "Libby, gal, yer heart's in the right place. I kin handle hosses."

He stood looking out at the mountains, letting the breeze push at his hair.

Libby gazed at the back of her favorite uncle, knowing that here was another addition to her daily prayers.

CHAPTER 14

The Call of the Lamb—June, 1941

Libby had been down on her knees in the cove, praying all morning. Jim had come home drunk the previous night, and had started in drinking again this morning. When she begged him to stop, he stalked off down the mountain.

Frank, who had taken the chore of keeping an eye on him since he and Cannie had come to live at the Golden Place, had left behind him, shaking his head.

Libby knew that cutting as much timber as Jim did in one day caused him a great amount of pain in his leg, especially in the evenings. She had an adversary that seemed to be winning the battle for Jim's soul.

"Lord!" Libby prayed aloud, "please help me! What kin I do? I'm been feelin' s'sick lately...I find it ever s'hard to git through the day. Even though Cannie's been here most of a month now, I can't seem to git what I want done.

"Cannie don't look to be as happy as I wuz when I first got married. I been thankin' it might be cuz o' Jim's drankin'...but I don't know. Frank seems to be doin' all right...sorta quiet, though. Ain't heard nothin' 'bout Uncle Sterlen 'n' Marthie. We been s'busy with Cannie gittin' married 'n' all. I worry 'bout Cannie...."

Libby's head dipped even lower until her forehead brushed the ground. Her hands pulled at her apron, as her knees sank deeper into the brown pine needles in which she knelt. She shivered, but didn't realize it.

"Lord...oh my Lord, I'm so in need o' Jim! He's s'busy feelin' his pain, he ain't got eyes fer m-m-mine...Oh, Oh! My...God!"

Libby's hands had flown to her stomach as she collapsed onto the ground.

"Cannie...." The sound of Libby's voice brought Cannie around to stare at her sister in surprise. Her mouth dropped open as she gazed at Libby's pale face.

"Cannie...I think somethin's wrong with me. The pit...o' my stomach...hurts somethin' fierce!"

As she spoke, the woman stumbled toward her, one hand outstretched.

"Oh, my God, Libby! Ye ain't but four months; it can't be the baby comin'!" Cannie ran to her sister, put her arm around her waist, and helped her sit on the edge of the bed.

"I...I fear somethin's' terrible wrong. When I...wuz a'prayin', I begun to feel odd...sick et my belly 'n' sorta...dizzy in my head."

"Libby, ye lean back 'n' I'll git a rag fer yer head. I thank ye got a little fever." Cannie bustled about, muttering to herself that Libby was all but burning up. Fear covered her face.

"Cannie! CANNIE!" Libby's voice suddenly filled the small room. "I want ye to go git Miz Ammons—ye hear? I can't lose this baby! I already lost one...'n' now, I'm...scared, Cannie!"

"But, Libby, I can't leave ye here all alone! Please don't make me go, Libby—please!"

"There's somethin' wrong...I know it, Cannie! Ye're not

old enough to know how to handle these thangs. Miz
Ammons is. Go git her...fast!"

Without another word, Cannie turned and ran out the
door. Libby knew it would be at least an hour before Cannie
could even make it to the Ammons homestead. With a
coldness rising in her heart, Libby lay back on the bed.
"What is this, Lord? Have ye forsaken me? Why,
Lord...why er ye takin' my baby? Ooooh...the pain...."

Suddenly, Libby's pain-filled eyes flew open. She could
hear someone coming up the path. Then, Cannie and Jim
burst into the room.

"My God! Libby, What's wrong?" Jim's concern shown
through bloodshot eyes as he leaned over his wife. "What is
it?"

"I got pain, Jim...awful bad!" Then, grimacing, Libby
turned her head from him. "Please go away, Jim. I...can't
stand the smell...it takes my breath."

Jim straightened and backed away from the bed, his face
covered in darkness.

Libby moaned. Jim shook as if she had slapped him,
turned abruptly, and left the cabin.

Hesitantly, Cannie ran to her sister, laying her hand on
her forehead. "Libby, yer truly burnin' up! I got to git a rag
to put on yer head! I run into Frank jest down the trail; he
wuz bringin' Jim home. Frank's gone fer his momma."

Libby's eyes rolled back, then fluttered open. Her voice
came almost in a whisper. "I wuz a'prayin' out yonder fer
the Lord to let Jim know I needed him. Mabbe I wuz...bein'
selfish. Cannie, I'm gonna...lose my baby...."

"Don't say nothin', Libby. Ye're gonna be all right...I
know it. God wouldn't do a thang like that to ye! Why,
Libby, ye've been prayin' long hours down on yer knees fer
months! How many people do that? None that I know of!"
Cannie's words belied the fear swimming in her eyes.

Outside, in the fullness of day, a hoot owl cried.

Blackberry briars pulled at Jim's clothing. He moved

away from the touch of the thorns, then continued almost blindly up the steep incline. Before him, the trail he followed dug deep into the mountain, a bank of damp earth and old leaves on one side, and a drop-off into a deep ravine on the other.

The haziness that had filled his head earlier as he'd climbed the trail behind Frank was gone. Instead, for the first time in a long while, Jim was praying as he walked.

"Lord, help Libby 'n' the baby! Don't let her hurt so bad, Lord...Lord!" He paused for a moment, drawing deep breaths, leaned down to touch his leg. He moved on and continued his pleading, "Lord, I'm the one ye oughta punish! I jest ain't no good. Not good enough fer that grace o' a lady back there. I jest ain't...no good, Lord! Oh, God...Oh, God! help her. Take away her pain! Her pain...her pain.... Lord! Lord, if ye jest take away her pain 'n' let her be all right...I'll quit this cussed drankin'...I swear I will!"

Just as his words touched the air before him, he staggered, lost his footing and began to slide. His eyes widened in surprise as he lost control and fell sideways, thrust out into what seemed like nothingness.

In his fall, he grabbed at the limb of an old jack pine, but the branch slid out of his hand, cutting flesh. His feet hit the bank and he pitched forward head first. He felt his clothes, then his skin, tear as he bounced from dried brush, back against rocks, and against the dead branches that littered the sharp slope. He slid downward, tasting gritty earth, then his own blood. He could no longer see objects, only bits and pieces of black and green, brown and blue, then black again. His body scraped against a huge rock, but the big object only slowed his fall.

Gradually, he stopped. His hands were out before him, buried deep in leaves, dirt, and unearthed roots. He had not lost consciousness. He wished he had, though, because there was not a place on his body that didn't hurt. He struggled to sit up, catching his breath in pain as he felt a rush to his head.

"Oh, God," Jim moaned as the throb attacked every corner of his mind. He brought his hands up to rest his head upon them, then stopped and stared. His hands were red—

blood-red. It was as if his palms had been raked with a pitch-fork. In the middle of the palms small stubs of sticks protruded. Squeezing his eyes, his teeth clamped together, the man in pain concentrated, then slowly began to pull the bloody pieces from first one, then both hands. Beneath his operation, the sticky wet circle on his torn overalls began to grow red.

It was then he heard it.

The sound was soft; he barely made it out. Slowly, the torn man turned toward the quiet noise. Was he now hearing things as well as feeling such sharp pain?

There it was again!

Jim blinked his eyes, and as his sight cleared, he realized he was in the midst of one of the largest tangles of blackberry vines and briars he'd ever seen. His eyes narrowed. Slowly, he surveyed his troubles. Then his gaze came to rest on a patch of white caught in last year's dried thorns.

The patch moved, and looking closer, Jim made out small eyes—pleading eyes. They burned into him.

The cry became weaker.

D. Ammons

A lamb! It's a baby lamb! He's caught in the thorns!

Jim's consciousness seemed to readily accept the lamb's existence. However, his pain still dulled his senses. He didn't move.

"Baaaa...." came the now clearly plaintive cry.

The sound seemed to attach itself to the pounding in his head. Jim struggled to think as he stared into the eyes of the imprisoned animal. He knew there was no way the lamb could ever get free by itself. But how could he get over there. Before him were years of old growth, woven so tightly the brambles seemed impregnable. How could he, in his condition, do anything to help.

"Ba..aa..a..." The innocent, diminishing sound and the now seemingly hollow eyes sent shivers throughout Jim's body.

I have to do somethin'! I can't let this lamb die! It's gotta be me to help!

Grimacing, Jim pulled himself around. Sprawling and then crawling on his stomach, he pushed himself deeper into the briar patch, helping himself along with his bloody hands. Pricks of briar parted his hair, scratched his scalp, caught his clothes and again cut through to his skin. As before, both cloth and skin tore. The slow work of growth and death, gravity and decay, had produced black humus on the floor of the briar patch. Soon, this humus had embedded itself into his wounds. For the moment, the bleeding stopped.

There, I'm here! Thank ye, God! I can do it! I can do it!

A fistful of briars, plunged deep into the heavy white wool of the lamb, at first resisted his eagerness. His hands became sticky again. Jim felt the lamb struggle feebly, tense, then a releasing sense of trust terminated his bleating. Finally he lay still, unmoving, as Jim pulled each thorn away, one by one.

The briar roof above Jim's head kept even the sun's rays from filtering through. In the dull greyness of tangled shadows, Jim felt the last prick of bondage give way—and yet the lamb still lay motionless. Completely released and free, the lamb waited for a sign from Jim, for direction from this man who had saved him from inevitable death.

In the dim light, Jim wiped his hands on his soiled britches, picked up the lamb, and placed it tightly against his side underneath one arm. He began to inch his way from underneath the mass of thorny branches.

The going was slow, but he finally made his way to the edge of the briar patch. Then, struggling to sit up, he took a deep breath. He found that the pain in his bad leg had now climbed past the hurt of the scratches and bruises, lodging in his chest.

He wiped his face with the back of one arm as he brought the lamb around to rest in his lap. Feeling the tremble in the small animal, he gently placed both hands on the lamb and tried to lift it. The strength was gone from his arms, and pain once again stabbed through his head, blurring his vision. He closed his eyes.

Suddenly, Jim felt a push of warmth. His eyes flew open as a strange wind descended, hiding man and animal in a swirl of flying leaves. A roaring filled his ears; he felt himself being pushed even farther back. His shoulder blades touched the heavy bark of an oak. In the midst of the bright funnel, a voice came to him. It was as if the voice spoke from within his own mind. It flowed over him, coating like honey. Commanding words filled his head, momentarily replacing the pain.

James, hearest thou Me!

Jim tried to turn his head; he could not.

James, console thy wife!

Again, Jim tried to move. He could feel wetness on his forehead. His will resisted, and his body refused to respond. Caught in a moment of time, Jim's mind stretched, cupping around the message. Again, came the voice.

James! Console thy wife...for as one is taken away, another is given.

Only Jim's eyes moved. The cocoon of wind and sound held him fast. In his mind he knew Libby had lost the baby. Another one is given...what...how? Libby lost the baby! As a strangled cry escaped his lips, the voice came again.

James, hearest thou Me! Feed my sheep!

And once again.

JAMES...FEED MY SHEEP!

Then it was over. The wind vanished, the leaves settled, and the lamb moved in his arms. In the quiet of the forest, Jim could hear his heart pounding.

"Baaaa...." the lamb cried.

Glancing down, the shaken man placed both hands on the animal, and this time, he lifted it easily. When he carefully withdrew his hold, the imprint of his bloody hands remained on the white wool.

Realizing he was free, the animal found its legs and scampered away into the underbrush.

In the stillness of yet unrealized truth, Jim's brow furrowed. Where had this lamb come from, here in the middle of the mountains. No one had any sheep up here, not since his daddy had killed the ram that butted him in the rear. His mother's sheep had slowly begun dying out, and then the flood last year got the last of them. And anyway, his mother would never have allowed any of them to come up this far into the denseness of the surrounding underbrush.

Jim pushed himself to rise. Then, gaining his feet, his gaze searched the terrain again for the lamb. So funny...not a sign of it.

Suddenly, deep in his mind the rush of discovery hit, overwhelmed him, and dropped him like a waterfall to his knees. His bad leg held him.

Oh, my God, my God!

Understanding splashed over him, to the ground all around. He allowed it to wash away the pain...the earthly pain. His hands sank deep into the earth in which he knelt as he let go of his own will.

Use me Lord! My hands are Yours!

Jim raised his eyes and then his released hands went above his head. He gazed at a sparkle of blue through a criss-cross of green. Libby's face took slow shape in the wind-touched leaves. He knew then. She needed him. He had to get to her.

Just inside the doorway, Cannie and Frank stood together. Beyond, in the shadowed corner of the room, Libby lay sleeping.

Suddenly, there came the sound of running steps. The sound came over the rocky path, up to the split-pine boards of the porch. Out of breath, Jim burst into the room, stopping to lean against the wall just inside the door. His eyes were wide, as if in shock.

For a moment, the couple stared at the sight of the wild-looking man. His clothes were torn. He was covered with dirt, and the scratches on his forehead dripped blood.

"J-J-Jim! My God! W-W-What's happened to ye?" Frank hurried to his brother.

"Never mind me...what's happened with Libby? Is she all right?"

Jim tried to see around Frank, his gaze searching the shadows behind him. The tiny house seemed so empty.

Frank swallowed. Jim could see that his brother's eyes were red. "I-I-I'm sorry, Jim," was all Frank could say, touching Jim's arm.

There was a stir of emotion on Jim's face as he stared at the younger brother. In a tight whisper, he said, "Ye mean she's...."

"O-O-Oh, no, Jim! L-L-Libby's all right! It's jest that...."

"That's okay, Frank," interrupted Jim. "I understand. I reckon we lost the baby, didn't we?"

Frank stared at the certainty on Jim's face.

"H-H-How did ye know?"

Jim's shoulders sagged as he experienced the sadness of losing someone that would have been a part of him. But then, he raised his now steady eyes to the questioning face of his brother. Straightening his tall frame, he shook his head, saying quietly, "What I've been through today has changed my life, Frank. I'm done with drankin'! I'm done with wastin' my life! I got more to do now than fool around. I got to do somethin'...somethin' fer this woman who's been prayin' fer me. Frank, I believe I've been visited by the Lord!"

"W-W-WHO?" demanded Frank in surprise.

"Frank," Jim began again, then hesitated, looking first at his blood-caked hands, and back again to his brother. "I've heard 'bout these kinds o' thangs, but I never did believe in 'em. Ain't ye heard them old time preachers say the Lord talked to 'em...that He told 'em what to do? I always laughed 'bout it, thankin' they wuz touched in the head. Wal, I got to change my way o' thankin', cuz I done heard the call! Frank! The lamb of the Lord called me...I thank He's called me to preach!"

From across the room, Libby's sister raised her eyes to gaze at her brother-in-law. Wonder lit her face. Quietly, the young girl crossed the floor to stand beside the bed of her sister.

"Prayin' 'n' trustin' makes all the difference in the world," she said quietly. "Ain't that so, Libby." Then, she leaned over and softly brushed away the pine needles that still clung to the knees of the sleeping woman.

CHAPTER 15
The Ragged Muffin

In His own mysterious way, God had answered Libby's prayers. The loss of her child had left a void, but with Jim's sudden commitment to his "calling," the emptiness inside her was replaced with hope. When he accepted an invitation to go and help her father in his ministry on Wolf Mountain, Libby's heart filled with happiness.

The Lord allowed the memory of the loss of her child to diminish. Then the new light in her husband's eyes began to hide the sadness that had lived within her. Libby knew the Lord had partially answered her prayer. She only had to give the Lord time—the second part of her prayer would come. As she gave thanks, the sun moved into Libby's soul.

It was Saturday morning, moving day for Libby and Jim. The Golden Place was full to overflowing. The Ammons womenfolk had come to help Libby pack. Marthie and Cannie were wrapping dishes in torn-out pages of the Sears Roebuck catalog, while Libby, sitting on the edge of her bed, folded clothes.

Retter stood in front of a cupboard in the corner of the kitchen, sorting through jars of canned vegetables. Some were to be packed for Libby and Jim, and some were to be left for Cannie and Frank. The young newly married couple would soon be living alone at the Golden Place.

"Lillie! Lillie!" shouted Retter out of the open window near her. "Git Nealie to git some more kindlin'! That fire's 'bout to go out!"

Outside, just by the corner of the house a large cast iron kettle hung on a tripod of oak. Steam rose, its vapor-like fingers reaching for the clear sky. As the fire died, red embers winked from underneath the crusted tub. A slender dark-haired girl of thirteen closely watched by a smaller sister, stood by the kettle, stirring the contents with a wooden paddle.

At the sound of her mother's voice, Lillie looked over her shoulder toward the window and answered, "Yes, Momma!" Then, turning slightly, she called toward the porch, "Nealie, Momma says fer ye to fetch some kindlin'. There's some out there under them apple trees."

Nealie crawled from underneath the porch, and began to dust himself off, turning his head and looking up to the window just above him.

With a grin on her face, Lillie watched her seven-year-old brother. He was young, but he was smart. He was old enough to know that his momma was set in her ways about her children's clothes. They had few garments—mostly well worn—but they were clean!

Nealie dashed off toward the grove of apple trees that surrounded the house.

Lillie turned her eyes back to the concoction she was stirring and wiped her brow with the back of her hand. The wooden ladle pushed the liquid soap into a churning yellow soup, burping thickly with the heat. She backed away slightly, pushing an anxious sister away from the fire.

"Corie, ye stand back, ye hear! If this stuff pops out on ye, it'll burn awful!"

A small shadow reluctantly moved away from Lillie, her

mouth screwed into a pucker. Corie eyed her sister a moment, shaking her head, stirring an almost white cloud of ringlets gathered around her face. Then, without a word, the ten-year-old turned and followed her brother.

Lillie pushed the ladle, stared into the bubbles and fell deep into thought.

She felt uncomfortable. The dark-eyed girl was just beginning to experience confusion about the changes in her body. She could feel the soreness of her small growing breasts underneath the tightness of her dress. She smoothed the front of her skirt, softly touching the faded patterns with a fingertip. She sighed. If only she could have a new dress! Earlier she had helped tear the pages from the catalog and had longed for each colorful fashion. Her momma had called the catalog the "wish book," and that was exactly what it was! Lillie had wished for everything she had seen.

The soap churned; Lillie stirred.

Tomorrow was Sunday, and in the afternoon Libby's daddy would be coming to help them move. Lillie remembered him. He had liked her hair the last time he'd come and had said, "What a pretty girl!" But he'd see her tomorrow in the same old ragged clothes again!

She raised her hand to the dark braids that hugged her head. How she'd love to have loose hair that would float in the wind. But Momma wouldn't let her cut her hair—it hung in long black plaits.

"Lillie! Quit that daydreamin' 'n' build up that fire!"

Retter's sudden words caused the girl to jump, jarring the new hair style out of her thoughts. In the quietness of her mind, Lillie absently listened to her mother talk to the women in the room above.

"We had to make the soap today, even though it's movin' day fer Libby. It's the full o' the moon! Good soap has to be made in the light o' the moon...makes it firm and white as lamb's wool. 'N' don't ye girls ever fergit—good soap's gotta be stirred with a paddle made out o' sassafras...makes it smell good."

Lillie looked at her paddle. It had been whittled out of a

small log by her daddy. Her momma had pushed him to get it done by the full moon. Now she knew why. Her daddy could make anything with his hands—little birds out of clay, little animals out of wood. He had even whittled out old Maude, the mule. In the evenings, he'd always sit and tell them stories or read out of the Bible. Sometimes he'd make up stories and work his hands just the right way, and the story would come alive with his hand shadows on the wall.

A long time ago, the doctors in town thought her daddy would die when he was knocked off of a railroad trestle, but her momma had saved his life with her herbs. Now crippled, he had to make white lightning to get money in the household for shoes and other things. Her momma always said it was too bad..."My Tom woulda outdone all them lumberjacks fer Blackwood Lumber Company!" Well anyway, he could get around pretty good with his cane—and besides, being crippled gave him time to tell stories! Lillie loved that.

Suddenly, Corie and Nealie came flying, their arms full of small branches and twigs, their cheeks rosy from the run.

"Momma—Momma! Somebody's comin'! There's two o' them!" Corie's small voice carried excitement as she dropped her kindling, looking over her shoulder.

Nealie dropped his load also, and crawled up the rock steps onto the porch. Then turning, he looked from his new position down the path beyond the barn. The thought of visitors excited and frightened him at the same time. He wanted to be near his mother, just in case she needed him...or something.

Lillie moved closer to the black kettle, trying to keep the pot between her and the unknown visitors.

The women in the house had all left their tasks and now stood in the open doorway and by the window, anxiously looking in the direction of Nealie's pointing finger.

"Poppy! It's Poppy!" shouted Cannie. She left the doorway, and was across the threshold before any of the others. Her feet seemed to fly down the path toward the man on a horse who had just topped the crest of the hill. A smaller figure rode closely behind.

From her position behind the kettle, Lillie's eyes quickly

settled on the small figure. All she could see at first was a flash of bright red. The rays of the sun had found a mirror. Lillie blinked her eyes.

Then all at once, she realized that the figure behind Mister Owen was a young boy not much older than she, the filly he rode pranced proudly. Her eyes grew round as she stared at the red-headed youngster in a tan suit. He wore a white shirt so bright that it hurt Lillie's eyes. And shining up in dark contrast was a chocolate-brown tie.

"He's beautiful!" thought Lillie as she tried to make herself small, shrinking still farther behind the cast iron pot. Looking at her faded clothes, she felt herself grow sick with embarrassment. "He can't see me...not now!" she moaned to herself as she watched the two dismount.

"Libby! Libby, look! It's Ray!" called Cannie as she slipped in and out of her father's arms and ran to her brother. The faces of the boy and the woman were alight with gladness. After a warm embrace, Cannie stood back from Ray, holding him at arm's length. "Ray! My, but yer growin'! Ye done caught me!"

"Wal, yer only one year older'n me, y' know! Anyway, since ye ain't t'home, I been eatin' yer share of Mommie's cookin'!" laughed the boy. His hair was lighter than the auburn hair of his sister. The white of his teeth sparkled in his tanned and freckled face. His eyes danced blue as he playfully cuffed his sister's shoulder.

Libby appeared on the porch, smiling broadly. "Poppy, ye 'n' Ray come on in 'n' make yoreselves t'home. Ain't ye a day early?"

"Yep, we're early—but we'll help pack today 'n' leave tomorrow...yer Uncle Blye's leadin' the meetin' at the church fer me. Couldn't help but come today, fer this young'un here wanted to go down to Sylvie this mornin'. Seems he sent away fer some home guitar lessons 'n' a guitar." Poppy came up onto the porch. "He saved five dollars cleaning out yer Uncle Sterlen's smokehouse, so we bought him a guitar with it." Poppy took his broad-rimmed hat in his hands, slapped it on his knee and nodded to Retter and Marthie, paused and continued, "Howdy, Miz Ammons...young lady. Right good seein' ye agin. How's Tom these days?"

As the attention of the women rested on Poppy, Lillie timidly peeped over the rim of the tub that hid her. She didn't want to be seen, but she was fascinated by this red-headed boy. Just the color of his hair made her swallow and blink in admiration. All her brothers had dark hair. It seemed so strange to see this vivid bright hair atop a smiling face of freckles! Suddenly, he was looking straight at her. Lillie quickly ducked back, hiding herself again, her face flushing pink.

"Hello, little doll, what's yer name?" the boy was saying.

As Lillie slowly looked around, her heart caught in her throat, she found that Ray was talking to her little sister.

"Corie...." replied the younger girl.

"Corie! That's a pretty name. My name's Ray...let's be friends, what'll ya say!"

"I say...yes! I'll be yer friend!" Corie was won over instantly. Her gaze had settled on his face, unblinkingly.

"How 'bout yer brother...'n' yer sister? Ye are kin...brothers 'n' sisters, ain't ye?" Ray paused for her nod, then continued, "What's their names?"

"This here's Nealie." Corie dragged her resisting brother closer. "'N' that's Lillie over there...hidin'!"

Lillie's face burned hot. "I'll kill her!" she cried to herself behind the kettle.

Suddenly, brown shoes were resting on the grass beside her. She felt his eyes on her even before she raised her gaze to his. Her face slowly lost the rosy blush as her body seemed to turn to ice. Her tongue grew thick in her mouth, preventing her from speaking.

"Hello, Lillie, I'm Libby's brother Ray. Looks like we're 'most the same age." The freckle-faced boy was smiling at her, not two feet away.

Lillie couldn't speak. Her eyes grew larger; then her gaze dropped to the ground. All she could think of was how awful she looked. Any minute now he'd laugh at her.

"I come to help with the movin'." He took a step closer.

"What're ye doin'...makin' soap? Smells good!"

His nearness caused her legs to weaken. Her heart sank with the heaviness of embarrassment.

Then, all at once, she handed the ladle to Ray, turned and ran as fast as she could down the path toward home. Her breath, caught somewhere in her ribs, slowly began to find it's way up, and finally she could breathe.

Just beyond a bend in the trail, out of sight of the cabin, Lillie slowed to a fast walk. Her breath now coming in quick gasps, she held her side to quiet the sharp pain of running.

Her heart cried out to the confusion of her thoughts. "Why did he have to see me like this? Momma calls me her 'dark-bread muffin'—what I really am is a ragged muffin!" Angry tears filled her eyes.

She shook her head, wiping at her eyes with the back of her hand. In her mind, she could see an image of the boy who had come into her life. She could once again see him coming up over the crest of the hill, his red hair gleaming. And such a pretty suit! She didn't think she'd ever forget the way he looked. It appeared as if he'd stepped right out of that Sears Roebuck catalog!

But wait a minute, he was going to be at Libby's tomorrow!

Maybe she could find something else to wear. Maybe he would look at her again and see a different girl. Lillie's heart began to swell. She raised her head and tossed her braids about in sudden determination. Her steps became quicker, then turned into a run. A smile covered her face as her bare feet flew, scarcely touching the rocky trail.

The girl in the faded dress was soon lost in the shadows of the quiet forest.

CHAPTER 16
A Purple Grin

That night lying in bed, Lillie couldn't sleep. The dark of the room had been lit by a fuzzy golden moon that hung in the sky beyond the silver curvature of the mountains—she could see it through the curtainless window beside the bed. There was a ring around it..."Hope it don't rain tomorrow durin' the movin'," Lillie suddenly thought, then shook her head. How could it, the sky was filled with stars!

In the bed next to Lillie slept Corie, and Nealie slept across from them in a small cot near the door that led to the front room where their parents slept. Marthie's bed sat underneath the steps to the attic that hugged the far wall. Above them, in the attic slept Bryson and Albert. There used to be three more bodies thrashing around on the mattresses up there, but Jim, Thomas, and then Frank had married...and left.

The house seemed almost empty now, especially since Frank had moved out. The ages of the three younger ones were so distant from the rest of the Ammons brood, that it had taken the outgoing Frank to link them all together even though he was still seven years older than Lillie. Marthie, almost eleven years older, lived in a world all her own, never allowing the younger children even a glimpse. So, when Lillie, Corie, and Nealie were sent to bed in the evenings, it seemed as if they lived in their own little midnight world in the back room.

Bryson, the eldest son, was all of thirty-one and after courting disaster for years with drinking, had surprised everyone by "getting religion," preaching his beliefs to one and all.

Albert, the third son, came after Jim. Four years Bryson's junior, he still liked to have his spirits whenever the urge called. His daddy and all the older sons had been making liquor for so long, it just seemed natural to always have it around, making it easy to sample. Once in a while, when he'd would get on the outs with the family, he would cook his own meals. Lillie loved to get up early any morning when Albert was cooking. She loved his fatback and pancakes.

Now, gazing at the stars through the open window, the sleepless Lillie could hear Bryson's snores above her and the quiet steady breathing of Marthie in the corner. She knew that the hyper Corie and Nealie must be asleep; there was not a sound from them.

All at once, someone came unsteadily through the cloth curtain that served as a door to the bedroom. In the moonlight, Lillie made out the form of Albert. He staggered past, groping for and then grabbed hold of the railing, pulling himself up the stairs.

Once above, his unsteadiness seemed to get worse, even to the point that he must have awaken Bryson.

"Al...Albert!" came the hoarse whisper. "What are ye doin'?"

"Jest...comin'...ta...bed," Lillie heard Albert say loudly.

"Shhh! Don't ya know everbody's tryin' ta sleep!" Bryson said in a whisper, then with a raised voice, he continued, "Shuuu-eee! Lord, yer drunk, ain't ye?"

"Shhhhhhhhhh, Bryson...I jest...hadda...little taste."

"If that's a taste, I'd hate to see ye chug a few! What

batch did ya cut yer jar out o' this time? Dad's gonna have yer hide!"

"Ain't been...in no jar, Bryson." Suddenly Albert's voice had laughter in it. "I...been...tastin' that barrel o' black...blackberry wine...inna shed...."

"Now yer gonna git it, Albert! That's Daddy's pride 'n' joy—that blackberry wine!" Bryson's voice rose. "Albert! yer shore enough goin' to hell! The Lord's gonna punish ye!"

"Shhhhhh...don't wake the...young'uns." Lillie could hear Albert sit down on his bed. One shoe came off, then the other.

"Albert, listen to me." Bryson had lowered his voice, but the words still managed to crawl down the stairway. "Ye need to repent o' yer ways! The Lord's gonna come any day now, 'n' ye havta git ready fer him. It says in Romans...."

"Alright...Alright, Bryson...maybe tomorrow. Now lessus git some shut-eye."

Bryson grumbled some more, but his voice died out. Shortly, a duet of snores filled the attic.

Lillie was now indeed wide awake. Suddenly a small hand touched her face. The chubby fingers traced her eyebrows, and a low whisper reached her ear.

"Lillie, are ye awake?"

"Yes," Lillie whispered back, removing the fingers from her face. "Whatta ye want?"

"Did ye hear?" Corie's soft voice carried excitement. "The blackberry wine's done—Albert's been drankin' it!"

"'Course I heard; how could I not help it! Even Bryson's whisper is loud! He's done jumped on Albert agin, too. He's after him to quit that drankin'."

"Lillie, lessus go check out this year's batch o' juice tomorrow...'fore Albert drinks it up! I wanta taste! It smells so good, 'n' I looooove blackberries!"

"Corie, ye know Daddy sets great store in that wine. He said to stay away from that barrel! We could get a good lickin'! Ye remember last year how mad he got when he caught Albert in the barrel! He took his cane to him and

Albert had to stay away from home almost a week!"

"Yer jest a fraidy-cat! It's worth it fer a drink o' that sweet smellin' juice. Come on, Lillie...I ain't never done it...'n' I ain't never wanted to taste somethin' as bad as I do that wine. Jest one taste, Lillie?"

Lillie sighed, "Corie, ye sound jest like Albert. But...I reckon one won't hurt."

Corie laughed under her breath, then hugged her sister. "Oh...yer jest the best sister!"

"Shore—shore. Corie, ye git me into all kinds o' trouble all the time. Don't know why I ever listen to ye."

The small girl beside her didn't answer; she'd already drifted off to sleep.

Closing her eyes, Lillie's thoughts blossomed again. It was the red-headed boy she'd met today that was keeping her awake. Again, her troubled thoughts settled on the problem of what clothes to wear the next day.

Earlier that evening, she had turned the house upside down looking for something to wear, but had found only the one other dress she had. In worse shape than the one she wore, she had donned it anyway in order to wash the first dress. Thinking about her small wardrobe, whatever self-confidence she had managed to build up, now began to disappear. Well, anyway, tomorrow she would just do the best she could. Besides, no one knew how she felt; she had kept her unhappiness well hidden.

The first touch of sunlight had fallen on the cheek of the worried girl before she'd finally dropped off to sleep. So, she slept later that morning than usual. Her mother tried several times before she'd finally roused the tired girl. Everyone else in the house had finished breakfast and had gone outside.

Amid the reproaches of her mother, Lillie rushed to do her morning chores. Finally, she sat down at one end of the long table to eat her now cold breakfast. But the rushing
had whetted her appetite, so the two cold biscuits still
to her.

tightening the kitchen, Lillie washed the dishes,

all the time gazing out the open window near her, watching for Corie. She had suddenly thought that her sister might slip out to the shed without her.

But, no, there she was, out near the barn with Nealie. Lillie could see they were busy shelling the early sweet peas. In the distance, Bryson walked behind the mule, still breaking ground for more garden vegetables.

When the dishes were dried and put away, Lillie brought the heavy black iron out from behind the stove and placed it on the warm burner. To heat the iron, she would need more wood, so she filled the compartment under the eyes of the burners. As the pop of the wood echoed through the room, Lillie unfolded a heavy muslin cloth and laid it on the table. This would be her ironing board.

She quickly pressed the dress and laid it out on her bed. Smiling, she felt pleased with herself. When her mother called her to go over to Libby's, she would be ready.

All the while Lillie had been rushing around to get her dress ready, Retter had watched her with curiosity. This was the first time she had ever seen Lillie wash a dress and iron it so carefully.

"She's shore actin' peculiar," Retter mused to herself. Then, "Ah-ha! I did see that young Ray talkin' to her yesterday. My little girl is smitten!" Retter chuckled to herself. "Maybe I kin help her a mite." A few minutes later, Retter laid a soft white bundle in Lillie's arms.

"I been savin' this here fer ye fer a while now. Why don't ye wear it today? It'll keep yer dress clean while we help finish the work fer Libby 'n' Jim."

Lillie's face shone with appreciation as she spread out a hand-stitched, full-length apron. There were ruffled straps that went over her shoulders, dropping down to tie with the apron strings at the pit of her back. The two pockets in the front were edged with narrow white lace.

"Oh, Momma! It's so pretty! Thank ye!" The words brought a smile to her mother's eyes.

"Ye best git dressed now. We're leavin' in jest a while."

Everything was ready for the move down the mountain, everything, that is, but the weather. From the doorway of the Golden Place, a group of long faces watched the downpour. A musty smell floated up as the raindrops danced across the bare ground around the porch steps. In the distance, a slow-moving blanket of gray crept over the rise and fall of the mountains, changing the green to pale blue.

"Aaahhh, looks sorta dismal, don't it," said Jim, from his position leaning on the windowsill. "Sorry state o' matters! I wanted to git this move over 'n' done with."

"Never kin tell what's gonna happen," spoke up Wiley Owen. "Take this war, fer example, did ye hear by any chance, that France surrendered?"

"S-S-Sure wuz a surprise, w-w-wuzn't it!" Frank said, nodding as he helped himself to another cup of coffee. "W-W-Woke everbody up! Nobody thought that would happen. France wuz supposed to have the strongest army ever has been!"

"Yep! And with all them other small countries going' under," said Jim, "Old England's gonna be standin' there nekkid as a jay bird!"

"Radio says Hitler sunk tons o' British ships," nodded Wiley. "Somebody's gotta do somethin' soon er he'll be sittin' in their backyard a'shootin' squirrels."

"B-B-Bet Roosevelt won't let 'em git away with that! We're gonna go to war, bet my bottom dollar on it!" Frank spoke with conviction. Standing behind her husband as he spoke, Cannie's face had gone ash white. Libby, sensitive to her sister's thoughts, quietly slipped her arm around Cannie's waist and led her to the kitchen table.

"Wal, somethin' is a'happenin' up there in the north," said Wiley, grimly, "up there where they make steel! My wife Ellie's sister Jurdie—she's been gone from home almost a year now. Anyways, she's got herself a job somewhere's up there in Connecticut...some big fighter plane plant!"

"Ye don't say! They're hirin' women now! Jurdie got a job?" Libby spoke up from the table. A disbelieving expression slid over her face.

"Seems since the draft started, there's openings all up 'n' down the Great Lakes up there. That's where all the car people are. Some of the older men have joined the women, goin' up there to work," Wiley said.

"P-P-Probably gonna be more women doin' the work o' a man," responded Frank.

"What do ye mean, Son! I been doin' that fer a powerful long time already!" said Retter from her position near the open door, "...since before ye wuz born!"

Then Retter burst out laughing at the look on her son's face. As the others followed her lead, the atmosphere in the room brightened considerably.

Lillie, who had been silently standing close to her mother, shyly looked over at Ray, who had likewise held back from speaking. He was smiling at the conversation, but kept on working. He had spent most of his time cleaning Jim's hunting guns and wrapping them for the journey. His presence in the corner of the room near the fireplace could easily have been overlooked, if it hadn't been for the bright touch of red hair lighting the shadows.

As the laughter ebbed, the conversation once more turned to the problem of moving in the rain, their voices all running together, floating above Lillie's head. Her gaze traveled over the hills of trees below until she was entirely oblivious to what was being said. Her heart heavy and burdened, her problem seemed more important than that war! She didn't understand her own feelings, and knew even less about how to deal with them. With the blueness of the wet forest mirrored in her eyes, she did not see her mother move away, leaving her in the doorway alone.

Minutes later, a pleasant presence suddenly awakened her from her musings. Slowly, she raised her head, and turned slightly, to find Ray standing beside her. Her legs grew weak. Quickly she averted her gaze. He spoke not a word, just stood there, his hands in his pockets not even looking at her.

After what seemed like long minutes, Lillie decided to risk another look at the boy beside her. He was smiling.

She stared openly, forgetting her fear. What was he

smiling about? Was he laughing at her? Anger rose. She straightened her back and gathered her breath, the blue in her eyes now bright and shinny black.

"Look at that blue-tick hound! Ain't he funny? That dog's jest a'rollin' in all that mud!" laughed Ray, pointing at the scene outside.

Lillie's harsh words caught in her throat. Her breast rose and fell in the swift change of emotions.

"I got a dog at home almost like that one. I shore do thank a heap o' him. Do ye like dogs?"

"Yes...yes, I do." Where her voice came from Lillie didn't know, but there it was; she heard it herself. Slowly she began to calm down.

"But I like music more'n I like my dog. My sister, Irene, bought me a pick—an ivory guitar pick—back a few months ago. Ever since then, I been wantin' my own guitar. I finally got it, ye know."

"I seen it yesterday." Lillie's words were low, but clear. She'd become interested in what he was saying.

"When I learn how to play my guitar, I'll play it fer ye." As Ray spoke, he moved slightly toward her, his full gaze now resting on Lillie's eyes. The softness of his smile slid right down into her heart, and rested there. She felt warm inside as she returned his smile.

"I don't git up here much, but I could send ye letters with my sister, Cannie, now that she's gonna live here, or with Uncle Sterlen. Reckon it would be all right to write ye? Then I kin tell ye when I'll be ready to play fer ye!"

"Okay," was all that Lillie said, but the remark widened Ray's smile.

"Lillie! Lillie Mae!"

The call came from behind the young people. Lillie turned to see her mother beckoning her. Quickly she hurried to where her mother stood with Jim and Frank.

"Lillie, I want ye to go back over to the house. It's quit rainin' now, 'n' I don't know why, but I feel it in my bones that somethin's not right at the house. I left Corie 'n' Nealie over there out o' the way o' the movin'. I'm thinkin' that yer daddy's not gonna watch them young'uns like he oughta."

"All right, Momma, I'll go. Ye don't need me no more?" Lillie's gaze darted to the silhouette of Ray, who was still by the doorway, and back again to her mother.

"No, they've decided to move everythin' tomorrow. It's too wet to walk that mule 'n' wagon down this evenin'. Ye git on now, ye hear! I'll be right behind ye."

Lillie walked to the door and looked up at Ray. "I got to git on home now."

"I'll walk with ye since we're stayin' another night."

Lillie's heart beat fast as they made their way down the wet sloping trail toward the Ammons' homestead. For a time, it was as if everything stood still. She could hear nothing but Ray's voice. She heard his every word, but at the same time, she seemed to be far away, listening only to herself. Her thoughts wondered...*how could his hair lie in such perfect deep waves...how was it that his freckles seemed to dance on his skin as he talked and laughed.* She asked herself if it could be true—this look in his eyes that told her that he liked her.

Then, the cabin came into view. Time took over again.

"Ye are shore far apart here on this mountain, Lillie. It's ever s'far over to Libby's...er, Cannie's house from here, but...." Ray paused, and then continued quickly, " I could walk it agin any time...with ye."

A warm blush spread over her face.

"Lillie," Ray's voice went on, his tone changing. "Lillie, stop jest fer a minute, 'fore we git to the house."

Lillie paused and waited, her eyes on Ray's face.

"I jest wanted to tell ye how glad I am that my sisters are married into yer family. I like ye Ammons...a lot." He took Lillie's hand in his and squeezed it gently.

The girl with the long braids trembled. To her, his hand seemed to spread warmth throughout her body. "I'm glad, too," she managed.

Suddenly, Ray's eyes opened wide and flashed. He was staring over Lillie's head toward the cabin. "Somebody's comin'...fast!"

Lillie whirled around and saw Nealie coming toward them, his arms flying.

"It's Corie! It's Corie! Come quick!"

Without another word, Ray and Lillie ran after Nealie. It was all they could do to keep up with him.

At the fork in the trail, he turned toward the shed out back of the house.

Deep inside her heart, Lillie began to dread what she might find. She feared that this sister of hers had been up to no good again.

Nealie flung open the door and led the way to the barrel in the middle of the room. Nearby, a small stool was turned over on its side.

"She's in there! Corie's done fell in!"

Ray wasted no words either. He righted the stool and stood on it, looking inside the huge wooden barrel. Quickly both arms disappeared as he reached inside. Almost immediately, he brought up a squirming bundle of purple, and helped her scramble over the rim, down onto the dirt floor.

Amid a lot of coughing and gagging, this purple ball of a girl fought to regain her breath. A strong smell of alcohol filled the closeness of the shed as the warmth of the little girl's body heated the wine that still clung to her.

"Corie, are ye all right?" Lillie had found her voice, as she drew near the girl.

"No! I don't like this...stuff!" she cried as she shook her head. Seeds went flying everywhere from her purple hair— then she turned and flung herself into Lillie's arms.

Lillie held her arms away from the little purple girl as she realized, with horror, that her new white apron now displayed the imprint of her little sister. Slowly her eyes rose to Ray's face and then passed down over his now purple spotted white shirt with the stained sleeves. His mouth was trembling. Was he going to cry?

Instead he burst into laughter.

That was worse. Rage grew deep inside Lillie. She turned hot eyes on Corie!

The younger sister recognized the look. She began backing away, crying out in self-defense, "Lillie, don't! Please! We couldn't reach the juice! It's all Albert's fault! He done drunk too much. I fell in cuz I couldn't reach it...it's not MY fault! Ye leave me be, ye hear...Lillie?"

"I'm gonna wring yer purple neck wunst I catch ye, Corie! Ye coulda drowned! Jest wait'll I git my hands on ye! COME BACK HERE!"

But the small girl was gone, her purple hair spitting purple seeds as she ran.

Lillie looked down at Nealie. He suddenly grinned...his teeth were purple.

Lillie's anger vanished in that moment, and she, too, burst into laughter. Who could resist a purple grin?

CHAPTER 16
Joe-Pye Weed

It had been over three months since Sterlen had talked to Libby about his feeling for Marthie. He had put it off long enough. Time would not slow nor wait. Fear of rejection had to be discarded—he must get on with it.

"Howdy, Retter." Sterlen stood on the porch in the doorway of the Ammons kitchen. Retter turned from the cook stove, a welcome smile on her face.

"Why, bless me, if it ain't the man of song agin...come on in, Sterlen." She came toward him, wiping her hands on her apron. "Ye been stopping by quite a bit lately. Shore am happy to see ye."

Sterlen's smile, covered by his now well groomed beard, twitched as he strode through the doorway to shake the hand of his friend.

"You hungry? Ye'll stay for dinner, won't ye! Come on in 'n' sit 'n' talk to me." Retter indicated a chair at the end of the long table. "Ye look like ye're either goin' to...er comin' from...somethin' important."

"Retter, ye got a way o' sizin' thangs up in jest one look!" Sterlen felt the pressure building within his chest as he pulled out the chair and sat down.

"Wal, if ye've come from Wolf Mountain this mornin', ye've come a fer piece on foot to be up here on this mountain afore dinner time," smiled the woman who had busied herself back at the stove. Pushing her pots aside, she reached for the iron lifter. Inserting it into the large eye of the stove at the left end of the cast iron surface, she removed it and deposited short pieces of wood inside.

The popping of the freshly-caught burning wood filled Sterlen's head, it's heat and Retter's sharp reasoning adding to his discomfort. He ran his fingers through his hair, felt it's dampness and gathered his nerve.

"Retter, I figger I better jest lay my cards on the table 'n' be done with it! I want to talk to ye 'bout Marthie."

The big woman slowly turned, her eyebrows arching as she stared at Sterlen with a pointed questioning look. "Marthie...what about Marthie? What's she done?"

Sterlen watched as Retter's whole demeanor became one of protection. He warmed to see it. Suddenly, his mission became easier, and he almost relaxed.

"Wal, I reckon she's done somethin' awful. She's stole my heart."

"They...Lord a'mercy!" Retter's mouth dropped open, her expression pure disbelief.

"Yep, it's a mercy all right, Retter! I been set in my ways fer a powerful long time! Who'd ever thought I'd have such feelings at this age!"

"Ye care fer her!" The mother swallowed, her hands now fisted within her apron. "How did...this happen?"

"Don't rightly reckon how it happened, Retter. Ye know I been comin' here to visit fer ever s'long, but seems I ain't never really seed yer daughter 'fore the other month when I wuz here. It's as if I wuz meant to really see her this time!"

"Umm...she don't stay 'round when people come to visit...mostly." Retter had begun shaking her head from side to side, muttering under her breath. "...'n' she wuz touched by yer song, too." Suddenly a smile lit up her expressive face. "My God! It's a miracle—if I ever seed one."

Sterlen continued as if he had not heard her. "I wanted to talk to ye...then Tom, if I could. Don't want to even git started bearin' my soul to Marthie, if I couldn't git yer go ahead." His discomfort had come back. He pulled at the collar of his shirt.

"Wal, Sterlen, ye got mine! But do ye know what ye're gittin' yerself into?"

"Now, think about this, Retter...I really want there to be no miscalulatin'! I ain't the young elk I used t'be. I've seen many a year a'tramplin' all the hills 'n' valleys 'round here. I've done seed a lot, 'n' I've heard a plenty."

Retter had sat down on the outside bench of the two that embraced the table. Laying one arm on the checked table-cloth, she learned toward Sterlen, fixing him with her direct-ness. "Does Marthie know ye feel like this?"

"Wal, we met in the woods a few months back 'n'...talked...wal, we...come to the place where I thank she knows I keer fer her. 'N' I wouldn't be here if I didn't feel there wuz some hope."

"Did ye talk about gittin' married?" Again came the directness.

"Lord, no! I gotta go slow with this gal! She don't have no idee what I got in mind...no idee a'tall!"

Retter smiled warmly. She placed her hand on Sterlen's arm. "Yer old enough to know what to do, I kin see. Age shore does make a difference, Sterlen. I'm forty-seven 'n' what I wouldn't give to go back 'n' tack on what I've learned to my young years! Ye sure 'nough got my blessin'! Tom's, too! I'll see to that! Fact is, as I think on it, yer exactly the person Marthie needs." She stood. "Now, let's see about dinner on this fine, fine day...afore the mornin' is completely gone!"

As Retter walked back to the stove and her pots, Sterlen's thoughts slid back to the time he had mentioned—in the forest with Marthie. Within the warmth of the kitchen he could almost feel once again the sweet touch of the lips she had placed on his cheek. Yes, he concluded to himself, he did have a fair chance.

Dinner had been served and the family was well into their noon meal when they heard Marthie's bare feet on the porch. The boards creaked as she deposited whatever she was carrying outside. She entered the room, prepared just to pause in her duties of harvesting the herbs her mother had sent her to find. She walked over to the table opposite the stove, and poured a dipper full of water from the pail into a small basin. Sterlen watched as she washed her hands. Her hair, combed only by the forest, fell onto faded overalls far too large for Marthie's slender figure. Instead of drying her hands, as she turned toward the kitchen table, she ran damp fingers through the wildness of her hair.

Even then, she failed to see Sterlen. When she stepped into the beam of light from the window, stopping the glare, she realized there was more than her family at this table. Shock paled her face as her dark eyes locked with Sterlen's.

Within this pocket of time the two connected without a sound. Retter had not mentioned why Sterlen had come to visit. No one had seen anything unusual in him being there, especially since one of his nieces still lived at the Golden Place. Talk went on as normal. The younger children knew to sit quietly when there was a guest. However, they crowded around Sterlen, sitting as close to him as possible. Marthie sat down at the far end of the bench, only one child away from Sterlen. Her gaze seemed glued to her food.

"Hey, Sterlen, did ye bring a paper this time?" Albert said, wiping his mouth on his shirt sleeve between mouthfuls.

Sterlen shook his head. "Still don't have a nickel, Albert. But I hear thangs down to Dock Moses store, people talkin' 'n' such. War's still a'threatenin', fer as I kin tell. Ye sure do git interested in them goings-on, Albert. Ye thankin' about joinin' up?"

"Never kin be too interested when it comes to yer country. Ever since I worked fer the CCC back when I wuz twenty year old, I learned that it takes workin' together to make thangs happen."

"Naw...ye worked for the CCC! Heard tell they done some good thangs fer the county here! What did ye do?"

Albert laid his fork down, chewing as he thought. Then, swallowing, he said, "I helped a little with building the rock wall that goes 'round the hill there below Sylvie's court-house, 'n' over in Webster...but mostly I worked out in the mountains, doin' this 'n' that. Good five years ago...yep, it wuz a good thang!" The young man's face showed great interest for a moment.

"Ye don't git involved in thangs like that nowadays, do ye, Albert?"

"Too far away...ain't got ary way to git there...'n' politics gits in the way of a lot of good thangs...sometimes." Accepting of his plight, Albert gaze dropped to his plate, "Don't much like politics."

"'Sides all that, we got a lotta land here to plow, sow seed, 'n' harvest!" spoke up Bryson. "Back breakin' work here on the mountain."

"Ah, Bryson...sounds like ye don't like it!" Sterlen grinned at the taller man.

"Shore I like it! But what I like most is to work in the fruit trees." He stuck his fork into the blue mason jar in the center of the table and pulled out half a peach and put it into his plate. "Take this peach here...come off that nice tree we got over yonder in the field. We got pears and apples, too. Like to git some more trees started this year."

"I'm out in the backwoods most of the time. I see some good young fruit trees 'round deserted homeplaces er where cabins have burned down. I'll brang ye some...next time I come." Sterlen's gaze slid to the side, to where Marthie sat, so quietly, yet intently listening.

Suddenly, Sterlen felt a tug on his sleeve. He looked down and saw the hazel eyes of Lillie. Shyly, she said, "Ye been over to the Owen house lately, Sterlen?"

"Shore have, little'un."

"Did ye see Ray?"

"Ye mean that young feller who's learning to play the guitar?"

Lillie's smile flashed; she nodded.

"Yep, jest sit a spell with him yesterday. We played our first duet...he's comin' on real good with his pickin'. I'll tell him ye said hello."

"Now, ye be careful, Lillie! Don't like to hear such talk!" Tom Ammons pounded the table with the palm of his hand, all the while his eyes twinkling at his daughter. "It's scary, Sterlen...all them Owens' er gonna wind up gittin' ALL my young'uns!"

Laughter filled the room as Lillie blushed red and slid back against the wall. No one saw the shy exchanged looks of Sterlen and Marthie.

"Ye gonna stay the night, Sterlen?" Tom asked as he turned his attention back to Sterlen. Tom leaned back in the chair at the head of the table, pushed his plate away and continued. "Shore would like to hear some o' yer songs."

"Wal...don't rightly know if I kin stay...yit, Tom. Might...gotta see."

"Ye don't..." started Tom.

"Marthie! ye find any joepye weed out there this mornin'?" Retter interrupted, stabbing a look at Sterlen.

The startled Marthie blinked at her mother. "Joe...pye...weed?"

"I need the roots o' it...fer my...wal...I jest need it." She turned to Sterlen. "Kin ye help her, Sterlen?"

"Shore kin, Retter." Sterlen nodded to Retter as he rubbed his hand over his mouth, further concealing his rising fear.

"Wal, git on with ye then," responded Retter. "I'll git these dishes."

"I'll help ye, Momma," said Albert as he rose. He began his customary after meal gathering of the plates and silverware.

The scraping of the benches and chairs muffled the mutterings of the young girl as she got up and quickly slipped out of the kitchen door. Sterlen hurried after her, not seeing the questioning face of her father as he watched them go.

"Marthie...wait!" Sterlen wanted to talk. He didn't want to run. "Slow down...please."

"Oh...I'm sorry." A high pink had grown on Marthie's face.

"Marthie, kin we find a place somewheres where we kin jest talk?" He wanted to touch her arm, but held back. He had to be so careful. His stomach churned with an emotion that felt akin to anguish, for he so wanted to hold her in his arms.

She stopped and stared at him. "What do ye want to talk about?" He could see her lips quivering.

Sterlen didn't want to get too personal right away. She could bolt any minute. "Marthie, I jest need to talk to ye!"

For a moment he became afraid that she would indeed run away. But then, she responded to him.

"I got this favor-rite spot o' mine. I only showed it to one other...person afore." Marthie seemed to fall into a reverie. Then she shook her head and turned to look him full in the eyes. He caught his breath. He could see danger. Something cold lived there in her eyes. He felt urgency rise within him.

"Lessus go, then...lead on!" he said and waved his arm.

Before long the couple had gone through a maze of animal trails, and over, in and around fallen trees and laurel thickets. If Sterlen had not been such a knowledgeable man of the forest, he would have lost his direction. No wonder Libby had lost her way.

But the feel of the earth came up out of the ground, through the soles of his shoes, into the back of his mind. There was no need to speak—only a deep need to experience this "other world," and to listen to the voices that called to him—they were all around. Somewhere in the trip up to Marthie's favorite place, the mountain man realized that this was the first time he had felt his unique kinsmanship with the forest while in the company of another. He reveled in it.

Suddenly, Sterlen stopped. He knew they had reached their destination even before Marthie had turned around to look at him, and he could see she knew he knew. Looking into her eyes, for the first time Sterlen experienced the wonderful thrill of knowing mutual appreciation and total understanding of that appreciation.

"Marthie," he breathed. "Your place is right nice, indeed!"

And wonders of wonders, the woman's barrier came down and she smiled.

CHAPTER 18
It Fell a Flood

"I love this place! It's my little corner of the world."
Marthie said.

To cover her nervousness, she ran around, her arms
flying out as she showed him each section. "I started comin'
here when I needed to think on somethin'! The sound o' the
water down below drowns out the rest o' the world, 'n' I kin
sorta straighten out my thoughts. Listen...listen to the
waterfall! It's just a little farther on."

She ran before him. Sterlen gathered his emotions as he
followed. He must keep his wits. She sat down on a rock
overlooking a beautiful cave-like rock indentation in the
mountain. From far above, icy, bubbly water fell like strands
of pearls, spraying into a foamy bed of glistening rock
encircled by a fairy ring of greenery.

Marthie smiled up at him; again they shared the
appreciation of each other's similarities. He dropped to the
rock next to Marthie to feel the satisfaction of the view.

Suddenly Marthie stood and, without warning, darted
down from their place on the bank, quickly jumping from

rock to rock to stop just in front of the splashing water. Her hair seemed to float out all around her as she spun around to sit on the wet rock jutting out from under the falls. She laughed to the heavens as she flung her head back to look up at the startled Sterlen. Then, just as quickly, she jumped up to run back along the same pathway—back to sit beside him. Breathing hard, Marthie lowered her head onto her lap to get her breath.

"Yer beautiful, Marthie." Sterlen's voice expressed admiration and a touch of awe. It was all he could do not to stroke her damp hair. "Yore a little sparrow sittin' here beside me. Ye won't fly away, will ye?" His tone had become wistful and uncertain.

"I'm not gonna run away," laughed Marthie as she lifted her head and looked up at him. "I jest got the urge to git closer—to touch the water...to touch what I wuz feelin'. Somehow I feel so peaceful here, jest like bein' in my bed on rainy nights and listenin' to the rain hittin' the tin roof above me."

"It's peaceful here all right," Sterlen replied. He wanted to touch her cheek. "There's places like this over to my mountains, too. Do ye think ye'd like to come with me sometime to visit my place?"

As he spoke, Sterlen witnessed the sudden stiffening of Marthie's body. He immediately knew he had already said something amiss.

"Jest cuz I kissed ye cheek the other day don't mean...." Marthie began harshly.

"Marthie" Sterlen interrupted. "I jest want to share my own special place with ye."

Marthie's shoulders visibly slumped. She refused to look at Sterlen, still not speaking. The sound of the waterfall grew intense, roaring in his ears.

"Marthie, I felt ye liked me...a little? Wuz I wrong?" he said.

Still no answer. Marthie kept her face averted, holding her body still and stiff.

Sterlen pulled himself up and quietly rose to walk a few steps away. He stood with his back to her, not speaking, deep in thought. After a long moment, he turned to look at the woman who had not moved.

"Marthie," he began, "I reckon I've gone a step too far."

"No...no, Sterlen. It's me. I jump into protectin' myself, 'n' then I'm too ashamed to say I'm...sorry. Please stay." Her face clear now, she patted the rock beside her, smiling at him.

He couldn't believe she had invited him to stay. He came back, but in doing so, he began to feel an uneasiness in the back of his mind. He brushed it away.

"What did ye want to talk to me about, Sterlen?" In her eyes he could see it...the coiled blacksnake. That's all right, he could handle snakes!

"Marthie, did ye know that if ye hang a blacksnake, head down, there'll be rain in two days?"

"No...sure 'nough!" came her surprised answer. "I gotta remember to ask Daddy if he knows that. Ye know any more such thangs?"

Sterlen smiled. It felt good to be back in control of himself. "Wal, if ye put a four-leaf clover in yer left shoe, ye'll met yer intended comin' down the road."

Marthie burst out laughing. "It'd take ye a month o' Sundays to find a four-leaf clover! Ye gotta work fer that one!"

"Have ye ever heard a hen crow, Marthie?"

"Now yer loco! Ain't no such thang as a hen crowing...is there? Well, I'll ask anyway...what'll happen?"

"If ye hear a hen crow, then ye better kill her..or else we menfolk are in fer a heck o' a lot o' trouble!"

Marthie almost fell over laughing. Sterlen chuckled, thinking that he could get this hurt-filled woman to laugh. He'd be good for her.

Now smiling wide, Marthie said, "Now, seriously, Sterlen, what did ye want to talk to me about?" She turned to him eyes that were no longer hard and cold.

"Wal," suddenly, his hands were clammy. He stood up.

"Wal...I very much like yer company, Marthie." He rushed on, "I would like to come a'courtin', if I could."

There they were. The words she wanted to hear from this man. The pit of her stomach turned into one of her momma's rolls of yarn. A part of her wanted to run to him...but another part of her wrapped itself around her feet.
God! Help me!

"Marthie...." Sterlen was saying. "Whatever ye say, I'll honor yer wishes. My intentions are good."

Marthie raised soft, intense eyes, and from somewhere she found the words, "Sterlen, I'll speak, if I kin. It'll be hard to listen...but please listen." She paused.

"I'm...a'feared. Ever since that time back when I wuz jest a girl...when...those... men...had their way...with me...." her voice sank lower, but the words came faster. "I've even been a'feared o' being' in the same room with any man. I have a wondrous longin' to be keered fer, but my mind jest turns black...when I thank o' anythin' beyond that. I cain't ever be courted."

"Marthie, what happened to ye is a tragedy! I could kill somebody over it, but it won't take it back. It's done. We'll start over...together."

"Sterlen, don't ye hear me! I'm not fit fer ye...if ye only knew what they done to me! I'm not fit fer any good man! I'm...used... Everbody says...so."

As she finished speaking, gentle, yet strong hands caught her hands, pulling her up from the rock. Deep compassion shone in Sterlen's eyes as he gazed on Marthie's saddened features. He wanted to draw her close, to let her hear the steady pounding of his heart, to feel the warmth of his body. Instead, he let her feel the absolute sincerity of his presence as he spoke.

"Marthie, I havta tell ye the truth. Please listen to me. I love ye...I would never hurt ye. 'N' my love fer ye doesn't come from jest the looks o' ye. I don't want ye jest cuz yer beautiful. There's more to it than that. There's a look in yer

eyes that sometimes takes my breath away. There's so much
sadness spillin out, I cain't begin to tell ye how much I want
to hold ye safe in my arms forever."

Sterlen paused, then continued, "Marthie, yer a
wonderful creature of great importance. For me, ye're the
link—the one who will carry on when I'm gone—through ye
will flow tomorrows." His voice grew more excited.
"Marthie! yer the earth...the water...the waterfall...the flood!"

Gazing intently into her eyes, he refused to let the
darkness come back. Softly, with his heart in his own eyes, he
said. "Marthie, ye asked me what I wanted to talk to ye
about. Wal, here's the truth! Yer're the one I love! I want to
marry ye."

Tears covered Marthie's anguished face. "Sterlen, don't
talk to me like that! Don't tell me such stuff! Ye say these
things now, but one day ye'll hear stories about me from
somebody in town, 'n' ye'll turn from me. I couldn't bear
that...bein' turned away from. Sterlen...people turn away
from me."

"Marthie! The good Lord has seen fit to let me feel a
touch o' the splendor I've sung about, to let me dream o'
havin' a partner in the spirit o' livin'...to become one with
another afore I die. What a wonderful thang! Mabbe if we
take it real slow...mabbe with time ye kin fergit. With time
ye'll learn to trust me. Ye'll find I'm the stayin' kind,
Marthie."

The look in Marthie's eyes had not changed. Visibly
shaken, Sterlen made still another attempt to speak. His eyes
glistened. Finally he continued, "What has happened before
is all behind us! Don't ye see that? Time is short; let me
give to ye what I have in my heart. Please, Marthie, let me
love ye...please?"

*I love ye too, Sterlen! I love ye Sterlen! Lord! let me
say it!* Marthie thought in despair.

Sterlen could see the battle that filled her. He knew she
cared for him, and yet, now he was sure that she feared him.

She feared all men. He was a man, one of the race that had harmed her, maybe beyond repair.

"Say it, Marthie...say what yer're feelin'!"

Moaning, she finally spoke, but the wrong words came out, "All the men I ever knowed jest wanted to paw me whenever my brothers warn't lookin'. Here ye are, tellin' me that ye love me fer no good reason at all...lovin' me in spite o' all I told ye about myself. How kin ye do that? How kin I believe ye?"

"Marthie, who ye see here is who I am. I don't go 'round sayin' thangs I don't mean."

"But I seem to have sadness stuck to me...everthang I've ever touched, everthang I've ever done...it's all come out in sadness!"

"If ye turn me away, there'll be sadness...big sadness."

Hot tears filled her eyes as she struggled. "I cain't...I cain't...."

Sterlen's hands dropped. His shoulders sagged. He stared at her for a moment. The roar of the waterfall beat against his chest. In deep despair, he turned from her, and began walking away.

He's going...down the trail...out of my life! He's leaving! NO!

Somehow she found her voice as she cried aloud, "STERLEN! I need ye!"

She watched as he stopped, whirled, and with long strides, was there, wrapping strong arms around her, holding her feverishly close to him. "God, I love ye!" he whispered, and then trembling lips hidden within a soft beard found hers.

The love she felt for this gentle man and the sound of the water hitting the mossy rocks seemed, for a time to obscure the pain. But the shadows were there, in her mind; she knew it.

I've warned him. What more kin I do?

Her skin rippled, repelled, her physical body still attached to that horrible memory. Tight! her arms, her legs, her stomach...all tight...and there's his scent...

Kin I do this?

But the longer the gentle man held her, the more she began to listen to the outpouring of his beating heart.

CHAPTER 19
The Legend of Horseshoe Rock

S terlen stood beneath Horseshoe Rock at the top of Wolf Mountain. Leaning against the bark of a red maple, he studied the area. Years ago, the Cherokee had lived all over the mountain. Before the Removal of 1838, the Cherokee had raised their families here, intermingling with the settlers—they had lived side by side in harmony. And then, greed brought loss of home and death for the most peace-loving people of all time. *It was so wrong...so wrong!*

Thereafter, when new pioneers arrived they listened to a fearful sound, for each night wolves would creep to the top of Horseshoe Rock and howl!

Horseshoe Rock was itself a puzzler. Embedded, top to bottom, in the hard rock that covered half the mountain, were barefooted horseshoe prints. So, they named the community Wolf Mountain, and the top of the mountain, Horseshoe Rock.

Now, in the cove before him lived his sister's mother-in-law–Elminia Mason Owen. Her husband, Isaiah, had passed away in 1935. The Owen homeplace had stood since two years after the Civil War when Jackson Owen, Isaiah's daddy, had come across Tanasee Gap from the next county. Fact was that the father of the local Owen clan, John Owen, Sr., had received a land grant way back at the end of the Revolutionary War, giving him the whole mountaintop. Living all around in this territory were kinfolk of these pioneers of Wolf Mountain—people of Scotch-Irish descent who had carried a sack of creativity on their backs with them when they came...for it was the main ingredient in settling this land so far away from civilization. Sterlen's family, the Galloway's, were among them.

As far as Sterlen knew, all these families had made their living as farmers. This specific part of the community was called "Little Canada," because a French Canadian who had done some trapping on the East prong of the Tuckaseigee River had told his partner that it was as cold as Canada up there, and the image stuck. Along with farming, livestock was kept on natural balds, and they supplemented their incomes by trapping and hunting. His grandfather had owned herds of sheep, as did the Owen family. He could remember his mamma carding and spinning wool by the light of the fireplace. And he had helped his daddy by grinding corn and making sorghum, after which they'd go fishing!

For entertainment, families gathered at corn shuckings, revivals, picnics on the ground, decoration days, house and barn raisings, community socials at the school house, home-comings, and evenings on front porches—where everybody sang, picked and fiddled (when allowed to play string music), clogged—and preached a little, too. The only way they had of getting to the gatherings was by walking, by horseback, on wagons drawn by oxen or horses, in buggies, and now by motorized vehicles.

Sterlen had lived his years mostly alone, in a modest home he built himself. He had engaged in little farming, preferring to trap, hunt, and harvest herbs. He loved being out in the forest, walking, free to experience the ways of nature. He received his greatest joy watching young and old faces come alive as he played his banjo and sang and told his mountain stories.

Now—his life as he knew it was ending.

Sterlen watched the scene before him, dropping down into deep reverie. It had been almost three months since that day in July when he'd declared his love for Marthie. Since then he had been preparing a home for her where only he had lived for these many years. During the first month he had produced much change in his dwelling, the excitement of his newly found love guiding his every effort.

As the second month came along, his gaze had strayed to the warm summer trails leading out into the hemlock cove forest beyond his cabin. He'd heard the call of the ruffled grouse and bob white, and seen the eyes of raccoon and red foxes looking back at him out of the recesses of laurel thickets edging the forest. He began to realize that he missed the musty aroma of damp earth and his many nights of sleeping under the stars.

Then, the third month had placed him in a deep quandary, slowing his handiwork and his enthusiasm. He was almost fifty years old; he had not lived the life of a farmer for most of his years. Besides, he did not possess any of his own land. Could he make a good enough living trapping and harvesting his herbs to take care of Marthie? And how about a family? When he died what would he leave them? Was he really doing the woman he loved any favor by marrying her? But then, what would it do to Marthie if he didn't marry her?

The warm sun of October decorated Sterlen in speckled shadows as he lingered under the shade of the red maple, lost to the wonder of the glorious autumn leaves all around. Never had his heart felt so heavy.

Absently, he glanced up to the fading deep blue sky. The sun was going down, sending a halo of pinks, lavenders and golds across the mountaintops. The beauty of the scene immediately brought him out of his thoughts. He stood full and present in the admiration of nature's handiwork. It seemed only moments until twilight was upon him, and only minutes more when the largest moon he believed he had ever seen rose right over the crest of Horseshoe Rock—big, round, yellow, perfect.

"Sterlen."

The big man jumped. Startled, he turned toward the voice. Standing there in buckskins was a Native American with long white hair covering his shoulders like snow.

"Sterlen, I come to ye in friendship. I am Cooweesucoowee, Cherokee medicine man," he said, his gaze sinking deep into Sterlen's.

Incredulously, the mountain man stared at the medicine man.

Sterlen had seen many unusual happenings and unexplainable forces while in the mountains alone, but never had he been approached by one he knew to be...a spirit.

"Retter's girl child, woman with crying heart, cares for ye. All heritage comes through woman—encourage her, support her. She must be made strong!"

The Native American took a step closer.

"It is Nuwatiegwa [Great New Moon] in October sky. Strange things will happen tonight on A ni wa yah [Wolf] Mountain," he said, and then raising his arm toward the ridge opposite Horseshoe Rock, he continued, "Oh great storyteller...listen and watch!" And the spirit vanished.

Sterlen felt almost unable to move as an ominous stillness created such tension that it hurt his eardrums. He heard it then—coming from afar, slowly growing louder and louder. It sounded like a horse...coming over the ridge—a horse in a dead run!

Then there he was... a Cherokee astride a galloping pony, coming in a powerful way. He slid to a stop, only feet from Sterlen. Black hair and eagle feathers spread out like a dark cloud around his face. He said nothing but his eyes, wet with tears, pierced into Sterlen, stabbing him through to the heart.

And now the wind picked up strong! Leaves whirred like flocks of birds taking off in flight. A sound like thunder jerked Sterlen's gaze away from the Native American. Over the ridge came hundreds of Cherokee--men, women and children—riding bareback, hair flying. As they came closer and closer, Sterlen glanced back to the lone rider, but he was gone—galloping toward Horseshoe Rock!

The first of the on-coming tribe began passing him. He could hear them calling..."Sterlen, Sterlen, Sterlen!" Their heads turned toward him—in the moonlight he could see the sparkle of tears on their faces. It hurt him! But, they went on by, following their leader, who had reached the mountain sided with rock. The lone Cherokee didn't stop! He went straight up the rock! Clouds of dust and pieces of rock almost hid the rider. Sterlen's heart thumped loudly in his ears.

The lone rider reached the top and disappeared over the horizon, going right over where his hollow log of old had been.

The whole tribe of Cherokee rode right behind him...straight up the rock! And then...they galloped right into the moon! A soft mist seemed to rise from the trail left by the band of Cherokee, as if their tears had hit the rock, warmed with their passing.

Suddenly, the lone rider appeared at the top of the mountain. He sat sideways, his black shadow pasted against the yellow of the moon. He raised his hand to Sterlen...Sterlen knew it was for him. The mountain man threw up his hand in return. Then, the lone rider and his horse turned, and leapt into the moon!

And the yellow of the moon turned red.

Sterlen dropped to his knees. His senses had been hit with so much so fast, he had to collect himself. He must understand what this all meant! Then it all came so quickly he almost fell to the ground.

The Native Americans had been driven out of their homes, forced to go—thousands dying on the "Trail of Tears." Horseshoe Rock would always be a reminder of that. No wonder the wolves howled at the moon!

But the lone rider had thrown up his hand in a gesture of friendship! Sudden words filled Sterlen's head: "Forgiveness must come before healing."

Never had Sterlen been more certain of a message, not only for mankind, but for his own life; for Marthie! He must go to her!

CHAPTER 20

The Simplest Thing in the World

O
n foot, from Wolf Mountain to Ammons Mountain, the trip took more than a day, especially when traveling by the way of Sylva. Sterlen followed the dirt roads mainly, but sometimes he'd veer off to go his own way through the mountainous terrain.

At the top of Ammons Mountain, the road divided; the road to the left running around between the forest and wild grass, over a log bridge, to the front door of the Ammons' cabin—the road to the right, past the old Connor house, by way of the spring, lead to the back door of the Ammons' cabin. Just beyond the spring, the road continued up the mountain to the Golden Place.

As Sterlen arrived at the top of the mountain on the rocky dirt road, he could hear voices and laughter coming from the spring area. He decided to follow the sounds. He passed the old Connor house. Thomas lived there with his young wife, Evie. She was the daughter of Doc Watson, whose home was almost at the foot of the mountain, along Grassy Creek Road. Sterlen had seldom seen the friendly

Evie since she married, for Thomas was known to be jealous of her.

He stood just under the old hemlock that was part of the protective covering for the spring that bubbled out of the side of the mountain. The spring house, consuming part of the indentation in the rock and bank, had been built to handle large quantities of milk, butter, and cheese—enough to supply all three extended Ammons families living on and near the original homestead. Controlling the water flow was a large pipe that had been inserted within the bank itself, through which a steady stream of water, dancing off the slick rocks, created music for the peaceful knoll.

Just to the side of the trail that led over to the Ammons' cabin was a large well-used area designated for doing the family wash. Here were gathered all the women on the mountain—Retter, Marthie, Evie, Cannie, Lillie, and even Corie. Tin and wooden tubs set with clothes in them in various spots and blackened iron pots hung in tripods over burning fires.

Sterlen set his gunny sack down, leaning it against the hemlock. Boxwood bushes planted to line the pathway covered the presence of the mountain man as he took time to gaze at the one he loved unobserved. The conversation he heard brought a grin to his face.

"Ye don't mean it!" Evie was saying. "Lord, how did ye catch 'em?"

"Why, we hid out in the hay up in the top o' the barn," came the maturing voice of Lillie. "I would bang 'n' make a lotta racket, then Frank would hold out the socks Momma had made 'n' catch 'em as they'd run out. Frank would put 'em in a cage he'd fixed while he made the harness out of Daddy's old reins."

"That boy! He's too smart fer his own britches!" Retter's face looked thunderstruck. "If I had known...."

"Wuzn't he afraid they'd bite him!" Evie said, her nose pushed up into strong disapproval.

"Frank's not afraid of anythang!" chimed in Corie, dancing from one foot to the other.

"But how'd he hold them when he put on the

harness...'specially the bridle...'n the bit?" Cannie incredulously shook her head.

All work had stopped as the attention of the women zeroed in on Lillie. Sterlen leaned closer so he, too, could hear the answer.

"Wal, let me git this all straight fer ye," said Lillie, in her glory at having so much attention. "He'd have a sharp piece o' a broken plow tied up with a stick all ready to go. The reins wuz tied to the stick. He didn't go fer 'nough to make a bit, it'd be jest a little hole to stick the face into. Then, he'd hold the rat real tight with one hand, slip the harness on, turn loose...'n' there that rat would go...with Frank a'hangin' onto the stick 'n' that rat a'plowin' as straight a furrow as I ever seen!"

"Lord a'mercy!" exclaimed Retter. "I'll kill him!"

"No! Don't do that!" laughed Cannie. "I'd lose my husband!"

"Why'd ye do sech a thang?" Evie still didn't seem to want to believe it.

"We wuz jest playin'," Lillie smiled, loving the shocked expressions. "Never had s'much fun!"

"How come I didn't know 'bout all this!" Retter began scrubbing on her washboard with strong sweeps of her hands, the water in the tin tub splashing all around, her face just as stormy. "Ye young'uns coulda got bit with rabies!"

"Wal, we didn't, Momma," Lillie responded, happy to make such a statement.

The silent Marthie who had stood slightly apart from the group wringing out clothes from the rinse tub, suddenly smiled. Sterlen, watching with storytelling interest, felt the smile from where he stood. He experienced great satisfaction in being where he was at this very moment.

"Punch them clothes!" Retter demanded of Lillie, still exclaiming, "What kin we mothers do! We cain't be everwhere, a'watchin' ever move! Who'd ever thank yer young'uns would catch rats 'n' play with 'em? I'll be hog-swattled! Wait'll I see that boy o' mine!"

"Miz Ammons...," began Cannie, hesitantly, coming over to stand near her, "I been wantin' to tell ye since Frank 'n' I went down to Sylvie last week...but...."

"I know, Cannie." Retter's face had lost it's storm. She pulled her hands out of the water, dried them on her apron, and put her arms around Cannie. "Yore with child."

"Oh, Cannie!" exclaimed Evie, running over, followed by Lillie. Corie, not wanting to be left out, started jumping up and down, trying to get inside the group embrace.

At this, Sterlen thought it was time for his entrance.

"What's a body gotta do to git some attention 'round here!" He sang out as he walked down the incline. "Coulda been a wildcat comin' upon ye, 'n' youns woulda never heard it!"

"Sterlen Galloway! Did ye hear?" Retter welcomed him. "This niece o' yourn is gonna have my boy's child! I'm gonna be a grandma...," Retter's gaze switched to Marthie, and she continued, "...agin!"

Marthie's face swiftly expressed changing emotions. Sterlen couldn't make out if she was happy or sad about the news. But then, their eyes met. He knew her feelings then. Her spontaneous smile warmed him all the way through.

"Ain't it good, Cannie!" he said as his young niece ran into his arms. "Frank's gotta be...uh...chomping at the bit...if ye know what I mean!"

"Ye heard my story, Sterlen, didn't ye!" Lillie shouted

as everybody laughed, glancing at each other.

"Yep, heard 'bout them rats as I come 'round the old hemlock," he smiled as he saw the women's relieved expressions. Must've been some good stories before he got there, he thought. "Child, with stories like that, yer gonna be the second best storyteller in this part o' the country!"

"Oh! that sorry no-good...flyin' killer!" suddenly shouted Retter. "Look at him...here he comes!" She pointed back over Sterlen's head.

He turned to see a spec in the sky. Watching closely, he could see then that it was a chicken hawk, coming in low.

"He's after that new batch o' dibbies. That old settin' hen hatched out a brood o' the prettiest red chicks ye ever seed...'n' s'late in the year. I cain't let anythang happen to 'em. Best go git the old man's riffle!" Retter started off down the path.

"Retter, wait!" called out Sterlen. "Take this!" He turned and ran up the trail to the spring, picked up a loose stone underneath the spout, and ran back down to Retter.

"Here, take this with ye," he said. "Put it in the ashes o' the fireplace. Won't be no more chicken hawks a'gittin' any more o' yer hens! It'll ward'em off!"

"Ary ole rock?" Retter accepted the stone, looking closely at it. She then dropped it into her apron pocket as she headed out toward the cabin in a run.

"Naw...jest gotta be outta the sprang!" Sterlen's gaze once again connected with Marthie's. He called to Retter's back, "I want to borrow Marthie for a little while!"

"Reckon that'll be fine, Sterlen," Then, Retter yelled came over her shoulder. "Girls, I'll be right back! Won't take me but a little while...mabbe I kin wing this flyin' chicken lover!"

"Marthie, kin ye take a walk with me," asked Sterlen. He smiled wide and patted the breast pocket of his jacket for her to see.

Marthie's forehead wrinkled. She looked at him with a question written on her face. "What's wrong...does yer chest hurt?" she asked, coming quickly to him.

"Naw, Marthie. I jest got somethin' fer ye to see."

As he spoke, he realized that all eyes were upon him—the women and the girls were hanging onto each word. He grinned and winked at them, flipping his jacket open to show them papers stuck in his pocket.

"Come on, Marthie...walk with me." He took the tall woman's arm, drawing her up the path toward the road to the Golden Place.

He waited until he found just the right place—a small glen just off the main road. At the edge of the glen, he brushed away the dead leaves from an old log so Marthie could sit. In trying to form just the right words, Sterlen hesitated.

Marthie watched him. He was such a handsome man. The sun filtered through the umbrella of tree limbs and leaves, lighting the white hair of the muscular man. His blue eyes, a little absent at the moment, were otherwise clear and open. He had said it himself—here was a man who meant every word he said. She now had no doubt of it. He would do what he said he would do.

She stopped her tabulating. When had she begun to believe him? What a wondrous thing...she believed him! And suddenly, the world opened for her.

The sky...oh, the sky...it's so blue. The leaves are like fire! The colors...oh, the colors—so many! Look...look at the squirrels, so big and frisky! Oh, Sterlen!

"Marthie. Marthie!" He had put his boot upon the log, leaning toward her with a question on his face. "Marthie, what 'er ye thankin' about?"

"Uhhh...I wuz jest lookin' at the squirrels jumping in the trees up there over yer head," she said. "They're s'big."

"Wal, they got a heavy coat this year. Gonna be a cold winter!" He brought his leg down, and ran his fingers through his hair, seemingly unsettled. "'N' if ye look around, ye'll see lots o' acorns, 'n' hickory nuts...'n' spiders! Lots o' spiders! 'N' wooly worms, ye seen the fuzzy coats on them boogers! Yep, we're in fer one heck o' a winter!" He paused, and then began walking back and forth in front of the attentive woman. "Marthie! we're in fer a heck o' a winter, too! I been thankin' an awful lot."

Marthie looked at his discomfort and grinned.

"Ye got it in fer me, do ye?" she said.

"In...in fer ye? Now, listen, Marthie...this is serious."

"All right, Sterlen, I wuz only foolin'."

"Wal, here goes!" He ran his fingers over his beard, turned to her and began. "Marthie, back in July I told ye how I felt about ye, and that I wanted to marry ye. Since then, I've been workin' in my cabin, tryin' to make it the kind o' home ye'd like to have. Jest recently, I begun to thank that I had to give ye another chance at tellin' me no.... Now, I see ye shakin' yer head...let me finish.

"I done figgered it out. I'm twenty-five years older'n ye...I could be yer daddy! Yer daddy...ye hear! I been livin' an awful long time alone! I could be a real humdinger to live with. What if I git lonesome fer the woods, 'n' take off fer a time...what would ye do? I ain't a farmer—I'm a trapper, an herb gatherer, a sanger, a picker, a storyteller! Lord, what kind o' a father would I make!" He paused for air, then, stopped his pacing, and squarely faced the woman he loved.

"So, Marthie, after I talked ye into lettin' me court ye...what do ye say after I try to git ye to see the truth about me?"

"Sterlen, what ye got in yer pocket?" Marthie smiled at him.

"What have I got in my pocket? That's what ye gotta say?"

"What did ye try to show me awhile ago?"

"Wal," he said as he pulled out a folded document. "It's a marriage license." And he began to laugh aloud.

Marthie placed both hands on her knees, joining his laughter. "Took me fer granted, huh?" she said between breaths.

Sterlen sobered. "Marthie, seriously now...do ye have

any doubts? I wouldn't hurt ye fer the world."

"Listen closely, Sterlen, fer I ain't said this to ye afore, fer I...jest couldn't." Marthie now stood, and going over to the mountain man, she gazed deeply into his eyes. "Sterlen Galloway, I love ye with all my heart. I would trust ye with my life, 'n' that's all there is to that!"

Such an emotion filled Sterlen's heart that he thought it would crack open right there and spill out. The document floated to the ground between them, as he opened his jacket and enclosed her within the innermost part of himself—and still he was not close enough. His arms tightened as he poured his spirit into this dark one who would soon be his wife. "Marthie," he whispered. "Will ye marry me?"

To know love...to be loved...never had Marthie felt that she would ever experience these emotions first hand. Her deepest despair had now been equaled by the simplest thing in the world...the knowledge that another human being loved her for herself alone.

The woman now filled with purpose, validated by another's complete acceptance gave the man her answer, an answer for his ears alone.

In the distance came a clear, resounding rifle shot, echoing many times over.

CHAPTER 21
Death by Nightfall

Tom Ammons leaned over to his younger children who sat on the warm hearth at his feet, and said, "See that fire in the fireplace? See how the logs seems to talk. That fire's got somethin' to say. It's gotta story to tell. If the fire sorta sobs, it's gonna rain. If it kinda sputters, then it's gonna snow. 'N' if the fire jest jumps 'n' leaps 'n' roars up the chimney, sure 'n' certain, there's gonna be a fight. But if the flames turn blue, like it's doin' now, ye better be leery, fer there's gonna be...death by nightfall."

"Daddy, who told ye that?" asked Corie, pulling her knees up under her chin, wrapping her arms around her legs. "Is somebody really gonna die?"

"Them old sayin's er the renderin's o' years 'n' years o' life lived through...better pay mind to 'em! They're sorta alertin' ye to sit up 'n' take notice. Lord knows! Anythang could happen!

"'N'...ummm...let me see...that sayin' there comes down through the family...where did it git it's start? Ahh, I thank it

130

wuz my momma's great grandma," and here Tom grinned a toothless grin, "Great great grandma taught it to my great grandma, who taught it to my grandma, who taught it to my momma, who taught it to me...'n' I'm teaching it to you!"

"That's a lotta people!" said Lillie, drawing closer to her dad. "We—Corie 'n' Nealie 'n' me—we don't have but one grandma now ...do we, Daddy?"

"Wal, no, Lillie, they're all gone except my momma out in Washington State. You younger ones come along when yer old man here wuz already in his fifties. Yer momma 'n' me both done lost most o' our parents pretty early on."

"Why, Daddy? Where'd ye lose 'em? Where er they?" piped up the small Nealie.

"What I mean to say...." Tom grinned again, and leaned forward to spit into the fire while quiet laughter sifted the darkened room behind them. "What I mean to say is that all yer grandmas 'n' grandpas 'cept one have passed on...died a long time ago, but they've left us with some outstandin' stories. Yer momma's great grandma Bryson's an example!"

"Grandma Bryson! That's a man's name...that's Bryson's name!" Corie popped up to her knees, intent on making her point.

"Wal, Corie, yer momma named yer brother 'Bryson' after her momma's maiden name. Let's see, now where wuz I...uh...yer great grandma Bryson...Yep, she shore wuz one heck o' a woman! She had her young'uns on her own. Even though she finally married a white man., some say that's how the Cherokee blood got into the family's veins. Nobody knows fer sure...."

Retter, who sat to the side, her darning in her lap, looked up at her husband and shook her head, but kept silent, smiling to herself as she watched the happy faces of the children.

"We got Indian blood in our veins!" whispered Nealie to his sisters, looking at his arms. "It's right in here!" His smile growing large with wonderment.

Tom continued. "Least ways, Grandma Bryson warn't talkin', even after her young'uns wuz born! She wuz already along in years during the Civil War. When that war between the states broke out, ye had to go either one way er the other.

Weren't no strattlin' the fence. Ye either had to be on the side of the "Rebels" er be sympatric to the "Union" side."

"What side wuz we on, Daddy?" Lillie said, pushing even closer. Around the outside of the circle of firelight other chairs had been drawn up. Marthie, Albert, and Bryson were all there, listening.

"Wal, North Carolina had gone over to the Rebel cause–this wuz 'round '61...uh, 1861. Still, some folks didn't want to be Rebels, er jest didn't keer to fight. The hills wuz full o' men who didn't want to go off 'n' leave their women-folk 'n' young'uns alone...they wished the whole thang would jest go away. Most o' the young ones left to fight, though. Like always, yer grandma had to take keer o' her farm 'n' her least little'uns by herself. She wore them old timey bonnets 'n' long dresses. Right feisty red-headed woman, she wuz.

"In them days there wern't much to make a livin' at, 'specially fer a woman by herself. So she started making liquor 'n' sellin' it. She had to be crafty, too—fer there wuz some Rebels who went huntin' fer those hill people who didn't want to fight. Sometimes, under cover o' the war, these men would take a lot o' the stuff that belonged to these hill folk fer themselves. 'N' naturally they heard about that good ole brew yer grandma wuz turnin' out. But yer grandma done thought it all through afore hand. She had found herself a right nice hidin' place fer that still o' hers! Instead o' in the brush, or in a cove on the mountainside, she buried the still in the Tuckasegee River!"

"Naw! She didn't!" laughed Bryson. "She shore used her haid!"

"Yep, right smart o' her. She knowed that no matter what, these hill people would want to have a drank er two ever onst in a while. She grew her own corn; sold some o' it to buy the sugar 'n' the jars 'n' had herself a good business goin'. Sometimes 'stead o' money, she'd take a swap o' somethin' she needed, but everbody paid her fer her hard labor. She had a shotgun up above the door, jest in case a feller didn't want to pay a woman fer his brew...'n' believe ye me...she could use it!"

"Did she ever git caught by the law, Dad?" Albert said.

"Wal, they did round her up one day 'n' took her to court, the story goes. While she wuz bein' tried, they asked her if she wuz guilty. She took her bonnet off and hit her lap and said, 'I might be...but then agin...I might not. Ye prove it!'"

"Did they prove it?" grinned the imaginative Corie.

"They never did!" Tom said, and spat emphatically into the fire again. Then he pulled the chaw of tobacco out of his mouth with his finger and threw it into the fire, spitting again.

"1861...ye know, Dad," said Albert, "it's 1941 now. That story happened exactly eighty years ago! Reckon Grandma Bryson would be pleased. Her story's still being told!"

"I thank she might be interested in the fact that what she did fer a livin' is still goin' on," spoke up the quiet Retter from the corner, her gaze hard on her husband.

"Now, Retter...ye mind what yer sayin' in front o' these young'uns," cautioned Tom.

"But, Daddy," came the small voice of Corie, "we all know there's a still up yonder in the cow pasture. Mabbe ye better hide it in the creek!"

Sudden laughter crowded Tom into a sheepish corner. "I thank ye young'uns oughta hit the sack!" he exclaimed. "That's enough o' a lesson in yer heritage fer a Sunday night!" He coughed, covering his grin with his hand.

"See there what ye did, Corie!" Lillie groaned as she got up from the floor, leading the children toward the back room. "Ye always talk too much!"

Retter spoke up. "Marthie, ye all set fer tomorrow? Ye picked out what ye want to wear?"

Tom and the brothers turned their attention to the quiet girl near them. It was the first time that they realized she had not been sitting in the back of the room.

To suddenly be the focus of everyone's attention brought pink to the cheeks of the young woman. With a half-smile she answered her mother, "Sterlen brung me what I asked fer last week."

"What wuz it?" Retter laid her darning in her lap and leaned closer. Even Marthie's brothers seemed interested in her answer.

"Ye'll all laugh!"

"Laugh at what ye're gonna wear to git married in ?" Albert looked quizzically at his sister.

"Ye'll jest laugh, Albert!"

Now everyone had been hooked, even the younger ones who had come back in dressed in their nightclothes. They all began clambering, begging Marthie to tell them about her wedding.

"Hold it...hold it!" exclaimed Tom, hitting the wooden floor with his cane. "Let Marthie breath!" And then, as everyone quieted down, he continued, "Now, Marthie, tell us about yer wedding tomorrow. What's Sterlen got planned fer ye."

"Wal...," the excited woman began, looking at all the faces turned toward her, happy that she could tell the news that had been about to explode within her. "Jim's jest been ordained to preach—he's gonna marry Sterlen 'n' me!"

"Lordy, Lordy!" Retter smiled big, leaning back in her rocker, making it squeak in her rush of energy. Smiles made the round of faces.

"Praise God!" said Bryson.

"Sterlen, Jim 'n' Libby er comin' tomorrow. Sterlen 'n' me er gonna git married right out there on the porch...betwixt the front room 'n' the kitchen!"

The now quiet Retter wiped at the happy tears that had slipped out of the side of her shining eyes. Her action went unnoticed by the semi-circle of smiling faces.

"Frank 'n' Cannie er comin', too!" It was all Marthie could do to contain herself.

Retter's rocking chair stopped rocking. "Lord a'mercy! I better plan what to cook fer all you young'uns! What a celebration...we'll have Christmas early this year!"

Marthie's countenance had now settled into one of complete contentment. The encouraging sounds of her family brought luster into her eyes. Her gaze went from one to the other, gathering their happiness to her like roses, and storing the harvest in her healing heart.

"But, Marthie, ye didn't tell us what ye're gittin' married in!" protested Corie, with hands on Marthie's arm and gazing at her with questioning eyes.

Marthie burst out laughing. "I'm gittin' married in a brand new pair o' overalls!"

Bedlam broke out in the front room of the Ammons cabin.

"Ye got to be foolin', Marthie!" gasped Retter, stopped short in her ascension from the chair. She stared at her oldest daughter in disbelief.

"No, Momma," Marthie smiled. "Jest thank on it. I really needed a new pair o' overalls cuz I'm gonna be out in the mountains with Sterlen s'much. Sterlen sorta liked the idee, cuz he said the first time he told me he loved me...I had a pair o' yer overalls on."

"Marthie! it's so romantic," Lillie ran over and hugged her sister for the first time she could ever remember.

"How come yer gonna get married on a Monday, Marthie?" asked Bryson. "Always thought womenfolk liked to marry on a Sunday."

"Jim had to preach his first message today, fer Verge Massingale's funeral. Tomorrow he don't have to worry none 'bout his preachin'. We're gonna git married sometime in the afternoon...soon as they git here, I reckon." Marthie stood up and smiled at her family. "yer all invited to my weddin' tomorrow. Ye don't have'ta go far!"

Just beyond the ring of excitement, from deep in the blackened fireplace, blue flames leaped high, dancing unnoticed.

CHAPTER 22
Monday, December 8, 1941

Marthie's wedding day dawned clear, but cold. Retter arose long before daybreak, rattling the banister that led to the attic.

"Bryson! Bryson Ammons! Ye git out o' that bed 'n' take that rifle o' yourn out to the woods 'n' git us a wild turkey! We need somethin' special today!"

Knowing better than to complain, Bryson was up and out in no time.

The children, awakened in such a fashion, found it difficult to go back to sleep.

"Marthie, ye awake?" said a muffled voice suddenly.

"Yes, Corie...I'm awake."

"Where er ye 'n' Sterlen gonna live?"

"Over to Wolf Mountain, in Sterlen's house he built."

"Er ye ever comin' back home?"

"'Course I am, ye little duck! This mountain is my home. I ain't lived nowhere else my whole life through."

"Kin we come see ye?"

"Any time Momma lets ye...but I'm gonna be out with Sterlen a lot. When he first asked me to marry him, he thought that I'd be stayin' there at the cabin all the time. But I set him straight right off...I love the woods, too. Been learnin' from and doin' fer Momma all these years. So, we're gonna go out trappin' 'n' grubbin' fer herbs together! Ain't that wonderful! I'd be happy doin' it ferever!"

The little girls were quiet for a moment—Marthie had never confided in them like this before. Then, Lillie responded, "I guess it's really good fer ye, Marthie. Me...I wouldn't keer to do it all the time, though."

"Why not, Lillie." Marthie's voice crept from underneath the stairway.

"Cuz it's cold, 'n' wet, 'n' scary out there sometimes. 'Course I love our mountains, but I reckon I'd like to go see what's over yonder on the other side o' them mountains some day."

"Not me, I never want to leave!" Marthie emphatically stated, then more softly, "I want ye two to come visit me often...I'll miss ye."

This statement, totally surprising, held the two younger girls in awe. Corie propped herself up on her elbow to gaze into Lillie's face. Her eyes were wide. Lillie nodded at her, and then as she lay back down, she said, "We'll come...Marthie...we'll come."

"Good! Now let's git up 'n' go help Momma! It's my weddin' day!"

It had not taken Bryson long to comply with his mother's wishes. He made short the preparations and soon the wild turkey, plucked 'n' stuffed, went into the oven just as the sun came up. While Marthie helped Retter in the kitchen, Lillie and Corie rushed about cleaning the house.

Tom came in from milking the cows and stoked the fire in the front room. While he was waiting for breakfast, he prepared for his usual ritual. Bringing a large glass of warm milk to the front room, he found his chair beside the fireplace toasty from the dancing blue flames. He settled himself in and turned on the battery-operated radio to listen to the morning farm news. As he sat, he leaned over and pulled a well-worn encyclopedia out of the bookcase built into the wall beside the hearth. Listening to the announcer, he absently fingered the dull cover.

Around noon, Frank and Cannie showed up. By this time, the aroma of the baking turkey wafted through the kitchen door, onto the back porch, and into the living part of the house.

"M-M-My goodness, Momma!   Does that smell good! Did ye kill yer old rooster fer this weddin'? " Frank came in and turned to help Cannie remove her coat. "Ye still got yer sanity, Marthie?" He continued, grinning at her nod.

Retter, in her glory when she was cooking, shook her head. "No, son, yer brother brought in the biggest wild turkey ye ever did see. It's a young one too, so I'm cookin' it slow. It'll be good 'n' tender." She continued to stir the cake batter in the bowl in her arms. "Come on in, Cannie...ye feelin' all right today? Yer beginnin' to show now, ain't ye?"

"I'm doin' fine, Miz Ammons...fer bein' five months along. My clothes er jest a'gittin' a little tight."

"Hello, Cannie...thanks fer comin'." Marthie came over to the young girl and reached for her hand.

Her eyes wide with surprise, the curly-headed woman smiled. "I wouldn't have missed it fer the world!"

"M-M-Momma, January 1st is Cannie's birthday!" Frank had found some leftover fatback in a plate setting on the bread saver of the cookstove. Helping himself, he continued, "She's gonna be sixteen on New Year's Day!"

"That's a birthday we won't fergit anytime soon!" Retter poured her cake batter into a cast-iron skillet. "I'll have to make another cake fer yer birthday, Cannie."

"Momma, Momma!" Lillie came running into the room. "Sterlen 'n' Libby 'n' Jim er comin' up the road yonder. They're early!"

When Sterlen entered the kitchen, he had eyes for only

Marthie. This was the most important day in his life; he wanted it to be the same for her. She stood about center of the room, near his niece, Cannie. Her cheeks flushed, she turned to look at him as he entered.

How beautiful and happy she looks! Our wedding day is going to be everything I wanted it to be. Never to worry, Marthie, you and me...we're going to take it nice and gentle. We have lots of time.

He smiled, coming to stand beside her. "Howdy there ye pretty thang," he said, and then joined the laughter at his greeting.

"Shoo now...all ye young people...outta my kitchen. I gotta make the biscuits, 'n' I need some elbow room." Retter flapped her apron at the crowd in the kitchen. "Yawl go on in yonder with Tom 'n' the boys while I finish this feast we're gonna have. 'N' Marthie...ye go on now...git ready fer yer weddin'! Ye need to tie that knot afore we kin eat."

Then, as they all turned to leave, Retter put her hand on Jim's arm and spoke softly, "Son, I'm s'proud of ye...a preacher 'n' all."

"Thank ye, Momma." Jim leaned down and kissed his mother.

At one o'clock, Sterlen and Marthie were married by Jim on the porch of the Ammons' homestead. The onlookers, crowded close together, kept each other warm on the crisp December day. Marthie, in her new overalls overtop a warm woolen sweater spun by Retter herself, made a lovely bride. Then, blushing from her happiness and the cold, the newest Mrs. Galloway kissed her husband. As the couple turned to the family, Sterlen said, "Marthie 'n' me--we thank ye all fer witnessing our weddin'. It's a day we won't ever fergit. We're much obliged fer everthang."

"Wal, now that's done...let's eat!" Tom held his cane up and shook it, smiling his full approval. Then he led the way into the festive-smelling kitchen.

"P-P-Pass that turkey 'round agin, Bryson," said Frank.

"Ye got a hole in that long leg o' yourn, Frank," Bryson fussed, giving up the platter to his younger brother.

"Y-Y-Yep...been tryin' to stuff it full fer a long time. It's still holler!"

"Ye know, there sure er a pile o' wild turkeys this year, Dad," Bryson said, passing the potatoes to him. "Most I seed in a long time."

"Used to be hundreds of 'em 'round here," his dad responded, passing the plate on to Sterlen. "Why, many's the time I heard the story 'bout yer great, great uncle John Bryson driving a big flock of 'em from Grassy Creek Road all the way down to Walhalla, South Carolina."

"Where's Albert gone?" Retter asked Frank.

"How'd they do that...drive wild turkeys...how'd they keep 'em from flyin' away?" asked Lillie from her seat on the bench near the wall.

"A-A-Albert stepped out awhile ago...said he didn't want to miss the news on the radio, Momma." Frank kept eating.

"When they'd catch 'em, they musta clipped their wings," Bryson answered.

"How'd they catch them?" Nealie was instantly interested.

"More'n likely they'd sneak up on 'em et night. If yer real good, ye kin catch 'em roostin' in the trees—like I done this mornin'!" Bryson said in between mouthfuls.

Tom set his coffee cup down on the table and wiped his mouth with the back of his hand. "Now, let me tell you the real way they herded them turkeys," he said. "First, ye gotta be there when day comes...the turkeys fly off their roost 'bout sun up. When they come flying off, ye gotta feed 'em right then to keep 'em from scatterin'. When they're hungry, they'll find somethin' to eat, so good turkey herders brang a goodly supply of sacked corn. Give them turkeys somethin' to eat, 'n' they'll foller ye any...."

Albert suddenly burst into the door, shock etched deeply into his face. "HEY YAWL! Come listen...come listen to the radio! Somethin' awful's happened! The president is gittin' ready to talk on the radio!"

Within minutes, the kitchen emptied and all were settled around the radio in the front room. Albert turned the volume up. "Listen to what the announcer's sayin'...."

"....Stemming from the Japanese attack, the total casualties in the Hawaiian island of Oahu yesterday are believed to be about 3,000, including nearly 1,500 killed, with one battleship capsized, one destroyer and a large number of planes put out of commission..."

"We've been attacked by Japan! That's what I heard when I came in here 'n' turned on the radio to catch the news. I heard they bombed that big Navy base at Pearl Harbor that I've been readin' 'bout!"

Lillie could see from where she sat on the floor that Albert's fingers, holding his cigarette, were shaking as he spoke. Corie had scooted in beside her, frightened at not understanding what was going on. Nealie had pushed himself close to his mother's knees, and Retter's sharp penetrating gaze kept going from son to son to son.

"Listen," Albert was saying, "It's the president."

"...Yesterday, December 7, 1941—a date which will live in infamy—the United States of America was suddenly and deliberately attacked by naval and air forces of the Empire of Japan...."

As the mellow voice of President Roosevelt continued, the hearts of all listening began to fill with several emotions: shock, deep sadness, growing fear. They listened intently, each reacting to his or her own situation.

"...attack yesterday on the Hawaiian Islands has caused severe damage to American naval and military forces. I regret to tell ye that many American lives have been lost. In addition, American ships have been reported torpedoed on the high seas between San Francisco and Honolulu.

"Yesterday the Japanese Government also launched an attack against Malaya.

"Last night Japanese forces attacked Hong Kong.

"Last night Japanese forces attacked Guam.

"Last night Japanese forces attacked the Philippine Islands.

"Last night the Japanese attacked Wake Island.

"And this morning the Japanese attacked Midway Island.

"Japan has, therefore, undertaken a surprise offensive extending throughout the Pacific area. The facts of yesterday and today speak for themselves. The people of the United States have already formed their opinions and well understand the implications to the very life and safety of our nation.

"As Commander in Chief of the Army and Navy I have directed that all measures be taken for our defense.

"Always will our whole nation remember the character of the onslaught against us. No matter how long it may take us to overcome this premeditated invasion, the American people in their righteous might will win through to absolute victory. I believe I interpret the will of the Congress and of the people when I assert that we will not only defend ourselves to the uttermost but will make it very certain that this form of treachery shall never again endanger us...."

The voice of the President continued as the family members stared first at one another and then, slowly, their eyes glazed with each of their own internal realizations. Lives would be quickly changing.

As Albert turned the sound down on the radio, Sterlen reached over and took his wife's hand. She moved closer to him, unsure as to what would happen in their own near future, a future she had already begun planning. She caressed the hand of the man who had made her his own.

Libby and Jim huddled close together, as Cannie looked up at her now stern-faced husband. The young mother-to-be placed a hand on her stomach and grew dreadfully afraid.

In the quiet that ensued, Lillie could hear the clock on the mantle ticking; the sound grew louder, louder, and louder, until it seemed to fill the room.

"Wal," said her dad suddenly, shaking his head. "We're goin' to war! The Lord help us all." Then, he too gazed at his sons—his young fearless sons.

CHAPTER 23
The Fifth Strawberry

Reality set in gradually for the entire country. America was at war. The draft intensified. Enlistments were now for the duration. Headlines of newspapers screamed... BOMBED! WAR! DEATH! CAPTURED! INVASION IS ON! DEFEAT!

During the next few months, hundreds of young men came down from the mountains and enlisted in the armed services, including the Ammons boys...all except the twenty-year old Frank, and his older brother Thomas. Knowing he would at some time have to go, Frank listened to his mother and his young pregnant wife, and reluctantly decided to wait until he was drafted. Since Thomas' wife, Evie, was also newly pregnant, he decided to also wait for the draft.

Jim, denied for combat because of his leg turned with power to his preaching. His past indiscretions and his prowess with the spoken word brought many people closer to the word of God and enlisted comfort to many during a time of loss and grief.

Bryson got as far as Asheville, but then he was rejected because of an old injury. He, then also turned to the word of God in a much more determined way.

Albert alone walked away, filling an army uniform.

Sterlen, rejected—too old he was told—poured his energies into his new marriage. The two, Marthie and Sterlen, became almost inseparable and the forests of the mountains became their home. They spent a great amount of time visiting their families, first on Wolf Mountain and then on Ammons Mountain.

When Frank rode by on the mare to get the doctor for Cannie, he passed Marthie and Sterlen on the way. He didn't make it back with the doctor before his little girl was born.

Cannie named the child, delivered by Retter with Cannie's sister Irene looking on, Violet Irene Ammons, but Frank later decided he would call his little girl, Mildred. So...on April 1, 1942, Retter's first grandchild since Jhon Fred, came to live at the Golden Place.

"Sterlen, I want to go visit Cannie 'n' see her new baby," said Marthie early that May morning.

Sterlen, laying out roots on a table to dry, turned to look at Marthie. "That's a good idee. Let's git our packs ready 'n' go by the old copper mine on the way. There's some plants I got to git...."

"Sterlen!" Marthie interrupted, "Don't always think 'bout gittin' herbs! Let's jest go 'n' visit!" She turned a face working with the beginnings of displeasure toward the older man.

"But Marthie...it's on the way...." Sterlen couldn't understand what was making her so angry.

"No! I jest want to go see the baby!" Marthie now seemed to be seething with uncalled for exasperation. "If ye don't want to go, I'll go by myself!"

"What's makin' ye so....?"

"Then I'll go by myself! Ye wouldn't go the day the baby wuz born...we were right there...we watched Frank go by." Marthie's voice, now filled with grievance, had lowered but held something like fury within the folds of its telling language.

"Marthie! We didn't know where he was going. We only found out later." The deeply surprised Sterlen didn't know how to deal with this new aspect of his wife. "Marthie, what is...."

"No! Never mind! I'd rather go by myself!" And she threw on her jacket and stomped out the door.

"Marthie...." Sterlen, shocked and rooted to the spot, listened to the woman's retreating footsteps until they were gone. In the quiet of the room, Sterlen began to rationalize that his wife would soon walk out her anger, regain her senses and come back home. He hadn't done anything wrong. He then shook his shoulders, and went back to work, one ear tuned to the door.

But...Sterlen did not know his wife.

Seven hours later, the woman's footsteps were still being planted firmly, but now it was into the soft earth of Ammons Mountain. Almost to the crest of her climb, the dark-eyed, stubborn Marthie, did not even realize that she felt any fatigue. Her mind, filled with the urge to do what she wanted to do, continued to berate the unsuspecting Sterlen.

She only slightly hesitated at the crossing of roads—she'd see her mother later—she turned to go directly to the Golden Place.

Beside the spring she could see the gourd that hung on a branch near the cool water. It called to her, but she passed it by..

The baby! The baby! I have to see the baby!

Energy born of determination, pushed her to climb even faster. Before the hour was up, she saw the Golden Place come into view. With only one thing on her mind, she bore down on the cabin under the apple trees.

Oh! Oh! The apples trees are in bloom. It's beautiful here. And the sounds...so welcome...bees buzzing, birds singing, chickens clucking. And the baby....

Marthie spent a wonderful hour with Cannie and little Mildred. The new mother, tickled to have the first visitor since Irene had gone home, treated Marthie like a queen. She shared her child with her freely and even welcomed the break from holding the infant. The two women talked about their lives. And all the while Marthie played with the child, cooing, and talking jibberish. By the time she left, Marthie's anger seemed to have finally run its course.

But, as soon as she walked beyond the sight and sound of the Golden Place, suddenly, her legs would no longer hold her. She dropped to the ground, completely overcome. In deep despair, sobs filled the air all about her. Her heart felt broken.

What is wrong with me! Am I losing my mind?

The thought came to her that she should go to her favorite place. With no worry of the time, Marthie pulled herself up and began covering ground with that same determination that had brought her so far away from Wolf Mountain and Sterlen. Up and up she walked, tears so intense she fought to see, but the way had been ingrained into her—she had even found it in the fog.

There, by the waterfall, Marthie fell forward onto the ground and finally allowed herself full freedom to cry. And afterward, lying there in the cool of nature, Marthie slept.

Something woke her. What was it? She scrambled to her knees, straining to see in the coming twilight. She looked closely at the trees, the underbrush, the sky that looked as if her mother had thrown out pink and lavender dishwater across it's horizon. She stood, and moved beyond the stump at the edge of the clearing, not knowing why. And there, almost in homage to the setting sun, she found a strawberry patch. The tall green leaves clutching it's ripened fruit stretched a good way down the natural knoll, beckoning her.

Leaning down she quickly picked a handful, and then continued, eating as she went. Then carefully watching each step, she removed herself from the strawberry patch and sat on the stump.

They're sweet...these heart-shaped strawberries...they smell go good!

And then, without knowing why, Marthie turned around.

"Woman with Crying Heart...ye have returned."

The Native American stood straight-backed and proud. His wrinkled face, framed with white hair, held nothing to be afraid of but Marthie feared all men except her husband. With this spontaneous thought of Sterlen, she felt her first regret at walking away from him that morning.

"Who er...ye?" rolled past that fear. The strawberries were crushed in her hands; she felt the pulp run through her fingers.

"I am Cooweecoosuwee...Cherokee medicine man. Call me 'Charlie'."

"What do ye want?"

"I want nothing. What do ye want?" The penetrating gaze consumed the fear within her eyes.

"Wh...what do I want? I don't understand."

"Ye are here, away from mountain man. What do ye want?"

"I don't want anythin'. I wouldn't tell ye if I did want somethin'!" Marthie's anger began to come to the front as she knelt to the ground and wiped her hands on the grass, never taking her eyes off the brown-skinned man.

But somehow, on her knees, her rekindled anger vanished.

"Strawberries are good...very important to Indian. Please sit. I will tell ye a story passed down over many years by my people."

Marthie watched as he directed her to sit beside him on the ground. She moved to the spot he indicated, and still not knowing why—except for her vivid curiosity—she sat. He lowered himself, sitting cross-legged beside her.

"Long time ago," he began, laying five strawberries out in front of them, "man and woman lived together in peace. Husband and wife were happy, filled with love for one another. One day, woman gets angry at man. He does not understand why she is angry, so he does not stop her when angry woman stomps away."

Marthie began to grow uncomfortable, squirming around where she sat. He failed to notice and continued.

"Soon when she does not come back, he begins to worry. He drops his tools and goes running after her. But when heart is heavy ye cannot run so fast. He could not catch her. He goes up and down the mountains, calling her name. She does not answer, for when anger drives, it takes one far." He paused to study the strawberries.

Now Marthie had begun to feel terrible. In her own anger she had not even thought once about what Sterlen would do when she did not come back right away. Her eyes grew dark with worry.

"When problems come that people cannot handle, some people do good thing. They fall to knees, crying out for help. No one can gain world alone. Must have help.

"Now, this man falls to his knees and cries out 'Oh, Creator, help me.'

"Creator comes fast. He stands by man, saying 'What is wrong?'

"Man crys out that his woman has left him and he cannot find her. She has gone too far.

"Creator says 'Did ye harm her?'

"Man says he does nothing to hurt her, and wants to tell her he is sorry she is angry. Then maybe she will forgive what he did not know he did.

"Creator says 'It is good. ye rest, then soon follow behind me.'

"And the Creator runs on ahead to find the woman."

Marthie, now completely entranced with the Native American's story, leaned forward in her interest. The Cherokee's eyes twinkled as he picked up one of the strawberries, ate it and then continued.

"The Creator finds woman, still stomping away through the mountains very far away from the man. He brings image of her mother into her head. Woman does not even slow her steps."

Marthie dropped her head. Another strawberry was eaten by the Cherokee.

"Still farther on, the Creator places a cool spring in her way, coming right out of ground. He wants the woman to cool her anger with cool spring water. She does not respond and still goes on and on."

One more time, the Native American eats a strawberry.

"And then, in desperation, Creator makes the apple tree grow up in her path to see if she will stop to smell the flowers. She sees it but keeps going."

The fourth strawberry is eaten.

"So Creator now must think out his war weapon. He thinks 'What does woman or man have to do to get over being angry? They have to bend knee and bow head. Woman's weakest spot is curiosity. Creator brings about big patch of strawberries, puts them right in path of stomping woman. She sees them but stomps on through.

"But soon, the smell...so sweet...makes woman curious. She stoops down on knees, picks the berries and eats them. Soon, she has no more anger.

"Creator makes patch grow back the way her husband is comin' and soon man comes upon woman, who has now picked a leaf cup of strawberries. She sees man coming, and runs to meet him. She wants to tell him what she has found and to share her strawberries.

"Man knows Creator has helped him. He harvests some of the plants to take back with him so that his wife will always have nature as sweet as strawberry."

The Cherokee leans over and picks up the last strawberry, then stands. Seriously, he speaks slow and clearly to Marthie.

"Fruit of sorrow is bittersweet. Young child who kept heart from breaking long ago...gathered much in short time. His job is over now."

He hands the strawberry to Marthie and suddenly smiles. "Here, eat, and forget anger. Mountain man comes soon. Let man heal wounds, O Woman with Crying Heart—wounds put there by man."

Marthie gazed into his compassionate eyes, and ate the fifth strawberry.

CHAPTER 24

In the Misty Distance of Blue Ridge

W hen Marthie had not returned in a short time, Sterlen had gone after her. It hadn't taken him long to know that she had indeed left for Ammons Mountain. He thought about what she had said, why she had been angry, and suddenly, he felt sure he knew the problem.

It's not me. She's hurtin' bad. I gotta git to her!

When he didn't find Marthie at the Ammons homestead, nor the Golden Place, and he had not passed her going down as he had come up, Sterlen knew where Marthie had gone. She had followed her instinct and returned to where she could renew her spirit. He set out, going on up the now darkening mountain path.

As he walked, he continued to think about his wife's strange behavior. The old feelings had not surfaced since they married; he had been proud of that. He had refused to give her something else to have to face...not yet. But God, how he wanted her! He wanted her desperately...he wanted to get so close to her that neither one would know where the other ended or began.

But before they married he had promised himself that he would wait for her to want him. It would be so much better for her, if she was the one to suggest intimacy rather than himself. At this thought, a half-smile came to his lips. It was sort of ironic, married for the first time at his age and still waiting to taste the truth of total union.

Since her outbreak this morning, however, Sterlen knew the time had come for a change of some kind. It had come from her, so whatever it was, it was good. He realized that he must get Marthie to talk about this time in her life that still held her captive. It must all be discussed and brought out into the light...she needed to grab hold of it and run it over the scrubbing board a couple of times, rinse it and then hang it out to dry.

Lord! it's gonna be painful...painful fer us both!

The cool May evening began a waltz of twilight sounds—tree frogs and hoot owls and far off panther crys. He heard none of this. He looked ahead...Marthie's favorite spot lay just over that next rise. The sound of the waterfall grew louder. He trembled. This eposode unnerved him much more than his marriage. Sterlen squared his back and stretched his legs. Painful or not, he wanted to find his wife and hold her and tell her he was sorry if that was what it would take.

As he came over the crest of the hill, his gaze went directly to the bank where they had sat so many times. Marthie was not there. Sterlen strained his eyes in the fading light...no, she wasn't there. His heart sank. He had been so sure she'd be.....

"Sterlen, here I am!" came her voice and around to the right of him came the sound of running feet.

The big man turned and Marthie ran into his arms. She clung to him, her breath full and warm against his neck. He moaned.

"Sterlen. Sterlen," she whispered, "I'm ever s'sorry fer my temper. I shouldn't have run off like I done. I wuz wrong."

"Ye skeered me, Marthie!" Sterlen spoke through trembling lips.

"I'm sorry...I'm so sorry. I stomped off cuz I wanted something 'n' didn't know how to explain it to ye. I got mad, I reckon, at myself."

"I love ye with all my heart, Marthie. Nothin' ye could say er do kin change that." Sterlen held her out from him. "But, I been a'thankin' whilst I walked...mabbe we should talk 'bout what happened long ago...git it out 'n' see if that will help."

"I caint! I cain't! It's too hard!" Tears welled up in her eyes.

"Marthie, ye've got to help yerself. Ain't nobody kin help less'n ye help yerself. 'N' that means to face it 'n' git it over with. It won't be so bad after that."

She gazed at his face for what seemed to be hours, but in reality was only a few minutes. "I will." she said.

"Don't listen to me if it's not what ye want to do!" Already he felt the guilt.

"Will ye still love me...afterwards?"

"More than ever! There is nothin' ye kin tell me that will make me love ye less. I'll love ye ferever. Ain't a man livin' could love ye more!"

Marthie gazed at him long and hard. It seemed to Sterlen that she was still gathering the courage to face the story she must tell. His heart bled for her.

"Come, sit with me by the waterfall," he said.

She followed him, sitting as close as she could. He held her warm in his arms, providing her the place in which she could tell her story in complete safety. Cradling her head against his chest, he waited...almost holding his breath.

She then told him the story of Bell and how she loved her...and how Bell loved her back. She told about trying on the lipstick, dressing up, and going to town with Bell. She had the best time just being with Bell. It was so different...it was her birthday! The movie had been alright, but wasn't anything she'd care to do too much. Then Bell had told her that they were getting in the car with these two men and that the men would take them to Doc Watson's house in their new car. Marthie's voice slowed as she searched for just the right words to describe the next scenes to Sterlen.

"I had never been near a man afore who put his hands on me like this Bill did...he never even asked me. He touched me in all the wrong places...I know this cuz I could feel it wuz wrong. My whole insides wuz hollering, 'n' then I wuz able to holler somethin' cuz Bell finally looked back 'n' asked Bill what he thought he wuz doin'. But that Lester stopped her. He must o' hurt her bad, cuz she didn't say anythang more!

"Then we stopped near some kind o' cabin. That...Bill...he pushed me down on the rocky ground 'n' he got on top o' me. Told me to pay attention, that I might learn somethin'. I told him my brothers would kill him, but he jest laughed.

"I screamed. He kept on laughin'...'n' then the bad thangs started to happen...not...only by him...but later on...by the other man...too. I...I ain't never hurt so bad...never so bad."

Marthie's head dug into Sterlen's chest, her hands balled up into his shirt. He caressed her with his big hands, gritting his teeth, his heart for the first time black with hate.

"Ever once in a while I kin see their faces when I'm tryin' to go to sleep! It's jest plain...awful!" Marthie wiped her nose with the back of her wrist and then plunged on.

"I must've really blacked out that night, cuz the next thang I knowed this Bill wuz pullin' me to the river. He had aholt o' my hair, a'yankin' me into the icy water. I couldn't thank...all I could do wuz cry out. He pushed my head under the water, a holdin' me down whilst I wuz a'trashin' 'n' a'strugglin' about. Then all to onct, he let go 'n' I come up outta that riverbed, jest eatin' the air. There she wuz...Bell. She grabbed holt o' me, a'draggin' me through the water to the other side. I looked back 'n' seen that Bill sprawled out on a big rock with blood on his head. Bell had laid him out flat! Wal, I don't know how we done it, but we got clean away...but we wuz lost, 'n' in no shape to stop 'n' ask fer help. Bell wuz a'cryin', askin' me to fergive her."

Marthie took a breath. "Fergive her! I loved her. How could I fergive her? It wuzn't her fault...wuz it? If it wuz her fault, then it wuz my fault, too, fer I had come with her. Oh, but I hated them men fer the longest time. Ever man I looked at, looked like them. I couldn't even stay in the same room with a man....

"Anyway, we finally figgered out where we wuz, 'n' made our way home. Bell left me at the bottom o' Ammons Mountain. She hugged me afore she left walkin' down the road toward where her family lived. She wuz afraid to face Jim...'n' she wuz right!" The woman's eyes blazed.

"I hated Jim fer what he did to Bell. He wuz like all the rest o' the people. They believed what they wanted to believe—that we did somethin' to brang this onto ourselves! Wal, mabbe Bell made a mistake 'n' trusted the wrong men...'n' played with fire too much, but she didn't ask fer what these men did. Jim wuz wrong....dead wrong. But I couldn't tell him...cuz he jest put me out o' his life. I didn't exist anymore to some people in my family...even my momma changed t'ward me. That hurt the most. She couldn't look me in the eyes.

"'N', Sterlen...I hated myself cuz I felt like my own body wuz taken that night. When they did what they did to my body, I felt as if it didn't belong to me anymore—it was no good, soiled by two rotten, filthy men.

"When my bleedin' time come, 'n' I didn't bleed, it skeered me plain to death. I thought fer sure they had ruined me fer all time. I wuz only sixteen years old! Weren't too long that Momma told me I looked sorta suspicious, 'n' asked me 'bout my bleedin'.

"That's when she told me I wuz goin' to have a baby by one o' them men. What wuz I to think? I had all kinds o' idees...I wanted to kill myself...but something told me I could be stronger than that. I stayed home so nobody could see me, but it got out. I wuz a damned woman!." Again there was fire in Marthie's eyes. But another thought changed her... softened her.

"When Jhon Fred wuz born, he wuz the most precious thang in the world. That's when I learned that men don't have to be that way! They got a choice! Jhon Fred wuzn't like whoever his daddy wuz. I loved him with all my heart. I thought he wuz worth all the pain. He became my little man, tryin' to take keer o' me cuz he knew there wuz nobody to do that." She swallowed. "But, he died. Sterlen, he died! My baby died! Sterlen...he...died!"

The stricken woman began to sob, burying her face into his chest even more. Sterlen wiped tears from his own eyes and rested his hand upon the head of the woman he loved. After a while, Marthie slowly quieted. It was then that Sterlen picked her up and brought her deep into his embrace again, holding her until the tears were gone.

"Sterlen," came the muffled voice.

"Yes..." he answered.

"What do ye thank o' my...story?"

"It wuz hard to take...Marthie," he said, swallowed, then continued. "Fer all I wanted to do wuz kill 'em! These 'men' ain't men...they ain't even animals...fer animals take keer o' their young. They only wanted to gratify themselves with takin' that which had never been taken afore. It made them feel powerful in their own weakness, 'n' by usin' force, pickin' on somebody who couldn't fight back, they felt they wuz in control. They're the buzzards that swoop down 'n' take without regard to any human feelings, even to takin' a life.

"You, my little lovely girl, were the one to pay the most fer this terrible wrong done to ye. Ye were the victim...the most innocent...the one who took everbody's slop. Wal, it's time to rise above it, to look at 'em all, one by one, 'n' fergive what wuz done."

"Fergive it! How kin I, Sterlen?"

"Think, now. Whose the one bein' hurt? Ain't them chicken-livered men! Ain't that Bell! Ain't Jim! Now, there's jest you carryin' the whole picture 'round in yer head 'n' heart. Ye gotta fergive the whole th from the inside out. I know it's gonna me! I kin help. I'm yer 'other part.'"

"Kin ye still love a...used woman, Ste

"Marthie, ye ain't like that at all. Ye own. I ain't like them other men. I carry a totally different way. My union with ye will only come when ye want it, not before. 'N' even if it never comes, I'll love ye still." He paused and then went on. "I'll keer fer ye when yer sick, 'n' I'll keer fer ye when ye git old. Marthie, yer my wife. From now on, I'll protect ye. Won't be nobody ever hurtin' my wife! It'd take death to separate us!"

His voice, filled with fervor, slapped against the splashings of the dark waterfall in the little cove on the mountain.

Marthie's heart leapt at his intensity, listening to Sterlen's heart beat against her ear. She felt his body heat...it saturated hers. She wanted to be closer to this man who had come to love her...this man who stood head and shoulders above all else.

"Sterlen," she said, "I love ye so much." She brought her hand up and felt of his face, his beard, his hair. "Ye only make me happy."

"Marthie," Sterlen said, pulling her up so she could see the workings of his face. "I'll make ye even more happier...fer I'll play fer ye, I'll sing fer ye, I'll be there when ye need me."

"I'll need ye always, Sterlen."

"Marthie," his voice had grown suddenly husky with his need, "Let me jest look at ye." As he gently brought her face around toward him, he turned to place her within the new light of the moon. In the smudges on her cheeks, he could see the tear stains. He laid his cheek against hers, muttering soft words of love and support, his arms holding her tightly. Then he just as suddenly pulled back, looking into the face of a responding woman. Her arms went around his neck...the look in her eyes drawing him still closer. He gently kissed those eyes, her cheeks, her lips...over and over again. The soft arms of the woman became strong and her heart was full of surprised desire.

His body, heavy with the months of passion denied, cried fer his wife; he molded her into himself, his spirit struggling. How could he wait any longer?

"Marthie, oh God!" His voice, anguished and tight, filled the cove. Then, with all the power he possessed, he pushed her from him. And there in the moonlight, the mountain man trembled in the presence of total manifested love.

Dark eyes stared at the man. His silver hair nested within a background of woven night-blackened limbs, while the bulk of his shoulders against the deep grey outline of the horizon would frighten anyone or anything coming upon him in the depth of this cove. As these thoughts flew through Marthie's mind, briefly, the darkness reminded her of what had happened to her years ago, out in the forest. But some-how, the images were only vague shadows.

Her body, still tense and warm from his embrace, didn't want to be away from him any longer. She wanted to be there...within his arms, within his protection...she wanted to be as close to him as she could get. There came a certainty into her mind. This man loved her as surely as she loved him. He had said he would never hurt her. She realized at this point that there would be no turning back. Whatever she decided to do at this moment would change the rest of her life, one way or another. And as that certainty entered her thoughts, she suddenly accepted what she wanted more than anything in the world.

"Sterlen!" she cried, and with the strength of the one who bore her, moved into complete womanhood.

The yellow moon rose higher and higher in a cradle of blue satin as it's gleam gently caressed the flowering of the natural response of love between a man and a woman.

In the misty distance of Blue Ridge, an old Indian spirit smiled.

CHAPTER 25

Almost Grown

Bryson walked across the porch into the kitchen carrying a large box. He sat the box down on the kitchen table and came back out onto the porch where his father sat, whittling an axe handle.

"Dad, I don't know what Lillie's doin', but here's a box addressed to her. I jest carried it all the way up the mountain from the Post Office down in Tuckasegee. Got pretty heavy that last mile er two." Bryson sat down on the porch near Tom.

"Who's the box from, son?"

"Says 'The Rose Company,' er something like that. Ain't got no other markin's."

"She'll be back here in a minute er so. She's brangin' my hickory wood up from where I got it stashed in the creek. This axe handle's most done now." Tom ran his hands down the texture of the handle, feeling it's smoothness with satisfaction, then stretched it out toward his son.

"Dad, I been meaning to ask ye...why do ye put them pieces of wood in the creek. I see ye do that year after year,

160

'n' fer some reason, I never asked ye afore." Bryson accepted the axe handle and also ran his hand down it in admiration.

"Jest makes it last longer when the handle is whittled out...water makes the wood tough. Now, I use water in another way to cane the bottom o' chairs. Ye have to take white oak, peel off long pieces o' the wood...I use my pocket knife...then ye soak the splints in water to git the wood to bend. While they're soft, ye kin cane a chair er make a basket er anythan' ye want. It'll dry powerfully strong, yes siree!"

"Yer good with yer hands, Dad. Ain't seed nothin' like it." Bryson handed the axe handle back to Tom just as Lillie and Corie came around the path carrying some pieces of wet wood between them. Behind them, at a distance, Nealie could be seen dragging his piece on the ground, struggling to keep up.

"I'll have enough fer ye to take to town by day after tomorrow. Ye remember that, son." Tom indicated to Lillie where to put the wood. "Young'uns, yer doin' a fine job!"

"Hey, Lillie, ye got a package on the table in yonder...from the Rose Company. Whatta ye doin'...ah...?" Bryson was interrupted by two girls running by him so quickly that he had to move fast not to get stepped on.

"Oh! It's come! Corie, it's come!" Lillie's voice followed them.

"Lord, young'uns!" Retter came out of the front room. "What on earth is the racket?"

"The girls got a box in the mail, Retter," said Tom, grinning at her.

"What's in the box?"

"Any minute now we're gonna know," chuckled her husband as he propped a new piece of hickory up on the large rock protruding out from underneath the porch and began to chip away at it.

Suddenly the two girls came out of the kitchen with their arms loaded with small round tins. Lillie's face, bright with hope, caught in a large smile turned toward her mother.

"Look, Momma...Rose Salve. Corie and me...we're gonna sell Rose Salve and make us a pile o' money!"

"Yep, we shore are! Gonna have so much money, we kin buy whatever we want!" Corie's determination matched her sister's.

Tom Ammons' eyes twinkled as he saw the enthusiasm of his daughters. "Hey son, mabbe we kin bottle some o' that ...git up 'n' go...'n' sell it. Make us a heap o' money, too!"

Bryson laughed. "Hey girls! Who's gonna buy that stuff. Ain't anybody got any real money in these mountains."

"Don't never ye mind, Bryson! We know what we're gonna do...we done planned it all out." Corie said emphatically. She sat on the porch and stacked her tins one on top of the other.

"Wal, whatever ye do," said Retter going into the kitchen, "git yer chores done first. Run out yonder to the hen house 'n' see if we got any eggs. Might make us a cake today."

"I'll do it, Momma!" called Nealie, jumping off the porch in one leap, then running down the path.

"A cake!" Tom's bowed head hid his smile. "Wonder why anyone would want to bake a cake? May 23rd...ain't no special day, is it?"

"None that I know of...leastways none of importance." Bryson laughed outright.

"It's my birthday! It's the most important day I know, fer I'm all o' eleven years old! 'N' don't youn's laugh! 'Sides, tomorrow's Daddy's birthday! I'm the lucky one, cuz I kin celebrate with my daddy! Ha! Ha!" Corie jumped up, stamped her foot, and all her tins fell, clattering down the rock beyond the porch.

"Corie! ye be keerful with that salve!" Lillie called from within the front room. "Ye cain't sell somethin' that looks used. Brang it all in here...I got it on Momma 'n' Daddy's bed. Let's count it 'n' make sure we got what they said we're supposed to have."

Four days later, Lillie and Corie, came home with a

paper sack in each of their hands. Their faces were covered with satisfaction, but they watched furtively for any of the family. They were in luck, for they could see Retter over at the wash area and Tom at the barn below the cabin. Bryson was nowhere to be seen.

Inside the house, the girls ran back to their bedroom, and dumped the contents of the paper sacks onto the bed. Lying before them were four tubes of lipstick, two a piece. They looked at each other with deep satisfaction.

"We did it, Lillie!" Corie's eyes were big with happiness. "We went all over the mountains...worked like a dawg! Sold all our salve, paid for it, 'n' had 'nough left over to buy what we wanted!"

"Wal, I wanted to buy the lipstick, maybe ye should have waited awhile." Lillie shook her head. "Momma might not like it cuz yer...."

"I'm almost grown, Lillie!" Corie demanded. "I'm eleven now 'n' as big as you too!"

"All I'm sayin' is, we better be real keerful 'bout how we do this."

"Lessus try it, Lillie...we worked hard fer this." Corie picked up a tube, and wound it out to it's full glory. She found the mirror they used in the back room, and leaning close, painted her lips bright red with great care.

Soon, Lillie stood beside her sister, applying the same color to her lips. Then, after carefully rewinding the tubes, they capped them and put them back on the bed with the other ones. Only then did they turn to look at each other.

"Lillie, yer beautiful!"

"Oh, Corie...with yer white curly-looking hair, ye remind me o' a movie star!"

Corie grabbed a pillow from the bed and began prancing around Lillie.

"Ma deara, ye may have my autograph...but first, ye have to kiss my ring finga!" She held out her hand to Lillie...who promptly kissed it soundly...leaving her lip prints on the girl's hand. Then, both broke out in laughter. They were laughing so hard they did not hear Bryson walk in.

"MY GOD! WHAT HAVE YE GOT ON YER FACE?" he suddenly yelled.

And before they could think, the man had confiscated all four tubes of lipstick and was headed out the front room door.

"Bryson, that's ours!" Lillie went running after him, closely followed by a recovering Corie, yelling, "Give it back! Give it back!"

As they ran into the kitchen, they saw Bryson lift the eye of the stove and throw the tubes of lipstick down into it's recesses.

"The devil's in that stuff! Don't ever let me catch ye with that paint agin! Momma sent me to tell ye to come help her with the wash! So, git out there!" he said, and stomped out of the room.

Corie and Lillie looked at each other, tears sliding out of their eyes. The room grew quiet, except for the popping of the fire. Lillie went over, picked up the eye of the stove and gazed inside.

"It's burnt." she said, sadly. "All that work...."

Corie sniffed, going to stand beside her sister to look into the stove. Then, she looked up. "Ye still look beautiful, Lillie." she said, reaching up to touch Lillie's lips.

"Ye, too, Corie. It ain't gone yit."

"So, Lillie...ye always say somethin' good comes out o' everythan'." Corie walked over to the table, sat down solidly and put her face into her hands. "What's the good that's come out o' this?"

Lillie stopped by the table, thought a minute, then said, "Wal, we know we look pretty good in lipstick, don't we! We don't have to guess any more. But Corie, take a gander at my hair!" She had gone to the mirror that hung up on the wall near the wash basin, and stood looking at herself. Immediately, she turned to Corie and said, "I cain't stand my hair in plaits, Corie! I'm gonna cut 'em off!"

"Lillie, no! Momma will kill ye, fer shore! Fer shore!"

But the cry went unnoticed. The scissors were already in Lillie's hands. She held one plait out, and cut it off close to her neck. And just as quick, the other one had been clipped.

Corie's face had turned pink, then white, then pink again. She could not believe she had seen her sister's unhappiness end up with her chopping off her hair.

"Ohhhh, Lillieeeee! Momma's gonna scald 'n' cook ye fer supper! I swear she will."

"Yer momma's gonna do what?" Tom stood in the doorway, a pail of milk in one hand and his cane in the other. His gaze followed Corie's and he saw Lillie standing there holding a braid in her hand.

"Whoooeee, Lillie...Corie's plumb right! Ye ain't gonna sit down good tonight, I'm afeared."

Their father came in and set the bucket of milk on the table, then he came to look at Lillie's hair. He rubbed his chin, and then surprisingly, he winked at her. "Git yerself a towel, 'n' come out here on the porch 'fore the sun goes down, soes I kin see—brang the scissors. Corie, ye run on out there 'n' help yer momma with the last o' the wash."

"But, Daddy, I wanta watch!"

"Corie, git now, ya hear! We don't want yer momma suspectin' somethin'...at least fer a while. 'N'...I'd wipe that paint off yer lips 'fore I'd go, if'n I wuz you." Tom lead the way out to the porch.

Since Sterlen had stopped by on his way up the mountain looking for Marthie, Retter had been worried. Neither one had showed up, going or coming, so she had been distracted all evening.

All during supper, Retter kept looking at Lillie, wondering what bothered her about her daughter...yet in her state of mind, she couldn't figure out the problem. Suddenly, it hit her.

"Lillie! It's gone! What have ye done with your hair!" Thunder clouds loomed on Lillie's horizon. Retter stood up, her eyes on the strap that hung on the wall by the cabinet.

"Momma...." she began.

"Retter!" Tom spoke up from the head of the table. "She started it, I reckon, but then I cut the rest. 'N' that's that! Unless ye want to whoop me!"

Corie's eyes, large and unbelieving, stared into Lillie's; then they quickly turned to watch the interaction between their mother and father.

"Wal...."

"Retter! Sit down!" he said. "Jest look at her...ain't she pretty with short hair? 'Sides, it's done now, ain't no changin' it."

Retter refused to look at Lillie the rest of the meal, and even into the evening hours. Afraid to go near her, Lillie sat on the opposite side of the front room, looking at the encyclopedia her father was sharing with her. Absently, she listened to him talk.

"Lillie, these books er wonderful books fer stories. They got all kinds o' information in 'em, told like a story. Look...look at this one...."

Suddenly, they heard footsteps on the porch, and Sterlen came in followed by a woman they assumed was Marthie. Everyone stared at her...was it really Marthie!

Damp dark hair framed her face...a face that spoke of soft happiness, blushing with laughter when Sterlen spoke.

"We got caught out in the wilds. Thank ye could spare a bed fer two way-farrin' strangers?" He grinned to all in the room, and put his arm around his wife.

"Yer as welcome as rain, Sterlen. Did ye brang your banjo?" Tom spoke up, motioning for them to sit.

As Sterlen turned to Tom, Marthie walked over and sat down next to Lillie. She smiled into her eyes. "Yer hair shore does look pretty, Lillie," she said. "Don't ye thank so, Momma?"

Lillie hesitated, then gazed at her mother, to find her eyes on her.

"Ye know," Retter said, looking at her two changed girls together, "the more I look at it, the better I like it. Yes...I reckon so. I reckon so."

"Oh, by the way," said Sterlen, coming over to Lillie, "here's somethin' fer ye. Ray sent it when I went by his house on the way here today."

Lillie, her eyes glowing, ran out to read her letter.

CHAPTER 26
The Lean-To

The summer of 1942 flew into winter for the people on Ammons Mountain and Wolf Mountain. The chores of making a living went on while the war overseas filled their radios and newspapers.

On Wolf Mountain Jim sat every evening...Bible in his lap...listening to the radio. He listened to announcers tell how America was handling the war at home.

"Everyone is saving everything: scrap metal, waste paper, toothpaste tubes, tin cans, old tires and even women's nylons. Americans have gone on the biggest scavenger hunt in our history. They're ransacking their attics, their basements, their garages—everything and anything can be used. Hey, out there, even if you want to get rid of bacon grease, bring it on in to your nearest grocer. The government can use it for making ammunition."

"Libby," he called, "what do ye do with your bacon grease?"

"Why...I put it in with the pinto beans, I use it in my corn bread, I pour it over greens...why? Why do ye ask?" Libby had come to the door of the front room.

Jim grinned at her. "Did ye know the government uses bacon grease in making ammunition?"

"Well, so do I," she exclaimed, and joined Jim in his laughter.

Suddenly there came a knock at the door, then the door opened and Talmadge, Libby's ten-year-old brother ran in.

"Libby, here's a letter from Cannie. The Golden Place has burnt up!" he exclaimed...breathing fast from his run over from Libby's mother and father's place.

"Burnt up! The Golden Place!" Libby's face had gone white. "Wuz anybody hurt?"

"No, but they done lost everthan'! Ain't got no furniture...ain't got no clothes. They lost everthan'! It's in the letter...gotta go...Poppy needs me...," he said as he turned back to the door. "Oh, Cannie 'n' Frank 'n' the baby...they want to come live on Wolf Mountain if they kin find a place." And the boy was gone.

"My Lord, Libby," Jim turned his head and rolled his eyes, speaking slowly, "read the letter 'n' see what Cannie said happened!"

Libby quickly drew the letter out of the opened envelope. She scanned the letter and then said, "She says the house caught fire in the attic when she and little Mildred were there alone...Oh Jim, she says she carried all the furniture out by herself...'n' ye know, she's six months pregnant again! Oh my God! After she carried out all that furniture 'n' their clothes, the burning house fell down on top o' it! They really have nothin' left...." Libby's voice trailed off.

"Wal," said Jim after he had cleared his throat, "we kin ask at the church Sunday fer donations o' clothes fer them. There must be somewhere to bed them down. In this rickety old house, ain't nothin' but one old bed. There's what's left of a couch in the corner. Wouldn't be much fer a woman with child...though." He hesitated then continued, "Ain't it funny, Libby, how little ye got when it's time to share it."

"All l know is, my sister 'n' her family will be taken keer of," responded Libby emphatically. "We'll all see to that!"

A week passed. One day, in the bitter cold of late January, 1943, an old logging truck stopped out by the mailbox. After the truck pulled away, Frank and Cannie came down the lane toward the Owen cabin. Frank carried a small bag and Cannie carried their baby.

All the Owen family welcomed the threesome with hugs and little squeals of delight at seeing how the baby had grown since they'd last seen her. After everyone had heard the story of the fire again, the men and the three Owen boys went outside to cut some more wood for the fire and the women settled down at the kitchen table to catch up with each of their lives.

Behind the women, near the pot-bellied stove, eleven-year-old Lucy and three-year old Dohonov, played with the baby.

Ellie ran her fingers through Cannie's hair and smiled, "Cannie, yer hair is still ever s'wavy 'n' pretty."

"Oh Mommie, it's s'good to be home here on Wolf Mountain. I feel better all ready." Cannie smiled deep into her mother's eyes.

"We been askin' the kinfolk, tryin' to find a good house fer ye 'n' Frank," Libby said as she drew up a chair and sat down next to her sister.

"It's awful close in here, I know, Mommie," Cannie said apologetically. "We'll try not to stay too long."

"Ye'll stay as long as it takes, Cannie," her mother said. "The boys er gonna have to share their beds in that back room where all ye young'uns used to sleep."

Cannie and Libby laughed. "It's different now, Mommie...Cannie's got a husband 'n' a baby!" Libby said.

"I know...I know...still, things have to be done in their own time."

Cannie looked around the room. It didn't look near as big as it had before. Her smile faded a little and her gaze locked with Libby's. The older sister shook her head, feeling helpless.

There had to be a place somewhere, she thought.

And within the week, a place came. Granny Owen sent word that Cannie and Frank could live in the lean-to over at the Owen homestead beneath Horseshoe Rock—it was small, but, it would be their own place. When the mountainfolk in the community heard about the fire, clothes and food came from everywhere. One of their own needed help!

Frank set about making all their new furniture. With his daddy's ability to work with his hands, Frank quickly fashioned all the furniture the little lean-to would hold, even a bed for Cannie and himself and a smaller bed for Mildred. She would no longer be allowed to sleep with her parents—a new child would be coming soon.

Granny Owen furnished the couple with shuck mattresses and feather pillows. Libby and Jim brought quilts and jars of honey as their gifts to the couple. Ellie brought over a well-used cast iron skillet which Cannie loved. It had been in the family a long time.

About three weeks after Frank and Cannie had moved into the lean-to, Sterlen and Marthie showed up one day smiling widely. Pelts were tied to the horse Sterlen was leading.

"We're on our way down to Sylvie to sell these skins," said Marthie, as she walked in dressed in overalls and a warm coat. "We brought ye somethin'!" she beamed, then added, "Where's the baby?"

Frank, followed by Sterlen, came in the house with the happiest face Cannie had seen in a long time. In his arms was a bear skin, black and shiny. "L-L-Look what yer gonna have on yer bed, Darlin'," he said to his wife.

Marthie, bouncing little Mildred in her arms, said to her brother. "Frank, I bet that's the bear that surprised ye that day awhile back over at the copper mine—fer that's were Sterlen got him. Now, he kin keep ye warm at night!"

"Hello the house!" Jim and Libby stood in the doorway.

"Ye always leave yer door open in this freezin' cold?" Jim stretched out his hand to Sterlen.

Libby squeezed in and shut the door. "Not to worry, Jim," she said, "Our body heat will keep us warm as an Armstrong heater!"

"Jest look!" Cannie smiled wide. "We're all here...six o' us out o' two families...all married to one another. And we're already starting to multiply."

Without realizing what she had said, Cannie kept on talking, proclaiming the values of their unique situation. But Marthie and Libby, almost at the same time, found each other's eyes. Both had been praying for a child, and both had been unsuccessful thus far. And here Cannie, only seventeen, would, by April, have two children.

For the first time ever, Marthie and Libby felt total kinship. When Libby reached out her hand to Marthie, the dark one gratefully took it. The warmth of the close room moved into their eyes.

CHAPTER 27
Pure Nakid Rich

O n April 22, 1943, Cannie, with help from Libby, gave birth to Doris Ellen Ammons. And then, in August Frank received his draft notice. Three days before his twenty-second birthday, on August 26, 1943, Frank was in the Navy...little knowing that he had left Cannie once more with child.

"It's a sure sign of rain when the chickens gather on high ground and trim their feathers," said Sterlen to Marthie.

She looked at him for a moment, muttering, "Er ye shore," and then continued to dig up the sweet potatoes in her garden.

"Yep, it's gonna come a good downpour, ye wait 'n' see!" Sterlen sat on the ground nearby, running blades over his knife sharpener—a rock set between a white oak strip tripod with a turning apparatus.

Marthie straightened, pulling her hoe up and leaning against the handle. She absently watched her husband's mastery of the sharpener. "Libby says that Frank's gonna take Cannie down to the flat lands o' South Carolina when he comes home on leave after his basic trainin'.."

Sterlen stopped his work and stared at his wife. "Lord, Why?"

"He told Cannie that while he's gone overseas, he wants her around a lot o' people, 'n' in walkin' distance of a store. He'll be sendin' her money soes she kin buy fer them babies."

"What's Cannie say 'bout this?"

"Reckon she's resigned to go. Libby says she thank's she's skeered to leave the mountains, but at the same time she's skeered to be alone if somethin' happens. I don't rightly blame her. Frank's asked if Lillie kin go stay with her, too, 'n' it looks like Momma's gonna let her." She dug her shoe tip in the red earth, and sighed. "Frank don't know Cannie's gonna have another young'un yit, either."

"Would ye want to leave the mountains, Marthie?" Sterlen suddenly asked, watching his wife earnestly.

"Heavens, no! I never want to go away from this...." She threw out one arm, her face lighting as she looked at the woods edging the clearing. "Jest as I never want to be away from you."

"But I won't be here fer as long as ye will, Marthie...ye know that, don't ye?" His gaze hard on her face, he learned forward. "There's an awful lot o' years betwixt us; I know there'll come a time when ye'll be without me. We both got to face that 'n' make out a plan fer ye."

"Sterlen! It ain't time to talk 'bout that yit! I don't want to thank on it!" Marthie went back to digging. "We ain't been married but two years come December! Talkin' 'bout stuff like that dulls my eyes!"

Sterlen stepped on his pedal, holding the small wooden machine still with his knee, turned the handle, and for a moment listened to the sharp scoring of blade against stone. Then he halted his work and grinned, "Marthie, I got to fix ye somethin' to help yer dull eyes!" he said.

"What's that?"

"Wal, fer dull eyes ye steep the bag that comes from the musk of a skunk in a cup o' water. Then, ever so often durin' the day, ye pat yer eyes with it."

"Ye got to be outta yer head! A skunk! On my eyes! No siree!"

Sterlen burst out laughing at the expression on Marthie's face and the now furiousness of her digging.

"Wal, then, how 'bout boiling a handful of bramble briar leaves in a quart o' sprang water. Ye jest put drops of this in yer eyes ever hour er so. Thank ye kin handle that?"

"Bramble briars?"

"Jest the leaves...jest the leaves!"

"Sprang water?"

"Yep...leaves 'n' sprang water."

"It all sounds like ye made it up, Sterlen! Skunks 'n' bramble briars!"

"Naw, Marthie...what I know has been passed down through the family. I follered Granny 'round 'n' listened...some o' her remedies come from the Cherokees. Fer example, see them strawberry plants over yonder...."

"What strawberry plants!" Marthie's body straightened like the releasing of a bow. She spun around to stare at her husband again.

"Why, those I planted over yonder...there, by the edge o' the woods. Ye know they're good fer what ails ye in any kind o' season...the leaves 'n' roots, biled in white lightnin' stays the bloody flux; the berries help with a bad stomach, fer fever, fer yellow jaundice. The juice helps to fasten loose teeth...'n' even works fer sore eyes!"

"Where'd ye git them plants?"

"Up there on Ammons Mountain. At yer favorite place...why?"

"Why did ye git 'em there?"

"Marthie, why er ye so...."

"Tell me, Sterlen, why'd ye git 'em there?"

"Wal, I sorta wanted to remember that place. I'm fond o' thankin' 'bout that night...'n' eatin' the strawberries afterwards." Sterlen leaned forward again, smiling softly at his wife. "In the sprang, I'd like to pick some o' them strawberries 'n' brang 'em to ye."

Marthie grinned at the big man. "Oh, go on with ye!" She blushed and found herself getting lost in his eyes. Shaking her head, she pulled herself away, and returned to her job, muttering, "...thought ye might have talked to the Indian."

"Indian? What Indian?" Sterlen was immediately interested.

"He called himself...Coowe...uh, Charlie."

"Ye seen him, Marthie? He talked to ye?"

"Yeah...jest 'fore ye got there that night. He wuz wonderful." Marthie kept on digging, not looking at Sterlen.

In the quiet that followed, Sterlen smiled deep within himself. The spirit had talked to Marthie...she was going to be all right now. Happiness flooded him...he wanted to dance...he wanted to play!

He jumped up and walked quickly to the cabin. Then to Marthie's surprise he came fiddling out the door. The sweetness of the strings glided through the air as he came closer and closer to Marthie. He swayed to the tune, his big body moving as if he were a reed swaying with the wind. The music entranced the woman, reaching way down to where movement lived. Soon, she began to sway with him and then to dance all around him in the clearing in the forest...twirling to the sound that grew from the magic hands of the mountain man and his fiddle.

Much later, the almost exhausted dancer huddled within the arms of the gifted musician, resting in a deep purple haze of perfect contentment. Sterlen, also rested in this—his world. Gazing around him, he could not believe his luck. Here, after all these years he had been given a gift such as he'd never dreamed. In his reverie he studied his youth...no, he would not have been ready, he would not have appreciated what he had here within the circle of his arms.

Appreciation comes only after getting what ye truly want

with all your heart, but not realizing it until it is manifested.

Takes a lot of livin' to understand that nourishment o' the heart! Sterlen thought, and turned his gaze upon the damp head of his wife.

The rain, sudden and steady, came down hard upon the two by the edge of the forest. The coldness it brought immediately soaked the pair through and through. Sterlen pulled himself erect, lifting the slim form of his wife as if she were his cure-all sack high in the air. He quickly had her cover his fiddle within her lap as he walked solidly toward their cabin.

"It's that gully washer I warned ye about!" he said to his bundle.

"Sterlen, I'm glad ye hadn't talked to Charlie 'bout them strawberries; it means more...."

He didn't want to study on what she meant.

"We're s'wet, reckon we'll jest have to strip 'n'...." he continued.

"Sterlen," again came the muffled voice at his shoulder, "yer firmly rooted in indecent thoughts!" He felt her shoulders shake.

He threw back his head and laughed to the rain.

"We're jest pure nakid rich!" echoed through the clearing behind the closing of the door.

CHAPTER 28
The Quiltin' Party

One day, the last of October,1943, Libby made a sweet potato pie from the fruit of Marthie's garden, and invited Marthie, her mother, Ellie, and her sisters Lucy and Elmina over to her house. She had sent word to Cannie and cousin Nellie to come also. Frank had taken Cannie over to Nellie's house to stay until he returned from boot camp. *This quiltin' party's gonna be so nice,* Libby thought as she placed the coffee pot on the stove...the last of her preparations. *Everbody together in this beautiful season...jest look at them leaves!*

She walked out onto the porch. Off to the side were tables strewn with sliced dried apples, peaches and pumpkin. Absently, she thought she'd better get those fruits onto the shelf above the stove to continue drying in the house. "The killin' frost ain't come yit...probably be a mild winter this year," she muttered to herself, turning her gaze to the rocky path leading out from her house. Her foot touched the cream-colored stone jar that was filled with fresh milk. She leaned down and pulled the wooden lid up to check if the milk had clabbered yet. *Not quite ready...good,* she thought. *Gives me more time to spend with my guests today.*

"Hey there, Libby!" Down the path came Sterlen and Marthie. "Brung ye a young lady who's anxious to git started."

"Good! I got the quilt pieces all cut out 'n' ready to go. Thought we'd do "'Round the world"—it's an easy one to start with. I want to do this agin next year, too.

Sterlen hugged the smiling Marthie, "Where's Jim?"

"Out down to the barn, a'waitin' on ye."

"Wal, I'm off then...pick ye up long 'bout dark, Marthie."

"Ye have a good day, Uncle Sterlen...I'll take good keer o' Marthie." Libby invited Marthie into the house and indicated a chair by the table in her small kitchen. "The coffee's 'bout ready."

Before any more conversation could be started, the others began showing up. Soon the small room held almost too many bodies but Libby rearranged some of the furniture. Everyone could finally sit so they could see each other, and they all began talking at once.

"Where's Jim?" said Elmina, the sister after Libby in age.

"Gone huntin' with Sterlen."

"Where's Cannie?" Elmina grinned, teasing her sister.

"Ain't heerd from her...hoped she'd be here today."

"Who all ye waitin' on?" came the smaller voice of Lucy.

"Everbody's here, 'ceptin' Cannie 'n' Nellie. Everbody! Have some coffee, now. Soon as ye git yer cup filled, I'll make some more."

"Lord, how we gonna fit two more people in here!"

There came the sounds of cup hitting saucer, spoon hitting cup, and then the smooth sound of many sips melting into one. The voices began again.

"Where's Dohonov, Mommie...who's takin' keer o' her?"

"Ray done volunteered...ain't that nice!"

"How ye been, Mommie?"

"Fair to middlin', 'ceptin' fer my rheumatism...been actin' up some. 'N' ye, Libby, yer stomach any better'n the last time I seen ye?"

"It's 'bout to kill me, Momma! Don't know what to do fer it!"

"Mayapple'll help rheumatism, Sterlen says...the root of it." spoke up Marthie for the first time. "Gotta be keerful o' the joints, tho...they're poison. He says to use only the pieces betwixt the joints."

Everybody stopped talking and directed their gaze to the dark-headed woman in the corner of the room. She looked almost odd, sitting among all the other fair-skinned females, each with a different shade of red-hair.

"Ain't that interestin', Momma," spoke up Libby. "Ye ever heerd o' that?"

"Come to thank on it...I have. Sterlen used to tell me that when we wuz young'uns. He's still a'sayin' it. Ain't that good. He's got somebody to listen, now. Yes, Lord, ain't that good." The mother of the women in the room beamed at Marthie.

Marthie blushed with pleasure, remembering for the first time, that this was Ellie, Sterlen's younger sister. She looked closer at the most interesting lady. Her face, filled with faded freckles, was framed in red hair laced with white, braided and wrapped around her head. The gaze from her brown eyes, full of life and twinkle, blanketed the room. Her grin, slightly crooked, pushed her cheeks in, showing high cheekbones. *She looks almost Indian!* she thought.

"Wal, lessus git to work on this quilt, yawl...we got a lot to do! Over here on the table I laid out some extra needles 'n' some scizzers, 'long with the pattern squares I cut out. Lucy, ye pull that battin' 'n' linin' outta that back room yonder. Yes, brang it on over here where we kin all git a'holt of it."

"I brung my own needles 'n' thread 'n' scizzers," said Ellie. "Here, Marthie,use this needle, it's a good size fer ye."

And so, four red-heads and one dark haired woman bent over a job that had been a mainstay of mountain living for decades. The fingers flew.

For a while the conversation covered all the ailments that could be mentioned and their possible cures—each woman trying to outdo the other in the description of the worse, most excruciating pain.

When the subject was exhausted, the conversation turned more intimate.

"Ye know, now that my boy Carroll is born, Demus is admittin' how happy he is that he really did want a son. But he wouldn't say that afore." Elmina's wonderfully deep voice spread out overtop the quilt. "But I'd been happy no matter what I had. Seems ye always want to see the eyes o' another generation a'walkin' 'round."

Libby and Marthie glanced up at each other and then went back to sewing.

"Wal, try havin' nine o' 'em runnin' 'round! Look at me, jest turned forty-nine 'n' still got a four-year-old. Shore is a good thang I had girls first! Don't know what I'd done." Ellie kept sewing and didn't notice the looks passed around by her daughters.

Then, the older woman raised her head and smiled. "Lord, I love my young'un's! They've made my life s'special. I always thought we had to be here on earth fer some reason...reckon mine wuz to birth s'many good young'uns! Ain't that good!"

"Wal, Cannie's comin' 'long after ye, Mommie— married two years, got two young'uns and another one on the way! 'N' Marthie 'n' me jest a'cryin' fer one!"

"Libby, I didn't tell ye...didn't want to spoil yer day here. Somethin' jest awful happened last week over to Nellie's. I got the letter yesterday."

All sewing had stopped, all gazes directed toward the older woman.

"Frank come home from boot camp. Seems it wuz a surprise fer him to find Cannie with child...she wuz already showin'. They all celebrated a little, singin' 'n' playin' old songs. Cannie went to bed early 'n' left the others. Sometime later there wuz a loud noise that frightened her, 'n' she jumped, rolling off the bed onto her stomach. She lost the little boy she wuz carryin'. She wrote me that Frank...buried it...in a shoe box over there on Tensaee Mountain."

Tears rolled down Marthie's face. She could hardly see around her hurt. Libby laid her head onto the crook of her arm. The atmosphere of the room hung in sadness.

"How's Cannie now?" asked the saddened Elmina.

"Frank's done took her to Pickens, South Carolina. The letter came from down there. Frank's only got a few days left o' his leave. He's gotta go back and finish his training...said somethin 'bout shippin' out fer the Philippine Islands in a few months."

"I thank we all got to pray fer Cannie, Mommie!" Elmina laid down her needle, leaned back against the chair, and gazed at all those around her. "Prayer is powerful, especially in a group such as ours here. Let's hold hands."

For the next few minutes, the walls of Libby's home felt the depth of five voices in prayer. The children of Ellie and Wiley Owen turned to the only answer they knew in a crisis...sincere and loud prayer, and the child of Retter and Tom Ammons, followed them in her own silent fervent offering.

Afterwards, in the silence ebbing the circle, the flash of needles took to cloth again. And then the soft, almost bass voice of Elmina, filled the room with song:

> *"Keep me close to thee when storm clouds rise*
> *Keep me close to thee when temptation rolls high*
> *Keep me close to thee let me lean on thy breast*
> *In the shadow of thy wings let me find sweet rest*
>
> *Keep me close to thee when the tempest appears*
> *Keep me close to thee when I cry cold tears*
> *From thy side, dear Lord, let me never stray*

Lead me on forever to that blessed day

Keep me close to thee when the shadows fall
Let me forever heed your blessed call
When my life is done, dear Lord hold my hand
Keep me close to thee, lead me on to that land

Keep me close to thee, Lord, hold my hand
Until I reach that wide golden strand
Let me never stray from the narrow way
Until I reach that land of your perfect day"

When she finished her song and the last note from her mellow voice ended, the hearts of all in the room had been moved to such tenderness and joy. Libby, tears in her eyes, was the first to speak.

"Elmina, I ain't heard that since way back yonder when ye 'n' Irene 'n' Cannie used to sing it at Poppy's revivals."

"We were called the 'Cardinal Trio from Wolf Mountain' cuz o' our red hair," Elmina laughed, and one by one, the others smiled. "We, each o' us, wrote a verse 'n' then we sang it that way, too, joinin' all up at the end. What a time we had, then...huh, Libby! What a time...."

"Now, Irene's married to Rufus, 'n' off to Army camp somewhere's in Tennessee. Cannie's in South Carolina, and ye're off down the mountain in yer own home, too, Elmina. Time goes a'flyin', don't it." Libby shook her head, dipping her needle into the cloth.

"Wal, I been a'lookin' at Ray here lately," said Ellie, gazing at her daughters. "He's seventeen now, a'playin' that guitar like Sterlen taught him, a'lookin' out fer his brothers 'n' sisters, a'carin' fer ever livin' thang. He's got s'much earnestness in takin' keer o' others, it skeers me. Seems our gentle mountain people wind up sometimes with troubles jest cuz they're backward 'bout talkin'...'n' cuz they trust s'much. Ye know, tho, the Bible teaches that—to trust.

"I jest trust that the war ends soon...'n' Ray's path is

strewn with the goodness he gives out."

"Libby, hand me that log over yonder," suddenly spoke up Marthie. "There's a chill comin' from somewhere. I kin feel it in my bones. Jest look at that cat sittin' with it's back to the fire...it's gonna be gittin' awful cold...comin' up soon."

CHAPTER 29

The Tree That Had Been Lying Around

"Timber cut in the dark o' the moon lasts longer...ye know that, don't ye, Sterlen?" Jim asked that dull February day as he harnessed his team of mules.

"Yep! Been helpin' many a man cut timber a passel o' years, Jim." Sterlen walked around to the other side of the mules, holding the leather straps tight for the younger man. "Now's a good time to fall some timber! Ye fixin' on doin' that? Where ye goin'?"

"Them Owen boys over to Tanasee Camp Creek want to git out a few yeller poplar 'n' hemlock today. I told 'em I'd help. Seems my reputation has traveled on up here to Wolf Mountain."

As Jim worked, Sterlen couldn't help but admire the strength he saw in the shoulders of his brother-in-law. "Say, Jim," he said, pulling himself out of his reverie. "I come over here today to help Wiley work on his traps while Marthie's visitin' with Ellie and Libby. More'n likely, we'll be here when ye git back tonight. Ye thank ye might do me a favor?" Not waiting for an answer, he continued, "Ye thank

184

there might be a birch in the midst o' that hemlock cove over yonder?"

"Might be...don't rightly know. Ain't seen this stand o' timber yit. What ye thankin' ye want with a birch?"

"I need jest a little bit o' its bark. The spring run o' sap might've loosened it up soes it'll come off easy." Sterlen walked back around to stand beside Jim. "I want to git myself enough bark to make a bowl fer Marthie. If I start now, I might git it done by her birthday in April."

Jim chuckled. "Takes ye over a month to make a bowl? That birch hard to fool with?"

"Aww, Jim. It won't take much onct I kin git to it. I gotta find time when Marthie's not around. It's gotta be a surprise."

"Ye really thank the sap is running? Ain't late February a mite early yit?"

"It's been a pretty mild winter, Jim...so could be. If not, there could be a tree that's been cut down 'n' jest layin' around...it'll do jest as good." Sterlen took a bandanna out of his pocket, and moved closer to Jim. "To pull the bark off the trunk, ye gotta cut a straight line and then pull it apart with yer fingers. Pound the black spots with a wooden maul ...it'll loosen it. Onct ye git the bark off, roll it up fer me. I only need 'bout this much." He held up the handkerchief.

"Ye got a maul, Sterlen? Don't know where mine is...'n' I gotta hurry on outta here." Jim finished his chore and began loading his saw and axe onto the sled. "By the by, what if there ain't no birch...won't a white oak do...er even one o' them yeller poplars?"

"Shore 'nuff, Jim. But I got a story I want to tell Marthie 'bout that birch...ye know me 'n' my stories!" He laughed, then continued, "I seen yer maul over yonder by the shed. I'll fetch it fer ye!"

Jim grinned as he watched his brother-in-law walk away. He had sure added to his sister's life...and disposition. He could remember when she hadn't been very huggable. Then, just as suddenly, Jim frowned, for it crossed his mind that he couldn't remember the last time he had hugged his sister.

Marthie walked ahead of Sterlen as they slowly made their way home that evening. Avoiding the dirt road, the two preferred to follow their own trail through the forest. Shadows, clinging to the limbs of the pines, brushed against them as they passed while the darkened moon, cradled in starlight, slipped in behind them. Screech owls sent out their quivering, whistle-like calls while in the distance came the howl of the wolves that had given the mountain its name. Neither woman nor man spoke, allowing themselves to be freely interlaced into the night's natural black-silver web.

From the edge of the clearing, Marthie and Sterlen, in complete accord, stopped to gaze at their small world below. In the darkness, the cabin seemed to melt into the crook of the cove, while faint starlight shimmered through the laurel bushes, illuminating the leaf-padded pathway before them.

"Ain't it pretty, Sterlen?" Marthie's voice came in an almost breathless satisfaction. She moved to put her arm in the crook of his.

"Shore is," he answered as he quickly shifted the roll of birch to the other arm.

"It looks like a star fell out of the heavens and ran right down our trail." She hugged his arm close to her bosom.

"Ye 'n' me, Marthie...we got it made." Sterlen shared his contentment. "We got the best o' all worlds here...beauty o' nature...all we want to eat, food we provide fer ourselves...'n' free to do what we want to do. Cain't thank o' what I'd want more."

The pressure of Marthie's hand lessened. She stood still for a moment, looking up at her husband. "Free to do what we want to do...what do ye mean?"

"Why, I mean that we are...how would I say it...that ye let me be free, 'n' I let ye be free." Sterlen, in the black of the night, did not see the danger in Marthie's eyes.

"Free to do what?" Marthie pulled away from Sterlen.

"Whatever we want to do, I reckon."

"Whatever we want to do! Ye mean ye're free to do 'hatever, whenever ye want to?"

Startled, Sterlen suddenly realized something was amiss. He quickly began to try to edge his way out of his predicament. "Wal...I guess. Ye know what I mean, don't ye?"

"No...I don't." The woman's words dripped like icicles, while her eyes, dark holes in an upturned face, stabbed shivers into Sterlen's backbone.

"What I mean is...if ye want to...go over to see...say, Cannie 'n' the baby...ye kin go jest as if I want to go 'sanging...I kin go, too." He swallowed.

"What I want to know, Sterlen Galloway, is what do ye thank 'freedom' really means?" Her hand went to her head as a grimace crossed her high cheek bones.

"Free...to do...what ye want to?" The same words eased out in a question.

"There, ye said it again! Free to do what ye want to! See! That's what I keep hearing! Free to do what ye want to! Don't ye see, Sterlen...there's more to it than that. Here in the mountains, them men wuz free to do what they wanted to do to me! I never heerd that anythang happened to them fer what they did! 'N' then, cuz o' what I had done, my brothers wuz free to treat me like I wuz nothin'...like I wuzn't around! The whole country wuz free to talk 'bout me behind my back 'n' stare at me with them funny looks on their faces! I'm sick to death o' that kind o' freedom. Fact is, jest thankin' 'bout it has done caused my head to pain me somethin' awful...it's killing me now!" Marthie stalked off, the anger lodged in her head pushing her down the trail toward their cabin. Over her shoulder came the words, "You, Sterlen, o' all people, should know how to talk 'bout being free."

Stunned into immobility, Sterlen stared after his wife. Her wrath had happened so fast with no apparent reason, that he felt as if he'd been rained on and put away wet. What had he done? What had he said? 'And what about all those words of things that had happened years ago? This was the first time she had even brought up the past since that day...that day of the strawberries. Suddenly Sterlen knew that Marthie still felt the shame of it all. It had been lying around all this time...she had not forgotten.

"This ain't gonna do...no siree, it jest ain't gonna do!" Sterlen muttered aloud. "I can't be on the watch fer ever-thang I say! This pain o' hers needs to be treed, shot down 'n' skinned! I better hit this thang straight on!" And with steps full of determination, the big man who had stomped down the mountain and destroyed that liquor still years ago plunged forward, down a dimly lit trail.

CHAPTER 30
Freedom

As Sterlen's heavy, determined steps stirred the browned leaves of autumn past, their reflections slowed him to a more thoughtful walk. By the time he had arrived at the cabin, he'd realized that he must stay completely calm and in control of himself—an angry man is momentarily a foolish man. Emotion would block out logic. He also knew that he had to steer away from what was causing Marthie's irritation until he and she could talk constructively about the problem. Now that he knew how she felt, he would watch and bide his time. But, he resolved, it would be this night that it would be settled. Time waited for no man...especially at his age.

He entered the cabin. The kerosene lamp on the small water table had been lit, but he could not find Marthie anywhere within it's dim shadowy circle. His gaze dipped behind the kitchen table in the center of the room back to where the quilted cover of their one bed was hidden in their one-room home. There she lay on her back close to the far side of the bed, one arm covering her eyes.

"Marthie," he began softly, moving forward. "Kin I help ye...with yer headache."

For a moment, the silence continued. Then, Marthie moved slightly, and the concerned man heard, "I...reckon. But, first, ple...please build up the fire in the fireplace."

As Sterlen moved to do her bidding, he concentrated. What she needed was...water from the walnut tree. Not very much...just a few sips every ten minutes or so.

Yep, that'll do the trick! No matter how bad the headache is, that stuff will halt it...'n' it won't take long!

"I got jest the cure, Marthie," his voice rose above the hungry lapping of the firewood, each word precise and soft. "It's stored over yonder in the cabinet. I bored a hole with an auger into the trunk o' a walnut, 'n' caught it's water in a mason jar. It tastes a little bitter, but it'll stop that pain in yer head."

Within only a short span of time, Sterlen had removed his coat, found his cure and administered the first dose to Marthie. Sitting on the side of the bed, not saying a word, he began to gently rub her temples, then her cheeks, her chin...even her lips. After a few minutes, under the now glazed eyes of the one he loved, he once again gave her the walnut water, one sip at a time.

The treatment continued for almost an hour. Both man and woman had grown warm and vulnerable. The lamplight teased the two with its far-reaching caress, lingering on the hand, the arm, and the cheek. Her headache long since gone, the glazed look in Marthie's eyes had been replaced with sharp alertness. From behind half-lowered eyelids, she followed the intentness of Sterlen's gaze, surprisingly realizing her heightened pleasure.

Marthie, her body now steeped in the magic of the moment, was in complete control of her thoughts. Sterlen's warm, healing hands, had kindled Marthie's skin like wood to a fire...burning hot as he began removing her clothing, piece by piece. He covered her white skin with the quilt. Her skin, soft to the touch, responded to Sterlen's hands underneath it. She moaned.

Never had she felt this way...not even the first time she had been with her husband. Quick thoughts, like rabbits, jumped through her aroused consciousness.

He'll never be like the others...

I know this man!

He's a good man.

He loves me...he loves me.

He didn't take me to him 'til I wuz ready.

'N' then, it wuz I

I who brought him to me!

Marthie's thoughts collided with the position of Sterlen's hands as his strokes reached her stomach, her thighs. "Ster...len. Ster...len." The choked sound of his name followed the movement of his energy as she voiced the brim of her rising passion, all fears once again evaporated.

"Yer headache?" he whispered.

"Gone." Her hand slid along the heavy muscle of his arm.

"How do ye feel?"

"Warm...so warm."

"Kin I take the cover...?"

"Off?"

He nodded, and swallowed.

"Ye...yes...take the cover off."

Slowly he slid the cover to the side. Above them, a pattering of raindrops ran across the tin roof, playfully enticing any who would listen. As if in answer, thunder cracked, shaking the cabin in its unseasonal intensity. Then from the distance came the footsteps of heavy rain running through the forest, down the path, and suddenly... overtop the cabin. Above them, it beat, passionately!

She brought her hands up to the buttons on his shirt, fumbling, quickly unbuttoning them to expose the wide, smooth chest of the man above her. She touched him, brought her hands to her face...breathed warmth around her fingertips, and then spread her fingers out like daisies onto his chest.

"Marthie?" He breathed as his arms opened, stretching toward her. And yet, he waited.

"Come...to me," she whispered as she rose to meet him.

Into the night they gave into the cycle of love underneath the out pouring of the heavens. At times, a high wind swept fervently through the cove, while in other moments, only a close steady pulsing dominated time.

Finally as two wakeful souls rested one within the arms of the other, courage eased into the room.

"Marthie," he said softly, "freedom is being able to choose freely to go after our own good...in our own way."

He waited.

The wind had died down...the rain now a low murmur. In the corner of the room he could hear the ticking of Old Ben. Low, yellow flames hissed at charred wood, licking hungrily and silently.

The woman within his embrace formed her body more closely into the crook of his. She laughed, warm breath against his chest.

"I understand," she said. "I choose..." and then, once again, tasted freedom.

CHAPTER 31

Ray's Victory Garden

At the beginning of World War II, when the Secretary of Agriculture, Claude R. Wickard startled Americans by suggesting that U.S. Civilians who wanted fresh vegetables on their tables should plant "Victory Gardens," they did more than he ever thought. Because commercial farmers were busy feeding the Army, people rationalized that this was the least they could do to help with the war effort.

So, millions of home-front citizens who had never known a hoe from a trowel began planting lettuce, tomatoes, beets, carrots, peas and radishes in such unlikely sites as their own backyards, the Portland Zoo, Chicago's Arlington Racetrack and the yard of the Cook County Jail. In 1943 alone, Sunday farmers planted 20.5 million plots and produced at least one third of all the fresh vegetables consumed in the country.

The winter of 1943 had passed with the war continuing to bring better times to the people of Jackson County, North Carolina. Rationing of gas and products like tires was probably the biggest hindrance, resulting in people riding around on bald tires at great risk. The nation had caught onto the planting of fresh vegetables, with pictures of Victory Gardens appearing in all the magazines and newspapers. The spring of 1944 brought more of the same.

"We always plant a garden, Ray...why er ye callin' this yer 'Victory Garden?'" Lucy watched while her older brother manipulated the reins of the mule, holding the plow handles, and guiding the spade of the plow. His shirt, wet from exerting control, clung to his back.

"Wait a minute...I'm done when I git to the end o' the row!" called Ray, pulling his mule to a stop and reaching for the bandanna dangling from his back overall pocket.

Lucy ran over and handed him a jar of water. He drank deeply and returned it empty. Wiping his brow, he grinned at her, then looked at his handiwork.

"Yep! we always have planted a garden. The rest o' America is jest now doin' what we've always done. Shows we have known it wuz a good thang all along. 'N' 'sides, I want to be a part o' gittin' this war over with."

"But, I don't understand. How kin plantin' a garden git the war over?"

"Lucy! Jest thank! We're takin' keer o' ourselves; ain't nobody havin' to take vegetables from the Army to feed us. So, the Army gits fed...'n' we do too. By takin' keer o' ourselves, we're helpin' feed the people in the Navy and the Army...like Frank and Albert, like the Galloway brothers, our cousins down the road, 'n' on 'n' on. By growin' our own garden, we're helpin' with the 'victory' o' the war. Understand?"

"I thank I do. It means when ye plant this garden, ye're helpin' all the soldiers that are in the war eat, cuz we ain't takin' their food...ain't that so?"

"Ye got it! Now, look at this. When we take keer o' this garden...every time we hoe the carrots...every time we pick beans...every time we grabble potatoes...we're helpin' to win the war, jest like we wuz soldiers ourselves!"

"I ain't never looked at it that way before." Lucy shook her head, causing her braids to swing back and forth. Her bare toes grabbed at the loosened earth as she continued to ponder what her brother had just told her.

"Help me with the mule, 'n' I'll tell ye what I want to do when I git older," the boy grinned at his sister. "I been thankin' a lot 'bout it this sprang while I've been plowin'."

"Yeah! I wanta know!"

"Gee, haw! " Ray called to the mule so he could move the plow out of the way until the next day. "Whoa!" he called again. Then he unhitched the plow and gave one of the reins to Lucy, inviting her to help him walk the mule.

"Come on, be keerful now...stay close to me. We gotta go down by the creek to git Mable some water, then over to the barn."

When their chore was completed, Ray asked Lucy to sit on the side of the creek bank with him. The two looked out over the rolling hills of the Wolf Mountain community. It seemed to be on the top of the world, it's pastureland just coming to new life with the season. From where they sat, they could see the budding of the apple trees, and here and there, white and pink dogwood trees were still in bloom.

"I love this mountain, our homeplace, Lucy. But, some-how, I know I won't live here when I grow up. I got something big to do...don't know what yet...but I know it." Ray, sitting on a grassy knoll, had become so intense that Lucy kept quiet so she could catch every word.

"It's in my heart to help keer fer people...like be a doctor er somethin'. 'Course that would take a lot o' money, 'n' I ain't got any...but I know if I join the Army I kin go to school. I done looked into it."

"Ray! Mommie wouldn't let ye do that! Ye could git hurt...'n' ye jest turned seventeen in January! Why don't ye jest go back to working in that old copper mine like ye did last year?" Lucy's eyes had grown big and unhappy.

"I ain't goin' in the Army now, silly goose! It'll be a year er two yit but it's never too early to start plannin'. It's funny, but I kin almost see it now. Knowin' what it'd take to save a life! That's big stuff, Lucy! Working in a copper mine...why, anybody kin do that!"

"I wonder what made ye thank to be a doctor. Ummm...ye got so many sisters who's gonna need one, maybe that's it!" Lucy laughed, pushing at her brother's knee. "Less see...ye got Libby, Elmina, Irene, Cannie...older'n ye; 'n' then ye got me 'n' Dohonov younger'n ye. And say...how 'bout Marthie! I jest heard Mommie tellin' Poppy that she's finally gonna have Sterlen's baby!"

"Ye don't say!" Ray laughed aloud. "Marthie's gonna have a baby! She don't look it...ye know when?"

"Mommie said she's jest over two months along...she jest figgered it out, she said." She paused. "How do ye tell if yer gonna have a baby, Ray? Yer gonna be the doctor!"

"Lord! ye better ask Mommie, Lucy," Ray laughed again. "Let's see...this is May...guess she'll have that baby in November. Bet she's happy! Heard tell she really wanted a baby."

"Wal, ye won't be a doctor by then!" Lucy jumped up to skip around him. "But, Ray, besides all them girls...I thank it's our little brothers Talmadge 'n' Cecil who's probably gonna be the ones who'll need a doctor the most...'specially Cecil! Ye remember when he climbed up on the fence 'n' somehow got on the horns o' that ole bull? He weren't any older'n Dohonov is now."

Ray grinned at the memory. "Mommie skeered him the most. When Poppy grabbed him off'n that bull, Mommie tuck off after Cecil with a stick. Lord, he run! Mommie never caught him either. By the time he got back, she wuz grinnin' 'bout it. I thought Poppy would jest die laughin' at the sight o' Mommie runnin' after Cecil...that brave boy who rode the bull at four years old!"

Lucy stopped her skipping and dropped to the ground. Her breath came in short spurts. She joined her brother's reverie, both relishing the memory of their brother's escapades, as the sun slid down behind the farthest mountain. The air grew cooler.

"Ray," said Lucy suddenly, "what if ye cain't be a

doctor. Is there somethin' else ye want to be?"

"Wal, I could become a guitar player with a band 'n' tour the world...I sing fair to middlin', I reckon. 'N' I thank I could be a good artist. I draw good, Mommie says. 'N' I like to write...I got this poem I'm gonna send to Lillie."

"Kin I hear it?" Lucy leaned closer.

"Wal, I don't rightly know if that's proper...I wrote it fer her." Ray teased his sister.

"I wanta hear...please, Ray!"

"I wrote it this mornin'...it's kinda funny."

"Tell it to me, Ray...please."

"All right, all right...settle down. Here it is in my pocket...listen...

"I met ye there, stirring the soap
Your big brown eyes gave me hope
Of knowing you, becoming your friend
But you run off around the bend
I thought you were gone forever that day
You didn't even hear me say
Lillie, Lillie, please come back
I really like you...that's a fact
But the next day, there you were
Such a pretty girl, yes sir!
Standing over there by the door
I had to look at you all the more
Them plaits, long and black
Hanging over your apron, down your back
I walked over to talk to you
We were laughing before we were through
Then we went down to your mom's place
And I got to look straight in your face
I told you then I liked you a lot
But a lot of words I ain't got
Then your brother run up and we tuck off

To the barrel where we heard her cough
Down inside was your sister Corie
Oh, this is such a funny story!
She was full of wine, and seeds, too
When she hit the ground, running to you
She splattered you purple, through and through
Lord, I ain't seen nothing prettier'n you
Your eyes flashed when you whirled around
A'making that madder than a hornet sound
I won't ferget us laughing that day
That's why I wanted to write and say
Lillie, Lillie kin I come back
I like you....do you like me back?"

"Oh Ray, that's the best story I ever heard! She'll like it s'much!" Lucy's eyes sparkled with her admiration.

"Wal, I don't ever want to ferget the time I met Lillie. It wuz s'funny 'n' happy. I like to write down things soes I kin remember 'em. I jest started writin' 'n' this is what come out." Ray folded his paper and put it in his pocket, grinning again at his sister as he stood up. "Now, don't go tellin' ever-body 'bout this, cuz I'll never hear the end o' it from Talmadge 'n' Cecil."

"When ye gonna mail the poem to Lillie?"

"Today...the mailman runs this afternoon. I thank I kin git it over to the box 'fore he gits there." His gaze slid sideways to fall upon his sister to see her reaction. "Been goin' to see her down to Cannie's ever once in a while."

"Ray, this is so romantic!" Lucy rolled her eyes.

"Now, don't go gittin' mushy on me, Lucy. It's jest a lotta fun."

"But, ye like her a lot, don't ye!" Lucy wouldn't be sidetracked.

"I reckon I do. Ain't seen anybody I like better. She usta have real pretty plaits...like yourn, Lucy...'cept her's was black...like I wrote. But she got her hair cut. It's grownin'

One week later, an excited Lucy stepped off the Trailways bus, and ran into the open arms of her sister.

"Oh, Lucy," said Cannie, pressing her lips to the red hair of the thirteen-year old. "I'm so proud to see ye. Corie came in last night. She and Lillie are at the house sitting with Mildred and Doris. Uh...what is that with your suitcase?"

"That's Ray's old guitar, Cannie! He's been teaching me to play on it. He's got him another, better one. Ray said to tell ye that he's sent me down here to brighten up your day with a song!" Lucy's freckles danced on her smiling face.

"Oh, how good! Lillie's got one, too. The two of ye can play together." Cannie picked up the suitcase tied with a piece of cloth. Lucy lifted the guitar case and the two of them set off down the street.

"How far is it to your house, Cannie?"

"It's...'bout a couple of miles. It'll take us some time to walk it, but...we kin do it. So ye kin play now...'n' sing?"

"Ye bet! I cain't wait to show ye. Ray says I'm real good."

As the two walked down the paved streets of Pickens, Cannie and her little sister caught up on all the news from Wolf Mountain. Then, when Lucy heard that Frank wrote wonderful letters, she had to hear all about what Frank had to say about where he was and what he was doing.

"Well..since he's in the Navy, he's been out to sea a lot. He says that sometimes they sit there in port...er sometimes out in the sea somewhere, waiting fer orders, 'n' it's so pretty the fellers take off their clothes, get into swimming trunks and dive into the ocean. In shaller places, Frank goes all the way down sometimes 'n' gets oysters that they jest eat raw!"

"Raw? Off the sea bottom? Yuk!" Lucy's nose wrinkled.

Cannie stopped to change sides with her load. The excitement of seeing her sister had helped her so far to forget the long journey back to her little house on the edge of town. Now, however, the weight of the suitcase began to take its toll.

Lucy noticed that Cannie was limping. "What's wrong, Cannie? One leg don't seem to be able to keep up with the other'n!"

"A vein in this leg busted...er something. It pains me an awful lot. But, don't ye worry none...I'll make it fine. It's jest that...with this new baby comin' I really got to take keer o' myself...soes I kin take keer o' it ...'n' my two girls."

"I'll help ye so much ye won't haveta git up...er even walk anywhere, Cannie!" Lucy's enthusiasm brought a wide smile to Cannie's lips.

"Ye sound just like Lillie 'n' Corie! But—I need to excercise. This walkin' is good fer me, Lucy! Cain't let ye girls do everything fer me...cuz then ye might want to have my baby fer me!"

"Nope! Ye kin do that all by yoreself!" Lucy swung her braids. They sailed back and forth around her head, slapping against her cheeks.

Cannie laughed, then swung out her arm, indicating a small white house just beyond a mailbox beside the road. "Well...here we are. I gotta git these shoes off. There's a blister on my heels from them shoes sliding up 'n' down while I wuz walkin'."

Bedlam broke out as the two came through the front door. Lillie and Corie rushed to get to Lucy while at the same time the little girls, Mildred and Doris, ran over each other to get to their mother. Two-year old Mildred reached Cannie first, hugged her legs, and then turned to help her one-year old sister, Doris, grab hold of their mother's legs also. Cannie dropped the suitcase on the floor then found the nearest chair and sat down, children and all.

At first shy, the small children hung back and watched this new red-headed girl who had come into their midst. Soon, however, the young girl had the babies up in her arms, talking and dancing around the house as if they'd been together forever.

Lillie helped Cannie make a noon meal for everybody. Then, afterwards, when Cannie went to lie down in the back-room with her babies, the three young girls sat for some time on the front porch.

"I got something here fer ye, Lillie," said Lucy, grinning knowingly. And from out of her suitcase, she pulled the letter. "It's from my brother...special delivery. He said to say that!"

Lillie grabbed the letter and ran back into the house. Corie and Lucy exchanged looks and rolled their eyes.

"Guess she needed to be alone to read it!" Corie laughed.

"I don't know what all the ruckus is between them. They each think the sun sets in the other one! Silly, ain't it! I never thought about somebody liking my brother like that. Ye think he's good-looking? I reckon...now that I think on it...he probably is."

"I know what ye mean...Lillie's jest my sister," Corie shook her head. "She looks all right...I reckon. Jest a sister."

Then, flushed and happy, Lillie came back out onto the porch. Her cheeks glowed pink as she withdrew her hand from her skirt pocket, patting down the bulge of the letter. She chose to ignore the eager expectant looks of the two younger girls and didn't mention what was in the letter from Ray. Instead, she said, "The man Cannie rents from lives up at the farm over that hill yonder." She pointed to the dim, grey farm house in the distance.

"Yep," continued Corie, forgetting quickly about her sister's love affair. "Lillie says we git to go over there in a while 'n' see his great big barn. She says his barn is bigger than our house is up on the mountain."

"When kin we go see?" Lucy jumped up, indicating that she was indeed ready for this adventure.

"Guess we could go now...he wanted me to help him clean that chicken house o' his. Told him I'd start on it in a day er two. Now's as good a time as any. I'll tell Cannie, and then let's go!"

Later that afternoon, there were three tired girls who made their way back to the little house. They had helped the farmer around his barn, gathered pumpkins out of his patch, and cleaned the chicken house...but in their hands they carried jars of canned goods, a gallon of fresh milk and a basket of large brown eggs.

"Oh, what fun!" sang Lucy, as she seemed to forget how tired she was and began to dance around Lillie. "I ain't never seen so much food before. 'N' there were chickens, hogs, cows, horses, 'n' lots and lots of pumpkins! Them folks got to be rich!"

"Let's cook supper fer Cannie 'n' surprise her!" Lillie directed the two where to put their acquired treasures. "She's not feeling too good."

Later, as the family of four young girls and two children were just finishing their evening meal, Cannie suddenly looked up and smiled.

"Hey, ye two guitar-playing girls," she said, "why don't ye play for us out there on the porch. I would love to hear ye play together."

"I'll get mine, Lillie!" Lucy jumped up, pushing her chair back, almost tripping over her feet in her hurry.

"Slow down, Lucy...let's git there in one piece!" laughed Cannie, picking up Doris in her arms.

"Me, too...me, too," Mildred pulled at her mother's dress, wanting her to carry her.

"I'll git her, Cannie," said Lillie. "Ye git my guitar, Corie...okay?" As Corie dashed toward the back room, Lillie swung Mildred up into her arms. "Say...," she continued to the child, "do ye know that yer still my little apple blossom?"

The children grinned and threw her arms around Lillie's neck. "'Gin, Lillie! Tell me 'gin!"

Lillie balanced the child on her hip and began her story, talking on their way to the porch, "Well, ye hadn't been born long when I first got to see ye. Yer momma 'n' daddy lived in the prettiest place in the world—in the middle of an apple orchard at the Golden Place. Ye wuz born on April 1st...when all the apple trees wuz in bloom. All ye could see wuz apple blossoms and smell apple blossoms. I wuz waiting outside when ye wuz born...I wuz in the oldest apple tree, the one that wuz next to the front porch. Finally, Mamma came out and said 'It's a girl!' I sure wuz happy. I couldn't wait to see ye. Then, Irene came out and said I could go in. To me ye looked like all the apple blossoms all rolled up in one 'n' I said we should call ye "Apple Blossom," 'cause ye smelt just like one 'n' your mouth looked like the petals of the blooms. Ye shore wuz the prettiest thang I had ever seen. Your aunt Irene said I wuz crazy...that ye jest didn't name babies 'Apple Blossom!' Frank, yer daddy, called ye 'Mildred' instead. But I thank yer still my Apple Blossom! Don't ye ever fergit that yer special to me!"

The little girl hugged Lillie's neck, giggling, then began a sing-song, "Appy Boss'um, I'm a appy boss'um."

Lucy sat on the steps, tuning her guitar, with Corie one step below, holding Lillie's guitar. Cannie sat down in a chair, turning Doris around in her lap so she could watch the fun.

As Lillie let Mildred down to join Corie, she took the guitar, and ran her fingers over the cords.

"What do ye want to play, Lucy?"

"Why not 'I'll Fly Away,'" spoke up Cannie. "Kin ye play that, Lucy?" Getting her nod, she continued, "Corie, let's you and me sing...won't to?"

For over an hour, the singing and strumming girls entertained themselves, singing one hymn after another. Finally, when the children were sound asleep, the tired troop sang their last song. And then in the still night, from across the road, came the faint applause of the neighbors who had gathered on their porches to listen.

Smiling, Cannie and the girls on her porch waved to the neighbors, then gathered up the sleeping children and went inside the house.

"I'm so glad I come, Cannie," Lucy said to her sister as she got ready for bed that night. "I've had so much fun since I got here."

Cannie smiled. "I'm glad yer here, too. It's awful hard

not to have Frank around. Lillie and Corie and you make it easier fer me. I've been so homesick fer the mountains...ye three sorta saved my life. Wonder how Marthie's doin'...she's out there in the woods, far away from her neighbors. 'Course she's got Uncle Sterlen there with her, but it's 'most her time, now, ain't it?"

"I seen her jest before I come down. She's powerful big in her belly, but her arms 'n' legs er jest as thin as they always wuz. She's set on havin' her baby in jest a week er two, Mommie says."

"Oh, she did want a baby in the worse way. Did Mommie mention what kind o' child Marthie's gonna have...a boy er a girl...she kin always tell, ye know."

"I ain't heard tell, Cannie. Mommie ain't said." Lucy paused, pondered, then smiled and continued, "I did hear tell that Uncle Sterlen's done asked that granny woman over on Savannah Ridge to help in the deliverin'. He's gonna go git her when Marthie's time is near. Reckon he's tryin' to thank o' everthang!"

"Ain't that good!" Cannie said. "I never thought o' Uncle Sterlen as a daddy. Shore is gonna be funny! But, come to think on it, I never thought I'd ever see him married!"

Lillie stuck her head in the door. "Ye all talkin' 'bout Sterlen 'n' Marthie, ain't ye? I heard what ye wuz sayin'...Mommie thought the same thang 'bout Marthie. She said it wuz a miracle...'cuz Marthie wuz so afeered o' men. But then along came Sterlen!"

"He wuz s'funny when he come over that time when he brung the marriage license," laughed Corie as she pushed past her sister to sit on Lucy's bed. "Ye remember that day, Cannie?"

Laughter filled the room as three of the four nodded their heads.

"I wuzn't there!" said Lucy, looking at each. "Tell me 'bout it!"

"Let me tell it, Cannie!" Lillie pushed Corie over and sat beside her. "We wuz washin'...'n' Mommie wuz watching fer that old chicken hawk at the same time. All o' us wuz there. I wuz tellin' a story 'bout Frank 'n' me catchin' rats 'n' them a'plowin'."

"Now don't git started on that story," said Cannie, noticing Lucy's heightened interest.

"All o' a sudden, there stood Sterlen, grinnin' at all us women. He asked Mommie if he could borrow Marthie fer a little while. He kept pattin' his chest, a'lookin' at all us women! He seemed to be so proud o' what he had done. Finally, he opened his shirt, 'n' showed us this paper he had in his pocket. We found out later that it wuz the marriage license. He jest looked so funny...it wuz like he had tickled his funny bone!"

All three girls looked at each other and burst out laughing.

Finally, Cannie said, shaking her head, "Now, seriously...Uncle Sterlen is the most gentle man I've ever known. He's come to our house in times of sadness, toting his banjer on his shoulder. He'd sit 'n' play 'n' sing...'n' it wouldn't be long until he had all o' us smilin' 'n' singin' with him. He's never gotten the credit he deserves fer bringin' joy all over the mountains. He makes me think o' the mountains themselves, fer they're gentle too, ye know."

"Yer right, Cannie. I ain't never thought 'bout it that way...but, I kin see it." Lillie had sobered, nodding her head as Cannie spoke. "He's got a way 'bout him. He shore made Marthie smile...'n' like Momma said, that wuz a pure miracle!"

Cannie's gaze brightened at Lillie's words, "The Lord always marks folks to favor a purpose," she said. "Reckon it took somebody like Uncle Sterlen 'n' his gentleness to put the joy back into Marthie."

Lucy had dropped to the floor as she listened to the others talk. "So, Uncle Sterlen," she said softly, "is the gentle man from the gentle mountains. I don't thank I'll ever fergit that."

And in the quiet that followed, all four girls smiled.

The little hill where Cannie lived in Pickens grew to be called "Happy Hill" by the neighbors, because there was always so much music, song and laughter from the girls who lived there.

CHAPTER 33
The Granny Woman

Sterlen met her coming on the trail across Savannah Ridge above Cullowhee Gap.

"Howdy, Annie!" he said. "How ye doin' this fine day?"

The old woman pulled her glasses off, squinted her eyes at the mountain man, and set her basket on the ground. She threw back her blanket coat, let her hood fall onto her shoulders, and gathered her apron in her mittened hands...wiping clumsily at the glasses.

"I'm doin' good, Sterlen, now that I kin see," she said, placing her glasses back onto the tip of her nose. "The world has opened up since I got these here spec's!"

"How'd ye git 'um, anyway?"

"Why, Retter's Tom got 'um fer me," Annie placed her hands on her hips and grinned. "He gits 'um fer many a poor person in these hills. 'N' he sure knowed how much I needed 'um in my job up here in these backwoods."

"Wal...that's why I come lookin' fer ye, Annie." Sterlen

set his towsack down. "Marthie's time's 'most here. I really need ye...cuz I shore don't know what to do in birthin' a baby!"

"Ye want me ta come on over to Wolf Mountain?"

"She done asked fer ye, Annie. She said ye wuz the only granny woman she wanted. She sets a lot o' store in ye."

"Wal, lessus go on, then...lead off!"

"Don't ye wanta git a change o' clothes...er somethin'?" Sterlen didn't budge; he seemed rooted to the spot.

"I got everthang I need right here." Annie leaned over and picked up her basket, hooking it over her arm. "I got my flannel shirt 'n' wool socks fer sleepin', my beechwood sticks fer cleanin' my teeth...'n' all my paraphernalia, leggings 'n' wool shearings I always carry jest fer this kind of emergency. Lead off!"

Relief, like a spring rain, flooded over Sterlen. Still he hesitated.

"But, Annie! Where ye been...where ye goin'? I ain't takin' ye from somethang ye need to be doin', am I?"

"Jest hush, Sterlen. Marthie's my kin! Ain't nothin' more important right now! Git on with it!"

The older woman flung out her hand, waving him on like a broom sweeping the trail. As Sterlen swung his sack over his shoulder and the two set off down the trail, the granny woman's voice became a canopy of words that shielded him for a time from the elements of the cold November day and his growing apprehension.

"I been birthin' babies s'long!" she explained. "I got all kinds o' stories. Why, I remember one time when Old Joe Wike come 'n got me when that young second wife of his had her first young'un. Fact is, I won't ever fergit it till the day I die! All them young'un's from Joe's first wife wuz jest like wild thangs! When I come up onto the porch, they tuck off, their brown legs jest a'flying.

"That little girl—she warn't no more'n fifteen—wuz stuck back there in that dark room with no light in the place a'tall. 'N dust! there wuz dust everwhere. She shore wuz glad to see me, reaching out to me with her hand, asking me to help her. My insides jest cringed!

"She warn't too big, 'n her pains warn't too close yit, so's I begun to thank we might be in fer a spell of it. I went to work on that room, throwing open them winders, gitting me some light, 'n cleaning out all that dust. None of my babies have ever been born into a dirty room...there's enough dirt in its world afterwards!

"Joe hung 'round out in the kitchen. I 'spect he kept that jar of brew warm with his sweating hands. Ye'd thank with all them young'uns he's got, he'd git used to child birthing...er learn how to stop fathering s'many!"

Sterlen grinned. He did love a good story.

"With that girl looking fer the world like she wuz gonna have trouble, I figgered I'd git my incubator ready...shook out them wool shearin's from my basket...fer keeping that baby warm wuz a'gonna be the thang.

"Wal sir, in amongst her pains, I put the legging's I make fer these mothers-to be on that girl. She didn't fight me a'tall, poor little thang. There wuz tears coming outta her eyes, but she warn't doing nothin' but whimpering a little. My heart went out to her. I told her to yell it out...that she'd feel better fer the release of it."

Annie grew quiet, her feet brushing the ground. Then in a softer voice, she continued, "The time whiled away with that child growing weaker ever minute. I didn't like it a'tall. It wuz way into the night sometime that the baby all of a sudden decides to come."

Sterlen could hear the excitement rise in the telling of the story.

"Lord, I wuz ready! I had everthang out onto the table— pans, strang, soap, sizzers, disinfect. I hollered fer some water from old Joe.

"I asked the child how long she'd been in labor. She told me fer most of two days. My heart done sunk. She wuz powerful weak. I knowed I wuz gonna have to help her in the deliverin'. Shore nuff, I almost had to reach in 'n pull it out. It wuz the quietest birthin' I ever done."

Again, Annie's voice ceased. And then, the words eased

out , "That child-mother never hollered a bit...but afterwards, I found where her hands wuz all bloody...from her fingernails bitin' into the middle of them fists. 'N that baby, he come out still as death! I knowed what to expect...'n' I wuz right! There wuz a veil over his face! "

Electricity filled the air! Annie's story had reached its climax.

"As quick as a rabbit I flipped that little piece of thin skin back over his head so's he could breathe. I cleaned the little feller up with him a'squirming 'n yelling to make up fer his size. I knowed then we wuzn't gonna need that incubator after all...thank the Lord! 'N that new mother...she jest beamed et me from that old bloody bed. It's them looks that pays me fer the long walks back into these mountains."

Sterlen could hear the tears. The skin on his neck crawled, as the granny woman slid right inside his heart.

"Then agin," she was saying, her voice chocking, "I like to meet them...young'uns I've birthed...on the back trails sometimes. They wave to me 'n my basket...a'calling out, 'Howdy, Miz Coggins, ye take care now. Don't want any harm coming to my granny woman!'

"Them piny woods er full of my young'uns! I done birthed over 2000 of 'um...." She paused, then continued, "Now I'm set to birth Marthie's 'n' yer young'un. The good Lord has blessed me mightily, Sterlen Galloway! He's blessed me in my callin'! I praise Him!"

Her words rang through the forest. The lump in Sterlen's throat refused to allow him to speak. He had been acquainted with Annie all these years, and until this day, he had never truly known her. Marthie could not be in better hands.

CHAPTER 34

Libby, Sing Fer Me...Sing Fer My Baby

L ibby sat on the side of the bed, her soft gaze upon her sister-in-law who lay covered with only a sheet. The very pregnant woman's hands lay gripped on her bulging stomach.

"It's yer time, Marthie!"

Marthie's face had paled. Her pains had begun almost as soon as Sterlen had gone beyond the clearing. "I called out to Sterlen...but he didn't hear me. He's gone off to git the granny woman. I...I'm s'glad ye come by to see me. I don't know what to do. I seen Momma git her pains, but...I always run off. I didn't like to see Momma hurt." Marthie paused, then reached for Libby's hand. "I...I'm skeered, Libby."

"Sterlen's gonna be back afore ye know it, Marthie." Glancing around quickly, the red-headed woman's first instinct was to get the place ready for the forthcoming birthing. With surprise, she found everything needed in position.

"Why, Marthie...it's all here...yer all ready! How...When..?"

"I run off with Momma's pains, but not before I got everythang ready...like she told me to before her pains got s'bad. I got all the thangs ready fer four least young'uns, ya know. Daddy is the one who helped her with all o' 'um."

"Good fer ye, Marthie." Libby paused as she saw the water boiling on the wood cookstove, and then squeezed the hand she was holding. "I can't even holler 'git the water boiling!'" She laughed. "So, now what do we do?"

"Talk to me, Libby...tell me something...anything."

Still smiling, Libby said, "How much time do I have? How often are yer pains comin'?"

"They ain't too bad, yet. My back's killin' me, though." She closed her eyes for a moment, then turned her gaze back to Libby. "Wish Sterlen wuz here to play fer me...er yer Momma. They both make me feel real good when they play."

"I know, Marthie! I'll tell ye about Sterlen' s old holler log!"

"What log?"

"The log he hid his banjer in when he were'nt no more than nine er ten years old. Ye know it wuz Sterlen who taught Mommie how to play.

"Ye see, Mommie can play jest about ever instrument there ever wuz...the accordion, the piano, the organ, the juice harp, the guitar...she can even play the banjer. It wuz Sterlen who took the time to teach her. Ye see, Sterlen 'n' Mommie both loved music. They loved it better'n anythang in the world. But being as Mommie's mother didn't hold with strang music, she made no allowances fer it to be played at home.

'So's Sterlen decided he'd jest take matters into his own hands, 'n' not let Granny know. He slipped off out into the woods, 'n' found hisself a piece o' cherry wood. Then he climbed the mountain behind the cabin...way up to Horseshoe Rock so's nobody would know where he went.

"On yon side of the mountain, he found a clearing in the woods. Jest to the side of that clearing laid an old holler log. Wal, Sterlen sat hisself down on that old log 'n' commenced to whittling...'n' shaping... 'n' polishing that piece of wood.That's ho he allus tells it!

" Weren't long 'til he'd done whittled hisself out a banjer! Why, some say he went fer enough to kill a cat to git the cat's skin to made the head of that banjer!

"Lordy! what a time he had then, picking 'n' strumming that banjer. He would throw back his head 'n' let his happiness flow outta his mouth in a song. Even the birds would hush to listen!"

Libby felt Marthie tense up with a contraction. She held her hand tight until she felt it subside, then she continued with her story.

"Well, unbeknownst to Uncle Sterlen, Mommie had been follering him! She hid out in the bushes, a'watching her brother...wondering what matter of a miracle he'd done brung about. Never in her life had she seed a strang instrument afore, 'n' never in her life had she seen her brother enjoying' hisself s'much!

"'N' then one day, Sterlen jest happens to look up in the right way 'n' he sees Mommie's longing eyes hiding there in the bushes. Wal, he laughs to hisself 'n' hops down off'un that log, still picking 'n' sanging. Then he commences to dance all around that clearing in the woods, cavorting around something fierce. All the time, he's gittin' closer to Mommie. 'N' then, when he's within spitting distance of her big eyes, he stops his pickin' 'n' his sangin'...'n' he bows to the bushes, 'n' he says, 'Come on out, Ellie! I'm a'gonna learn ye how to play!'

"Talk about a happy little girl! Mommie came out dancing!

"Sterlen let Mommie sit on his log, 'n' then he learned Mommie everthang he knowed about music. Mommie would pick 'n' sang while Sterlen would dance all around that clearing in the woods. Mommie said the mountains jest rang with joy!

"Then, when Uncle Sterlen got big enough, he trapped hisself enough pelts fer a little bit o' money. One day, he came driving two mules up to the cabin, toting a pump organ on the back of the wagon, 'n' he called out to Mommie,

'Come on out, Ellie. Come see whut I done brung ye!'

"Granny shore wuz surprised at how quick Mommie learned how to play that organ! "N' sure enough, pretty soon Mommie wuz playing fer all the doing's on the mountain, even at all the revivals! 'N' that's how Mommie met Poppy!

"Poppy come to Wolf Creek Meeting House as a visitin' preacher. To Mommie he wuz the handsomest feller she had ever seen. 'N' he shore loved to hear Mommie play that organ. She even played fer their wedding. It wuz all she could do not to git up 'n' dance down the isle of that one-room church!

"Poppy 'n' Mommie had eleven children...me included! Uncle Sterlen would come to see us...'n' I kin remember how Mommie 'n' Uncle Sterlen would play fer all us young'uns! I kin remember Uncle Sterlen picking that banjer and Mommie pumping that old organ. I kin remember Mommie sangin'...seemed as if the words fastened themselves to rafters of my mind...'n' now they're dropping down...one by one. I kin hear the words...."

Libby began to sing,

"By and by...when the morning comes,
and the saints of God are gathered home,
we will tell the story, how we overcome,
And we'll understand it better by...."

Suddenly, Libby felt Marthie's fingers tightened around hers again and she moaned. This time underneath the pressure of Marthie's hand Libby experienced the contraction as if it were her own. She moaned also. "Lord, we ain't got any bys and bys...it's gonna happen right now."

Marthie caught her breath as the pain subsided. "Libby," she whispered, "sing fer me...sing fer my baby. He'd like to come into the world that way. He's Sterlen's son."

In the quiet November evening, Libby's high soprano voice once again echoed in the one-room cabin.

CHAPTER 35
Fanning the Fires of Faith

Fire popped in the fireplace, it's flames fanning the charred wood. In its flickering light, Libby held watch over Marthie, who lay sleeping now that her immediate job was complete. Beside her, wrapped in a small quilt, lay Sterlen's son. Libby had sung right up until his birth. The child had decided to arrive in the middle of the fifth verse, specifically just as Libby sang... "when the morning comes."

Libby stopped blinking back the tears that had been forming since Marthie and the baby had slipped off to sleep, and let them flow. Now that she sat alone in the dimly lit room, the red-headed woman could allow herself the luxury of totally feeling her own need, her own desires of motherhood. She didn't know how many times her dreams had been slashed...she had lost count of the miscarriages.

Lord, where are ye? Er ye listenin'?

It didn't seem fair to Libby that everyone had already birthed a child, everyone except her. Naturally, as the eldest of her siblings, she had thought she would be first in having a

child. Now, here was Cannie with two children and another
on the way. Elmina had Carroll, and Irene had Jo Ellen. Even
Thomas' wife Evie had given birth to a red-headed son,
Charlie.

Now, here was Marthie with a new son.

*Just look at him. So small and perfect. Little baby boy,
your daddy will love ye! Reckon I'm just gonna have to dou-
ble-up on my prayers.*

The longing woman stood and straightened the covers
one more time around mother and son and then stoked the
fire. She had long since cleaned the room of all birthing
evidence. Maybe she should make some corn bread or something. Sterlen should be back soon with the Granny
woman...who may also be hungry. Good! something to do.

"They...Lord a'mercy! The baby's done come." Annie
Coggins had entered like a whirlwind, then quieted herself
with the satisfaction of gazing at the pair on the bed.

"It's a boy!" Libby said, watching the expression on
Sterlen's face.

Sterlen stood as if in shock, staring at the miracle before
him. He had thought his love of Marthie had been his
greatest emotion...until she had loved him back. Now, this
wonderful feeling that consumed him could not even be
described. This son...his son...had brought him another
dimension of joy.

"Sterlen," came the soft voice of the new mother.
"Sterlen...do ye want to hold him?"

As Sterlen accepted his son, he realized that here he was
holding the future in his arms. He thought of the war, the
rationing, the lack of pelts in his traps, that he wasn't a good
farmer and that his age would never let him live to see his
own grandchildren.

The mountain man shook his head to get rid of the
bullets of thoughts that seemed to shoot through his mind.
*No...No. Let me enjoy this moment. I'll worry about
tomorrow...tomorrow.*

"Well, now," he said, smiling at Marthie, "what will we

call this brand new Galloway son o' mine?"

"I don't know yet...I can't thank.... What do ye thank?"

"Don't rightly know. We'll come up with it later." Sterlen laid the child back down on the bed beside his mother and kissed her on the check. "How er ye...er ye alright?"

"I am...yes. Tired...thank I'll sleep some...." She dozed right off.

"Want something to eat, Sterlen? Got some cornbread here, and I cooked ye up some greens." Libby waved him over to the table.

He felt suspended in time, nothing seemed real. With glazed eyes, he did as he was told.

"He's in shock!" Annie laughed and sat beside him at the table. "Just look et him...Libby, is it? Ye Jim's wife?"

Getting her nod, the Granny woman continued. "I seen it many a time, 'specially with the first born...'n' at his age." Suddenly, the quick gaze of Annie darted into Libby's. "Ye look like ye've been cryin', chile. Did the birthin' go all right?"

The quickness and swift change of conversation disarmed Libby. She had nowhere to hide, so, she simply burst into tears. "Marthie is fine," she sobbed. "It's me that needs help."

"What's the matter, chile? Maybe I kin help."

Sterlen sat quietly, totally confused, as the story unfolded in front of him. he and the granny woman heard how hard Libby had tried to have a child...about how every-one else in child bearing age had been successful...how the Lord had answered Libby's prayer about Jim and had not answered her desire to have the child she wanted. The story, laced with tears, came to an abrupt end when Annie held up her hand.

"Law, child, ye ain't praying fer the right thing." Annie took off her bonnet and reached for the greens. "Ye thank ye got it all figgered out. Howsomever, I've lived long enough to know that most of us don't know how to pray. There ye were down on your knees all those days praying fer Jim to become a preacher...that must have been His plan all along. I kin see that yer a prayer hoss." Annie patted Libby's hand. "Good fer ye! But let me give ye a lesson in how to pray."

Annie reached for the cornbread. After taking a bite of greens, followed by the cornbread, she chewed mightily, swallowed, then leveled her gaze into Libby's eyes, now dry and wide with apprehension.

"I want to tell ye a story about this great preacher by the name of Elder F.M. Jordan. He used to come 'round here all the time...he wuz a circuit-riding preacher. He come on his walking horse some times 'n' some times in a horse and buggy. He'd stay with us in our homes, nigh onto three weeks at a time. I wuz jest a young'un, but I remember."

Annie sipped her milk, glancing at the attentive Sterlen.

"He did right good fer our parts...he wuz a Baptist and started s'many churches that folks say it wuz 'cause of Preacher Jordan that our mountains has s'many Baptists.

"Well, he'd preach and holler...sometimes all day 'n' all night...and git everbody s'happy that they'd holler right along with him. When he stayed with us, I heerd him say he wished they'd holler when they had something to holler about."

Annie paused again, took another bite of greens and cornbread and chewed heartily.

"So how does this tell me how to pray?" Libby said. "My daddy taught me that sometimes the only thang we kin do is pray...'n' I been praying a powerful long time."

"Well, chile...so ye have. I jest want ye to thank on what I'm gonna say." She finished chewing and drank some more milk. Then, she wiped her mouth on the tail of her apron and leveled her gaze once again into Libby's waiting eyes.

"'Remember when I said Preacher Jordan said he wished they'd holler when they had something to holler about? I asked him about it...'n' this is what he toled me. He said that folks jest hollered sometimes when everbody else hollered. They want to have what everbody else is havin' so they do like they do. Ye git it? Ye holler fer the sake o' hollering! So yer hollerin' fer the wrong reason! Ye don't git salvation...alls ye git is a sore throat!"

"But, Annie, I'm not prayin' fer the sake o' prayin'...I'm asking fer what I truly want!" Libby's eyes filled with tears.

"Now, chile, listen...." Annie leaned over the table into Libby's space. "'Er ye prayin' fer what GOD wants fer ye?"

"Fer what...God wants fer...me?" Libby stared.

"When ye prayed fer Jim, ye wuz praying fer what God wants fer all o' us...to witness fer him. When ye prayed fer a child, ye were prayin' fer what ye want fer ye, not fer what God wants fer ye. Preacher Jordan said we must wait on the Lord...He's got a plan fer all of us. When we pray, we must pray fer His will to be done...'course we gotta tell him our druthers...but, we gotta be satisfied in waitin' on whut He wants fer us. He knows yer heart."

"Sssso, I should pray fer His will to be done," began Libby, "and then have faith that He hears my prayers. I shouldn't question if he's listenin'.."

"Ye got it! Ye gotta fan the fires o' faith, chile! Heard Preacher Jordan say that many a'time!" Annie took another bite. "Ye shore er a powerful cook...best greens I had in a passel o' Sundays!"

Sterlen watched as Libby's face began to beam. He smiled, knowing that this daughter of a circuit-riding preacher had just learned a lesson she'd somehow missed. Fact is, he seemed to have missed that lesson himself. He turned slightly so he could see his own small family better from his position. Here, in the prime of life at fifty-one years old, he had the world. He thought back to when he had been simply a mountain music man, going by way of the great outdoors from cabin to cabin with his songs and stories...sort of like a circuit-riding preacher...or like a jaybird flying from one cabin to another. He had not known true love, nor had it known him. And now...he still had a similar life, but he was no longer alone. Love made all the difference! But he'd never have had what he has now...if he had never visited the Ammons Cabin...if he had never been that jaybird!

"The Lord's been good to my family, Annie," Sterlen smiled and nodded toward his wife and son. "When folks love each other, thangs have a way of workin' out. Yer right, all we gotta do is jest fan the fires of faith!" He paused, then added, "It jest come to me...I think I'll ask Marthie if we can call our son 'Jay.'"

CHAPTER 36
Little Blue Baby

Against the side of the South Carolina hill, the weathered house seemed almost a part of its surroundings. Bright moonlight dropped, heavy and chilled, into the dead grass of February, 1945. Stillness cradled the luminance that sifted the night.

From the steps of the front porch a worn path of ruddy-red clay wound its way through crystals of frost to the edge of the highway. And there, like a lone sentinel, a young, spindly yellow poplar pushed against the post of a rusty mailbox. Even in its slender and struggling growth, the frail arms of the poplar reached protectively toward the home.

A pale ray of lamplight shone from a curtained window at one corner of the house, sending its tiny point toward the shadow of the little tree. High above, the coming of day outlined the distant mountains, slowly beginning to paint the horizon an icy blue.

It was almost day.

And then, as the moonlight paled, a soft wind spiraled

through the quiet. In the twilight between the end of night and the beginning of day, the poplar's shadow stretched, touching the beam of light. And from behind the curtains, there came the cry of a newborn.

Inside, the lamplight sputtered and flickered faintly. In his intense study of the weakened woman lying on the bed before him, the doctor ignored the waning light. He simply leaned closer to the woman.

"Miz Ammons....Miz Ammons!" he called in a husky whisper. "Are you strong enough to hear what I'm saying?"

Cannie's eyes, reddened with distress, opened and moved quickly toward the doctor's voice. "My...baby?" Fear caught at each word.

The doctor leaned closer still.

"Your son was born a blue baby...probably because of...well...it's not important...now." He sighed, then straightened.

"Blue? My baby! Is he all right?" The anxious woman tried to raise herself, straining to lift her head toward the doctor.

"He'll be fine. He's breathing normally. The bluish skin is caused by inadequate oxygenation of the blood. He'll be just fine. In fact, he's sleeping. That young girl has him out there in the kitchen." He paused, then leaned again toward the relieved woman who had fallen onto her pillow. "It's not the baby I'm worried about, Miz Ammons...it's you! It's you who's in trouble." His voice still carried a husky quality.

The young woman turned her head away from the persistent man. Her words were scarcely more than a whisper. "I'm tired, that's all. No need to worry none 'bout me. This is my fourth birthin'...I'll do all right."

"Miz Ammons, you are little more than a child yourself! And you've had trouble before with your birthings, haven't you? This one just about did you in. Are you listening to me?" The doctor once again hovered over the bed. "You simply can not allow yourself to go through this again!"

"What do ye mean?"

"You're not strong enough to come through another childbirth. You must have a hysterectomy!" His words were clear in the closeness of the small room.

"I cain't do...that," her voice cracked. "There ain't no money for that." Cold of the unknown trembled through her body.

"The government will pay for it! Your husband is fighting in the war, isn't he? That's the least his country can do for him! The government is paying for my visits already. They'll pay for the operation."

As he spoke, the doctor finally turned away from the woman. He began putting his instruments into a black bag that sat on a table near her bedside. Then, from over his shoulder drifted words that cut the heart of the woman behind him. "Think it over, Miz Ammons. I'll be back tomorrow. We can do the operation here...in this room. You won't even have to leave your home."

Cannie stared at the ceiling. She longed to go home, back to the winding trails of Wolf Mountain, to see Mommie and Poppy. The mountains, the faces crowded her mind.

Frank! When will ye...come home to me?

But then all images faded. Wolf Mountain, her parents, her husband had no realness at this moment in her life. Now, her world began and ended here...with her children. She had to be strong; she had to be able to take care of her girls and her new son. A tightness grew over her face, a tightness of determination. She would have to have the operation.

"Cannie."

The young woman turned her head on the pillow toward the quiet voice.

"Cannie...are ye awake?"

"Come on in, Lillie. Come...sit on the bed so I kin see ye good. I'm weary."

"I got the baby here, Cannie. He wants to see his momma!"

"Let me see...let me see his face." Cannie tried to smile, and struggled to pull herself farther up onto her pillow.

"Here...here he is." Lillie leaned close. "Watch now, I'm gonna lay him here in the crook o' yer arm."

As Cannie's arm tightened around the baby, she caught a movement at the door. Her tight smile holding true, the young mother looked into Lillie's face. "I think we have other visitors," she whispered.

With almost no sound, the door opened slowly and a youngster peered in at Cannie. Underneath the reddish curls, two wide eyes questioned the mother. But just as the child began to speak, she tumbled forward, pushed from behind by her younger sister. The small figures landed on the floor in front of the bed.

"Muffer, Muffer...Dars pushed me!"

"See...see, too!" Doris said eagerly.

The two children scrambled to their feet, each girl still pushing at the other, each trying to get to the bed first.

"Girls! Don't fight!" Cannie said. "Come here...be still now. Come see yer brother." She moved the baby slowly to her other arm, pulling the receiving blanket away from the tiny face so the girls could see the child.

Crowding close, the children gazed at the infant, a curious awe on their faces. The older girl, almost hesitantly raised her hand and touched the baby's face with one chubby finger. Quickly, the younger girl followed her sister's movement.

"Look, Cannie, Doris' yeller hair is almost the same color as the baby's!" Lillie said from the foot of the bed.

When Cannie didn't answer, Lillie began pushing the youngsters toward the door. "Mildred...ye and Doris must leave yer momma alone now. The baby's done tuckered her out. Corie and Lucy have gone back to bed. Go git in the bed with them. We'll let yer momma sleep."

Amid cries of disappointment, Lillie herded the girls out of the room, closing the door on the mother and her son.

In the quiet that followed, Cannie pulled the child closer and cradled her bundle against her breast. Her face softened with new-mother curiosity, she looked at her son.

He's tiny...much more so than the girls were. His hair is almost white, curling against his pink face. Look! look at his long eyelashes! One day the girls won't like it that he's got longer lashes than they do!

A warm smile grew on the tired mother's lips.

"My baby son...welcome to the world," she said aloud. "Looks like yer gonna have some dimples in these chubby cheeks. Yer lips are smooth, like the leather o' Poppy's shavin' strap. 'N' yer fingers have a good strong grip. Reckon ye won't have yer daddy's dark hair, though...yer gonna have hair like mine! I knew ye wuz gonna be a boy! I jest knew!"

Cannie's smile had grown until her countenance seemed to show no fatigue at all. She shifted the child so she could get a better look at his profile.

"David...that's what I'm gonna call ye. David Franklin...has to be Franklin after yer daddy. Son, that's yer own rightful name...David Franklin Ammons. I'm right proud o' the name. David wuz the Lord's chosen man in the Bible. When he wuz young, he fought the biggest man with just a little weapon and won! He understood the emotions of the king. He wuz good to his family. 'N' 'though he wuzn't perfect, he shore knew how to ask fer forgiveness!

"Are ye listenin, David? I want ye to hear me well. Yer a special gift to me. My girls are special, but ye...yer even more precious. Ye see, the doctor tells me that ye have to be my last child. I cain't have...any more.

"My little blue baby, yer gift to me is that I'm now complete. I have a boy so I can give yer daddy his name back. Seems there's a need fer a man to have a son, 'n' a need fer a woman to be able to give her husband that son to carry out the family name. It's been almost a year since...I lost yer brother."

Cannie's voice faltered. She swallowed...then continued, "I got the quairest feeling that the Lord has given ye all that wuz to be yer brother's, and all that's yourn too! 'N' like David in the Bible, yer gonna have to fight a big giant. Yer Daddy! He's gonna expect a lot outta ye. He'll want ye to live up the idea of them 'mean fightin' Ammons boys!'

"But son, part o' yer problem will be me...cuz, ye see, I got a lot o' love inside of me, love that I'm gonna give ye. If ye got love buried somewhere deep in yer heart, how kin ye be mean...how kin ye fight. So, baby mine, I have to teach ye how to win yer battles in other ways...I have to teach ye how to use a slingshot!"

As Cannie's voice died, the baby's eyelashes fluttered, and suddenly she was gazing into blue eyes.

"Ain't ye a pretty thang," she laughed.

Unbuttoning the top of her gown, Cannie drew the child still closer to her breast. Moments later, the struggling ended as the wet mouth found the nipple, hard with new milk.

"Oh, my baby boy," she sighed, "only hours old, 'n' what a load ye got on yer shoulders!"

Then suddenly her eyes brightened and she said, "But son, jest ye wait 'n' see, yer gonna grow up with yer daddy's instincts 'n' yer momma's staying power. Jest ye wait 'n' see, little blue baby, someday the whole family will come to depend on ye. I jest know it."

Outside, in the early morning, the sky had turned gray. Snow clouds, pushed by a northern wind, rolled across the sky. The little poplar trembled.

A mail truck came over a rise in the road, slowed, and then stopped. The rusty mailbox door squeaked open and shut. After a moment, as snowflakes began to dot the overcast earth, the truck pulled away.

CHAPTER 37

Fate Steps in and Lingers

Lillie looked at the closed door. She couldn't hear anything that was going on inside the cold room. The room had to be cold, for it was clammy cold there in the kitchen.

"Corie," she said, "why don't ye make us all somethin' ta eat. The little'uns need some soup er somethin'."

"Ye want me to cook? Ye must be sick!" Corie stared at her sister.

"I cain't do it, Corie! I gotta keep myself ready to go help the doctor if he needs me. Cannie's havin' that operation right now back there. She ain't none too good from havin' that baby already and this shore ain't gonna help none."

"All yer doin' is rangin' yer hands, Lillie!" Corie shook her head of curls and looked at Lucy, who she suddenly noticed had tears in her eyes."What's wrong, Lucy?"

"It's my sister he's cuttin' up in there!"

"Who told ye anythin' 'bout cuttin' anybody up?" Lillie

immediately demanded, casting an accusing glance at Corie.

"It wuzn't me, Lillie...I didn't' say no sech a thang!" Corie's eyes now full of concern latched themselves onto Lillie's. "He's not cuttin' her up....is he?"

"I heerd some women talkin' the other day whilst we wuz a'waitin' in the rationin' line at the store down in town," Lucy said as she stood and looked at the closed door, then back at the two Ammons girls. "They were talkin' 'bout what the doctors were doin' to young wives of the military."

"What did they say!" asked Corie, putting her hand on Lucy's arm.

"They said that there wuz no money at all fer doctor's visits since the war had gone on so long...that the only good money wuz what the government paid fer treatin' the soldiers wives." Lucy turned her wet gaze to Lillie. "They said that a lot o' women wuz gittin' cut up."

"What else did they say?" Lillie's stomach didn't feel so good.

"That's all 'bout the doctors...they started in on complainin' 'bout the government's rationin'...the er... point system 'n' not enough sugar 'n' coffee...'n' then talked 'bout some new dresses made by somebody called Door...I thank they said."

The door suddenly opened and the doctor came out. He had already donned his coat and carried his black bag.

"Mrs. Ammons will recuperate quickly. She has nothing to worry about. Just allow her some bed rest for a few days. But she must not lift any of her children for a month or two. Will you young ladies be here to help her?"

"Y-y-yes, we will," stammered Lillie quickly.

"Do you have any other family close by...an older woman of the family?"

"There's Aunt Minnie, my daddy's sister!" spoke up Lucy.

"Maybe this Aunt Minnie should be advised of Mrs. Ammons' condition. I recommend that you ask your aunt to help out." The doctor looked strongly at the young girls. "You're all children yourselves...includin' Mrs.

Ammons'...jest teenagers." He shook his head and cleared his throat. "Is your Aunt Minnie close by enough to come and visit on a regular basis?"

"She lives on the other side o' Rosman Highway," Lucy said.

"Well, Mrs. Ammons needs a lot of rest and certainly should not lift these two young girls...and then there's the baby. My goodness! What is this world coming to...kids having kids."

"Did ye cut up my sister?" The independent Lucy spat the words toward the doctor.

"Cut her up? Young lady, your sister has had a hysterectomy. She will not be having any more children...that's all. I'll be back in a week to check on her. In the meantime, get word to your Aunt Minnie. Good day." The doctor quickly opened the door and in only seconds, he was gone.

"Awwwwwww!" Lucy almost screamed. "I could kill him!"

Lillie grabbed hold of Lucy's arm and then Corie's arm. "Let's go check on Cannie. Come on."

The girls tiptoed into the room, shadowed by the two small daughters of Cannie, also on tiptoe.

Through a shaft of light from the window, they observed the matted red hair of Cannie on the pillow. This mother of three had once been the most beautiful eligible girl on Wolf Mountain. At one time the courting boy Frank had sung to her..."*Five foot, two...eyes of blue...but oh, what those five foot can do...has anybody seen my gal.*"

Now, far away from home, she had just received a hysterectomy in the back room of a small four-room shack, without a husband near, attended only by three teenage girls.

"H-h-ey...," came a weak voice, "come...over...here."

The girls rushed to comply.

"Cannie, ye all right?" they said together.

"I...I'm weak as a wet dishrag," she said.

"That doctor wants us to go git yer Aunt Minnie to help

ye git better," said Lillie.

"No...don't do that," said Cannie as she moved slightly, adjusting her pillow. "She's got a big family of her own. We don't need to go botherin' nobody. I'll be up 'n' a'bout in no time."

"We...all o' us...will keer fer ye, Cannie," said Lillie with Corie and Lucy echoing the same sentiment. Mildred and Doris, the children below the girls, somehow knew to be silent and still. They stood, holding hands, simply listening.

"Couldn't ask...fer better keer," smiled Cannie as she closed her eyes. "Bring me...my baby," came her last words before drifting off to sleep.

"We can't bring her the baby...she's asleep." Corie looked at Lillie.

"Oh, come on...when she wakes up, she means," Lillie said as she herded them all out o the room. "Corie, why don't ye and Lucy start dinner, er...supper now, while I change the baby's diaper. Okay?"

Suddenly, there came a knock at the door.

The girls looked at each other in surprise, then rushed to look out of the window. Outside, near the road a taxicab was just turning onto the highway. They couldn't see who was at the door. Quickly, they all ran to the door, just as the knock sounded again.

The girls righted themselves, as if answering the door was no great thing.

And then, when Lillie turned the doorknob and opened the door, there stood Ray.

"Ohhh," she said and couldn't believe what she saw.

"Howdy, girls," said the grinning Ray, dressed in the garb of the US Army. "I've been in the Army fer a month now. I come on my first leave...thought I'd stop by and see my favorite girls in all the world."

The excited Lucy and Corie promptly threw their arms about him while Lillie simply stared in shock. When the least little girls decided they didn't want to be left out, they grabbed his legs.

"Well now, although I like this a lot, I can't move if'n ye

don't let go." The grinning GI gently removed the arms from around his legs and came in. As he shut the door, he asked, "Where's Cannie?"

While Corie and Lucy proceeded to tell him of all the happenings of the last few months, Lillie watched from a distance. Taking it upon herself to check on the baby and then to begin supper, Lillie kept herself busy and just a little detached from the group.

When supper was ready, Lillie called, "Mildred, ye git Doris 'n' come and set the table. The dishes are on the table already."

The children scurried around under her feet, climbed up on the chairs and finally had the table ready for their meal.

All this time Ray's gaze had barely left the dark-haired Lillie as she worked. The grin had been replaced with concern for his sister who lay abed and with this lack of conversation from Lillie.

As they all set down for supper, Ray suddenly changed the subject. "Did yawl know that Marthie and Sterlen had a baby boy...Jay, he's called...born in November."

Lillie's joy automatically fell out on the table. "A boy! That's wonderful. Corie, ye hear! Marthie's had her son. I bet they're happy." Lillie fell to eating her supper, finally smiling at Ray.

Not knowing how he had achieved it, Ray felt the rush of accomplishment received from the look on Lillie's face. The ice had been broken and now he could talk to her about what he had actually came for...after everyone had gone to bed and they were alone. He could hardly control his need to touch her, to look in her eyes. Never had he wanted anything more. But, he must wait until the time was right.

With supper completed, the girls cleaned the kitchen while Ray ventured in to visit with Cannie. After Lillie brought David into Cannie, she bathed Mildred and Doris, then dressed them for bed, helped them hug their mother, and put them between the sheets side by side in the back room.

When she left the room, the girls had already cuddled up...back to back...almost asleep.

With the evening too cold to sit on the porch, the young group gathered in the kitchen once more, bringing out their guitars. For hours, the trio of pickers played and sang. They sang old songs of the mountains, hymns that spoke of faith, of keeping on, of going home again.

"I've written my first song," said Ray to the awe-filled eyes of the girls. "I had to write it cuz I miss home so much. Listen...I'm gonna sing it fer ye. I named it *"Blue Ridge Mountains Call Fer Me."*

"There's a touch of gold--in the Carolina sun
Laurel buds unfold--where the Tuckaseigee runs
How I long to flee--to the childhood days of yore

Blue Ridge Mountains call for me--to return once more

"I can hear the lonesome tone--whispered by the breeze
I can see my cabin home--shadowed by the trees
Through the days of distant past--I can never more
 restore.
I will always hope at last--to return once more

"Songs of whippoorwills-- that I heard so long ago
Echo in the hills--where the Tuckaseigee flows
How I long to flee--to those blessed days of yore
Blue Ridge Mountains call for me--to return once more

"Honeysuckle fills the air-- with its fragrant smell
Misty mountains tall and fair--cast a magic spell
Blessed days of memory--time no long can restore
Blue Ridge Mountains call for me--to return once more."

The song, with its poignant words and rhythm, filled the hearts of those listening.

"Oh, Ray....ye've said it all," said Lillie, as the other girls nodded.

Smiling,, Ray suddenly stood up and laid his guitar down on the table. "Girls," he said, "it's past my bedtime...yourn, too. I want ta talk to Lillie a little."

"Kin we listen, too," said Corie, raising her eyebrows at Lillie.

 Lucy giggled.

"No," said Ray, pulling her hair, "ye can't. This is my time with her."

Lillie, already slightly red, turned another hot look on her sister and nodded toward the bedroom where the little girls slept. "I'll be in a bit, Corie...Lucy...go on with ye."

After everyone had been settled as to who was going where, Lucy stuck her head out of the bedroom door and called, "Ray, yer going to spend the night, ain't ye? Yer gonna sleep on the couch?"

"I'm not goin' till mornin', " he laughed, motioning for Lillie to sit beside him on the couch. "Go on to sleep, Lucy," he said.

"Ray," called Lucy again.

"What is it?" he answered, now almost impatiently.

"Are ye gonna be a doctor now?"

"I'm gonna be a medic in the Army...that's sorta like a doctor. But, I'll be helpin' in the field...the battlefield."

"Oh." Lucy swallowed the rest of her thought, and slowly closed the door.

"Ray, are ye...goin' to...war?" Lillie's words dripped with sudden unspoken fear.

"I'm in trainin'. If the war ain't over soon, I guess I will go. Don't rightly know."

"I'm afraid to even thank what could happen to ye out there in the...battlefield."

"Before I left, I had to come see ye, Lillie. We've been writin' all these years. I know ye've more'n likely seen other boys...but I want to git one thing straight before I go! I haveta tell ye how I feel about ye."

"Well, I'm a'waitin'."

Ray took her hands and squared up his gaze with hers and his intention to speak his mind. "Ever since I laid eyes on ye, up there at the Golden Place...I've loved ye. Can't nobody else come near my feelin' fer ye. It wuz love et first sight."

With Ray's directness, Lillie's heart had stopped, she was sure of it. She could hardly breathe. But then, she gasped and the air came rushing out. "Ray! at first sight! Why, I wuz sech a ragged thang! I wuz so ashamed of how I looked. I remember it like it wuz yesterday!"

"Didn't ye hear me, Lillie! I love ye!"

"I did, Ray Owen...I heerd ye. I love ye, too! Y-you and yer brown suits!"

Ray couldn't hold back any longer. His arms went

around her and almost crushed her to his breast. "Oww," moaned Lillie. "yer uniform hurts when ye hold me so tight."

The red-headed man with the brown freckles pulled back to smile crookedly at Lillie. "Ye love me, do ye! I knew it! I jest knew it!"

With her face suddenly filled with indignation, the dark-headed girl tried to pull away. "Ye knew it...what makes ye thank ye knowed so much!"

"Ye had to love me...cuz I love ye s'much it hurt. I tried to tell ye in everthang I ever did, but I wuz too backward." Suddenly the young man became still. "Now, I'm gonna leave not knowin' if I'll git back anytime soon. I want to take keer o' ye the rest o' my life...'n' I wanted ye to know it. Ye had to love me back...ye jest had to."

"Well...I been meanin' to tell ye to yer face that I liked ye back...ever since ye sent me that poem."

"Will ye...," Ray paused and looked directly into her eyes, "will ye marry me?"

Lillie hesitated.

Ray's expression began to show worry when she didn't answer right away.

"Ye know, it's our fate, Ray. Your sister, Libby, met and married my brother Jim. Then, 'cause o' that, Cannie met and married my other brother Frank. Then yer Uncle Sterlen met 'n' married my sister Marthie.

"Now, Libby's and Cannie's brother is asking me ta marry him. It's fate! Ye see, we're really part of a bigger thang. So, Ray...I will marry ye...yes, I reckon, I will. "

And for the first time in their courtship, Ray Owen leaned over, tilted her head toward him and kissed the upturned lips of Lillie Ammons, the girl he loved and would always love.

CHAPTER 38
Jack Tarr Poinsett Hotel

Three years, eight months, and 22 days after Japan bombed Pearl Harbor, World War II ended—September 2, 1945.

And yet, Ray would still be sent to help with medical operations at home and abroad. So, before his duties started in earnest, Ray and Lillie were married in Pickens, South Carolina at the home of a local Justice of the Peace on January 13, 1946.

Ray had it all planned. After the marriage he would take his young bride to the fancy Jack Tarr Poinsett Hotel in downtown Greenville, South Carolina. While in boot camp, he had heard of its grandeur and wanted to impress his little mountain girl.

Lillie, very nervous already, did not know if she liked the idea. She had never been that far away from home in her life, and suddenly, here she was not yet eighteen years old and married to someone who had changed from being her friend to her...husband. Everything was happening so fast.

"But, Lillie," Cannie had said that morning before they left, "things happen quickly onct yer growed. Why, I wuz only fifteen when I married yer brother. Now, here I am just turned twenty on January 1st, 'n' got three young'uns. Lord a'mercy! All I'm hopin' fer now is that Frank will come home soon, now that the war's over."

"Lillie!" Ray was saying. "They've done put us on the 12th floor. Thank goodness they got this thang called an elevator. We git to ride on it up to our room." He picked up the only suitcase they had, working his fingers around the rope that had held it together. "Ye take the guitar case, Lillie...I got this."

They passed an entrance to a dining room. The two of them peeked in and saw a black lady with a bandanna over her head serving what looked like pudding to the customers. What grace and style she had, even smiling at them when she saw them looking.

Quickly going on to the elevator, Ray caught Lillie's hand with his and grinned in his excitement of the day. All Lillie wanted to do was shrink into a dandelion puff and float away from it all.

The elevator took her breath away, and stirred up her heart.

Lord, don't leave me now!

Their room had a window that looked out over the town. Evening had arrived and there were lights all over the horizon, some bright and some soft and faint.

Mommie! I like it on the mountain. Ain't no light at all except the fireflies outside and the lamp inside. I don't like this place. What am I doin' here?

Lillie watched her new husband put the suitcase on the bed. He hurried around doing what she should have been doing. But, he seemed to like 'doing' for her. No one had ever done that before.

Now, what wuz that...that Mommie had said...don't worry, jest lay down and let him do what he wants...'n' soon ye baby will come. Is that all there is to this? Lord, I'm skeered. If I knew my way home, I thank I'd go right now!

Her fingers had glued themselves to the guitar case...the only thing separating her from the unknown.

Ray had finished scurrying about and turned to look directly into her eyes, as he had a disarming way of doing. "Why don't ye set down over yonder in that chair. I'll take the guitar and pick a few tunes fer my new wife!" He grinned openly at her.

"Here," she said and pried her fingers loose so she could hand him the case. *Thank God he didn't say set on the bed!* She almost ran to the chair and plastered her back tightly against the cushion.

And so, the red-headed mountain boy played and played to his dark-headed sweetheart.

"Lillie," he said, resting his hand on the strings of the guitar after playing *'John Henry, the Railroading Man.'* "What wuz that story ye told me 'bout yer uncle who worked on the train?"

"Ye...ye mean my uncle Jim Ammons? My daddy's brother next to him?"

"Yep...tell me that story agin."

"Well, he wuz an engineer, ye know, 'n' used to come to Sylvie to see my daddy ever onct in a while. We'd wait fer him under that big ole tree on Main Street. We'd see the smoke comin' from a far piece...'n' walk down to the station. There he'd come...a' dancin' across the cars as they come rumblin' down the track! Whatta sight to see! He always brought me a huge sack of chocolate candy, 'n' he'd tell my daddy...'Tom, ye got a pretty girl here...she looks jest like our momma!'"

Some of the tension had gone out of her face as she remembered and told her story. Ray smiled again.

"'N' Ray, I fergot to tell ye," she continued, "that when he retired, he got a gold watch. He gave it to Daddy." She pondered on the statement for a moment. "Now, what I remember 'bout Daddy's oldest brother Clum wuz a different story."

"Why? what do ye mean?"

"He wuz the first person I ever seen who had false teeth!" Lillie giggled. "I remember how he swept his hand over his mouth, took his teeth out 'n' grinned at us, then his hand would go back over his mouth and the teeth would be back! It wuz the funniest thang I ever did see."

Ray ran his pick over the guitar strings and sang, *"All I want fer Christmas is my two front teeth!"*

More laughter!

"What 'bout the time President Roosevelt came to Sylvie...do ye remember that, Ray," said Lillie.

"Yeah, I do. All the people wanted to see him, so they climbed all over the buildings and stood on the rooftops, hung out of windows and shinnied up the light poles. Ain't nobody more important than that ever had come afore. I thank I wuz eight years old...but that wuz one man Daddy wanted to see...so, we come down off Wolf Mountain fer that!" Ray played and sang *"He'll be comin' around the Mountains when he comes,"* and they both laughed once more.

"Say, remember, Lillie...the flood of 1940!" He had stopped playing and began to draw her words out again. "What happened up on yer mountain?"

"Lor-r-r-dy! did it rain! It rained and rained and rained. It wuz somewhere near the end o' August, and all our corn fields wuz covered up. We didn't save nary a thang. The house wuz high enough up that it didn't git in the door, but the water got so high in the surrounding fields that Bryson had to swim across the back yard to git to the Connor house near the spring. The springhouse had washed away when it wuz all over with...'n' some o' the livestock wuz never seen agin."

"I recollect that the Post Office at Tuckasegee wuz washed away, along with all the records!" Ray hit his guitar strings to keep the momentum going.

"Yeah! 'n' Dock Moses' store wuz picked up by the waters comin' down the Tuckasegee and floated on down the river with his lamp still lit and lightin' up the room as it bobbed on by!"

The two young people began to laugh again at the thought of the store riding along on the river. Then, Ray cleared his throat and began to play again. This time he sang the words directly to his wife...*"I love ye truly...truly, dear."*

By this time, with the stories and the laughter, Lillie felt as if she had her friend back...and she relaxed, smiling as she listened.

That night as she lay contentedly alongside her friend, her husband, she thought of what her mother had said.

Hummmm...I wonder if it's gonna be a girl er a boy....

It took longer than she had been told or had expected. Well over a year and a half of laughter later, almost a year after Marthie gave birth to Sterlen's second son, Steve, a curly-headed Linda Elaine Owen arrived in the month of September, 1947. And everyone wondered why she smiled and laughed all the time.

CHAPTER 39

The Birch Bark Bowl and a Pennyroyal Turnaround

A very pregnant Marthie leaned against the porch rail, set her sack in a straight-back chair, and called loudly, "Libby, er ye about?"

Libby slowly materialized in the shadows just beyond the screen door of her home, her countenance haggard and dark. "I'm...here," she said.

"I heerd ye been sick, so I come to see if'n I kin do anythang fer ye." Marthie could hardly believe that the woman she was looking at was the same Libby she knew. "Lord, Libby...ye ain't nothin' but skin 'n' bones! What's a'ailin' ye?"

"Among other thangs, Marthie. I come down with the croup in the winter, 'n' I can't seem to come back frum it. I been throwin' up somethin' like bile...my stomach ain't none too settled...but come on in the house. I need somethin' to take my mind off'n my ailments."

Marthie gingerly removed herself from the railing, breathed deeply and picked up her sack. After a moment, she moved on across the porch and into the house.

"What er ye a'doin', Marthie, walkin' over here when yer so far along with this baby? Uncle Sterlen got the other boys with him?"

Marthie decided that a straight-back chair would be the best chair to choose. In her condition, she needed to have something solid and sturdy to sit on to help with the maneuvering.

"Sterlen's got them boys sure enough, Libby. I don't know what I'd do without him." Finally settled, Marthie set her sack on her large stomach and continued, "He helped me put together this little sack fer ye."

Libby's sunken eyes flickered as her expression registered warmth at this thoughtfulness. "Ye want fer me to make us some coffee?"

Marthie pulled a nearby table closer, set out a large birch bark bowl, and then hesitated, making eye contact with Libby. "I thank ye, but no...I thank not. Goes right on through me these days. Come...jest sit a spell, Libby...don't stand over there where I kin hardly see yore eyes. Sit here so I kin tell ye the story o' my bowl."

Libby did as she was told, the thought coming to her from nowhere that Marthie had begun looking for the world like her mother Retter...same piercing eyes...same directness, too.

"Look et this, Marthie...look at this bowl. It's been a few years ago now, but Sterlen made it fer me out of birch bark that Jim got fer him from off Tanasee Camp Creek. It wuz to be a surprise fer me...'n' et first, I paid no mind as to what he wuz a'doin'. When he thought I noticed, he'd quit 'n' pretend to do somethin' else. That's when I really begun to pay attention...thought he wuz a'sneakin' one on me, he did! Without him a'knowin' it, I watched him out there by the washpot, jest a scrapin' away."

Marthie paused as she smoothed the bound rim of the bowl with her fingertips. "He put the birch bark in the washpot and soaked it in hot water so he could shape it without breaking it. I knew what he wuz doin', fer I'd seen Daddy do it many a'time. I noticed he put some slit willow and some spruce roots in the water, too, 'n' then I wondered what he wuz gonna do with them. My curiosity wuz a'risin'!

"Ye know, Libby, mountain folk haveta to make do with jest 'bout anythang, a doin' and a'learnin' at the same time. They learned the hard way that it jest takes time 'n' patience.

"Lord, he worked and worked on this bowl...jest kept on reshapin' till it suited him. Then he scored the rim with his huntin' knife, 'n' cut holes jest below the rim. I watched him put that slit willow around the rim and lace the spruce roots over and 'round, binding it all in place. He wuz so into his work, I even slipped up on him 'n' watched from behind, 'n' he never knew."

Marthie's eyes were damp now. Libby waited, intent on where the story was headed.

"Ye know, Libby, I had been s'hurt...s'hurt that a part of me had died. But watching this man put so much into this simple bowl, and knowin' it wuz fer me...did somethin' to me. I kin hardly explain it...fer with ever twist o' that root binding that bowl together, I felt the pain...lettin' go."

The woman's dark eyes swam as she gazed at her sister-in-law. "Ye'd thank it would take some big thang to break up 'n' scatter the kind o' pain I'd gone through. Instead...it wuz this birch bark bowl that done it." Marthie wiped her tears with the back of her hand. "That's how special this bowl is! Sterlen wuz makin' it fer my birthday.

"When he gave it to me, he said, 'Marthie, I made this fer ye...cuz yo're like this bowl...tuff 'n' strong, made o' all natural thangs, 'n' like the bowl, ye hold all my world. Yer my Marthie.'"

Marthie picked up the bowl as she spoke, brought it to her breast and smiled through her tears...gazing at Libby.

"Libby, today is my birthday agin...April 5, 1948. I'm thirty years old, 'n' I come to share my birthday with ye."

"Oh, Marthie!" Libby's smile spread wide.

And then, Marthie pulled out a bouquet of violets from her sack and laid them in the bowl. "Happy birthday to me!" she sang, and laughed out loud.

"I ain't the same woman I wuz, Libby...fer I have Sterlen

who really loves me...fer me...no other reason...jest me. I got two boys...'n' another right here." She patted her stomach. "He's due this month...soon."

Libby stood and wrapped her arms around the shoulders of this woman who had at one time scared her just by looking at her.

"I'm s'proud fer ye...what a gift ye've brought me today. I can't say how glad I am." After a moment, Libby backed away and for the first time that day, smiled broadly at Marthie.

"I may have a present fer ye, too, on this ye thirtieth birthday!" Libby said, her hands on her hips.

"Ye do? What?"

Libby's lips trembled suddenly and she swallowed. "Of all the people 'round me, ye've understood the most jest how much I craved a child. Well, Marthie, I'm with child agin...that's one o' the reasons I'm s'sick."

"Praise the Lord!" sang Marthie as she slapped her hands together. "Happy birthday to me!"

"I know whatever happens is the will o' the Lord...but, I'm still prayin'...down on my knees. I'm sick as a dawg, but, I'm a'prayin'!"

Suddenly, Marthie brought her hands together and gazed at Libby over her fingertips.

"Oh...I fergot, Libby. Sterlen sent ye some Pennyroyal leaves to make ye some tea. He says whatever is wrong with ye, Pennyroyal leaves is jest the thang to smooth ye out 'n' give ye a new turnaround...that's what he said...a Pennyroyal turnaround! 'N' he said to give ye a double dose!"

CHAPTER 40
A Double Dose

L ibby looked outside at the snow. This Christmas had
been like no other she had ever seen...or hoped to see
again. The pain in her back and feet had gotten so
sharp that there had been no way she could cook, hang deco-
rations, do anything for the season. She grimaced and tried
to change positions on the bed. This having a child was not
all she had imagined. Her prayers had finally been answered,
and in a big way. This baby was one huge child, and during
the last month, she had not been able to get around much at
all.

"Lord, I'm s'sick I kin hardly stand it! I know I asked
fer this, but...now, at this very minute...I'm not s'sure I
wuzn't addled in the head."

Marthie had been here helping to cook and take care of
her, even though Sterlen had finally decided to get his own
place down near Wolf Creek Lake. Even with her three boys
to care for, Marthie had still come at least once or twice a
week, more this past month, as Libby had seemed to fall
apart with the heavy burden on her legs and back.

"Not to worry," Marthie had told her when she had protested, "I'm gonna take keer o' ye." She had patted her feet with a strange look on her face,

Again, she looked out at the new snow that had fallen this Christmas morning. Jim had long since been up and about, taking care of the lifestock and chopping wood. She could hear the sound of his axe.

Absently, she had realized a nagging dull pain that kept causing her to readjust her position as she sat gazing outside. The sun's rays seemed to be caressing the snow, brushing it until it was beginning to shine like new money. Crack! went the axe!

Awwwww! What on earth was that!

A sharp pain had hit her back with the sound of Jim's axe hitting wood.

No...it cain't be. It's not time yet...I got a week er two...don't I?

She had to go! Where was that bedpan?

When Jim came in a while later, he found his wife wet with perspiration and moaning, "It's time...it's time, oh God, it's time."

"They...Lord a'mercy! The baby! But, it's Christmas!"

"Christmas! Fergit Christmas! Send...fer...the granny woman, Jim! Send fer...Mommie. Send fer...Marthie! Send fer somebody! I'm a'dyin'...God, I'm a'dyin'!"

"I...I...I'll run over to yer mother's 'n' git Talmadge er Cecil to go git the granny woman. Yer momma had said that we should go git Gertie Shelton over to Rosman to come help ye when it wuz yore time. Then, I'll come back 'n' wait with ye. I don't want to go off 'n' leave ye, Libby! Ye cain't hardly move, ye're s'big with this young'un."

Jim paced up and down, wringing his hands as he planned out loud.

"GO ON then, Jim! GIT ON WITH IT!" The frightened woman wanted to push him, to somehow get him to understand her desperation. She'd delivered babies herself, but somehow she knew this one was going to be out of the ordinary. It had come to her...something her daddy had said long ago..."When the Lord stalls on answerin' prayers, look out when he finally hears 'um!'"

Without another word, Jim ran from the house, hit the deep snow with his long legs, and, to Libby, looked like a grasshopper going across the fields toward the senior Owen's cabin. If she hadn't been in so much pain, she'd have laughed.

Talmadge left, going down the mountain to find a neighbor who had a vehicle. In this snow and ice, it would take a while to get to Rosman and bring back Gertie. Mommie came over as quickly as she could, traveling through the snow in the trail Jim had left coming and going. Cecil had been sent to get Marthie.

All they could do now was wait. In the sudden seriousness of the moment, the clock sitting on the old organ struck twelve times.

Twelve hours later, the clock struck again. Marthie and Mommie looked at each other. They had prepared all they could prepare. Gertie had not arrived. Every once in a while, Libby interrupted the quiet with a series of moans and gritting sounds that made the hairs stand up on all their necks.

Outside, a new moon had broken from behind the heavy dark clouds, it's beams covering the glazed snow with a glistening blanket of diamonds. As Jim walked to the window to once again check if anyone was coming, Marthie slowed him with a hand on his sleeve.

"Be keerful, Jim...ye don't want to look et a new moon fer the first time through the trees...it's bad luck. Look at it over yer left shoulder. We don't need any bad luck here tonight."

Jim did as he was told, but saw no one. His face had taken on an ashen countenance. "Miz Owen, ain't they anythang we kin do...this waitin' is awful."

"Jest keep on a'prayin'...cain't quit now! The Lord

works in mysterious ways."

"It's been over twelve hours! She's plum wore out!"

As they turned their gazes back toward the bed, there came a shout from outside.

Jim quickly flung open the door, and two figures loomed up in front of the cabin.

"Made it, Jim! Had to walk the last mile er two up the mountain, but I brung her!" Talmadge tramped up onto the porch. His red hair gleamed in the light from the kerosene oil lamp shining through the doorway. "Did we make it in time?" He helped a middle-aged woman up the rock steps.

"Come on in, Gertie. Talmadge, ye stay out there; it's too tight in here. Close the door," said Mommie. "The baby ain't come yet...it's got to be soon, though. Thank ye fer comin', Gertie...fer walkin' s'far. We're beholdin'."

"Ye'd do the same! Now, let me see Libby. Good Lord...she's big!"

Gertie looked around at the semi-circle of faces. "Yawl, jest move away...give me room, here...go on in the other room. Shut the door behind ye. I best check out the sit-che-ation!" The heavy-set woman rolled up her sleeves and began to pull down the covers from the woman who had been trying to control her sounds of pain. "That's all right, honey. I'm here, now. Ye go ahead 'n' yell! Let's have this baby!"

Just after four o'clock in the morning, the screams of Libby filled the cabin, shot out through the cracks in the sawmill boards of the walls and slid across the crystallized snow. Chills ran up and down Jim's spine, and he moaned, "Oh, my Lord...Oh, my Lord...help her." He dropped his head onto his Bible which lay open on the kitchen table before him.

Silence...then the screams again, louder and more intense. Gertie's voice could be heard, coaching, soothing, singing. Then, there came the cry of a new born.

Everyone looked at each other, smiles quickly replacing the concern.

Then...there came another scream, not quite as loud, but it was a scream. But then, in a moment, the child cried again, and almost as one, they sighed.

"This havin' a baby is killin' me," moaned Jim.

"You! Killin' you?" Marthie said, "Fer a moment there, I thought my big brother wuz thankin' he had gone through the pain o' pushin' out his own child. Ye weren't thankin' that, wuz ye?"

Before Jim could answer, the door opened and all eyes turned toward Gertie and she came through the door, carrying not one bundle, but a bundle in each arm.

"Congratulations, Jim Ammons! Ye got two big healthy sons! Yer wife jest made up fer lost time."

Later, as Libby lay holding a twin in each arm, the pain of child birth already dimming in her eyes, Marthie experienced a feeling such as she'd never had before. Jim stood by the bedstead, looking down at his family. Marthie had listened to their conversation...the naming of the boys...James and Joseph, good names from the Bible...and seen clearly how powerful unconditional prayer could be when wrapped in faith.

Lord, this is more than an answer to prayer. What wuz it Sterlen called it...a double dose!

Sterlen. She should get home. Turning, the suddenly anxious woman walked to the window. Snow. Snow and ice. Everywhere. And look, the snow had begun again.

Listen...that's the wind...it's beginning to blow. It's getting deeper out there.

How would she ever get home? Home to Sterlen, to the boys.

Funny how we both, Libby and me, have all boys.

She blinked back sudden tears at the thought of what they had been through, alone and together. If it hadn't been for Sterlen....

I...I gotta git home!

Desperation filled her. She looked around for her coat. Finding it underneath the others piled on top, she quickly donned it and touching Mrs. Owen's arm, she told her that she was going home.

"Now, Marthie, don't ye want to wait till daybreak. I'll git Cecil or Talmadge to walk ye back."

"No...I gotta go on home. I kin do this...I've done it all my life." And the willful woman slipped out of the door,

The edge of the house protected the porch somewhat. Tying her scarf more closely, Marthie buttoned her heavy coat tightly against it and her chin, and stepped out into a blast of wind that almost took her off her feet. Marthie turned her head against it, squared her shoulders, and headed off down the lane, past Mrs. Owen's cabin, on through the lane to the dirt road that led down the mountain toward Wolf Creek.

She'd walked this road many a day, yet tonight she now knew she had stepped out into an unknown challenge.

Snow and wind swirled around her. There were no lights...she couldn't see. She couldn't see anything except snow and more snow. It came around her like sheets of sleet...like blue fire! Her legs were numb now. Cold...she was cold! Sterlen! Sterlen! It's...a...blizzard....

Sterlen! Where are ye?

CHAPTER 41

My Mountain Music Man—The Blizzard of 1960

"**S**TERLEN! I NEED ye!" the cry tore from her throat. The grief-stricken woman suddenly awoke to the room with the dying embers. From her crouch in the corner, her glassy eyes swept the room with a gaze hot with need. He had to be there!

One by one, she took in all four quilt-covered forms in the room now bare of all furniture. They were huddled together—Jay, Steve, and Robert. Who...was the fourth?

Ellavee. It's our youngest daughter, Ellavee.

She blinked. In her mind, she had been back in the blizzard of 1948, coming from Libby and Jim's house...going home to Sterlen. She remembered...that somehow, he had known to come for her. He had found her there in the snow.

Oh, my Sterlen, always saving me.

She could see his face, feel his hands, his arms as he had rubbed her body there in the blizzard to warm her before bringing her home. She remembered his words; they coated her like sweet honey.

"Marthie, listen to me. Stay calm 'n' listen. Ye must survive...keep yer eyes on me. Follow me...follow me even though ye can't see beyond. I'll lead ye home. Follow my back."

Sterlen, I cain't see yer back!

And then, suddenly, the truth of now...the blizzard of 1960...came twisting through her mind like a black snake.

Sterlen had been cutting wood fer the fireplace...more and more wood...fer the blizzard had choked their cove with foot after foot of snow. The chickens had gathered underneath the house to be near the warmth of the floor boards and the rock of the chimney, and had died there, frozen like Wolf Creek Lake had frozen so hard a man could walk overtop it.

Cold. Wind. Snow.

Marthie watched as Sterlen's chest heaved with every swing of the axe. The wind took the cold down into his chest. Marthie had told him; she had said that he should come inside...but there was no wood unless he cut it. Stubbornly, he refused to allow the boys to help him. He would take care of his family...until he could no longer raise his arms. Then, and only then, would he come inside.

He lay there, breathing so hard, so rough that it shook the bed. After awhile, he grew quiet, and then, he had laid that way for three days. She had waited beside him, listening to the sound of the wind off the lake howl around the house, thinking about all the ups and downs they had experienced together, about all the places they had lived, going from Wolf Mountain around to John's Creek to live near the Queens, and then coming back again here...to Wolf Creek.

The roof creaked from the weight of the snow, while the darkness of it edged up, covering the window panes. Light in the room grew dimmer.

The wood Sterlen had cut slowly began to dwindle. Marthie refused to let any of her children outside the door. They began to burn the furniture.

Then, that very morning, Sterlen had opened his eyes, smiled at her and said, "Ye know I play the banjo. Would ye like me to play fer ye?"

She cried and smiled at the same time, "Oh, yes, please play fer me, my sweet mountain music man."

"I will...jest...as...soon...as...I wake up."

But he didn't wake up; he would never wake up again. He lay on the bed in the back room, still near, yet so far.

Sterlen, I cain't see yer back! What will I do?

Hearing no answer, the completely devastated woman balled herself up on the cold floor and cried and cried and cried until she could cry no longer.

"Momma," said Jay. "It's quit snowing. Kin we try to shovel out."

"Shovel...out...? Yes, shovel out."

When Jay opened the door, he found the snow packed almost to the top of the opening. He grabbed the ash bucket and began to shovel, putting the snow inside the cabin.

"Find anythin' ye kin use to dig with, boys." Jay called to his brothers. "We gotta git out...so we kin see if we kin go git help."

Marthie pulled herself up, swallowed, got herself a plate and with a passion drawn from years of survival, began to cut into the heavy softness of the belly of the storm.

After about a half hour, suddenly a sheath of sunshine lanced its way into the room. The children let up a yell, and dug faster.

Once they were able to get through, they found the world covered in about six feet of snow, with eight-foot drifts against the cabin.

Finally, the five of them stood outside. Marthie called her children over to her, and they stood in the sunshine, arms wrapped around each other like morning glories.

"Ma...ye know Pa's...." said Jay softly beside her. She

could hear the pain in his voice and feel it in the arms of the others.

"Yer pa has gone on, young'uns...to wait fer us on the other side," said Marthie, her eyes dry and sore.

"What will we do? It's plain nobody kin git up here...'n' we sure cain't go anywhere until the snow melts down some. Jest look over yonder at the ice cycles hanging from the banks...gotta be ice all over the road."

"We will move yer Pa, Jay. We'll put him somewhere safe till we can give him the respect and dignity he deserves in a buryin'. We'll hunt fer our food, so we won't starve. We might even have some o' them frozen chickens under the house. We'll find us some wood to burn. We'll go on like yer pa would have wanted. We will survive. So let's git busy."

As the children scurried off, Marthie saw a round handle sticking in the snow near the door. She scraped away the snow until she could pull out the broom Sterlen had just finished making for her. She studied it closely, once again seeing the craftsmanship that had made her birch bark bowl.

Oh, my mountain man...thank ye. Ye gave me life by giving me back myself.

She turned the broom handle upside down and placed it on the ground beside her, holding it like a staff. With the other hand on her hip, she planted her feet firmly on the ground in front of her cabin and looked out over Wolf Creek Lake.

After a moment, she spoke into the gold-red sunset, "I've had the bad and I've had the good. I survived it all." She paused, then continued. "And Lord, have I been loved! So bring it on...'n' follow my back!"

The story of Sterlen C. Galloway, the man who represents the many gentle-hearted music men of the mountains, came about as a result of the encouragement and support of Phillip A. Scopelite, Amy's husband who passed away on June 14, 1995.

RECORD of LINEAGE

The following pages contain the major lineage of my family—Owen, Galloway, Ammons, Bryson, Coggins. Most of the research has been done by my cousin Michael Owen of Honea Path, SC. Another cousin, Denton E. Higdon of Franklin,NC has also furnished some information. More information has been gleaned from *Journeys Through Jackson,* the official journal of the Jackson County Genealogical Society, Inc.

The historical notes listed in the Bryson lineage were reported by John Parris in his column *Roaming the Mountains* published in the Asheville Citizen Times in years past.

We believe these facts to be true, but some dates may vary, according to the facts posted in the many different genealogy records.

Other significant names found in the family line: Allen, Blaine, Bracken, Braxton, Countryman, Dawson, Devendorf, Frady, Glazener, Grant, Hargrave, Henderson, Higdon, Holmes, Hooper, McCall, Mathews, Mason, Mathis, Parker, Poston, Sebrell, Shelton, Young.

—Amy Ammons Garza

OWEN LINEAGE

1. William Owen, b. 1568 in Wales, d. 1641,
   Wales; m. ?
Their children:
 --2. William Owen* (see below.)**
--2. David Owen
--2. Walter Owen

2. William Owen, b. 1584, Machynlleth, Powys, Wales,
   d. 1674, Machynlleth, Powys, Wales,
   m. Ann Strator, b. ? d. ?
Their child:
--3. Thomas Owen* (see below.)**

3. Thomas Owen, b. 1667, Machynlleth, Powys, Wales,
   d. 1741, Henrico, VA,
   m. Elizabeth Brookes, b.? d.?
Their children:
--4. John Owen* (see below.)**
--4. James Owen
--4. Mary Owen

4. John Owen, b. 1694, Henrico, VA, d. 1804, Granville,
   NC, m. Mildred Grant, b. 1714, New Kent, VA, d,
   1804, Granville, NC.
Their child:
--5. Thomas Owen* (see below.)**

5. Thomas Owen, b. Jul 21, 1742, Henrico, VA,
   d. Dec 31, 1825, Elizabethtown, KY,
   Fought in the Revolutionary War, Battle of Eutaw
   Springs.

m. Isabella Allen, b. Dec. 17, 1748, d. ? NC.

Their children:

--6. John Owen, Sr.*** (see below.)

--6. Mary Ann Owen

--6. James Owen

--6. William Owen

6. John Owen, Sr., b. 1774 NC, d. 1814, Rosman, NC,
   m. Anna Right, b.? d.1838, Rosman, NC. Fought at
   the battle of Guilford Courthouse.

Their children:

--7. Elizabeth Owen

--7. Joseph Noah Owen

--7. John Owen, Jr.*** (see below.)

--7. Annie Owen

--7. James Owen

7. John Owen, Jr., b. Jan 26, 1797, NC, d. Feb 6, 1876
   Transylvania Co., NC. Once owned from the top of
   Wolf Mountain to Lake Toxaway.
   m. Lavinia Parker, b. 1798, Haywood Co., NC, d.
   1872, NC.

Their children:

--8. James Milford Owen, b. Apr 4, 1817, Transylvania
   Co., NC, d. Jun 1, 1892, Towns Co., GA. (Ledford
   Cem., Towns Co., GA)

--8. William Baxter Owen, b. Apr 9, 1820, Transylvania
   Co., NC, d. 1888, Transylvania Co., NC. (William
   Owen Cem., Transylvania Co., NC.)

--8. Jessie Roland Owen, b. Jun 7, 1822, Transylvania
   Co., NC, d. Nov. 17, 1892, Transylvania Co., NC.

--8. John Bishop Owen, b. Dec 27, 1823, Transylvania
   Co., NC, d. Jul 27, 1899,   Transylvania Co., NC
   (John Bishop Owen Cem., Transylvania Co., NC.)

--8. Elizabeth Owen, b. Nov 27, 1826, Transylvania Co.,

NC, d. May 1, 1912 ?

--8. Mary Ann Owen, b. Dec 12, 1827, Jackson Co., NC, d. Aug 16, 1915, Jackson Co., NC

--8. Rebecca Owen, b. 1830 Jackson Co., NC, d.1903, Transylvania Co., NC

--8. Andrew Jackson Owen*(see below.)**

--8. Washington Owen, b. 1832, Transylvania Co., NC, d.? Clinton, TN. (Union Infantry, Civil War. Became a Texas Ranger. Married widow of brother Rufus.)

--8. Polly Owen, b. 1834 Transylvania Co., NC, d. 1900, Jackson Co., NC.

--8. Harrison Huston Owen, b. 1836, d. ? Colorado. (Union Infantry, Civil War. Became a Texas Ranger.)

--8. Thomas Owen, b. 1836, Jackson Co., NC, d. 1849, Jackson Co., NC (Died of rabies after being bitten by one of his hunting dogs.)

--8. Francis Marion Owen, b. Feb 22, 1837, Jackson Co., NC, d. Nov. 24, 1923, Jackson Co., NC. (Co. L., 38th GA Infantry Reg., Confederacy, Civil War. POW at Point Lookout, MD, released at War's end. Macedonia Baptist Church Cem.)

--8. Susannah Owen, b. 1838, Transylvania Co., NC, d. 1863, Transylvania Co., NC., (Mack McCall Cem.)

--8. Rufus Ansel Owen, b. 1840 Jackson Co., NC, d. 1864 killed in the Civil War. (Lieutenant, 62nd NC Infantry, Confederacy, Civil War. Survived the fall of Cumberland Gap, to be killed in a later battle.)

8. Andrew Jackson Owen, b,. May 3, 1831, Gloucester Township, Transylvania Co., NC, d . Sep 18, 1905, Wolf Mountain, Jackson Co., NC. m. on Jan 15, 1854 in Henderson Co., NC to Mary Ann "Polly"McCall, b. Jan 9, 1832 Wolf Mountain, Jackson Co., NC, d. Mar 20, 1915, Jackson Co., NC (Wolf Mtn Cem.)

Their children:

--9. Eveline Owen, b. Feb 13, 1855, Haywood Co., NC

--9. Angeline Owen, b. Dec 1855, Haywood Co., NC

--9. Thomas Cleamon Owen, b. Feb 25, 1858, Haywood Co., NC

--9. Isaiah Owen*** (see below.)

--9. Jackson "Jacky"Owen, b. Oct 19, 1861, Jackson Co., NC

--9. James Milford Owen, b. Jan 13, 1864, Jackson Co., NC

--9. Caroline Owen, b. 1866, Jackson Co., NC

--9. Adeline Owen, b. 1869, Jackson Co., NC

--9. Martha Jane Owen, b Oct 25, 1873, Jackson Co., NC

--9. Dillard Owen, b. 1876, Jackson Co., NC

--9. John Owen, b. 1878, Jackson Co., NC

***Notes about Andrew Jackson Owen: Fought in the Civil War, originally as a Confederate, and then with the Union. Co. K, 62nd NC Infantry, & 7th Bttn. NC Calvary. Rank at induction with the Confederacy; Corporal.Busted to Private before changing sides to the Union. After fighting with the Union for some time, he went home for the birth of son, James Milford, in 1864, and never returned to his post, and so was AWOL and never officially discharged from the Union Army. Moved from Transylvania County to Wolf Mountain after the War. -Wolf Mtn Cem.)

9. Isaiah Owen, b. Jan 22 1859, Transylvania Co., NC, d. Jul 14, 1935 (Jackson Owen-Wolf Mountain Cem.)
m. on Mar 4 1882 to Martha Elminia Mason, b. Sep 25, 1863, NC, d. Jan 17, 1962, Jackson Co., NC. (Jackson Owen-Wolf Mountain Cem.)

Their children:

--10. Martha Owen, b. Jun 14, 1880, Jackson Co., NC, d. Jan 20, 1971 NC.

--10. Sinia Owen, b. Dec 4, 1882 Jackson Co., NC, d. Jan 16, 1883, Jackson Co., NC. (Jackson Owen-Wolf Mountain Cem. Buried next to father and mother.Rest in peace.)

--10. Levia Owen, b. 1884, Jackson Co., NC, d. Jul 1, 1941, NC. (Jackson Owen-Wolf Mountain Cem.)

--10. James Harrison Owen, b. Jun 11, 1888, Jackson Co., NC, d. Jun 13, 1983, Jackson Co., NC. (Jackson Owen-Wolf Mountain Cem.)

--10. Willie Walker Owen, b. Apr 1, 1890, Jackson Co., NC, d. Jun 16, 1891, Jackson Co., NC. (Jackson Owen-Wolf Mountain Cem. Buried next to father and mother. Rest in peace.)

--10. Wiley I. Owen *** (see below.)

--10. Blye Owen, b. Jun 4, 1894, Jackson Co., NC, d. Jul 5, 1985. Jackson Co., NC. (Jackson Owen-Wolf Mountain Cem.)

--10. Haylie Owen, b. Jan 1897, Jackson co., NC.

--10. Pearl Owen b. Aug 1899 Jackson Co., NC

--10. Elva Irene Owen, b. Jun 13, 1907, Jackson co., NC, d. Mar 8, 2000, Jackson Co., NC.

--10. Minnie Owen, b ?, Jackson Co., NC

10. Wiley I. Owen, b. May 23, 1892, Jackson Co., NC, d. Oct 13, 1950 Jackson Co., NC (Jackson Owen-Wolf Mountain Cem.) ***(see picture, page iii)
   m. on Sep 23, 1925 to **Ellen Canzadie Galloway,** b. Aug 12, 1894, Jackson Co., NC, d. Feb 17, 1975, Jackson Co., NC (Jackson Owen-Wolf Mountain. Cem.) ***(see Galloway, page 278)

Their children:

--**11a. Libby Owen,** b. July 4, 1916, d. July 4, 1992. (Wolf Mtn Cem.) ***(see page 288 for descendants)

--**11b. Lillie Elminia Owen** *** (see below.)

--**11c. Irene Owen** *** (see below.)

--**11d. Cannie Owen** *** (see below.)

--**11e. Ray William Owen,** b. Jan 20, 1927 Wolf Mtn, NC, d May 13, 1968 in Tay Ninh, South Vietnam, killed in action. Served in WW11 and Korean War. Burial: Daventon Ch Cem, Honea Path, SC *** (see

page 291 & 292 for descendants)

--11f. Lucy Ellen Owen *** (see below.)

--11g. Talmadge Owen *** (see below.)

--11h. Cecil Owen *** (see below.)

--11i. Dohonov Owen *** (see below)

--11j. Infant Owen (buried Wolf Mtn Cem., in an
   unmarked grave next to father and mother.)

--11k. Infant Owen (buried in Wolf Mountain Cem.,
   in an unmarked grave , beside father and mother.)

   --11b. Lillie Elminia Owen, b. Nov 23,
1919, d. Feb 15, 2002; m. June 12, 1941 to
Demus William Galloway, b. May 30,
1912, d. Aug 3, 1991 in Pickens, SC. (Burial
for Lillie & Demus: Shoal Creek Baptist
Church, Balsam Grove, NC.)

Their Children:

--12b. Carroll Daniel Galloway, b June 9, 1942, d. Feb
   25, 2001. Never married.(Burial for Carroll: Shoal
   Creek Baptist Church, Balsam Grove, NC.)

--12b. Shirley Ann Galloway *** (see below.)

--12b. Holly Emily Galloway *** (see below.)

12b. Shirley Ann Galloway, b Nov 18, 1947, m. Roy
   Leonard Hoots, b. Oct 3, 1935, on Jan 8, 1966.
Their Children:

--13b. April Annette Hoot *** (see below.)

--13b. Roy Leonard Hoots *** (see below.)

--13b. April Annette Hoots, b. May 31, 1967
   m. Artis Williams,b. Oct 1, 1957
Their Child:

--14b. Breanna Williams, b. Sep 9, 1998

--13b. Roy Leonard Hoots,Jr. b. Nov 13, 1968, d. May 22, 2003; m. Angela Gilbert, b. Mar 13, 1967. (Burial for Roy: Shoal Creek Bap. Ch, Balsam Grove, NC.)

Their Child:

--14b. Ryan Grady Hoots, b. Sep 10, 1987

--12b. Holly Emily Galloway, b Aug 17, 1957, m. on May 12, 1972 to Perry Lamon Corn, b June 24, 1952, d. Sep 14, 1994. (Burial for Perry: Shepherd Memorial Park, Hendersonville, NC)

Their Child:

--13b. Jessica Sarah Corn, b. Aug 12, 1983.

Holly Emily Galloway Corn married George Oden, b. Aug 30, 1960, on Aug 17, 2001. They have no children.

--11c. Irene Owen, b.Feb 16, 1923--d. May 30, 1994; m. July 4, 1942 to Rufus Arix Moore, b. Jan 11, 1920--d.May 28, 1998. (Burial for Irene & Rufus: Old Field Cemetery, Beta, Sylva, NC)

Their Children:

--12c. Ronald Eric Moore ***(see below.)

--12c. JoEllen Moore ***(see below.)

--12c. Ruth Elaine Moore ***(see below.)

--12c. Rebecca Jane Moore ***(see below.)

--12c. Marcus Floyd Moore ***(see below.)

--12c. Clifford Mitchell Moore ***(see below.)

--12c. Ronald Eric Moore, b. May 7, 1949 m. on April 5, 1979 to Nancy Gail Jessup, b. Feb 20, 1958.

Their Children:
--13c. Chad Eric Moore, b. Oct 10, 1980
--13c. Ericka Gail Moore, b. June 16, 1983

--12c. JoEllen Moore, b. ?, m. Jeff Blaine, b. ?
Their Children:
--13c. Stephen Blaine *(see below.)**
--13c. Sharon B. Blaine *(see below.)**

--13c. Stephen Blaine, b. ? , m. Tracy C. ?, b. ?
Step Children:
   Timothy, Laura, Harley, and Connor.

--13c. Sharon B. Blaine, b. ?, m. Jan Pettersen, b. ?
Their child:
--14c. Mackenzie Pettersen

--12c. Ruth Elaine Moore, b.Dec 30, 1944, m. March
   12, 1969 to James Thomas Pruitt, b. Sep 24, 1947.
Their Children:
--13c. Michael Thomas Pruitt *(see below.)**
--13c. Allison Kelly Pruitt   *(see below.)**

--13c. Michael Thomas Pruitt, b. Nov 16, 1969, m.
   Tamara Carol Potter, b Aug 18, 1973
Their Children:
--14c. River Owen Pruitt, b. May 31, 1997
--14c. Brooke Olivia Pruitt, b. Sep 2, 2003

--13c. Allison Kelly Pruitt, b. Jan 14, 1975
Her Child:
--14c. Grace Elaine Moore Pruitt, b. Jan 21, 1999

--12c. Rebecca Jane Moore, b. Jan 15, 1952, m.Sep 13,

1969 to Stanley Keith Kelley, b. March 29, 1952

Their Children:

--13c. Jeremy Glen Kelley *(see below.)**

--13c. Stacey Katrinia Kelley *(see below.)**

--13c. Jeremy Glen Kelley, b. July 11, 1970

His Children:

--14c. Kimberly Storm Kelley, b. March 17, 1995

--14c. Jeremy Glen Kelley, Jr., b. Sep 17, 1997

--13c. Stacey Katrinia Kelley, b. Dec 8, 1979, Everest
  Cooper, father of one child

Their Child:

--14c. Everst Trent River Cooper, b. May 16, 1999

Stacey Katrnnia Kelley married Daniel Blaine Muniz, b.
Dec 23, 1981 on December 31, 2004.

--12c. Marcus Floyd Moore, b. Aug 5, 1954, m. June 9,
  1973 to Patricia Lynn Koutsky, b. Aug 11, 1955.
  (div 1999)

Their Children:

--13c. Amanda Lynn Moore, b. Aug 21, 1978 m.
  Jermey Lefler, b. Mar 16, 1975 , on June 2, 2001

--13c. Melissa Beth Moore, b. July 28, 1981

--13c. Marcus Clint Moore, b. June 21, 1984

Marcus Floyd Moore married Sheila Ann Turner, b. July
22, 1956, on April 21, 2001.

Sheila's Children:

--13c. Charles Wayne Moore, b. June 30, 1978, m.
  Katherine Irene Wood, b. May 6, 1980.

--13c. Johnny Ray Moore, Jr., b. Nov 11, 1974, m.
  Melinda Louise Greeno, b. Nov 22, 1976.

Their Children:

--14c. Christopher Ethan Moore, b. Sep 30, 1997

--14c. Brandon Scott Moore, b. Sep 8, 1999

--12c. Clifford Mitchell Moore, b. Jan 31, 1958, m. June
     10, 1984 to Teresa Annette Yeargin, b. Jan 30, 1959.
Their Child:
--13c. Arix Mitchell Moore, b. April 8, 1995.

11d. Cannie. Owen, b.
January 1, 1924, Jackson Co.,
NC, d. Oct 13, 1977
Greenville Co., SC.

m. May 19, 1941 to
Franklin Lee Ammons, b.
Aug 26, 1921, Jackson Co.,
NC, d. Nov, 1968.

(Burial of Cannie & Frank: Standing Springs Baptist
Church Cem.,Simpsonville, SC)

Their children:
--12d. Violet (Mildred) Irene Ammons *** (see below)
--12d. Doris Ellen Ammons ***(see below)

--12d. David Franklin Ammons , b.
Feb 21, 1945, m. Frances Sherilyn Barker,
b. May 23, 1946. on Aug 16, 1969 in
Greenville,SC. No children.

12d.Violet (Mildred)
Amy Ammons Garza, b.
April 1,1942, Jackson Co.,
NC, m. Robert Garza, Jr.,
on Dec 16, 1960, b. Mar 7, 1942 (div.
1987)

Their Children:

--13d. Aurora Yvonne Garza ***(see below.)

--13d. Veronica Leigh Garza ***(see below.)

***Notes about Violet "Amy" Ammons Garza: Amy m. Phillip Anthony Scopelite (b. Jan 24, 1926) on April 9, 1988. Phillip passed away June 14, 1995, cremated, ashes scattered over the Tuckaseigee River. Violet "Amy" Ammons Scopelite, m. Robert Donald McCann (b. April 1, 1952) on October 28, 2000. (div. Sep 2002) Amy took back her maiden name: Violet Amy Ammons, however, uses her pen n a m e for writing: Amy Ammons Garza. Amy has written six books: *"Retter," "Cannie," "Sterlen," "Matchbox Mountain," "Catch the Spirit of Creativity,"* and *"I Am Somebody, the Story of Tony Queen."*

Amy and her sister Doreyl co-founded the non-profit organization, "Catch the Spirit of Appalachia, Inc." in 1989 working with Amy as the storyteller with Doreyl spontaneously illustrating the stories as Amy told them. See page 302 for more detail.

Amy's children and grandchildren 2004 from left to right— Daughter: Veronica Grand girls: Holly & Ashleigh Daughter: Yvonne Grand boys: Alex & Steven

--13d. Aurora Yvonne Garza, b. September 7, 1963, Williamston, SC, m. Michael Eugene Fortner, b. Mar 9, 1966, on June 24, 1989.

Their Children:

--14d. Ashleigh Irene Fortner, b. January 5, 1992

--14d. Holly Jeannine Fortner, b. January 5, 1992

--14d. Steven Michael Fortner (adopted 2000),
   b. March 25, 1996

--13d. Veronica Leigh Garza, b. July 17, 1967, East
   Chicago, IN, m. Ronald Lee Vlasic, Jr. on
   Nov 5, 1988. No children. (div. 1997). m. on May 6,
   2000 to Daniel Lee Flinn, Jr. (div. 2005)
Their Child:
--14d. Alexander Davis Flinn, b. March 5, 2001

--12d. Doris Ellen Ammons (Doreyl
Ammons Cain) b. April 22, 1943, Wolf
Mountain, m. John Quarnstrom July 18,
1964 in Riverside, CA (div. 1994)

Their Children:
--13d. DavidPatrick Quarnstrom,
   b. Sep 28, 1966,
Sierra Madre, CA

--13d. Erik Quarnstrom,
   b. Nov 26, 1970, Sierra
Madre, CA, d. Feb 29,
1999 NV

***Notes about Doreyl Ammons:
Doreyl married Jerry Cain, b. Feb 12, 1946,
on July 1, 1996, in Macon Co, NC. Doreyl
has written three books, two published:
*"Greatness in a Nutshell," "Catch the Spirit of
Creativity"* and one almost ready for publication, *"Erik."*
   Doreyl co-founded the non-profit organization, "Catch
the Spirit of Appalachia, Inc." with her sister Amy in 1989
spontaneously illustrating the stories as Amy told them. See
page 302 for more detail.

--11f. Lucy Ellen Owen, b. July 11, 1930 (d. April 24, 1988); m. Orion Clarence Owens, b. Jan 24, 1926 (d. Jan 4, 2002) on Sept 13, 1948.

Their Child:

--12f. Nancie Ellen, b. Oct 9, 1949, m. Luke Glen Edwards on Nov 19, 1968.

Their Children:

--13f. Kymberly Christine Edwards *** (see below.)

--13f. Heather Yvonne Edwards, b. Nov 7, 1974, m. John Glew on Oct 4, 1997.

--13f. Kymberly Christine Edwards, b. Sep 6, 1969 m. Clayton Gibson in June, 1987. (div.)

Their Child:

--14f. William Michael Gibson, b. Oct 21, 1988

Kymberly Christine Edwards Gibson married Tony Spitler on March 23, 1991.

Their Child:

--14f. Luci Jane Spitler, b. May 23, 1993

--11g. Talmadge Owen, b. Sept 30, 1933, d. Nov 4, 1997; m. Elsie Owen, b. May 1929, on June 5, 1951.

Their Child:

--12g. Samuel Talmadge Owen, b. Jan 13, 1953; m. Kimberly Henderson on Mar 19, 1994.

Their Children:

--13g. Ryan Alexander Mitchell Owen, b. Nov 7, 1990

--13g. Samuel Lucus Iommie Owen, b. May 17, 1995

--11h. Cecil Owen, b. May 20, 1935, m. Edna Frady, b. March 21, 1940, on June 20, 1956.

Their Children:

--12h. Timothy Wiley Owen *** (see below.)

--12h. Thomas William Owen *** (see below.)
--12h. Rheba Sheryl Owen *** (see below.)
--12h. Jerry Dean Owen, b Dec 30, 1960 (no wife)
--12h. Gary Gene Owen, b. Jan 21, 1962 (div.)
--12h. David Gain Owen *** (see below.)
--12h. Margie Owen *** (see below.)
--12h. Mitchell Owen *** (see below.)
--12h. Brian Stacy Owen *** (see below.)

--12h. Timothy Wiley Owen,b. Sept 9, 1957, m. Velvet
   Jean Ann Owen., b. June 18, 1962, on Sep 8,1979
   (div. July 13,1992)
Their Children:
--13h. Joshua Wiley Owen *** (see below.)
--13h. Stoney Michelle Owen, b. Aug 31, 1984

Timothy Wiley Owen married Sue Miller, b. March
   1, 1958, on January 14, 2000.

--13h. Joshua Wiley Owen, b. July 23, 1980, m.Yvettte
   Norris, b. June 13, 1972, on May 11, 2002
Their Child:
--14h. Melanie Diane Owen, Nov 5, 2001.

--12h. Thomas William Owen, b. July 22, 1958, m.
   Linda Saunders, b. April 28, 1960 (div 2000)
Their Children:
--13h. Natasha Gail Owen *** (see below.)
--13h. Heather Marie Owen *** (see below.)
--13h. Thomas Chad Owen, b. June 20, 1984

--13h. Natasha Gail Owen,b. May 17, 1981 (married &
   divorced)
Natasha's Children:
--14h. Vanessa Leanna Owen, b. Mar 15, 2001

--14h. Kalie Owen, b. ?

--13h. Heather Marie Owen, b. Dec 12, 1982
Heather's Child:
--14h. Kaylan Denise Fesperman, b. Feb 29, 2002

--12h. Rheba Sheryl Owen, b Oct 2, 1959, m. Harrison
    O'Shields, Jr. b..Mar 27, 1949 , on June 19, 1973 (div.
    Jan 13, 1999)
Their Children:
--13h. Mitchell Thomas O'Shields *** (see below)
--13h. Samuel Lee O'Shields *** (see below)
--13h. Harrison Ray O'Shields *** (see below)
--13h. Emily Leanne O'Shields, Feb 8, 1983, d. Feb 8,
    1983

  Rheba Sheryl Owen married Raleigh Joe Hinsley, b.
    May 12, 1960, on January 14, 1999.

--13h. Mitchell Thomas O'Shields, b. Aug 15, 1974, m.
    Teresa Holland, b. Jan 7, 1982, on Nov 4, 2002
Their Child:
--14b. Anna Cheyenne O'Shields, b. Jan 3, 2003

--13h. Samuel Lee O'Shields, b. July 29, 1975,
    m. Theresa Schifano, b. July 29, 1976, on June 5, 1999
Their Children:
--14h. Abigail McKenzie O'Shields, b. Jun 6, 2000
--14h. Savannah Leigh O'Shields, b. May 3, 2003

--13h. Harrison Ray O'Shields, b. Jan 6, 1979, m.
    Teresa Ivy, b. May 4, 1983 on Aug 4, 2001
Their Child:
--14h. Emily Nicole O'Shields, b. June 19, 2000

--12h. David Gain Owen, b. Sep 14, 1963
David's Child:
--13h. Corey Blake (Owen), b. Jun 27, 1990

--12h. Margie Ellen Owen , b. Feb 4, 1966, m.Steve
Edward Carter, b. July 16, 1963, on April 11, 1981. d.
Aug 31, 1983.
Their Child:
--13h. Stephanie Dawn Carter, b. Nov 15, 1983

Margie married Thomas Edgar Whitmire, b. May 14,
1957 on Sep 1, 1984. (div. Dec 13, 1995)
Their Child:
--13h. Rebecca Holly Whitmire, May 21, 1986

Margie married Louis James Stern, Jr.,, b. Oct 15, 1970,
on Nov 19, 1996

--12h. Mitchell Owen, b. July 6, 1967, m. Marquietta
Sutton, b. May 22, 1959, on May 10, 1998.
Mitchell's Child:
--13h. Samuel Ray Webb (Owen), b. Dec 26, 1985
***Note on Mitchell Owen: When Mitchell was born,
Cecil had been in a very bad accident, so Cecil's brother
Talmadge and his wife Elsie provided a home for the two-
week old Mitchell. It turned into a wonderful blessing.
Mitchell grew up a brother to Talmadge's son Samuel
Talmadge Owen, an only child.

--12h. Brian Stacy Owen, b April 27, 1969, m. Wilma
Garret, b. Dec 1, 1971, on April 18, 1990
Their Children:
--13h. Stacy Ricky Owen, b. April 23, 1990
--13h. Chessie Nicole Owen, b. March 8, 1992
--13h. Dustin Cecil Owen, b. Oct 25, 1994
--13h. Steven Brian Owen, b. Mar 6, 2001

--11i. Dohonov Owen, b. Nov. 2, 1938, d. Nov 17, 1999; m. Fred Enos Ansley, b. Dec 20, 1930, in 1954. (div.) (Dohonov is buried in Jackson Owen-Wolf Mtn Cem.)
Their Children:
--12i. Steven Eugene Ansley   * (see below)**
--12i. Galen Owen Ansley * (see below)**
--12i. Nancy Elisabeth Ansley,   * (see below)**
--12i. Robbie S. Ansley   * (see below)**

--12i. Steven Eugene Ansley, b. Nov 2, 1956, m. Melanie Jane Lance, b. Aug 19, 1961, on Jan 17, 1990
Their Children:
--13i. Zachary Michael Ansley, b. Feb 5, 1987
--13i. Jacob Elias Ansley, b. Oct 2, 1990

--12i. Galen Owen Ansley, b. March 21, 1960, m.? (div.)
Galen's Child:
--13i. Galen Forest Ansley, b. 1986

--12i. Nancy Elisabeth Ansley, b. July 13, 1965, m. James Hyde, b. July 9, 1969
Their Child:
--13i. Olivia Racheal Hyde, b. Feb 26, 1992

--12i. Robbie S. Ansley, b. July 27, 1967, m. Missouri B. ?, b. July 5, 1968
Their Children:
--13i. Khristin Nicole Ansley, b. Nov 9, 1992
--13i. Thomas Isaiah Ansley, b. Mary 14, 1997
--13i. Lilierose Jeanine Ansley, b. Oct 14, 2003

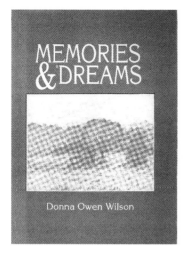

Donna Owen Wilson

***Notes about Dohonov Owen Ansley: Dohonov married James L. Wilson after her divorce from Fred Enos Ansley.

She has written one book entitled *"Memories & Dreams,"* (Winston-Derek Publishers, Inc.) Copyright 1991,under the name of Donna Owen Wilson.

In the book, Dohonov revisits the people and places of her childhood on Wolf Mountain, North Carolina.

Cannie Owen Ammons
The author, Amy Ammons Garza
Lillie Elimina Owen Galloway
Carroll Galloway

November, 1945
Wolf Mountain

GALLOWAY LINEAGE

--1. William Galloway, b. & d. ?, Ireland

Child:

--2. Alexander Galloway, b. 1746 Ireland, d. Jul 8, 1832 SC. m. Mary Millen, b. ? SC, d. ? NC

Their Child:

--3. William D. Galloway, b. 1763 VA, d. June 1, 1851 NC

  m. Sarah Harriet Essary, b. 1765, VA, d. 1842 NC

Their Child:

--4. James G. Galloway, b. 1790 NC, d. 1874 NC

  m. Sarah Parker, b. Aug 21, 1795 NC, d. 1880 NC

  (sister of Lavinia Parker, wife of John Owen, Jr.)

Their child:

--5. Augustus Eli Galloway, b. Apr 15, 1820, NC, c. Feb 28, 1892

  m. Elizabeth Owen, b. Dec 28, 1817 NC, d. Jul 17, 1881, NC

Their child:

--6. William H. Galloway, b. Mar 5, 1858 NC, d. Dec 24, 1932

  m. Sarah Dawson, b. May 14, 1858 NC, d. Sep 23, 1916, NC

Their Children:

--7. Sterlen Columbus Galloway *** (see below)

--7. Ellen Canzadie Galloway, b. Aug 12, 1894 NC, d. Feb 17, 1975 NC ***** (see page 264)**

--7. Jurdie Galloway

--7. Emmie Galloway

--7. Connie Galloway

--7. John Galloway

--7. Sterlen Columbus Galloway
  b. Feb. 28, 1893 d. Feb 19, 1960
  (Burial: Wolf Creek Cemetery, Jackson Co, NC)

m. Martha Jane Ammons
Dec 8, 1941, b. Apr 5,
1918, d. Oct 15, 1987
(Burial: Crossroads Baptist
Church Cem., Greer, SC)

Their Children:
--8. (Jay) J. W. Galloway, b.Nov 17, 1944, d.June
  14, 2002   (no marriage, no children)
--8. Steve Galloway * (see below)**
--8. Robert Galloway* (see below)**
--8. Ellavee Galloway * (see below)**

--8. Steve Galloway, b. Aug 26, 1946
  m. Carol Annette Turner in Feb, 1965 (div. 1970)
Their Child:
--9. Gary Allen Galloway, b. Sept 29, 1967, m. ?
Gary's Children:
--10. Vince Allen Galloway, b. Dec 18, 1987
--10. Crystal Dawn Galloway, b. Nov 1, 1991

Gary Allen Galloway has partnered with Nancy
Castell since 1993

--8. Robert Galloway, b. April 28, 1948
  m. Dorothy Thompson, b. July 11, 1953 (div. ?)
Their Children:
--9. Robert Lee Jr., b. Dec 14,1979
--9. Ricky Galloway, b. Dec 9, 1981

--8. Ellavee Galloway, b. Mar 22, 1950
  m. Clint Thomas (div. ?)
Their Children:
--9. Miranda Thomas
--9. Chris Thomas
Ellavee m. Don Jackson in 1977 (div. ?)
Their Children:
--9. Julie Ann Jackson
--9. David Lee (Davy) Vinson *** (see below)
  (adopted by Ellavee's first cousin Linda Owen Vinson
  when Ellavee's health began to fail. ***See Ammons***
  Lineage on page 292. *)*

--9. Davy Lee Vinson, b. April 22, 1980
m. Amber R. Riden on Nov 24, 2000, b. Jan 4, 1983
Their Children:
--10. Ethan Lee Vinson, b. Oct 24, 2001
--10. Emma Grace Vinson, b. Oct 13, 2003

AMMONS LINEAGE

--1. Jacob Ammons, b. 1689, Germany; d. 1743 ?,
   m. Anna? b. Germany, d. ?

Their Child:

--2. Jacob Ammons, Jr. b. 1720 Scotland, d, VA
   m. Barbara ?

Their Child:

--3. John Thomas Ammons, b 1748, VA, d, 1817,
   Buncombe Co, NC; m. Fertha ?, b. 1758 VA, d, ?
   Buncombe Co, NC

Their children:

--4. John Jackson Ammons Sr, *** (see below)

--4. Ephraim Ammons, b. 1778, SC

--4. Thomas Ammons, b 1792, SC

--4. Susanna Ammons, b ?

--4. Sarah Ammons, b. ?

--4. Mary Ammons, b ?

--4. William Ammons, b ?

--4. John Jackson Ammons, Sr. b. 1770, d. 1814
   Buncombe Co. m. Sarah Young, b. 1772, Laurens, SC,
   d 1814, NC. She was the daughter of John W. Young
   and Jane Montgomery.

Their Children:

--5. Sallie Ammons, b. Aug 6, 1793, NC, d. ?

--5. John Jackson Ammons, Jr., *** (see below)

--5. Thomas Ammons, b. 1798 in Macon Co, d. ?

--5. Rev. Joshua Ammons, b Feb 14, 1800 , Burke Co,
   NC, d Sept 27, 1877

--5. Young Ammons, b 1802, Macon Co., NC, d ?

--5. Polly Ammons, b NC, d ?

--5. John Jackson Ammons, Jr. b. 1796, SC, d. 1855 in
Macon Co, NC

m. Eda Peek, b 1803, Laurens, SC, d. before 1860,
Macon Co, NC. She was the daughter of David Peek
and Mary (Polly) Henderson.

Their Children:

--6. David P. Ammons, b 1821, Buncombe Co, NC, d ?
m. Mary (Polly) Carson

--6. Thomas Ammons, Sr. *** (see below)

--6. Ruth Carolina Ammons, b 1826, Macon Co, d ?
m. Hugh Roers, Nov 20, 1844 Macon Co

--6. John A. Ammons, b 1827, Macon Co, d 1879, NC
m. Rhoda R. Carson, b Haywood Co.

--6. Sarah (Sallie) Ammons, b 1831, Macon Co, NC
m. Govern Erwin Frady, ?

--6. Rhoda Ammons, b 1832, Macon Co, NC

--6. George C. Ammons, b 1835, Macon Co, NC
m. Mary A. ?

--6. James M. Ammons, b 1835, Macon Co, NC

--6. Polly Ann Ammons, born 1838, Macon, Co, NC

--6. William M. Ammons, Sr, b 1840, Macon Co, NC
m. Martha Mashburn, b 1843 ?

--6. Winfield Scott Ammons, b 1840, NC, d 1886, NC
m. Martha Ann Mashburn, b 1831 NC, d 1886 NC

--6. Marion Ammons, b Feb 22, 1843

--6. Joshua Ammons, b 1845, Macon Co, NC
m. Sally Buchanan, b 1848 Macon Co, NC, d ?

--6. Harvey Ammons, b 1846, Macon Co, NC

--6. Thomas Ammons, Sr., b 1825, Buncombe Co, NC
m. Catherine Kite, b 1830, TN, d ? NC. She was the
daughter of Benjamin Kite and Catrena Dolphelmier.

Their Children:

--7. Mary Ammons, b 1845

--7. James Washington (Pretty Jim) Ammons *** (see below)

--7. George L. Ammons, b 1851, Mcon Co, NC

--7. Mary Althia Ammons, b 1854, Macon Co, NC

--7. Eda E. Ammons, b 1855 in Macon Co, NC

--7. Elizabeth "Lizzie" Ammons, b 1858

--7. Ellen J. Ammons, b 1858, Mcon Co, NC

--7. James Washington (Pretty Jim) Ammons, b. Aug 25, 1848 in Ellijay, NC, d. Oct 15, 1937, Gold Bar, Snohomish Co., WA. m. Margaret Jane Blaine,Aug 4, 1872 in Macon Co, NC, b. Apr 1852, NC. d. Mar 12,1942,WA. (Burial: 100F Cem., Monroe, WA.)

Their Children:

--8. Lilly Jane Ammons, b Nov 10, 1875, Ellijay, NC, d Dec 5, 1954 Kennewick, WA; m. David Montgomery Mincey, Jr. Sep 27, 1895 in Ellijay, NC

--8. Columbus Ammons, b 1876, Macon Co, NC. d in Marysville, WA; m. Laura Henry Aug 15, 1900 in Macon Co, NC.

--8. Thomas Wilson Ammons *** (see below)

Lumberjacks on Cullowhee Mountain.

Tom W. Ammons is second from the right. This photo was taken early 1900's.

--8. James Albert Ammons, b. May 24, 1879, Macon Co. .d May 1942 in Monroe, WA.

--8. John Garfield Ammons, b. Mar 24, 1880, Macon Co. d. July 23, 1948 in Monroe, WA.

--8. Lydia Francis Ammons,b. Apr 12, 1881, Tuckasegee d. Sep 30, 1967 in Monroe, WA; m. Justice Samuel Clark in Snohomish, WA.

--8. Robert L. Ammons, b. Mar19, 1882, Macon Co., d. June 1964 in NC.

--8. Ella R. Ammons, b. Sep 12, 1883, Ellijay, NC, d. May 15, 1966 in Gold Bar, WA.; m. ? Smith. (Burial: 100F Cem., Monroe, WA.)

--8. Charles Harrison Ammons, b. Sep 21, 1889, Ellijay, d. July 14, 1937 in Monroe, WA. (Burial: 100F Cem., Monroe, WA.)

--8. Cora Ellen Ammons, b. Apr 22, 1892, Ellijay, NC, d. Nov 27, 1977 in Monroe, WA; m. James Irvin Parker June 14, 1912.

--8. Franklin Piercen Ammons, b. Aug 25, 1895, Ellijay, d. July 1, 1942 in Monroe, WA; m. ? (From Obit: Frank, 47 was the victim of an accidental drowning, while fishing from a boat on Cain Lake, about 5 miles from Burlington, WA. He was survived by 2 sons: Everett Ammons, 16, of Monroe and Kenneth Ammons, 15, of Wickersham. Burial: 100F Cem., Monroe, WA.)

***Notes about "Pretty Jim" and Margaret Ammons: Occupation: Surveyor. Margaret and her brother survived an Indian attack on the trek across country when just children by being hidden in a barrel of feathers.

--8. Thomas Wilson Ammons, b. Jan 22, 1878, NC, d. Sep 21, 1956, Jackson Co, NC (Tom was knocked off of a railroad trestle at age 39 in Jackson Co, and there after crippled.) Burial: Double Springs Cem.Cullowhee Mtn, NC

m. Retta Jane Coggins, b. 1894 Cullowhee, NC, d. May 17, 1974 Honea Path, SC. She was the daughter of Edward Filmore Coggins and Martha Jane Bryson. Burial: Double Springs Cem.Cullowhee Mtn, NC

Their Children:

--9. Bryson Louis Ammons *** (see below)

--9. James Edward Ammons *** (see below)

--9. Albert Abraham Ammons, b. Mar 3, 1914, Jackson Co, NC, d. May 8, 1970, VA (Double Springs Cem.Cullowhee Mtn, NC) (never married)

--9. Thomas Washington Ammons *** (see below)

--9. Martha Jane Ammons, b. Apr 5, 1918, Jackson Co, NC, d. Oct 15, 1987. (Crossroads Baptist Church Cemetery, Greer, SC). Child born: Jhon Fred Ammons, b. Sept 16, 1938, d. June 18, 1946.

*** (For further breakdown of descendants of Martha, *see Galloway lineage on page 276.*)

--9. Franklin Lee Ammons *** (For further break down of Frank's descendants, *see Owen Lineage*

on pages 267 & 268.)

--9. Lillie Mae Ammons   * (see below)**

--9. Cora Eleanor Ammons * (see below)**

--9. Nealie Roosevelt Ammons * (see below)**

***Notes about Tom Wilson Ammons:

Supper on the Mountain: *l-r. Tom Ammons, Amy, Frank, Nealie,Retter (standing), Lillie, Cora, Kenneth, Mike (unseen), David, Linda w/arm up (unseen), Doreyl. 1953.*

As a young man, Tom Ammons, left the mountains to become a gambler on a Mississippi riverboat. When he returned, he married Retta Jane Coggins and fathered eleven children (nine lived). At one time he owned 186 acres of mountain land on which he raised vegetables, field corn, fruit, goats, cattle, and childen. He tried his hand at about everything to provide for his family, including lumberjacking, milling, selling glasses and bootlegging.

After he was crippled at the age of 39, he became a great storyteller, always telling his eldest grandchild, Mildred (Amy) not to forget that her grandma was special. He eventually inspired Amy to write about the Ammons/Owen family.

--9. Bryson Louis Ammons, b. Mar 16, 1910, Jackson Co, NC, d. Oct 15, 1998 Tuckasegee, NC. m. Rena Coggins from Cashiers, NC, Sept 19, 1948, b. Aug 14, 1930.

Their Children:

--10. Eileen Ammons *** (see below)

--10. Lillian Ammons , b. January 12, 1953, m. Vernon "Eddie" Keeton (no children)

--10. Clifford Ammons *** (see below)

--10. Eileen Ammons, b. Nov 20, 1949
   m. Louie Sims, 1969 (div.)

Their Children:

--11. Ruth Ann Sims, b. Dec 20, 1970

--11. David Ray Sims, b. April 19, 1975

--10. Clifford Ammons, b January 31, 1960.
   m. Laura Foster on Sept 12, 1987

Their Children:

--11. Nathan Lee Ammons, b. Nov 12, 1992

--11. Joshua Lee Ammons, b. Jan 2, 2002

--9. James Edward Ammons, b Mar 25, 1912, Jackson
Co, NC, d. Sep 10, 1995 (Wolf Mtn Cem., NC) m.
Oct, 1940 to Libby Owen, b. July 4, 1916; d. July 4,
1992. (Wolf Mtn Cem.) *(See picture on page iv)*

Their children:

Joseph and James Ammons, 1995

--10. James Ammons, b. Dec 26, 1948, m.Sept 4, 1982
to Sandra Karen Praytor, b. June 5, 1948. (no children)

--10. Joseph Ammons, b. Dec 26, 1948, m. Dec 26,
2002 to Linda Bailey , b. January 28, 1953 (no
children)

--10. Daniel Ammons, b. May 29, 1952, m. Dec 18,
1982 to Debra Lynn Henderson , b. March 11, 1957
(no children)

--10. Mary Ellen Ammons, b Nov 28, 1999

--10. Donna Sharon Ammons * (see below)**

James Ammons
2000 — Wolf Mountain

--10. Donna Sharon Ammons, b Sept 5, 1959, m. Bobby
Carroll Owen, Sept 24, 1977 (div. 1982)

Their Children:

--11. Kevin Joey Owen, b. Nov 28, 1979

--11. Amanda "Hope" Owen, b. Oct 11, 1982
   m. Dec 18, 1982 to David Sheridon Kephart,b. April
   28, 1943. David is in the process of adopting Hope.

--9. Thomas Washington Ammons, b. Mar 3, 1914,
   Jackson Co, NC, d. June 1985, Jackson Co, NC
   m. Eva Watson b. ?. (div. ?) (Thomas' Burial: Double
   Springs Cem.Cullowhee Mtn, NC)

Their Children:

--10. Charlie Edward Ammons *** (see below)

--10. Robert Lee Ammons *** (see below)

1st Cousins & Friends:

Charlie Ammons
Kenneth Beasley, pg 293
Robert Ammons
David Ammons, pg 269

1963 decoration day,
Double Springs Ch Cem.

--10. Charlie Edward Ammons, b June 29, 1943, d. Aug
   3, 1997. m. July 3, 1967 to Willa Mae Hooper, b. Dec
   25, 1946

Their Child:

--11. Loretta Michelle Ammons, b July 8, 1969, m.
   May 14, 1988 to Chuck Norris, b. May 18, 1967 (div.
   1999)

Their Children:

--12. Charles Anthony Norris, Jr. (C.J.), b. Nov 12,
   1990

--12. Kayla Michelle Norris, b. Jan 7, 1993

--10. Robert Lee Ammons,b .Oct. 8 1945, d. Mar 26 1998, m. June 24 1969 to Lillie Mae Bryson, b. May 8 1950, d.Feb. 16 2004. (Robert's Burial: Double Springs Ch. Cem., Cullowhee Mtn.—Lillie Mae was cremated, her ashes scattered over Robert's grave)

Their Children:

--11. Corrina Gaye Bryson *(Lillie Mae's child when married Robert. Father was Fred Eugene Jones wo died Jan 4, 1968; Cornia was raised by Robert.)* ***** (see below)**

--11. Daisy Beaneace Ammons *** (see below)

--11. Evelyne Dee Ammons *** (see below)

--11. Robert Ammons Jr. *** (see below)

--11. Eva Annette Ammons, b. Nov 11, 1985

--11. Corrina Gaye Bryson b. Aug. 31 1968 m. David Todd Walraven,b. July 1963 (div.)

Their Children:

--12. Crystal Anne Walraven   *** (see below)

--12. David Levi Walraven, b. Dec 22, 1984

Corrina Gaye Bryson married Kyle John Blach, b.Aug 7,1968

Their Children:

--12. Gabrielle Li-Ann Blach, b. Dec 7, 1988

--12. Joshua Kyle Blach, b. Aug 4,1990

--12. Niccolette Diane Blach, b. Nov 13, 1992

--12. Crystal Anne Walraven, b. May 3,1983 m. James Alfred Walls Jr., b. ?

Their Children:

--13. James Alfred Walls, III, b. Feb 19, 2000

--13. Conrad Nathanial Walls b. Jan 21, 2001

--13. Jenniffer Nichole Walls b. Oct 7, 2004

--11. Daisy Beaneace Ammons, b. Sep 15,1970, m.
   Micheal Denver Rice. b. Mar 9, 1966, d. Apr 30,1996
Their Children:
--12. Micheal Wayne Rice, b. Oct 4, 1988
--12. Ashley Nicole Rice, b. July 27, 1995

Daisy Beaneace Ammons Rice is currently married to
   Robert Samuel Lowie, b. July 19,1967

--11. Evelyne Dee Ammons, b. Sep 5, 1972,
   with Matthew James Smith, b. July 13,1965
Their Child:
--12. April Dawn Smith, b. May 8, 1992

Evelyne Dee Ammons Smith is currently married to
   Charles Logan Ball, b. Oct 12, 1973

--11. Robert Ammons Jr., b. Feb 16, 1975
with Kathryn Crystal Atkinson, b. May 6,1973
Their Child:
--12. Robert Alexander Ammons, b. June 15, 1998

Robert Ammons Jr. with Sara Walls, b.?
Their Child:
--12. Robert Ammons, III, b. Dec 4,-2003

--9. Lillie Mae Ammons, b Sep 1,
1928, Jackson Co, NC, m. Ray William
Owen January 14, 1946, b. January   20,
1927 Wolf Mtn, NC, d. May 13, 1968 Tay
Ninh, South Vietnam--killed in action.
(Burial: Davington Baptist Church Cem.,
Honea Path,SC)

Their Children:

--10. Linda Elaine Owen   *** (see below)

--10. Michael Ray William Owen   *** (see below)

--10.Loretta Lucille Owen, b. Aug 6,1957, d May, 1961
(Burial:Davington Baptist Church Cem., Honea
Path, SC)

--10. Linda Elaine Owen, b. Sept 28, 1947, m. Charles
David Vinson April, 1971, b. Dec 15, 1942 (div.)

Their Children:

--11. David Ray Milton Vinson   *** (see below)

--11. Shane Ray Vinson   *** (see below)

--11. David Lee (Davey) Vinson *** (see below)

11. David Ray Milton Vinson, b. Feb 10, 1972 m.
Melanie Evelyne Short on Mar 22, 1998, b. Nov 2,
1974

Their Child:

--12. Kateyn Renee Vinson, b. Mar 22, 2000

--11. Shane Ray Vinson, b. Aug 30, 1976 m. Debra
Elaine Sims on June 14, 2003, b. Jan 30, 1974

Their Children (adopted by Shane):

--12. Clinton Shane Vinson, b. Jul 5, 1992

--12. Chad Lee Vinson, b. Feb 7, 1997

--11. David Lee (Davy) Vinson, b April 22, 1980
(Sterlen Galloway's grandson: mother—Ellavee
Galloway; adopted by Linda Owen Vinson soon after
*birth--**see Galloway Lineage page 280**)*
m. Amber R. Riden on Nov 24, 2000, b. Jan 4, 1983

Their Children:

--12. Ethan Lee Vinson, b. Oct 24, 2001

--12. Emma Grace Vinson, b. Oct 13, 2003

***Notes about Linda Elaine Owen Vinson: Linda has written one book *"A Pinch from the Little Brown Jar,"*(Ammons Communications) which gives "memories and recipes from the mountain."

a pinch from the

Little Brown Jar

Memories and Recipes
from the Mountain
by Linda Owen Vinson

Winner of hundreds of First Place blue ribbons for her canning, baking,sewing, photography, arts and crafts, Linda tells her story from the heart, saving the recipes of Grandma Retter, her mother Lillie, and her own as she stows them throughout the stories she has written.

--10. Michael Ray William Owen, b. June 3, 1951
   m. Millie underwood (?) (div. ?)
Their Child:
--11. Tommy Ray Owen, b. Aug 4, 1975
   Michael m. Mary Michael 1995
Their Children:
--12. Loretta Owen, b. March 5, 1996
--12. Matt Owen, b. June 5, 1997

--9. Cora Eleanor Ammons, b May 23, 1931, Jackson
   Co, NC, d May 2004. m. James Beasley April 16,
   1948, b. May 6, 1923 (Rt 25 Memorial Gardens, SC)
Their Children:
--10. Kenneth Beasley, b. June 25, 1951, d. Jan 31, 1986
   m. Linda Sullivan, b. Oct 2, 1953. *See Kenneth's*

picture as a young man on page 289)

Their Children:

--11. Chris Beasley, b. Aug 22, 1969, d. Oct 27, 2002
(Rt 25 Memorial Gardens, SC)

--12. Tonya Beasley, b. Oct 18, 1973

--12. Josh Beasley, b. June 2, 1977, d. Sept 26, 2004.
(Rt 25 Memorial Gardens, SC)

--9. Nealie Roosevelt Ammons, b Dec 15, 1933, Jackson
Co, NC, d Sep 14, 2004, SC. m. Aug 11,1989 to Ruby
Queen , b. May 19, 1940. Burial: Nealie was
cremated and his urn is to be placed inside Ruby's
coffin upon her death.

BRYSON LINEAGE

--1. William Bryson, b. 1720 . Co Antrim,Ireland; d. 1765 in Pendleton Dist., SC,

   m. Isabella Holmes, b 1720 in Lancaster Co, PA., d 1790 in Pendleton Dist. SC.

Their Children:

--2. James Holmes Bryson, b between 1740-1750 in Lancaster Co, Pa, d between 1830-1840 in Macon Co, NC *** (see below)

--2. William M. Bryson, b 1750, Lancaster Co, PA, d Sep 19, 1817 Buncombe Co, NC; m. Susannah Bogle before 1775 in Rowan Co.

--2. Andrew Bryson, B 1752, Lancaster Co, PA, d May 5, 1835 in Cullowhee, NC; m. (1) Agnes Naill Dec 17, 1783 Rowan Co., NC (2) ? between 1796-1799 Pendleton Dist., SC, d between 1811-1817 Haywood Co, NC (3) Sally ? before Aug 9, 1817 Haywood Co., NC.

--2. Samuel Bryson, b 1753, Lancaster Co, PA, d May 10, 1835 Wilson Co, TN; m. Martha Bogle June 14, 1776 Rowan Co, NC.

--2. John Bryson, b 1755, Lancaster Co, PA, d Feb 20, 1824 in Pendleton Dist, SC; m. June Malone before 1755 in SC.

--2. Daniel H. Bryson, b 1756, Lancaster Co, PA, d Mar 26, 1844 in Macon Co, NC; m (1) Jane ? before 1790 in Pendleton Dist, SC (2) Martha Morrow May 5, 1807 in Pendleton Dist SC.

****Notes for William Bryson:

This Bryson line came from Athens, Greece. They were sent as missionaries of the ancient Christian Church to France and Scotland. In Greek the name was spelled "Bruson." In France, it was spelled "Brisson." In Scotland it was the House of Bryce. The "Bryson" spelling was adopted in Ireland. These Bryson's journeyed from Scotland to County

Antrim, Ireland, to the William Penn Colony in Pennsylvania. In the 1750's, they moved south, and were among the first settlers in Western North Carolina (Haywood County) shortly after the American Revolution. All sons were Revolutionary War soldiers.

--2. James Holmes Bryson, b between 1740-1750 in Lancaster Co, Pa, d bet. 1830-1840 in Macon Co, NC; m. Sarah Countryman, b 1755, PA, d Aug 1833, Macon Co, NC. She was the daughter of Franz Countryman and Elizabeth Devendorf. Burial: Sugar Fork Cem, Macon Co., NC

Their Children:

--3. John W. Bryson, b 1768 in Ninety Six Dist, SC, d July 23, 1851 in Macon Co., NC *** (see below)

--3. Isabella Bryson, b 1770, Ninety Six Dist, SC, d Jan 31, 1835 in SC; m. John Armstrong before 1790 in Pendleton Dist. SC.

--3. Elizabeth Bryson, b 1775, Ninety Six Dist, SC, d May 5, 1837 in Macon Co., NC; m. John Gabby between 1790-1795 in Ninety Six Dist., SC.

--3. William Bryson, b 1777, Ninety Six Dist., SC, d Feb 27, 1837 in Macon Co., NC; m Elizabeth Turner 1802, Buncombe Co, NC.

--3. James Holmes Bryson, Jr., b 1779, NC, d after 1860 in Whitfield Co, GA; m Rebecca Poston between 1800-1810 in Buncombe Co. (James first homesteaded on Cartoogah Creek, Macon Co.NC in 1811.) Burial: Sugar Fork Bapt Ch Cem., Macon Co.

--3. Sarah Bryson, b 1780 Ninety Six Dist, SC, d ?; m (1) Hickey between 1790-1797 SC; (2) Thomas Gross between 1810-1820 in Haywood Co.

--3. Margaret (Peggy) Bryson, b Apr 11, 1784, Ninety-Six Dist, SC, d Jan 16, 1847 in Haywood Co., NC; m. Henry Wood 1811 in Haywood Co, NC

--3. Andrew Bryson, b 1785 in Pendleton Dist, SC, d April 19, 1826 in Haywood Co, NC; m Margaret

White May 1, 1817 in Haywood Co., NC (Andrew first settled the Sugar Creek area in Macon Co. early 1800's.) Burial: Sugar Fork Cem., Macon Co., NC

--3. Daniel Granderson Bryson, b May 23, 1787 in Ninety Six Dist., SC, d July 27, 1880 in Swain Co.,NC; m Artie Virginia Dillard August 3, 1810 in Haywood Co., NC. Burial: Old Field Cem., Beta, Jackson Co, NC

****Notes about Daniel G. Bryson: He first settled in what is now Jackson Co., NC in 1811(on the banks of Scotts Creek near the mouth of Cope Creek). He moved his family and his household goods across the Balsams in a sled. He staked out his homestead at a site barely a mile from the Cherokee boundary. Jackson Co.'s first court convened at Daniel's homestead. Daniel had 5 children. One of his sons was Thaddeus, the founder of Swain County, the first rep. of Jackson Co. in the State General Assembly, and the man for whom Bryson city was named.

--3. Samuel Decatur Bryson, b 1794 in Pendleton Dist., SC, d Jan 1850 in Macon Co, NC; m Rebecca Caylor Dec 28, 1820 in Haywood Co. (Sam settled the Cowee Creek area of Macon Co.in the early 1800's)

--3. John W. Bryson, b 1768 in Ninety Six Dist, SC, d July 23, 1851 in Jackson Co., NC

m. (1) Ann Land bet. 1790-1798 Pendleton Dist., SC

m. (2) Jane Poston bet. 1802-1806 Haywood Co, NC

Jane Poston b Oct 17, 1785 in Iredell Co, NC, d 1873 in Jackson Co, NC. She was the daughter of John Poston and Rebecca Balbridge.

Their Children:

--4. Sarah Bryson, b 1806, Buncombe Co., d after 1870 in Fannin Co., GA; M Jesse Lavasque, Jr, Mar 8, 1825.

--4. James H. Bryson, b July 14, 1808, Haywood Co. NC, d Oct 29, 1864 in Walhalla, SC; m Margaret Hyatt between 1820-1828 in Haywood Co.

--4. Andrew Bryson, b Aug 27, 1809, Haywood Co, NC, d Feb 21, 1884 in Jackson Co, NC; m Sarah Rogers in Buncombe Co.

--4. Isabella Bryson, b Mar 7, 1812, Haywood Co, NC, d Dec 11, 1902; m James Houston Queen Oct 17, 1829 in Haywood Co.

--4. Robert Bryson, b Apr 10, 1813, Haywood Co, NC, d Aug 21, 1887 in Jackson Co., NC; m (1) Mary Ann (Polly) Cunningham in Haywood Co. (2) Judith C. Ensley Mar 3, 1870 in Jackson Co.

--4. Henderson Bryson, b 1816, Haywood Co, NC, d 1889 in Towns Co., GA; m (1) Letta (Lettie) Mathis (2) Caroline Davis in Macon Co (3) Rutha Jane Mathis before Aug 23, 1869 in Jackson Co.

--4. Daniel J. Bryson, b Feb 11, 1816, Haywood Co, NC, d May 16, 1890 in Jackson Co.NC; m Lucinda Jones Sep 25, 1837 in Haywood Co.

--4. Rebecca Merimon Bryson, b Mar 11, 1818, Hay. NC, d Nov 28, 1899; m (Sheriff) John Baird Allison Dec 24, 1835 in Macon Co.

--4. Uel G. Bryson, b Sep 10, 1819, Haywood Co, NC, d 1884 in Towns Co., GA; m Priscilla Kirby Oct 13, 1838 in Macon Co., NC.

--4. Samuel Bryson, b Dec 27, 1822, Haywood Co, NC, d Dec 10, 1849 in Macon Co., NC.

--4. Milton M. Bryson, b Oct 24, 1824, Haywood Co, NC. d 1965 in Camp Douglas, POW Camp, Chicago, Ill (Civil War). *** (see below)

--4. M. Coleman Bryson, B Mar 23, 1828, Macon Co., d Dec 4, 1866; m Louise Bumgarner after 1850 in Jackson Co., NC

****Notes about John W. Bryson. As a young man John homesteaded on Cullowhee Creek in Jackson Co. in the early 1800's. He served in the War of 1812. The first land grant of Cullowhee, NC on the west side of the Tuckasegee River was owned by John W. He paid 25¢ an acre for the land considered to be 700 acres (original land grant is in the Macon Co. Courthouse records). He deeded over to the Cullowhee Baptist Church the land for the building and 2 acres for a cemetery. Burial: Cullowhee Baptist Cem., Cullowhee, NC.

--4. Milton M. Bryson, b Oct 24, 1824, Haywood Co, NC. m. Mary Anna duncan Dec 26, 1850 , Haywood Co, NC. Mary Anna, b Jan 18, 1830 in McDowell Co, NC, d Aug 20, 1901 , Jackson Co, NC. She was the daughter of John Duncan and Mary Carr. Burial: Cullowhee Baptist Church Cem.

Their Children:

--5. John Franklin Bryson, b Sep 7, 1851, Jackson Co, d Nov 5, 1936 in Jackson Co., NC; m Rachel Magdaline Shuler May 6, 1877 Jackson Co.

--5. Columbus D. Bryson, b Apr 10, 1853, Jackson Co,, d Dec 8, 1927 Jackson Co., NC; m Sarah Artemesia Phillips Feb 5, 1878 Jackson Co.

--5. Merrit Worth Bryson, b June 29, 1854, Jackson Co, d. Oct 24, 1842 in Jackson Co., NC; m Nancy Jane Pressley Nov 6, 1882 Jackson Co.

--5. Sarah Jane Bryson, b Apr 3, 1856, Jackson Co, NC, d. Jan 25, 1938 in Jackson Co.

--5. Martha Jane Bryson, b. Dec 2, 1857, Jackson Co, d. Feb 23, 1925, Cullowhee, NC *** (see below)

--5. Mary Ann Bryson, b Mar 20, 1859, Jackson Co, NC, d Mar 2, 1922 in jackson Co., NC; m Elbert M. Painter Nov 26, 1878 Jackson Co.

--5. Hugh Robert Bryson, b Feb 3, 1861, Haywood Co,d Jan 17, 1942 in Jackson Co., NC; m (1) Nancy Bell Pressley Jackson Co. (2) Martha Ellen Pressley march 10, 1887 Jackson Co.

--5. Coleman Vance Bryson, b Aug 7, 1862 Jackson Co, d Oct 4, 1950 Jackson Co., NC; m Caroline Palestine Bowen Jan 24, 1902 Jackson Co.

--5. William Richard Bryson, B Nov 20,1865, Jackson Co, NC, d Jan 23, 1914 in Jackson Co., NC; m Mary Alice Woodring Sept 22, 1885 Jackson Co.

****Notes about Milton M. Bryson, from the Bryson Family Book, located in the Macon County Historical

Society Museum, Franklin, NC, & some information was taken from the history of Cullowhee Baptist Church:

In 1854 the first contract for a school held in Cullowhee, NC was signed by Milton M. Bryson, the first teacher W. Hamilton Bryson, his nephew. Milton served in the Confederate Army during the Civil War and was captured. Imprisoned at Camp Douglas, IL, he died there in 1865. Burial: Oakmont Military Cemetery, Chicago, IL.

--5. Martha Jane Bryson, b Dec 2, 1857, Jackson Co, d Feb 23, 1925, Cullowhee, NC

m. Edward Filmore Coggins, b Nov 1, 1864, Speedwell, NC d Dec 5, 1832, Cullowhee, NC. He was the son of Marcus Lafayette (Fate) Coggins and Sarah Narcis Mathis. Edward married Martha Jane Bryson Apr 1, 1885 in Jackson Co.

Martha had two sons before her marriage to Edward:

--6. Charles J. Bryson, Speedwell, NC

--6. Walter Henry Bryson, Speedwell, NC

Children of Martha & Edward:

--6. John Columbus Coggins, b July 2, 1886, Cullowhee,d May 9, 1967 in Erastus, Jackson Co.; m Lora Stewart, Jackson Co. Burial: Pinecreek Cem., Cullowhee, NC

--6. Dovie Coggins, b Jan 112, 1887, Cullowhee, Jackson Co., d June 1975 in GA; m Ferber Moss, Jackson Co.

--6. Alex Montgomery Coggins, b June 25, 1888, Jackson Co., NC, d January 27, 1958 in Asheville, NC; m Annie Bennett Pressley Feb 8, 1914 in Cullowhee, NC. Burial: Woodlawn Cem, Franklin, NC. *(See page 305 for more information)*

--6. Daniel Coggins, b May 1, 1892, NC., d. Nov 1981 in Taylors, SC; m Rita Hoxit, NC.

--6. Retta Jane Coggins, b Feb 18, 1894, Cullowhee, d. May 17, 1974, Honea Path, SC *** (see below)

--6. Western Bryson Coggins b Mar 20, 1896,

Speedwell, NC, d Dec 31, 1969 in Cullowhee, ND; m
Callie Delia Mathis Sep 4, 1921 in Millshoal TWP,
NC. Burial: Doublesprings Cem., Cullowhee Mtn

--6. Samuel Edward Coggins, b Apr 13, 1896,
Speedwell, d Jan 1984 NC; m Lucy Mamie Owens
April 3, 1930 in Millshoal TWP, NC.

--6. Houston Coggins, b Sep 23, 1898, Cullowhee, d
April 1970, NC; m Violet Mathis, Jackson Co.

--6. Gertrude (Gertie) Coggins, b 1902, NC. d 1951 NC;
m William Jackson Berry, Sr. Macon Co.

--6. Retta Jane Coggins, b Feb 18, 1894, Cullowhee,
d May 17, 1974, Honea Path, SC. (Burial:
Doublesprings Cem., Cullowhee Mtn)

m. Thomas Wilson Ammons, Sep 18, 1909, Macon
Co, d Sep 21, 1956 in Jackson Co. (Burial:
Doublesprings Cem., Cullowhee Mtn)

(See page ii for pictures of Retta and Tom)

Their Children:

--7. Bryson Louis Ammons, b Mar 16, 1910, Jackson
Co, NC, d Oct 15, 1998 Tuckasegee, NC

--7. James Edward Ammons, b Mar 25, 1912, Jackson
Co, NC, d Sep 10, 1995, Wolf Mtn, NC

--7. Albert Abraham Ammons, B Mar 3, 1914, Jackson
Co, NC, d May 8, 1970, VA

--7. Thomas Washington Ammons, b Mar 3, 1914,
Jackson Co, NC, d June 1985, Jackson Co, NC

--7. Martha Jane Ammons, b Apr 5, 1918, Jackson Co,
NC, d Oct 15, 1987, Greer, SC

--7. Franklin Lee Ammons, b Aug 29, 1921, Jackson
Co, NC, d Nov 1968, SC,*** **(see below)**

--7. Lillie Mae Ammons, b Sep 1, 1928, Jackson Co, NC

--7. Cora Eleanor Ammons, b May 23, 1931, Jackson
Co, NC, d 2004, SC

--7. Nealie Roosevelt Ammons, b Dec 15, 1933, Jackson
Co, NC, d 2004, SC

--7. Franklin Lee Ammons, b. Aug 29, 1921, Jackson
Co, NC, d. Nov 1968, SC, *** *(see Owen Lineage on
pages 269-271)*

COGGINS LINEAGE

--1. John Coggins, Sr. b.? in Chesterton Oxon,England,
d 1786 in Weston-on-the-Green, England.

m. Grace Craker, b ? in Weston-on-the-Green,
England, d 1787 in Weston-on-the-Green, England.

Their Child:

**--2. John Coggins, Jr., b 1750 in Weston-on-the-
Green, England, d 1832 in Weston-on-the-Green,
England.**

m. Ann Thomas, b 1758 in Weston-on-the-Green,
England,d 1801 in Weston-on-the-Green, England.

Their Children:

--3. Alfred Coggins, b 1790 NC, d 1832 NC
*** (see below)

--3. Thomas Coggins, b ? England, d 1867 England

--3. Grace Coggins, b ?

--3. John Coggins, b ?

--3. Mary Coggins, b ?

--3. Joseph Coggins, b ?

--3. Richard Coggins, b ?

--3. James Coggins, b ?

--3. William Coggins, b ?

--3. Alfred Coggins, b 1790 NC, d 1832 NC

m. Sarah Sharp, b 1795 NC, d ?. She was the daughter
of John Sharp and Martha Young

Their Children:

--4. Zodiac Coggins, b 1816 SC

--4. Sarah Coggins, b 1819 GA

--4. Alfred Coggins, Jr., b 1825 SC

--4. Caroline Coggins, b 1830 NC

--4. Marcus Lafayette (Fate) Coggins *** (see below)

--4. Marcus Lafayette (Fate) Coggins, b June 3, 1831 GA or NC, d January 18, 1894 Jackson Co, NC

Fought in Civil War-Co. G, 62nd NC Infantry

m. Sarah Narcis Mathis, b January 13, 1832 NC, d January 29, 1918 Cullowhee, NC. She was the daughter of Peter Mathis, Jr. and Sally Sarah Frady.

Their Children:

--5. M.J. Coggins, b 1852

--5. William Thomas Coggins, b 1854.

--5. Wiley F. Coggins, b 1856.

--5. Columbus J. Coggins, b 1858.

--5. Mary Caroline Coggins, b 1860 Jackson Co., NC
Burial: Fall Cliff Cem, Speedwell, NC

--5. Marcus Lafayette Coggins, Jr., b July 8, 1863 NC

--5. Edward Filmore Coggins, b Nov 1, 1864, Speedwell, NC, d Dec 5, 1932 Cullowhee, NC *** (see below)

--5. Sarah Elizabeth Coggins,b June 9, 1867 Macon Co.

--5. Edward Filmore Coggins, b Nov 1, 1864, Speedwell, NC, d Dec 5, 1932 Cullowhee, NC

Burial: Cullowhee Baptist Church Graveyard

m. Martha Jane Bryson on April 1, 1885 Jackson Co, NC. Martha was b Dec 2, 1857 Jackson Co, NC, d Feb 23, 1925 Cullowhee, NC. Burial: Cullowhee Baptist Ch Cem., Cullowhee, NC.

Children of Edward & Martha Jane Bryson:

--6. John Columbus Coggins, b July 2, 1886, Cullowhee,d May 9, 1967 in Erastus, Jackson Co.; m Lora Stewart, Jackson Co. Burial: Pinecreek Cem., Cullowhee, NC

--6. Dovie Coggins, b Jan 112, 1887, Cullowhee, Jackson Co., d June 1975 in GA; m Ferber Moss, Jackson Co.

--6. Alex Montgomery Coggins, b June 25, 1888, Jackson Co., NC, d January 27, 1958 in Asheville,

NC; m Annie Bennett Pressley Feb 8, 1914 in
Cullowhee, NC. Burial: Woodlawn Cem, Franklin,
NC. *(See below for more information about Alex,
his wife Annie and the lifestyle of the time)*

--6. Daniel Coggins, b May 1, 1892, NC. d d Nov 1981
in Taylors, SC; m Rita Hoxit, NC.

--6. Retta Jane Coggins, b Feb 18, 1894, Cullowhee,
d. May 17, 1974, Honea Path, SC ***** (see below)**

--6. Western Bryson Coggins b Mar 20, 1896,
Speedwell, NC, d Dec 31, 1969 in Cullowhee, ND; m
Callie Delia Mathis Sep 4, 1921 in Millshoal TWP,
NC. Burial: Doublesprings Cem., Cullowhee Mtn

--6. Samuel Edward Coggins, b Apr 13, 1896,
Speedwell, d Jan 1984 NC; m Lucy Mamie Owens
April 3, 1930 in Millshoal TWP, NC.

--6. Houston Coggins, b Sep 23, 1898, Cullowhee, d
April 1970, NC; m Violet Mathis, Jackson Co.

--6. Gertrude (Gertie) Coggins, b 1902, NC. d 1951 NC;
m William Jackson Berry, Sr. Macon Co.

****Notes about Alex Montgomery
Coggins written by his grandson, Denton
Higdon of Franklin, NC:*
Alex was a farmer by trade which moved
him to buy 60 acres in the steep mountains of
Ellijay Community in Macon County. Vance
Jennings and other neighbors helped build the
four room house from rough cut lumber and
spilt oak shakes shingles. The out buildings
were made of logs that were cut and notched
on the site. The chimney for the house, made from rock and
mud, still stands today and is being used in a modern cabin
owned by his grandson Teddy Marshall Higdon.

The household belongings were moved by wagon on a
stormy May day in 1939. Everything was soaked. Their new
home was incomplete, so quilts were hung in the doorway to
keep the rain out.

That spring, Alex and some of the older children cleared
the mountainside and tried to raise crops which did very

poorly. In the years to come they raised corn, cane and garden vegetables for their own use.

The banjo was a large part of the family entertainment. Alex and his two older sons would pick while the girls sang. The children loved to watch their father buck dance, an activity for which he had won prizes in his youth.

In the lean years before and during the depression, Alex fell back on an old trade most mountain men knew too well. He distilled an illegal elixir, providing for his family.

Alex and Annie had eight children:

--7. Grace Candis Coggins, *** (see below)
--7. Eldon Montgomery Coggins, *** (see below)
--7. Bessie Gertrude Coggins, *** (see below)
--7. Pearl Geneva Coggins, *** (see below)
--7. Ellis Edward Coggins, *** (see below)
--7. Stella Denver Coggins, *** (see below)
--7. Irma Rose Coggins, *** (see below)
--7. Everett Eugene Coggins, b. Feb 4, 1936

--7. Grace Candis Coggins, b. July 31, 1915, m. Fred
	Rogers
Their Children:
--8. Kenneth Rogers
--8. Maquita Rogers

--7. Eldon Montgomery Coggins, b. May 3, 1917, m.
	Virginia (Ginger) Franks.
Their Children:
--8. Lester Coggins
--8. Mary Coggins
--8. Loretta Coggins
--8. Olivia Coggins
--8. Truman Coggins.

--7. Bessie Gertrude Coggins, b. May 5, 1919, m. Roy
	Stiwinter

Their Children:
--8. Geralene Stiwinter
--8. Lavauhn Stiwinter
--8. Dean Stiwinter

--7. Pearl Geneva Coggins, b. Sept 18, 1921, m. Ted
  Higdon
Their Children:
--8. Steve Higdon
--8. Teddy Marshall Higdon
--8. Lawanna Higdon

--7. Ellis Edward Coggins, b. July 24, 1923, m. Janet
  Putman of Michigan
Their Children:
--8. Ewilda Coggins
--8. Charlotte Coggins
--8. Wayne Coggins

--7. Stella Denver Coggins, b. May 2, 1926, m. Sam W.
  Higdon
Their Children:
--8. Sammy Ronnie Higdon
--8. Lonnie Higdon (died in infancy)
--8. Denton Eugene Higdon

--7. Irma Rose Coggins, b. Mar 1, 1929, m. Patrick
  Theodore Rogers
Their Child:
--8. Deborah (Debbie) Rogers

--6. Retta Jane Coggins, b Feb 18, 1894, Cullowhee,
  d. May 17, 1974, Honea Path, SC *** *(see the
  Ammons Lineage on page 301 for Retta's children)*

Catch the Spirit of Appalachia, Inc.

WESTERN NORTH CAROLINA

In 1989 Amy Ammons Garza and Doreyl Ammons Cain established Catch the Spirit of Appalachia, Inc. (CSA) as a nonprofit organization.

Together the Ammons Sisters, by becoming visiting artists in the schools, began to encourage children everywhere to honor and revere their heritage. Their methods were simple: while Amy told stories of growing up in the mountains, Doreyl spontaneously illustrated them. Children were fascinated with hearing and seeing stories come alive.

Establishing a CSA Board of Directors, many of whom are still with them 15 years later, heritage work in Jackson County began with festivals, summer drama camps, creative writing and visual art workshops, and publishing writers.

In 2004, Catch the Spirit of Appalachia joined forces with Appalachian Homestead Farm & Preserve, founded by Vera Holland Guise, another strong advocate to preserve the local mountain heritage. She has been successful in securing part of her family's original 250-acre farm on Tilley Creek in Jackson County—52 acres which is now placed in perpetuity for conservation and education purposes. Plans are to establish the Spirit of Appalachia Folklife School and Living History Farm, and provide a permanent home for CSA.

The shared dream is to be good stewards of the land, to inspire mountain families to keep and care for the land, to honor the heritage of those who came before, and to develop viable ways of earning a living in the new heritage tourism economy.

308